REBECCA PATER

THEY THOUGHT THEY WOULD NEVER BE SUCKED IN...

THE COLLECTIVE

Ark House Press
arkhousepress.com

Cataloguing in Publication Data:
Title: The Collective
ISBN: 9781763620162 (pbk)
Subjects: FIC042040 [FICTION / Christian / Romance / General]; FIC042000 [FICTION / Christian / General];

Design by initiateagency.com

To Andrew and Jack
who had to live through this too.

Chapter one

For the rest of her life Lauren would continue to ask herself the same question, "should I have said no?" If she had known what was coming, would she have done something different? Would she have decided that she was happy with her wonderfully ordinary life and said thanks, but no thanks? Would she have told Jamie that compared to the rest of the world they were already rich and didn't need more? But it would remain a question that she would never be able to answer. Knowing the pain that was coming, she should have said no. But then she would have missed out on the benefit of the lessons learned and the growth that comes from suffering. And that's why for the rest of her life she couldn't decide if she would have changed her answer and not said yes.

~ ~ ~

She heard the front door open and the man she had lived with and loved for over twenty years greeted the waiting dogs and then stopped for a minute to say hey to the children sprawled on the couch in front of the telly.

"Hello love," Jamie called out as he dropped his briefcase onto the battered desk in the family room. "What's for dinner? I'm starved."

"You're always starved," she said as she lifted her cheek for a kiss while swatting him with the tea towel as he lifted a pot lid.

"Well, today I really am. I didn't get a chance to have lunch. I was too busy taking a very interesting call from Patrick Belling."

Great, Lauren thought as she rolled her eyes. "And what did he want this time? More tax advice for free? Seriously, I wish you'd send him a bill. Every other accountant on Earth would have their stop watches out and charge him by the minute."

"He wasn't ringing about tax this time," he replied as he pinched a cherry tomato that was meant for tonight's salad. "He had a proposition for me, and it actually sounds like it might be viable."

Fantastic. She knew what this meant. Hours and hours of work for Jamie. Running the numbers, he called it, and every time it was a bust. He spent his evenings working for free for their friends and nothing ever came of it. Their real estate ideas, start-up businesses and plans to manufacture the next big thing always lost money on paper, and Jamie had to be the one to tell them their scheme was a bust and politely decline their offer for him to invest. As much as he dreamed of retiring before he was fifty, a get rich quick scheme from one of his mates wasn't going to be the way it happened.

"Don't be cynical," he said, catching her eye roll and her exaggerated sigh. "I actually think his idea might have some merit and it would be worth investing in if the numbers add up."

Lauren bent over and pulled the roast chicken from the oven, deciding it was done.

"Before you go and round up the children for dinner you better let me in on this fabulous idea that's going to make our fortune. Is it organising flights for people to the moon?" Jamie shook his head with a no.

"Right then. So Pat isn't going into business with Elon Musk. Is it a robot that does the washing? Cause I might actually get behind that one."

"Nope," Jamie replied as he went to the drawer and pulled out the cutlery to set the table.

"Then I give up. I'm too tired and too busy to waste brain power trying to figure out which stupid way Pat is trying to entice me to part with my money this time."

"Solar panels."

"Um, I don't mean to burst your bubble love, but I think someone already invented those," she teased.

"Really, I didn't know that," he replied sarcastically. "I'll go call the kids for dinner. Maybe they want to hear how we're going to make our fortune."

"I wouldn't tell them," Lauren called to Jamie's retreating back. "They'll have the money spent in five minutes."

~ ~ ~

"Delicious as always darl," Jamie said as he put his knife and fork down. They hadn't been able to continue their earlier conversation as neither child wanted to hear about solar panels and monopolized dinner with talk of school, with Emily trying to slip one by her parents. She wanted to attend a year twelve party, but knowing that the olds would say no, she had tried to hide where she was really going and had told her parents that she was sleeping over at her best friend Stacie's on Saturday night. What she didn't know was that Stacie's mum and Lauren had talked at school pickup last week, and Lauren knew all about the party. Emily was only in year eleven and the rule had always been no parties where alcohol would be available. Being an eighteenth birthday that was a given. Even her father, who more often than not gave in to his little girl, was adamant

3

that this was one party she was going to miss. This meant at least a week of sulking and snarky comments about how boring her parents were and how they never let her go anywhere but church and school. Oliver was two years younger and wasn't pushing the boundaries quite as hard yet, but it wouldn't be long. Lauren knew life would be easier if she gave in once in a while, but being the cool Mum just wasn't her. If she never heard the phrase just chill mum again she would be a happy woman.

"So, are you going to abandon me as well?" she asked as she picked up Jamie's plate and stacked it with the rest. Those lazy kids hadn't even bothered to take their dishes to the kitchen, disappearing the second they had finished their dinner.

"I'm happy to help darl, and it will give us a chance to talk about the Patrick opportunity," he said as they walked the few steps from the dining room to the kitchen.

"Sure. I'm always up for a good story," she chuckled as she started loading their ancient dishwasher. "Are we going to be millionaires?"

"Not this time," he sighed, thinking of the years and years ahead of him that he would still be working. "But we might be able to get rid of our mortgage."

"Doubtful," Lauren scoffed. "We'll be paying this place off until the children put us in a home." Lauren looked out the kitchen window to the tiny backyard. They could barely afford the house in Homebush and the renovations that had been needed had pushed them to the brink financially. The still undone kitchen was going to be a gut job. Lauren was tempted to go ahead and use a little of the money from her inheritance. After two years using an oven that often burnt the outside and left the inside raw and such bad storage that pots had to be kept in the hall closet, she was over it. The last time their hundred-year-old house's kitchen had been replaced was in the seventies and they were now well into a new century.

"I'm serious darl. Patrick has stumbled onto the investment of a lifetime and he wants us to be a part of it. He told me he's been praying for a while for an opportunity to come up, and he really believes he's supposed to build a small team of men around him that can invest and make a good profit. We've known him a long time and he might be impetuous, but he's also honest and Godly. And you know I wouldn't do anything that would put us in financial danger. You can trust me, even if you don't trust Patrick," Jamie reasoned.

"But solar panels. How can you make money from that? I'd understand if it was ten years ago when the technology was new, but now everyone seems to have them."

"Agreed," Jamie nodded. "A lot of people do have panels. But new houses are being built all the time and people love thinking they're saving the environment."

"Sure. But how are you going to sell them? Do you even have any contacts in the building industry?"

"Patrick knows a guy who owns his own building company. He's approached him as another investor."

"I don't know. Where did these panels come from? It's nothing dodgy I hope?"

"No, of course not. A guy in Melbourne who had just imported a massive lot of panels died last month. The bank wants their money back fast and the widow is desperate for someone to take them off her hands."

"That sounds a bit cutthroat of Patrick. Ripping off a widow to profit."

"Except that it's not," Jamie responded. "She's desperate, but she was the one that set the price. She had another buyer lined up, but they couldn't raise the funds in time. Patrick found out about the deal from the widow's nephew, who he knows through a mutual friend. Doug, the nephew, would buy them himself in a heartbeat but has no way of paying for them. This is going to be a first in, best dressed thing. She isn't interested in a bidding war, just getting enough money to save her home. The guy has left his wife in a real mess. Pat thinks we can buy at her price and still make a really good, quick profit even if we sell below market value. He's also talking to a few other guys who are in a position to invest."

"Speaking of which, how much is this investment going to be?" Lauren asked.

"I still need to spend some time checking Patrick's figures, and I need to do it quick or someone else is bound to buy them. That said, if we have seven investors, we will each need to come up with two hundred and fifty thousand, cash. We should be able to fund the rest through a bank." Jamie began wiping down the benches, not wanting to make eye contact with his wife. He knew just how much this was going to freak her out. Lauren, like most women, needed financial security, but she needed it more than most. Her childhood had been a seesaw of either feast or famine. Donald, her father had been a gambler, betting on anything that moved. He passed away when Lauren was only ten, leaving her family destitute. Lauren's mother Paula did the best she could, working any job that she could get so she could feed her two daughters, but sometimes she couldn't make ends meet. For a short time, they had even lived in a borrowed tent at the local caravan park because they couldn't afford to pay the rent and lost their tiny house. That might be all right for a week in summer, but trying to do her homework in a leaky tent in the middle of a Sydney winter had changed Lauren. She had been the happiest of little girls, not really understanding what her father's gambling was doing to her mother while he was alive, but being homeless for that awful month when she was thirteen taught her that you should always plan ahead, and save for that wet, cold, rainy day so that no-one could ever put you out on the street. She desperately needed to know that there would always be enough money, enough food and somewhere decent for her and her children to live. When she was a new parent the fear of not being able to provide properly for her children had almost paralysed her some days. Lauren had been determined to make sure that Oliver and Emily never lived the way she had. Paula had eventually landed on her feet, marrying a widower she met when she started cleaning his house. He had loved her and been kind to her two daughters. He wasn't rich, but he owned his own home, and when he died, he left his modest house to Paula. When she had died three years ago Lauren and her sister Penny had inherited the home. With the price of real estate in Sydney skyrocketing the girls had been able to sell the house for over seven hundred thousand dollars. Lauren and Jamie had used one hundred thousand of that to help with a deposit for their current home. The rest had gone into a term deposit, not to be touched, in case Lauren ever found herself in a difficult situation. They hadn't wasted it on holidays, or even used a cent to reno the house. Just knowing it was there meant Lauren could sleep at night.

"And just where is this two hundred and fifty thousand dollars coming from Jamie? We don't have that kind of money."

"But we do have the money. We can use your inheritance," Jamie pleaded. "It could change our lives forever."

"Our lives are just fine, thank you. And don't forget, it's my inheritance. Not yours. Mine. And I can tell you it will be over my dead body that you will be using it for something so stupid." She slammed the dishwasher closed and tossed the tea towel on the bench.

"Can't we at least talk about this Lauren?" Jamie begged, as she left the kitchen, her face crimson with anger. He got his answer when he heard the bedroom door slam.

Chapter two

J amie turned over slowly, pushing the cushion under his neck, trying desperately to find a comfortable way to sleep on a couch that had not been designed for his six-foot one frame. The lounge suite was an old one, dragged around for over twenty years of marriage and it was just as ugly and unfashionable as it had been the day his Grandparents had bought it decades ago. When his Grandmother had been moved to a nursing home, as newlyweds, they had gratefully received several pieces of furniture that would not fit in the one room suite his family had found for his Grammy Newman. One lovely inherited piece, a china cabinet, had been painstakingly restored by Lauren and took pride of place in the family room. The rest of the room was a hodgepodge of mismatched furniture that Lauren had tried to pull together with cushions and throws, but that never looked quite right. His wife had done her best with what she had but was always embarrassed when they had guests over. About to turn forty, they were much too old to still be using hand-me-down furniture a desperate University student wouldn't bother picking up if they saw it on the side of the road.

He stretched his legs out, banging his foot against the timber turned posts on the end of the couch. Stained a deep mahogany, they would be better suited to a stairwell than a couch, or better yet the burn pile. Seriously, who had designed a such an ugly couch? It had probably cost a fortune at the time, and he remembered as a small boy how proud his Grammy had been of her fancy lounge suite. Coupled with tapestry look fabric covered in deep red roses, Jamie understood just why Lauren hated the suite so much. When it first came to live with them they had promised each other it would only be for a year. A year had turned into twenty-one as school fees and rent in high-priced Sydney took priority over what their furniture looked like. When they had finally pulled together enough of a deposit to buy their first home twelve years ago Lauren declared she had made her peace with the couch and the ugly matching wing chairs and stopped complaining about them. That didn't stop her lingering over catalogues when she thought he wasn't looking. They probably could have afforded a new suite if they hadn't needed to do so much work on the house. The bathrooms had been almost unusable and were the first rooms to be renovated. And now more than anything, Lauren wanted a new kitchen. She had started saving her meagre wages from the three days a week she worked as a receptionist for a local law firm, but it would still take her at least two years of work to earn enough to get the kitchen of her dreams.

Jamie threw back the blanket he had dragged over himself at one am when he finally finished going over the numbers for Patrick. He had dreamed of his comfortable bed, but the door to the master bedroom had remained firmly closed for the rest of the evening and he hadn't dared to sneak in and risk waking Lauren. She wasn't a great sleeper and any disturbance left her tossing and turning in frustration all night. She was already mad enough. He hadn't wanted to make it worse.

As he sat up, his back protesting at the treatment it had received at the hands of the torturous couch, he cracked open his eyes and rubbed his face in an attempt to wake up.

"Good morning," he heard.

His eyes bolted open as his hand gripped his chest in fright, and saw his wife sitting opposite him. She was still wearing yesterday's clothes, mum jeans and a white tee-shirt. Her dark, shoulder length hair was dragged into a loose ponytail and she looked just as crumpled and exhausted as he felt.

"You scared me half to death," he said. "How long have you been sitting there?"

"Not sure. About an hour, I guess. I've been up since five."

Jamie looked over to the clock hanging on the wall behind Lauren. It was ten past six. Only five hours of sleep, and he had several important meetings with clients today. Calling in sick wasn't an option when you were the boss and the only person clients wanted to deal with.

"Would you like a coffee?" Lauren asked. "I would have made some sooner, but I didn't want the noise to wake you."

"That would be great," Jamie answered. He stood, and stretched, feeling the pain in his left foot where he had kicked the end of the couch. He followed Lauren to the kitchen and sat on a bar stool at the bench that pretended to be a breakfast bar. The sun was already up, and Jamie glimpsed the last of the sunrise. The house was already warm, and Jamie guessed it would be another hot February day. Summer in Australia. Sunburn, bush fires and frayed tempers as day after day of over thirty-degree temperatures left people grumpy from lack of sleep and dreaming of April when it would finally be over. Hot spells were followed by wild storms, flash flooding, and power outages. Only to be quickly replaced by another run of hot days that left them wondering why they lived there. And yet he never seriously considered moving anywhere else. Melbourne's weather was even crazier, and Queensland seemed to be in drought or flood most of the time.

Lauren adjusted the milk jug under the steam wand, trying to keep the noise down. The kids were still asleep and didn't need to be roused for at least another hour. She had her back to him, so he couldn't tell if she was still as angry now as she had been last night. Nothing was ever going to make her use her inheritance for something that he couldn't guarantee was going to be one hundred percent safe, and while he believed the investment was not only good, but fantastic, he knew someone else was going to be given the opportunity to take his place and make the money. He would just be an advisor, yet again, and another chance at financial freedom would be lost. It's not like he didn't make enough for them, but the cost of living in Australia's most expensive city kept them in the just making it category. He knew they were blessed, but Jamie wanted desperately to get ahead and have the things he saw his more successful friends enjoy. Exotic holidays, beach houses, and a mortgage free home. Although right now, he'd just be happy if he could afford to buy a decent couch.

Lauren set the coffee mug down in front of Jamie. He picked it up automatically and took a sip, daydreaming about taking that holiday by the beach where someone else made the coffee and brought it to you.

"Are you okay Jamie?" Lauren asked. "You seem miles away."

Taking a deep breath in, trying to stifle a yawn he replied "just tired. I didn't get much sleep. I worked till one, and then, you know the couch isn't the best place to sleep. I'm too tall and it's too …" He stopped, not wanting to draw attention to the fact that they still had it after so many years, even though they kept promising each other they wouldn't drag it to the next home each time they moved.

"You could have come to bed. I didn't sleep much either and I don't like it when you're not there."

"You were already mad at me," Jamie pointed out. "I didn't want to wake you."

11

"I'm not mad anymore Jamie. And I owe you an apology. I should have listened to you, given you a chance to explain yourself." Lauren raised her head and looked into Jamie's tired eyes. "I'm sorry."

Surprised, Jamie thought maybe he had misheard her. Lauren didn't like being wrong and took almost pathological pleasure in being right, all of the time.

"No, I'm sorry," he replied. "I know how you feel about that money. It's our contingency in case one of us gets ill, or the roof flies off in a storm, or someone kidnaps one of the kids and we have to pay a ransom," he smiled, thinking of their long running joke that if someone ever did kidnap Emily the kidnappers would end up paying them to take her back just to get some peace and quiet. That girl could talk under water and assumed everyone was interested in every tiny thought she had.

"Yes," Lauren started, knowing she needed to be honest. "I've felt that in the past. But last night I realized that I was putting all my faith in money, not in God. I've spent my life expecting the worst to happen and always trying to plan and prepare for disaster. The money does make me feel secure. But God had words with me last night and I realized I had cut him out of the decision making in my life. And I had cut you out too. Instead of using the money to make our home what we want it to be, or invest in something that could mean you didn't have to work so hard to provide for us, I've held on to it as a safety net for myself and expected you to earn enough to cover everything. And that's not fair."

"I love providing for you Lauren. And for the kids. I see it as a privilege, not a burden."

"I know," she agreed, "but I don't want you to live that way forever. Working late each night and stressing at the end of the month whether you've billed enough. So, I'm willing to talk about Pat's investment, and if that doesn't add up, then let's look at getting someone to do the work that needs doing around here. We don't need to be wasteful, but our home is an investment. And somewhere I want to be comfortable in, and not be embarrassed to invite people over for dinner. And I want a kitchen that isn't orange. I really, really hate orange."

"Are you sure? You're not just saying this to make me feel better? I know you're tired and that's not the best time to make decisions. I don't want you to have regrets later and blame me if it all goes wrong. We have to make this decision together."

Lauren leaned over the bench and took Jamie's hand. "I'm sure. I want to stop holding on too tightly and start living. So why don't you talk me through those numbers while I get breakfast started."

Chapter three

J amie pulled into the parking building that was just a short walk to the restaurant. He was excited to be eating at the recently opened Chuuka on Jones Bay Wharf. Normally outside his budget, the Japanese and Chinese inspired menu had opened to rave reviews. Pat was shouting dinner tonight, but Jamie knew that at some point, if the deal went ahead, he would be expected to reciprocate. That was just the way these things went. And for seven guys, probably some with very expensive tastes, he wasn't sure he could justify the cost to Lauren, let alone actually be able to pay for it. He slid on his sunglasses as he left the dark of the car park, nervous about how tonight was going to play out. He only knew two of his fellow investors, men he considered friends. Pat of course, who had bought the idea to him was a long-time client, and Daniel Lawson who was also a client. Jamie sat on the board of his company Racers and had been his advisor for years. Lauren and Daniel's wife Felicity were also friendly. Not close, but the two couples got together once a year for dinner, and the girls always got along.

Knowing that he wouldn't be walking into a dinner with six complete strangers eased his anxiety a little. He was putting so much on the line here. If this deal didn't work the way he hoped, or the solar panels didn't sell, he was positive Lauren would never forgive him, or ever trust him again. She had told him she was happy to move ahead with the investment, but there was always a risk, and at the end of the day the blame would fall on him. Trying not to think about failure he looked out over the wharf. It was lined with boats, most of them probably worth much more than his home. He had never really wanted a boat of his own, but he did appreciate the lifestyle of the few who could afford to just go out and buy such a beautiful toy. What must their lives be like? No worrying about making the mortgage payments or hoping that the kids school shoes fit them the whole year. And here he was, getting to play with some of the big boys. It was just as terrifying as it was exciting.

When he reached the restaurant, Jamie was greeted at the door by a thin, rather effeminate man, the kind that populated exclusive restaurants all over Sydney, and after giving him Patrick's name, Jamie was quickly led upstairs. The waiter barely gave him a second glance, knowing that Jamie didn't belong here. The restaurant afforded magnificent views over the water and Jamie stopped to appreciate them. This was it. This was what he had been wanting since he was a boy. Just a tiny piece of this lifestyle. The people dining here tonight knew they did belong. The men exuded power and the women with them had a polish and glow that came from pampering and money. What must it be like, being one of these special people? Almost like us ordinary humans, but not quite. They belonged to a club that the rest of the population could only dream of being part of, with the knowledge that they could have whatever they wanted. They were better looking, smarter and richer than the average people out in the world trying to get on with their ordinary lives. Glancing around, he realized how overdressed he was in his suit. Most of the diners were dressed casual, but expensive casual.

The women looked like they had just stepped out of a Versace photo shoot, not a hair out of place and makeup perfectly applied. Jamie knew he was nice looking, tall and fit, with dark hair that was just beginning to grey, giving him a look of maturity that people trusted. But he was never going to be one of these people, and when he thought about it, he wondered if that was what he really wanted. It might be fun for a while, but dressing up to impress others, caring what they thought of you, it all sounded like too much hard work to him.

He saw Pat at a table in the back corner and worked his way across the dining room.

"Come straight from work?" Pat asked noting Jamie's attire.

"Ah, yeah. Busy day," he replied, not wanting to mention that there had been no point going home to change as nothing else in his wardrobe would have looked right here. At least half of what he owned now seemed to be splattered with paint from all the renovating he had been doing. And the few good casual shirts and pants he owned had come from outlet stores and would quickly be spotted for the fakes they were. Unlike the Ralph Lauren polo Pat was wearing. And then thankfully there was no more time to consider what he was wearing as one by one the other investors arrived and introductions were made.

Stuart, who owned a building company hadn't got the memo about how to dress either. This put Jamie at ease, and he instantly felt comfortable with the older man. About fifty-five, he was completely grey with a rugged face, aged from years outside in the Australian sun. He told Jamie he was no longer on the tools and left the physical work to his two sons, Nathan and Jake. The company had grown over the past ten years to a point where he now managed the projects from the comfort of an office. He expected Andrews Construction to grow by ten percent in the following year, as it had done for the previous five years, and shared that he was very excited to get his hands on some cheap solar panels for the houses he built. He also knew a lot of other builders in Sydney who would be very interested in buying from them at the discounted price. That explained why Pat had chosen Stuart as one of the investors. A ready-made market for them.

Also, new to Jamie was Harry. He sat down beside him and quickly introduced himself. One thing Harry wasn't, was shy. He was in sales and happy to admit that he had made a lot of money in pharmaceutical sales. He had spent the previous few years selling a ground-breaking drug that reduced nausea in patients enduring chemotherapy. He still worked for the company but was looking for something a little less stressful and less time consuming so that he could follow the call that he felt God had put on his life. He told Jamie that he was passionate about helping people get to really know God and have a deep and emotional connection with Him. The financial blessing he had received meant he could move his life in another direction, away from paid work and into the ministry. He looked young, maybe mid-thirties, with an energy and enthusiasm for life that made Jamie feel tired. But on first meeting, he seemed to be a genuine guy and Jamie looked forward to getting to know him better.

The youngest of the investors was Josh. Under thirty, he was a solicitor. Jamie had no idea how he could possibly afford to invest with Pat, but it wasn't his place to ask. He certainly had an ego on him, and of all the men he had met tonight, Jamie felt the least comfortable with Josh. Lauren would take one look at him and call him a peacock. He quickly monopolized the conversation with the story of his last successful case. According to him he was the one to win the unwinnable lawsuits and was quick to hand out his business card to Jamie. It was obvious why he saw himself as a rising star. He was young, brash and good-looking. Tall with blond wavy hair and blue eyes, Jamie could see why he was so confident. He was wearing a wedding ring though, which

Jamie took as a good sign. At least he had settled down with someone. And Pat had told him that all the investors were Christians. So, for now he was going to wait and see before he formed a firm opinion of Josh.

The final investor to arrive was another man that Jamie had never met. He pulled out the last empty chair next to Jamie as he greeted Pat, the only one at the table that he knew. Turning to Jamie he put his hand out.

"Hi, I'm Lawrence."

"Jamie," he replied as the two men shook hands.

Lawrence was also older. Probably about fifty with a heavy beard and greying at the temples. He looked warily around the table, taking in each man. "Well this is certainly a motley crew Pat has bought together," he stated under his breath to Jamie. "You're the accountant, right?"

"I am. What gave me away? I promise I left my calculator in the office." Jamie hated that people assumed he was boring because of his job, but now he wondered if people tell just by looking at him what he did?

"Your name did. Pat and I have been talking together for some time about putting together an investment group. We both bought names to the table and prayed over every one. Each of you here tonight was chosen, and not just because you had money to invest, but because this is something we believe God wants you to be part of. And then we began praying for an opportunity. We had planned on everyone meeting and seeing how we clicked together first, but we didn't have time. This was a now or never kind of deal that fell into our laps. So here we are."

Surprised, Jamie said "I had no idea Pat put so much thought into this. He's usually such a fly by the seat of his pants kind of guy."

"Not this time," Lawrence said. "And he was really happy that God gave your name the go ahead. He really trusts you."

"I didn't know he felt like that. I'm going to take that as a compliment."

"You should," Lawrence answered as Pat cleared his throat and called for everyone's attention.

"Thank you all for coming tonight. This is a very time sensitive issue, so I appreciate you making it here on such short notice. We need to decide by Friday whether we go ahead or not. But in some very good news a few of you have come forward and offered to put in the extra money required, which means we won't need to go to the bank. With such a short deadline I doubt we would get verbal approval in time, let alone any of the paperwork done. Which of course would have been a huge risk. If the bank turned us down, we would have lost the deposit that's due five pm on Friday. So tonight, I suggest you ask all the questions you have, then go home and pray about it. Talk to your better halves. It's important that you be in agreement with them before committing so much money. We need your final decision by lunchtime Thursday and if it does go ahead then we need you to be able to transfer funds for the deposit that day, which is not easy to organise, so please don't leave it too late. I have a meeting set with the seller at five pm on Friday at Josh's firm. He will be representing us and has drawn up the agreement. He will also draw up contracts for us each to sign. Jamie, this is where you come in. If you could sort out who will own what percentage of shares based on their investment, I'd be grateful."

"Sure thing," Jamie nodded in agreement.

"And now gents," he said as waiters approached the table, laden with plates. "I have organised with the chef a special menu for tonight. Tonight's on me in appreciation of your time and consideration. Hopefully soon the profits will be rolling in and dinner will be on the company. And if anyone has any ideas for the company name let me know."

As the men made their way through the six courses, friendships were made. They could each see qualities in the others that they admired, and Jamie was happy to sit back and listen, taking each one at face value and finding them to be genuine men, with their hearts in the right place. Harry in particular steered the conversation toward how they could use some of the profits to grow God's kingdom. Jamie hadn't even considered that. Of course he would tithe on anything that came to him. That was the way his family lived their lives, ten percent straight to their church before anything else. But asking them to consider giving away more than that seemed a bit over the top. It was early days though, and he would do his best to steer the group away from the direction Harry wanted them to take. Right now, it was just a bunch of guys talking, throwing around ideas, and they all understood they were doing this to make a profit. Why take the risk otherwise. By the time the last course was eaten Jamie felt like his stomach might explode. It had been a lot of unusual food, some of it he couldn't name, but liked. He enjoyed one very expensive glass of wine, conscious that he needed to drive home. But several of the others had indulged, ordering more than one bottle that cost over three hundred dollars. That kind of excess was something completely outside his experience and he found it irresponsible. It all tasted pretty much the same to him. Sighing, he realized that this was how the other half lived, but it confirmed his earlier feelings. There was having nice things, and then there was just being excessive. If this all did go ahead, and based on the conversations going around the table, everyone was in, he could see it would be up to him to curb their spending. If they wanted to waste that kind of money it would have to be their own. They were all great guys, but Jamie wanted to be sure that they were the right people to be in business with and their attitude towards money was definitely different than his. He just hoped that God was in it and would be the one steering the ship.

Chapter four
Earlier

After ten years of marriage Lucy had become very sensitive to Steven's body language. She could tell when he had good news for her. Yes, he was an ordinary looking man with brown hair that he kept a little longer than she liked, but when he was happy his blue eyes would light up and his smile would reach every part of his face. When he was troubled the smile would only reach to the corners of his mouth and his eyes would become dark. He never wanted her to worry about anything, but when he tossed and turned at night, he couldn't control his emotions as well as he did while he was awake, and Lucy could always tell something was up. For the last few nights he had been restless, but Lucy knew it was best not to ask Steven what the problem was. He would talk to her when he was ready.

It was always the same thing anyway. From the way he was behaving she could tell that it was going to be time for them to move on. Five different towns and five different churches in ten years. She realized it was just as frustrating for Steven as it was for her. But it was getting harder to move the kids each time they had to find a new home. Chelsea was eight and in her third primary school already. If they moved again this would be her fourth and Jonathan's third. It wasn't fair on them and it wasn't fair on her either. She loved their new church and this time they had only been there for six months. She had been appointed to the role of Children's Pastor and loved doing it. If she had to leave, she would be devastated. It was a real job, only part-time, but it brought in a little money and she felt like she was doing something important with her teaching qualifications. This time it wasn't only about Steven.

But she trusted Steven's leading and when God told her husband it was time to move on, then it was time to move on. Lucy understood why it was necessary, but that didn't mean she wasn't going to be sad about leaving her newly made friends. She understood that as his wife she came under his authority and anyway, she loved him so much that she would always follow where he led. But she wished it didn't have to be this way. Whenever they started in a new church everyone loved Steven. Most people had never encountered a man like him before with a gift that was so special, because Steven was a prophet. People flocked to him for a word from God. The modern church seemed desperate to hear what God was saying to His people. Many churches had neglected to teach the prophetic and their people were hungry for it. Twice Steven had even been blessed with a staff position, which meant he could give up the manual labour he didn't enjoy and that never paid enough. He didn't have any bible school training, and he didn't have a formal psychological degree, but as he explained it to Lucy, God had been honing his gift for many years now, and there was no better training than what came directly from God Himself.

He repeated to her often the story of the day when he was only twenty-two, when a stranger had called him out in a church service and told him that God said that he was going to be a great prophet. That he would be a blessing to many people. Steven was a new Christian, but Alan, also a prophet, had seen the gift from God on him. Alan had taught him how to hear from God, how to tune in and listen, and to filter out his own thoughts and feelings. To this day he remained his mentor and biggest supporter. If Steven ever doubted himself then it was Alan he turned to for guidance. And Alan never wavered once. Steven was a true prophet. God used him and would continue to. Steven spoke God's word, downloaded straight from Heaven.

Lucy knew of many men and women who had received freedom when they spent time with Steven in releasing sessions. Together Steven and the broken soul he was helping would identify the problem or problems they were experiencing. Steven would then guide them back throughout their life until they discovered what event from the past was causing their current issues. He could drill down to a specific incident, often receiving knowledge in a vision from God, and then he would help to create a replacement memory. He would ask the person to bring Jesus into the painful moment. By doing this a person could then deal with their current pain and understand how these experiences had influenced who they were and how to recognise why they mishandled current situations in their lives. Once they understood this, they could get out all the rubbish, and move on. Often God would give him words of knowledge for people as he led them backwards through their lives, until they could remember things that had been buried in the recesses of their minds. He had been such a blessing to many, and Lucy was proud to be his wife.

But at some point, someone in power in the church decided they didn't like what Steven had to say. One time it had been a Pastor who was called out for ungodly behaviour by Steven. Another time it had been because of raging jealousy of his God given talent. People in the church had turned to Steven instead of the leadership because they knew that Steven had a gift their Pastor didn't, and he couldn't stand being overlooked. Those times the family had been asked to move on. And they had always left the church quietly, and without fuss. If the people weren't ready to accept The Prophet, he would shake the dust of his sandals the way Jesus had taught his disciples and move on. God would deal with the unbelievers in his own way and his own time. But most of the time it was Steven who decided it was time to move on. He was so passionate about helping believers that occasionally he got ahead of himself and moved at a pace that some weren't comfortable with. Steven found it hard to comprehend why anyone who loved God wouldn't want to hear what He had in store for their lives and receive the freedom that He desired for them. But he also understood that everyone had filters that they viewed life through, and they couldn't see clearly if the filters were clogged with emotional junk. Maybe it was because of neglect or abuse at the hands of parents. Sometimes it was their spouse who had hurt them and the pain they experienced warped their perception of life. While many of the people Steven had a prophesy for received his words gratefully and cleaned their heart and head filters, there were a few who refused to address what was holding them back, denying there was a problem. And you can't help someone who doesn't want help. If only they had received the deliverance they needed, then they would have understood the words God had for them through Steven and their lives would be changed.

So Lucy didn't blame her husband when it was time to move on. It was the people who rejected him that she blamed for the instability in their lives. He was a good, Godly man. And she knew that one day he would not only be accepted but embraced for what he was. They would finally have the life God had promised, with all the honour that should be rightfully given to such a man – The Prophet.

Tonight it was obvious to Lucy how distracted Steven was. She heard him sigh loudly from the faded rocking chair that faced the television. It was turned to the news, but he wasn't listening to it. Instead he drummed his fingers against his leg, and sighed again, louder this time. Someone had obviously hurt her husband and she felt so frustrated for him. When would people start accepting what God had for them? Why did they not trust Him?

"Everything all right hun?" she asked, not being able to keep her promise to wait for him to come to her this time.

"Not really Lucy." He rubbed his hands roughly up and down his cheeks. "God's been talking to me about the church. I'm sorry to have to do this to you, but He's told me it's time to move on. They just aren't ready to receive what He has for them. They're so closed off to me and the message that I'm bringing."

"What happened?" Lucy asked. "I thought you were getting on so well with Bill and Laura. We had that great dinner at their home last month, and they were really receptive to what you had to say."

"Unfortunately they seem to have changed their mind. Three days ago, Bill called me into his office and asked me to stop having releasing sessions with people, and I'm not allowed to bring any prophetic words without checking it with him first. Can you imagine? Bill expects me to run the words God gives me for people past him first. He wants me to confirm with others what God has said to me before I can share it with the church. But you and I both know that isn't necessary. God talks to me, I listen, and then I pass it on. I'm the vessel He's chosen," Steven said, his voice heavy with disappointment and frustration.

Lucy didn't blame him for becoming upset and admired how he was able to stay the course God had chosen for him in the face of so much opposition. He quietly accepted people's disbelief, always the gentleman, he backed off, leaving it to God to get through to them one day. He was so passionate about helping people move into what God had for them and had such an assurance that he was doing God's work, but he never argued. If a person rejected God, then it was up to Him to deal with them. And here was another nay-sayer shutting down God in the church. How were the lost ever going to be saved if the Church wouldn't listen to the prophet that God had sent to them? They were just as deaf as the Israelites in the Old Testament that refused to listen to God's prophets.

"I am so sorry that you have had to go through this. I wish you had told me earlier." Lucy moved toward him and knelt down, taking his hands. "These people don't know what they're missing," she continued. "But that doesn't mean we need to leave the church. Just because a misguided Pastor tells you to stop doing something doesn't mean you should. I've fitted in there, and I love working in the kid's ministry. And the children have made friends. Surely Bill can't dictate to you what happens outside of the church. If people want to come to you privately then that's their business. Why don't we stay for a little longer? And Bill might come around once he sees all the good you're doing."

"It wouldn't be right Lucy. You understand how authority works. Bill has it and he is responsible for his flock. If I try to usurp that then I can't expect God to talk to me. And without God I have no gift. No. It's better I bow out now and move on."

"But if we move you'll have to find a new job. I thought you liked working for the Matthews. You said farm work gave you plenty of time to spend with God. The quiet made it easier to hear Him. What if we stayed in the area and found a new church?"

"It's a nice thought Lucy. But there isn't another church here that will accept me. They are all full of people with closed minds. None of them are ready for this new move of the Spirit."

"But where will we live? This job was so perfect because it came with a house."

"Come on Lucy. Be honest. You know this place is a dump. And you deserve better. I'll get work somewhere else. Hasn't God always provided for us? Trust Him. He's told me he has more important work for me to do anyway. Milking cows and fixing fences is a waste of my time. I've learnt everything I could here and now it's time to put that knowledge to use. It's a big world out there and people need to hear my message. Soon I'll be doing ministry full-time. But New Zealand isn't where it's going to happen. This country isn't ready yet."

"But Steven this is our home. This is where our families are. I don't want to move to another country."

Shaking his head Steven said "our home is anywhere God wants us to be. Chelsea, Jonathon and I are your family. And are you really going to miss your parents? You know how they make you feel."

"Yes, it's difficult being with them. But they are still my mum and dad."

"But all they do is make you feel guilty."

"It's just that they don't understand me anymore or the way I've chosen to live my life." Lucy's parents were children of the sixties. They had met at a nightclub in Auckland where the LSD was easy to come by and love didn't last more than a few days. When Lucy's mum had realized she was pregnant she tracked down the father-to-be through a friend and the two of them decided to make a go of it. Lucy had grown up in a mostly stable home, but her parents never completely gave up their hippy ways. They dabbled in the occult, flirting with Wicca, séances, and believed in mother Earth. Lucy still got the occasional call from them when they needed bailing out of jail because they had attended a demonstration which had gotten out of hand. She had met Steven when a friend dragged her to her first ever church service. She had been searching for something more than her parents had taught her, but didn't know what. Steven had been the one to introduce her to God and she had never looked back. When he told her that God had chosen her especially for him and that he had been waiting for her, she felt like the luckiest girl in the world. They were soul mates. Unfortunately, Lucy's parents hadn't taken to Steven, thinking that he had indoctrinated her with old fashioned, judgemental Christian theology that had no place in today's world. Lucy knew they were wrong. Steven had saved her.

"I know this is what we need to do," he said. "I haven't discussed this with you yet because I wanted to fully understand it myself, but Alan had a prophecy for me the other day. Soon, not yet, but soon, there is going to be a group of businessmen who will support me financially. But this isn't the country where they are and where God is preparing them for me. We need to be obedient to His call and move on."

When Alan had told Steven what God had in store for him he had been excited, but he thought he would have more time in New Zealand. But when Bill had called him into the office three days ago and told him he was no longer allowed to prophesy in the church or conduct releasing sessions, Steven took it as confirmation of Alan's word. God was pulling him out of this church because they weren't ready. Some of the individuals were, but as a congregation, they weren't. And he was sure he knew who had bought his ministry to a halt.

He had been counselling a woman named Alice. She was the wife of one of the elders in the church and had sought him out. She had been very generous, paying him for each session. This happened sometimes. People were so grateful for his time and his God given wisdom that they felt led to give him money. And why not? If they were seeing a psychiatrist they would pay them. And he was much better for them. He could guide them through the process of releasing their pain in a way a doctor couldn't. They might have the degrees, but they didn't have God.

The time he had spent with Alice had been amazing. She was very open to what he had to say. Until her husband became involved. He became defensive and ordered Alice to stop seeing Steven. He was probably one of the reasons Alice had needed to see Steven in the first place. He wanted to control his wife and when she had begun to receive freedom it meant her husband was losing his power over her. Steven only wished he had been able to spend some time with Alice's husband John. He would have gotten to the root of his problems in no time and bought healing to a hurting family. But he had been rejected. Again. So he had no choice but to move on. If the Pastor and his board wanted to silence Steven because they were afraid of the truth, he would go. Quietly so others, including his wife and children, wouldn't be hurt. Let them reject him and see how God would take His hand off their lives. Steven didn't want to be around people that weren't in alignment with God anyway. Steven had walked away from Bill's office, already forgiving him. He wasn't angry. He was heartbroken. Alice had been so close and now she was going to be left to fend for herself. Steven could only hope and pray that God would bring someone else into Alice's life that could complete the healing that he had started.

"I'm sorry Lucy. I know you're happy here. But I know it's the right thing to do. And We're not going far. Australia is only a quick flight away if your parents need you. And mine too. They'll be sad, but we have to think about what God wants for us."

"Australia?" she sighed. "I guess it's just a short plane ride away. And it's cheaper than living here. Do you know where in Ozzie we'll be going?"

"Queensland. Beaches and warm winters. You're always complaining you don't do well in the cold. You'll love it and so will the kids."

"Queensland? We don't know anyone in Queensland. Isn't it full of deadly spiders and snakes? Yuck."

"We're not moving to the bush. We'll be close to the city. We can both get jobs while we wait on God, maybe even buy a house of our own. And there's so much possibility. People are more laid back there. God's ready to take their receptive hearts and heal them. And I'm going to be part of that. Just imagine. We could be instrumental in changing a city. We could change a nation. They just have to want it and to believe that they deserve the freedom God wants them to have. I can hardly wait to go."

Chapter five
Later

" Do you think you'll be late tonight?" Lauren asked as she spooned pasta onto three plates. Another dinner alone with the kids. Between work, church commitments and this new solar venture, Jamie had been late at least three nights a week, if not more, in the past two months. She understood what he was doing was important, and it wasn't like he was out at the pub with mates, but she still got lonely spending so many nights alone with just the dogs for company. Emily was in her second to last year of high school and had finally realized it was important to buckle down and do some work if she had a chance at getting into university. Oliver had three years of high school left, but still had a heavy workload, or so he claimed. For a kid with so much homework he seemed to spend an inordinate amount of time on YouTube. For some reason Jamie seemed to think that Lauren should be the one monitoring how much time he spent in front of the screen. Perhaps if he spent a few more nights at home Jamie would realise it was impossible to get Oliver off his computer and reading a book. Every time

Lauren went into his room and yelled at him to turn it off, he claimed he was only watching something for school. And by nine at night she was just too tired and frustrated to argue anymore. So instead of bickering with her son, she spent her evenings alone in front of the television.

"Sorry. Don't know," Jamie answered. "I imagine it will be quite late. We have a tonne of things to discuss and decisions to make. And with seven different opinions it can be hard to decide on something. We still don't even have a name yet."

"How difficult can it be?" Lauren asked. "It's solar panels, so just stick that in the name. Pat came up with the idea, so call it Belling Solar. There, sorted," she smiled, happy she had solved their problem and wondered why it had to be such a big deal.

"Right, can you imagine? Everyone else will want it to be their surname and anyway, they want the name to mean something. There's talk of doing some more ventures in the future together and we want to be able to use the same name again."

Lauren put down the pot that she had been ladling out the pasta from.

"What do you mean more ventures? We agreed to this one-time deal. You never said a word about doing more projects."

"But wouldn't it make sense?" Jamie defended. "If we did one every year or so we could be set up for life."

"I never agreed to that," Lauren declared. "And this is the first I've heard of it. As far as I'm concerned, we get our money back, make some profit and move on. I'm already a nervous wreck worrying about whether we've done the right thing. Based on what you've told me we should be able to renovate, pay off the mortgage, and get back our initial investment. That's more than enough for me. We don't need to be greedy."

"Don't stress Lauren. Nothing's come up yet and maybe this will be a one-time deal. Lots of ideas are being thrown about, that doesn't mean anything will come of it. And we have other things to sort out. How the dividends will be paid out, the timing of it, and how much we want to give to some very worthy charities." Jamie had hoped the discussion about giving a portion of the money away to Christian charities would die a natural death, but instead it seemed to be gaining momentum. And with Harry leading the charge, the figure being thrown around to give out of the profits was way too much for his liking. Thankfully, he wasn't the only one who felt this way and he couldn't see how such a high figure would ever get everyone's agreement. He had been putting off telling Lauren about Harry's idea for two months now, but panels were starting to sell, and money was finally coming in. He had no choice but to mention it so he could manage her expectations of what they would receive if something actually came of Harry's wild proposal. Hopefully together the boys would land on a figure lower than Harry's suggestion.

"I'm sorry, what?" Lauren asked. Jamie had obviously been keeping this piece of information from her. She knew Jamie would call it protecting her, but Lauren knew the truth. He hadn't told her because she would tell him no, and he probably didn't want to have to disagree with his brothers as they had started calling each other, who always took first priority these days.

"Um, don't you think that's our decision?" Lauren exclaimed. "We decide whether we want to give away any of our money, and it is *our* money, and *we* decide *who we* want to give it to. Don't most of the guys go to the same church? What if they decide they want to build an auditorium for Living Water's Church? Some of that's my money. I would much rather that went to our church."

"Calm down Lauren. Our church will receive money from our tithes. There's just this feeling that we need to include God in the decision making, and a lot of them are hearing that we need to contribute to the kingdom. It won't be much. Probably more of a token than anything. We're going to make a lot of money out of this, and like you said there's no need to be greedy."

"Excuse me. I am calm," Lauren said, moving very quickly from surprise to anger. "And I'm certainly not greedy. I tithe, I sponsor a kid in Africa. I'm always making meals for sick people at church and you know we give money if we know someone's in need."

Jamie started to massage his temple like he always did when he felt a headache coming on. Exhaling he said, "Lauren I don't think you're greedy. This isn't about us personally, but the spirit of the group. We've all come into this wanting to make money and we should be careful that it's not our only focus. Giving a small percentage of the profits away will help keep us in check. We've all been praying about it, and together we will come to a decision. No one person is in control of what will happen. I get to have a say too."

Dinner forgotten and beginning to go cold, Lauren tossed the serving spoon towards the sink. Missing, spaghetti bolognaise sauce hit the bench, and splattered up over the kitchen window. Crossing her arms over her chest, her body language said it all. Her face was stony and her usually soft brown eyes had turned dark and pointed, fixed on Jamie's own.

"How long have you all been discussing this?"

"A few weeks," Jamie answered. When Lauren didn't respond, he knew she didn't believe him. She had a knack of knowing when he wasn't telling her everything. It was like being married to a human lie detector. Or maybe he was just too easy to read.

"We've been discussing this from the first night," he conceded. "I didn't tell you cause I knew you would overreact like this. Sometimes there's no reasoning with you. You haven't even asked what I think.

You've just flown off the handle as usual, so what's the point of telling you anything anyway. And for your information, I'm not keen, and I'm going to let them know that. I think it's the responsibility of each family to make their own decisions."

"I hope you mean that. Because I will never agree. You seem to think this is all your decision, but it's not. It's my money invested, and nobody seems to be asking me what I think."

"I will be conveying that to the others tonight Lauren. But I am only one voice in the group. And we also need to consider this may be what God wants? Do *you* want to go against Him? Cause I don't. He told *you* to do this investment. So maybe *you* should ask Him what He thinks about extra giving."

"What I think is that you should just go," Lauren yelled, her temper no longer in check. "Off to another important meeting at some fancy restaurant, while I stay here alone and eat food I don't even like. One of your favourites. I don't know why I even bother anymore." She turned her back to him and picked up a cloth. She started wiping up the spilled sauce, her hands shaking with anger as Jamie backed away from the kitchen and then turned away. He knew this was not the end of the argument, but for now there was no point trying to convince Lauren that it would all be ok. And he was already running late for dinner. The last thing he wanted was for the rest of them to start making decisions without him there.

Once Lauren heard the front door shut behind Jamie the tears came. She hated crying in front of him. It just re-enforced his opinion that she was a crazy woman, out of control and unreasonable. She hated that word. Unreasonable. Did other women's husbands make them feel this way? Over the years, she had tried to educate him that men and women needed different things in life and had a different way of looking at a situation. She needed stability and security. He preferred to take risks and was much more trusting of people, taking them at face value. Since the beginning, Lauren had had her reservations about investing all her money in this venture. But she couldn't deny that God had been clear with her that it was the right thing to do. But why should she trust these guys. She hadn't even met some of them, and there was just this feeling deep in her gut. And she trusted her gut. It told her she needed to be on guard. And Jamie needed to start telling her the whole truth. Because there was one thing in life that Lauren really hated. And that was being lied to.

~ ~ ~

By the time Jamie made it to the restaurant most of the others had already arrived. And contrary to Lauren's assertion that every dinner they had was in an expensive place, this one was in a small Italian local, with cheap wine and paper on the tables. But the food was always good, and the atmosphere was always warm, if a little loud. He had booked out the back room for dinner and pre-ordered the food and drinks. This way he could control how much the bill came to because tonight it was his turn to pay. Another thing he had neglected to tell Lauren. He'd meant to, but that same day he had made the booking the health insurance premium had come in and of course it had gone up for the year. That had definitely not been the time to tell her he would be spending hundreds of dollars on a dinner out, when they had decided to curb their own spending. Restaurants were out of their budget for the moment, and he only hoped he had some good news for her regarding dividends before she saw the credit card bill.

As the host tonight, he took his place at the head of the table. They were only waiting on Lawrence. He had texted earlier that he would be a little late, caught in city traffic. Jamie saw that Joshua was looking over the wine list, even though Jamie had specifically asked for no menus at the table. There was no need when everything was already ordered. Pushing his chair back, he walked over to where Joshua was sitting and tapped him on the shoulder. Turning, Joshua's face lit up, happy to see Jamie. Being a good ten years older than him, Josh looked up to Jamie.

"Hey mate. Good to see you." He put his right hand out to shake Jamie's as he held the wine list with his left.

"I'm just trying to find something decent to drink here tonight. Not too keen on this plonk they put out."

"Oh, um, sorry. I ordered those. Guess I don't have much of an eye for wine."

"No worries mate. I'll look after it for you. Not much to choose from here anyway. Hardly anything decent on this list."

Phew, thought Jamie. Even if Joshua picks the most expensive bottle, there was nothing over forty dollars. He couldn't break the bank here. And it wasn't true that Jamie couldn't recognize a good drop of red. He just didn't think because it had the most expensive price tag on it that it was better than something from a good local winery. He believed Australians could turn out wine that was just as good, if not better, than the French.

Retaking his seat, he pulled out seven copies of the agenda he had drafted last night and started handing them around the table. Most of the men gave it a quick glance and then resumed their conversations. Harry was the only one who read it thoroughly and even pulled out a pen and started making notes. Over the past two months as Jamie got to know Harry better he had really begun to admire the way he lived his life. He spent a lot of time with God, praying and worshipping, and God spoke to him more than anyone else Jamie had ever known. He had a level of relationship with God that Jamie desired too. Harry also had a presence about him that very few men did. He was incredibly articulate, and persuasive. It was almost impossible to disagree with him when he spoke with such logic and passion. Jamie could only dream of having a skill like that. It would make life at home more peaceful if Lauren was able to get on board with his views occasionally. And Harry wasn't only in this for the money. Harry was the one that had been strongly lobbying to give a big chunk of the money away. Knowing that, Jamie decided that tonight, despite how much he liked Harry, he needed to have his wits about him. He would not agree to anything he thought wasn't good for his family. Who, after all, were the reason he was doing this.

A few minutes later Lawrence arrived, taking the last place at the table. He apologised for his delay, but it was dismissed by the group. Sydney traffic was a nightmare, and everyone understood. One accident or breakdown in the wrong spot could throw half the city into chaos. Standing, Jamie tapped his fork on his glass and the babble of conversation stopped as everyone's attention was drawn to him.

"Thanks everyone for making it here tonight. I thought before we started I would say grace." Each man's head bowed as Jamie continued.

"Thank you Lord that we can all meet here tonight. We ask your blessing on the food that we are about to eat and for the staff who prepared it tonight. We also invite you into our conversations and our decisions. We are walking in your plan for us and we ask for your wisdom. Amen." More amens rang out across the table and then conversations started up around them.

After the first course was brought to the table, share plates of bruschetta, olives, mini capsicums stuffed with feta and prosciutto wrapped artichoke hearts, the volume at the table dropped to nothing but the odd murmur of pleasure. Pleased that they were all enjoying the food, Jamie took advantage of the quiet to bring the meeting to a start.

"Guys, we have a few points to go through tonight. I'm going to quickly go through them so we're all on the same page and hopefully we can come to some decisions tonight. The first thing we need to address is finding a name for our little enterprise. Has anyone had any ideas?"

"I've been sitting with this for a few weeks now and seeking God on a name," Harry began, predictably. He always seemed to know exactly what God wanted them to do.

"I'm sure you all know the story of Gideon. He was chosen by God from the least significant clan in Israel and he was the least significant one in his father's house. He was an ordinary man, but with God on his side he defeated the Midianites with only three hundred men. The seven of us are just ordinary men, but I know God is going to use us and this venture, to do something amazing for his kingdom. So, I suggest we call ourselves Gideon Solar. And in the future, we can apply the Gideon brand to whatever new opportunity God brings our way."

"Sounds good to me," Daniel confirmed. "I like it!" From the nodding around the table, Jamie could see that no one disagreed. He hoped that everything else would be that easy. There was a feeling of contentment in the room. Good food, good company. There was a small electrical charge running through the group and Jamie felt like God was here with them.

After the table was cleared and the glasses had been refilled, it was time to bring the next decision to the group. This was the one Jamie was most excited about, the reason he was doing this.

"Guys, the next thing we need to discuss is the timing and the amount, of paying out dividends. And what we think are reasonable overheads. We all know the main cost is Harry. We have him on a commission and from what I can see sales are already strong after being operational for only a month."

"Ah, sorry to interrupt you Jamie," Harry said. "Before we start talking about dividends, shouldn't we finish our previous discussions about our giving? That's an important decision, and once we agree on that, we can move on to the rest of the agenda."

"I agree with Harry on this," Pat said. "The two of us have spent quite a lot of time in prayer together and God has been very clear. At first, I was surprised at where God was leading us, but Harry and I are both hearing the same thing and the same amount. I'll be honest. I originally thought ten percent would be right. It's biblical and a lot of good could be done with that much money. But God is calling us to more than the minimum. He's going to stretch us in ways we never imagined and He's also going to bring blessing. But first He has to know He can trust us. And with that said, I think we should be giving twenty-five percent of all profits."

"Yeah, I'm not sure about that," Stuart called out as he shook his head. "I've said it before and I'll say it again, my decision to invest in this project was based on the returns. I don't mind making some sort of charitable contribution, it'll help with the tax bill. But twenty-five percent really cuts into what I was expecting, and I had plans for that money."

This had been the prevailing opinion at the first few meetings. Most of the guys were in it for the money. But slowly there had been a shift and now Jamie, Lawrence and Stuart were the only holdouts. Jamie felt himself tense up, the easy-going atmosphere from earlier was gone as all eyes turned to Harry.

"Is that *really* how we should be making decisions?" Harry asked, his voice gentle as he began to unravel Stuarts objections. "What would it look like to ask God what His plans are? Don't you want more for your life than just a one-off investment that yes, will make you some money now, but doesn't store up anything for eternity? Because we are called to store up our treasures in Heaven, not on Earth. There is more for us than just making a quick buck. Together we can change lives if we all agree to give a little more. It won't make much difference to us individually, but combined, this money will impact souls throughout this city if we seek God and do His will. After all isn't this the reason we're here on Earth? To win souls for Christ, not for a life of luxury and pleasure."

Jamie looked around the table. Apart from himself and Lawrence, everyone else was murmuring their support of Harrys suggestion. And even he, with all his objections, was finding it hard to argue with. Stuart, who was now nodding his head, had obviously had a change of heart too. As the staff started to bring out the main course Lawrence stood up to get the attention of the table.

"Guys, this all sounds very holy, but don't you think it's important to discuss this with our wives first? They have a vested interest and they *are* our partners. I don't think it's right to go ahead and make such an important decision without talking to them first."

"My wife is on board," Pat replied, "and so is Harry's. Yes, you will need to take this home and discuss it with your wives. But first *we* need to work out where *we* sit so you can have something to discuss with them. And when you let them know what's been decided, I'm quite sure they will all be in agreement with what God has asked of us."

Joshua was the first to answer. "I know Ashley won't mind. She doesn't really have a head for finances and as long as I keep her comfortable, she's happy. Harry if this is what God is telling you, then I'm all for it."

"Guys," Harry said as he rested his elbows on the table and wove his fingers together in a v shape. "Let's be clear. This isn't my idea. I'm just telling you what I heard. And if you are feeling uncomfortable about the amount, you might want to ask yourselves why. What issues are holding *you* back from fulfilling God's will? Does greed have a hold of you?" And then Harry leaned forward in his chair and helped himself to some dinner. He didn't force his opinion. It was never necessary. He knew God's will would prevail.

The others followed suit and started to fill their plates. Jamie had ordered a combination of pizza and pasta. Not fancy, but all delicious. After everyone was eating he decided he needed to take a vote. If they didn't agree, then at least they could continue the discussion at home and come back to it in the next fortnight. He wasn't looking forward to going to Lauren with this proposal. She would never agree to it.

"So, have we reached a consensus," he asked. "We take this home to our wives and come back next fortnight?"

"I don't need to," Daniel replied. "I'm good with twenty-five percent to the kingdom."

"Yep, me too," echoed Stuart whose backflip on his earlier stance was complete.

Jamie knew where Pat, Harry and Joshua stood. That just left Lawrence and himself. He looked over, hoping for some support from the only other one who was holding out for something more reasonable.

"I really think this is pushing it guys," Lawrence declared. "But Harry has made some good points. I'll agree to twenty-five percent, but there are some conditions. The money can't just be going to random charities. We need an oversight committee. And a way to make sure the money is used well. Maybe a foundation, governed by law, and accountable to a mission statement we *all* agree on. I don't want to see the funds wasted on people's pet projects."

"Absolutely Lawrence," Pat agreed. "I wouldn't have it any other way. And I think Harry would be the best one to bring us options for where we should sow the funds. He's the one with the heart for this. I'm positive he will come to us with the best possibilities and from there we can seek God together and give it a yah or nay. That seems the fairest way to move forward."

Nobody seemed to notice that Jamie hadn't said anything. He didn't even understand how this had happened. One minute it was Harry and Pat. And the next everyone else was on board. Decision made. Talk about blindsided, this had not been the outcome he had been hoping for, nor was it one that Lauren would say yes to. But there didn't seem to be any point to arguing. Not only were the others happy with the result, but they were excited about it. Taking this home to Lauren to discuss was going to be pointless. There wasn't any *discussion* to be had. She could disagree all she liked, but he could see this was a done deal. The volume in the room rose as he heard statements like amazing blessings, and extending the kingdom tossed around. The food on the table fast disappeared as the others chattered amongst themselves. After they had finished, and the staff cleared the table and bought out dessert Jamie decided it was his last chance to bring the discussion back on topic. He tapped his dessert spoon on his glass, hoping to get the groups attention. There were still other things on the agenda to be discussed.

"Hey, guys. Can we come back to the dividend issue?" When Jamie saw that he had their attention he continued.

"We still need to discuss how and when we are going to pay out dividends. I've done a lot of projections, obviously, I'll need to adjust them considering the last decision just made. They're attached to the agenda I've passed out. They are a best guess scenario, depending on how Harry goes with sales, but it will give a good indication of how much we are looking at."

"Jamie it's late," Pat said as he looked at his watch. "And at this time of night it's a bit much to be going over complicated numbers. I suggest everyone take the figures home, have a look and shoot around an email with your thoughts. And Jamie if you could update the numbers that would be great."

"But this is important," Jamie reasoned. "I don't know about the rest of you, but I need to go home tonight and give Lauren some sort of indication of when we can expect to see some return for our investment." *Especially if I have to tell her we are giving away twenty-five percent,* he thought to himself.

"She can wait a couple of days, can't she?" Pat replied. "We've been at this for hours tonight and made an amazing decision together. We can decide the how and when in the next two weeks and confirm it at the next dinner. Lawrence, it will be your shout. So, if you could let us know the restaurant by next week that would be great. Same night work for everyone?"

Heads nodded around the table as a couple of them finished up their gelato and the waiters started clearing the dishes. One by one the guys left, saying their goodbyes and thanking Jamie for an awesome dinner. He saw that more than one agenda had been left on the table. They wouldn't be looking over his proposal tonight. And then Jamie and Pat were the only ones left at the table. Coming over to say goodbye he noted the look of puzzlement on Jamie's face.

"Don't worry mate. We'll get to the figures in the next few days. It'll all be sorted."

"But I just don't understand Pat. This is an investment. I've put everything on the line for this. And I know you came into this wanting to make money. We never once discussed starting a charity at the start."

"It's going to be amazing Jamie. We will make more money than you can imagine. I've been praying with Harry and I'm connecting with God on a deeper level than I have before. I've just shifted my focus, that's all. And I think you will too. This thing is going to be bigger than we ever imagined. Don't stress. It's all in God's hands. You aren't even going to believe the blessing that's coming our way. And the blessing that we are going to be to others. It will make the twenty-five percent look small. Just email me the new numbers in the next few days," Pat reminded Jamie as he headed out the door and waved goodbye.

Jamie didn't have the energy to argue. Not with Pat, and certainly not with Lauren when he got home tonight. How was he ever going to explain what had happened? He couldn't quite put his finger on it, but he felt like he'd been railroaded. Unless? What if this was exactly what God wanted? He wasn't working with conmen. These were Christians. His brothers in Christ, and he trusted them. Pat and Daniel had been his friends for years and he had rarely seen them make a bad decision. *Maybe I just have some more growing to do*, Jamie thought. I know I want to obey God. And if Lauren can't see that giving God whatever portion He requires is a good thing, then maybe it's time for her to do some growing too. What if some of this is about her learning to let go of all her insecurities? I know she has trust issues, but perhaps this is the time for her to really trust God. And maybe Jamie would be able to help her see that this was a good thing. A tap on his shoulder bought his attention back to where he was and turned to find the waiter standing there. He was holding out a folder which no doubt contained the bill. Taking it as he thanked the young man for the wonderful service and food tonight, he opened it. Luckily there was a chair close enough for him to sink into. The food total was right, but the drinks portion was much more than he had expected. Someone, he assumed Joshua, had ordered two bottles of Penfolds Shiraz at one hundred and fifty dollars each. Where had the staff dug them up from? They certainly weren't on the menu. But tonight was on him, and he had no choice but to pay the bill. The cost of those two bottles alone was more than Lauren spent on groceries in a week. He fished his credit card out of his wallet and placed it in the folder. He reluctantly handed it back to the waiter and followed him to the front of the restaurant. Card swiped, he thanked Fabrizio, the restaurant's owner, and stepped outside into the cool evening. He pulled his jacket around him, hoping to warm up as he walked back to where he had left his car. His usual purposeful steps dragged as he hoped to delay the inevitable. Home was not somewhere he wanted to go tonight. There he would be faced with yelling, accusations, and the worst thing, his wife's disappointment in him. And while he didn't blame her, it was going to be an uphill battle to convince her to trust that he knew what he was doing. But he was the head of his house. At the end of the day it fell to him to make decisions. While this was not what either of them had originally signed up for, being part of something bigger for the Kingdom of God might turn out to be one of the best things they had ever done. Lauren had a lot of hang-ups to let go of, and money was her biggest one. It certainly wasn't going to be easy, but this would be an opportunity for him to lead her where she needed to go. He just wished for once that she would trust him, instead of arguing at every turn with his decisions. Why couldn't she just for once be like the other wives who believed in their husbands and were willing to do whatever God asked them without an argument?

Chapter six

J amie looked up from his laptop with a huge grin on his face. Finally, he had some good news for Lauren. Her reaction when he told her about the new foundation and the twenty-five percent of the profits it would receive, had gone as expected. For days, she had ranted that her money was being stolen. She insisted he refuse to contribute in any way, not understanding that the group had made the decision and there was nothing he could or would do about it. They were all in agreement now, including him. And it looked like their decision had been the right one. Once she'd calmed down and the stopped being hysterical, he had hoped she would accept that the foundation was going to happen. Unfortunately, her anger hadn't disappeared, but was hiding behind silence. She only spoke to him when it was absolutely necessary and the tension in the house was so thick he felt like he could reach out and grab it. Hopefully what he was about to tell her would thaw some of the frost coming from her.

"Lauren," he said. "Can I talk to you for a sec?"

She put her hand up in a wait-a-minute gesture as she continued reading the page she was on. When she finished, she slowly folded the corner down and closed the book. She looked across the room to where he was sitting, her face a mask of indifference.

"Yes?"

"Do you remember me telling you that Harry was in Melbourne meeting with a building company? Well, he's just sent through an email with a signed contract. They are buying a quarter of our stock. They are taking half immediately, and the other half in six months. And because we insisted on payment on delivery, they are depositing the funds into Gideon's bank account by the end of the week. We should have our investment back, plus a little more, by Tuesday."

"Are you serious?"

"Yep," Jamie nodded. "I think we might come close to an extra hundred grand on top of the two-fifty we invested. And," he paused wanting the moment to last, "I think we should use that money to do the kitchen."

Lauren leapt off her chair, tossing the book she had been holding in the air. Before he could brace himself, she launched herself across the room and onto his lap, throwing her arms around him.

"I get a new kitchen?"

"Yes, you get a new kitchen. And if we stick to a budget, I think we might even be able to swing some furniture as well. Maybe a new lounge suite."

"A new lounge suite. Woohoo. I know exactly what I want," she clapped her hands with glee. "The staff at freedom furniture think I'm a shop lifter cause I'm in there so often."

"Then let's go buy the couch of your dreams this weekend," Jamie smiled and kissed Lauren's cheek. "So, does this mean I'm off the hook, or are you still mad at me?"

"Of course I'm still mad, and you might as well get used to it. I'm going to be mad at you for a very long time. I don't know how you let yourself get pushed into agreeing to such a stupid thing. Nobody gives a quarter of their profits away. It's ridiculous."

"Okay," Jamie tilted his head to the side the way Harry did right before he announced something profound. "That might be true, and I can see why you would believe that. But look at what's just happened. We agree to give twenty-five percent away, and in one hit, twenty-five percent of our stock is sold. If that isn't God, I don't know what is. You only have to look at the fruit to see that we've done the right thing."

"Talk about conclusion jumping. You have no idea whether the sale was dependant on giving away so much."

"I think it was," Jamie countered. "Harry was doing really well with sales before this, but at that rate it would have taken us months before Gideon had enough to pay us back our initial investment. This sale also means we can take on a staff member to sell even more panels. Pat had a girl in mind, Jules, who has an amazing resume, and we all wanted to bring her on board, but we couldn't pay her. Now we can. And now we know we'll be able to take another big dividend in six months when the second half of the contract settles. Not to mention there will probably be another payment in the middle of all that. Just like that, half our mortgage gone. I don't think that's a coincidence. It can only be God."

"I'm not doubting this is God's blessing. But it's almost like you are trying to buy his favour. And I have huge misgivings about all this Foundation money sitting in one pot. I'm not going to have any say in where it goes. Neither will any of the other wives. You could all easily be taken advantage of."

"No way," Jamie shook his head. "Harry is one of the most honest guys I have ever met. And his heart is completely in the right place. He'll make sure that money goes to good, Godly causes. Now can you please let this go. What's done is done. You can be as angry as you like at me, but it won't change the outcome. All you're doing is creating tension in the house, and it's not good for us, and it's really not good for the kids."

Lauren knew Jamie was right. She hated being mad at him, and from what he had told her, he had tried to stop the whole thing. He said he had fought it, but with the other six in firm agreement, there had been nothing he could do.

"Fine," she said. "But you really need to consider asking us girls what we think the money should go to. I'm sure we're all clever women, with lots of great ideas. You boys seem to forget it's our money too. And you wouldn't even have been able to invest without my money. I should be the one making decisions, not you."

"Perhaps. But Pat didn't ask you. He asked me. And in a few days, I will be paying back every cent. And I might add, buying you a new kitchen," Jamie reminded her.

"I almost forgot," Lauren giggled. "A whole new kitchen, with everything I want in it. Should we go ultra-modern? Or country style? That would suit the house better because of its age. All I know is it has to have a scullery. And two dishwashers. I have always wanted two dishwashers."

"Why on Earth would you need two dishwashers?" Jamie asked.

"Because when we have people over for dinner there's nothing worse than not having enough space to do all the dishes and waking up to a mess."

"Am I going to need to buy you two fridges as well? Maybe two washing machines. Or two cars," Jamie teased.

"No, I think one very big fridge would be fine. But you might be onto something with the two-car thing. One for driving the children and one for when I'm on my own. Something sporty to reflect my new glamourous life now that we're going to be rich."

"Well, I'll get right on that," Jamie replied. "But first can I get you to organise some quotes for the kitchen. Maybe narrow down what you want. Because I think an ultra-modern, country kitchen might look a little weird."

Lauren jumped off his lap and started rummaging through the junk drawer in the lamp table.

"What ya doing?" Jamie asked. Lauren continued pulling out old school notes, paid bills that had never made it to the filling cabinet and paint charts that had been put away when the inevitable argument about which colour to choose got out of hand.

"I'm sure I put a house and garden magazine in here last year. It had an article about kitchens and what not to do. I remember there was one picture that was just beautiful. Aha. Here it is." Retaking her seat, Lauren began flipping pages while Jamie continued to read his emails. A companionable silence took over the room. Most of his mail was either Gideon or work related, and he quickly answered questions, tapping away quietly as Lauren uttered the occasional sigh of pleasure or disgust at the kitchens on offer in her magazine. He looked over to her, happy she was happy. Hopefully the argument about the foundation was behind them. It had been a horrible few weeks, but next week she would have her money back and with the kitchen reno to focus on, she would forget how angry she had been. This distraction would be perfect, and Jamie didn't think it would take her long to narrow down exactly what she wanted. One thing about his wife. She knew what she liked. As Jamie made his way through the long list of emails one caught his eye. It was a thank you from a Pastor he knew a little. He had called last week to ask some advice. And while he hadn't been able to tell him what he wanted to hear, it had been great to catch up with him and hear how he and his church was going. He had meant to tell Lauren about the call, but with all the tension in the house, there hadn't been a right time.

"Hey," he asked. "Do you remember Tim Rawlings?"

Lauren looked up from her magazine. The pages were now covered with notes she had made in the margin and the old paint charts had stars marked beside potential colours.

"Ah, Pastor over in the western suburbs, right?"

"Yeah, him. He called me last week. He was after some tax advice."

"And did you charge him for your time?" Lauren asked. "Or was this another freebie because he's a Christian?" It was a bone of contention between Lauren and Jamie. He wouldn't charge for phone calls and she thought he should because people were always ringing and asking him accounting questions. Time was time, whether you were sitting in an office face to face, or on the other end of the line.

"Please stop asking me to charge people when they ask for a little off-the-record advice. It was fifteen minutes of my day while I was driving and he's a Pastor for crying out loud. The advice was for his church, not him personally. Those guys work so hard for their congregations I think it's the least I can do."

"Sorry," Lauren mumbled feeling like a naughty child being reprimanded by her Dad. She was only trying to look out for Jamie.

"And as it happens, I couldn't help him anyway. He wanted to know if it's possible to set up a structure that would enable people to make donations to one of his church member's and make it tax deductable. I told them no. They weren't very happy when I told them as an individual, he didn't qualify for tax exempt status. They actually tried to argue with me that there must be a way to get around the rules."

"Who's they?"

"Oh sorry, Tim wasn't alone in the car. He was with the guy he wants the tax exemption for. And get this. Just before the end of the conversation Steven, that's the other guy, said he had a prophesy for me."

"Really. He's never met you, but he's got a prophesy. Was it that you would find a way to make the tax exemption work?" she asked sarcastically.

"Ha ha," Jamie said shaking his head. "No, it was all a bit generic. Let me think." Jamie paused a minute trying to remember what Steven had said to him. "He said he had a vision of a paint-by-numbers painting and that God isn't finished with it yet. I guess I'm supposed to be the painting. He said I was frustrated with the turmoil in my life that I can't control, but to not worry about it because the turmoil was from God and he was leading me to a different place and change would come suddenly in my life."

"I've never heard of anyone phoning in a prophesy before."

"No, me neither. And I'm not really sure what it meant. I'm pretty happy with the way my life is going these days. But I was interested in hearing about why he wanted the tax exemption. He does counselling with people. He called them releasing sessions."

"Oh. So he's a qualified therapist. Can't he just charge people through their health insurance. And why would he think he can get a tax deductable status? No doctor can get that, let alone a counsellor."

"I got the feeling he doesn't actually have a degree or any other formal qualifications. As they explained it, Steven uses a combination of prophesy and his experience to help people identify past hurts that may be causing the problems in their lives now."

"That's a different approach to counselling. I don't think I've ever heard of doing it like that before. Sounds a bit, I don't know, off. Is Tim cool with all of this?"

"Tim loves him. He would have Steven on full-time at the church, but they can't afford it at the moment. So instead people pay privately for the sessions. They think that if they could make them tax deductable Steven would have more clients. I was actually thinking it might be something we could consider."

"Consider?"

"Counselling."

"Why would we need that?"

"I thought it might be helpful for you. Maybe deal with some of the issues you have with your father. I'd be happy to go along with you."

"I don't need counselling Jamie. I'm perfectly sane."

"I didn't say you weren't. But everybody needs help sometimes. Maybe a chat with Steven would clarify some things for you and then you could move on. Not worry about money so much."

"You have got to be kidding me," Lauren snorted. "Under no circumstances am I going to let someone poke around in my head. I can't believe you would even suggest such a thing."

"*Sorry*. I had no idea you would be so sensitive," Jamie said.

"I am *not* sensitive. But I am surprised you would want me to get counselling from someone with no qualifications."

"He's had years of experience. That has to count for something?"

"Not to me. If, and I don't ever see that happening, if I went to see a doctor for counselling, I would want them to have years of University and a degree behind them."

"Fine," he said lifting his hands in surrender. "Let's drop it. I thought it might be a good idea. Clearly you don't. If Tim calls again for advice, I'll tell him I can't help him. Okay?"

"Good," Lauren exhaled. Why did Jamie do this? More than once he had suggested she needed counselling. Yes, she'd had a rough childhood. But she wasn't a child anymore. The last thing she wanted was to get bogged down in the past. Move forward and forget the bad had always been Lauren's motto. She had worked hard to forget what it was like to be hungry, afraid that there wouldn't be food the next day either. She tried not to think about the humiliation of going to school in hand-me-down clothes from a girl in her class. Of course, that girl had pointed out to her friends that Lauren was wearing her old clothes. Bronwyn's mother had probably thought she was helping a poor family, but unfortunately her generosity of spirit hadn't passed along to her daughter. Jamie didn't know, didn't understand. He had grown up in a nice home with stable parents. He had never gone hungry. He had been able to attend the same school throughout his entire education. He never had to experience sitting alone in the library at lunch because he had no friends after having been moved to yet another town and another school. But instead of being proud of how she had overcome the disadvantages of her childhood, he continued to pick away at her old, healed, wounds. If she really needed counselling, then she would get it. But it wouldn't be with Steven. Something didn't feel quite right to her about what he was doing. She knew Jamie would think she was over-reacting and not giving the man a chance. He would accuse her of being suspicious of anything new. But there was a niggle. Just a little one, but it was there. And she trusted that.

It wasn't until he was cleaning his teeth later that Jamie's thoughts returned to their earlier conversation about Steven. He thought it was exactly the kind of experience that could change Lauren's life. He loved her, but she needed some sort of help. Her money issues, her lack of trust, often held them back from opportunities. Lately he thought her behaviour was becoming erratic. Happy one minute, uncommunicative and angry the next. She wasn't happy about Gideon and often voiced her concerns. He was worried her behaviour would affect the way their kids lived their lives as well. And yet again she had dismissed him and accused him of thinking she was crazy. It didn't help that sometimes she acted like she was. Frankly, some days he found it exhausting.

Chapter seven

"I can't believe how beautiful this is" Lauren said as she gazed out over the grounds of Sipping Time winery. She breathed in the crisp Autumn air as she settled into the rocking chair that sat out on the deck of the second story suite they would be staying in for the next three days. She took a sip of the local Sauvignon Blanc that had been waiting for them on ice and felt instantly relaxed. *This was the kind of life I could get used to,* Lauren thought. It was made even more enjoyable knowing that they wouldn't be spending a cent while they were here. Everything was paid for, courtesy of Gideon Solar.

When Jamie had first told her that all the shareholders and their wives would be flying to New Zealand for the first, annual retreat, Lauren hadn't wanted to go. It sounded like a waste of money and couldn't the boys have just added in an extra meeting or two at home to discuss whatever it was that was so important. But now, overlooking the winery, the vines heavy with grapes ready to be harvested and the Autumn leaves a blaze of reds and oranges, she felt grateful that she was able to experience the beauty on display. The sun was about to set, and it looked like God was going to put on a magnificent show just for her.

Not that she wasn't still apprehensive about the trip. It had been made clear that the girls were to spend their time bonding and Lauren hated being forced into friendship. It reminded her of being paired up with a new friend every time she started yet another school as a child. Teachers would always pick the weird girl with no friends to show her around. The girl might have been perfectly nice but hanging around with someone already considered an outcast had made it hard to make real friends of her own. She was instantly labelled a loser to the other girls and it was difficult to prove she wasn't one. And now she was expected to make connections with new strangers. She knew Pat's wife Maria, and Felicity who was married to Daniel, but these weren't close relationships and she had only met the other wives once at a dinner the boys had planned as a social get-together. They had all been lovely, but they already knew each other outside Gideon. It was like being ten again and looking for somewhere she could hide during lunch until class started again.

She would have much preferred to explore the beautiful countryside and wineries with Jamie. But the boys had three full days of meetings to discuss what the future held for Gideon, and the girls were expected to bond over shopping in the eclectic stores that littered the Marlborough region, taking in the farmer's market and even spending some time in a local museum and art gallery. A small bus and driver had been hired for the long weekend and they had a tight itinerary. They would only see their husbands at breakfast and dinner. Lauren had no interest in the art gallery. She had looked it up on-line at home. It was full of awkward sculptures that people pretended to understand and paintings that looked like something Oliver had brought home from Kindergarten. She was interested in the farmer's market, but it seemed kind of pointless as she couldn't take any of the fresh produce home with her to Australia. The only thing she was really looking forward to was the spa day on Monday morning before they caught a flight home. The reviews were fantastic and from the pictures she had seen on the internet, the views from the treatment rooms were going to be magnificent. And it would give her some time to herself. She could already feel herself relax as she thought about the massage she had booked.

"I can't believe we're here," Lauren declared. "It's just so beautiful."

"It really is, isn't it," said Jamie. "And to think, you didn't want to come."

"I know, I know. I was wrong. But don't get used to me saying that. I'm just going to finish this glass of wine while the sun sets, and then I'm going to soak in that huge tub before I have to get ready for dinner."

"Okay, but don't be too long. Dinner is in an hour and I don't want to be late" Jamie said as he stood up. "I'm going to have a quick shower and wash the plane smell off me." Lauren watched his retreating back and thought to herself *how blessed am I. I have an amazing husband and while we have our ups and down, we get along great most of the time. Yes, the last few months had been stressful, especially with all the fighting about the Foundation but I've almost made my peace with it,* Lauren decided. *And now we are in the best position we have ever been financially. What more could a girl want?*

~ ~ ~

By the time dessert arrived, Lauren wasn't sure she would be able to fit it in. Dinner had been sublime. One of the best meals she had ever had, even surpassing last night's dinner which they had eaten in the winery where they were all staying. Tonight they had spent the evening in another beautiful winery, one which had opened their restaurant tonight just for them. Normally it was closed during grape harvesting time but somehow Harry had convinced them to make an exception. Rumour was he knew someone who used to live in the area, and they had put in a good word for Gideon. It meant they could make as much noise as they wanted, without needing to accommodate other diners. People moved around the table between courses to chat and a few, Jamie included, congregated at the open fire with yet another glass of exquisite wine that was so expensive Lauren was scared to look at the price list. Dinner had started with tasting plates of local produce, including award winning goat's cheese and cured wild game. Normally unsure about new kinds of food, Lauren had decided to throw caution to the wind and try everything she was offered. The mussels in a red chilli broth that followed the tasting plates had stretched her commitment to sampling everything but surprisingly they turned out to be delicious. The slow cooked lamb shanks for the main course, and perfect for a cool New Zealand evening, were much more to her liking, the mild Mediterranean spices giving the dish a depth of flavour she didn't often get in her own cooking. She was going to need to look up some new recipes when she got home and extend her repertoire.

As the staff bought out dessert, of course it was pavlova, good natured insults were thrown back and forward between the staff and their guests. It was typical between the two rival countries. Who had first invented the pav was a battle that had been going on for decades. As long as they didn't start arguing over who invented the Anzac biscuit. If they did, the whole evening could fall into disarray. Lauren took one bite of her dessert and then placed her spoon down. It was delicious but her stomach was actually starting to hurt she had eaten so much. If Gideon kept feeding her like this, she was going to need to buy bigger clothes and as she already struggled with her weight, that was the last thing she wanted.

"You don't like it?" Harry asked. He had sat down beside her after the mains had been finished, with his wife on Lauren's other side. They were a physical match that Lauren didn't really get. Louise was tall, slim and stunning. Her long blonde hair fell in waves down her back and her skin was the colour of honey. Unlike Lauren's own pale skin which burnt, peeled and then returned to its original pale hue. Harry was shorter than Louise, and stocky. Messy black curls framed his face, and whenever Lauren saw him she thought he looked more like a skateboarding teenage boy than a man in his thirties. But he had a kind face and Lauren had like him immediately the first time she met him.

"No, it's delicious. I love pavlova. But I'm just so full I don't think I can eat another thing. Plus, I'm going to get so fat if I keep eating like this."

"And it worries you, getting fat?" Harry questioned.

"Well I'm not exactly skinny, am I? The last thing I need to do is make it worse."

Harry shrugged his shoulders. "That's just your outward appearance. How important is it really?"

"Yeah right. Come on Harry. Look at your wife. She's gorgeous."

"She is. But do you think that's what really matters to me? I don't want to sound like a cliché but what's most important to me is what she's like inside. Have you considered that you might be uncomfortable with how you look because you aren't happy with who you are?"

"No one's one-hundred percent happy with who they are Harry. We all have area's that need improvement."

"That's true. But take me for example. I know how God sees me. No, I'm not perfect, but every day I ask Him to mould me into the person He wants me to become. And because I'm on that journey willingly I feel content with who I am right now." Harry tilted his head to the side. "Are you content with who you are Lauren? Do you think there's anything God wants you to work on and change about your inward appearance?"

"Talk about a heavy conversation. Isn't this supposed to be a fun evening out?" Lauren said with a nervous giggle. Harry didn't respond, waiting for an answer to his question.

"Look, I'm sure there's plenty God wants me to work on. I just never gave it much thought before."

"Don't you think it might be time to ask God? I haven't known you for long, but I can see that you have some deep struggles. And I feel like it's time that God wants to heal old hurts."

Appalled at herself, Lauren felt tears threaten. It must be the wine making her emotional. Harry reached over and patted her hand.

"Don't be embarrassed. We all need healing. And I can see that your pain goes deep. Why don't you tell me about it."

"I'm not sure this is the right time or place Harry."

"Why not? You can't let it fester like this forever. If you do your pain will continue to spill over until it starts to hurt Jamie and your family. Is that what you want?"

"No of course not. And it's nothing really. My Dad was a bit of a gambler, that's all."

"Ah. I thought it might be something like that. How did that affect your life?"

"It … Well" she paused. "Sometimes there wasn't enough money. For food and stuff."

"And I'm sure you make sure you have plenty of food in your house now that you're in control."

How did he know that, Lauren thought? Running out of food terrified her. The cupboards were always bursting with supplies, in case money got tight. She would at least be able to feed her children. Harry continued to look at her thoughtfully.

"And I think that might explain why you aren't the weight you would like to be. You get to be in control now and eat as much as you want. You never want to feel hungry ever again, do you?"

"No," Lauren whispered.

"Has trying to be in control of this situation made anything better? You might not be hungry now but are you happy? That little girl inside of you is still frightened of what might happen. Perhaps it's time you explored this issue. Really drill down into your feelings about your father and what his addiction did to you" he said, not unkindly. Lauren could feel his eyes on her, boring into the deep recesses where she kept her pain shut away in a little box that she never opened. What if Harry was right? If he could see it after only knowing her for such a short time maybe she wasn't hiding her hurt as well as she thought.

Looking back at Harry, her eyes shiny with unshed tears, she gave him a weak smile.

"You could be right. Perhaps I do have some issues with food. Maybe it is time I dealt with them."

Nodding his head gently in agreement Harry replied.

"You don't have to do this alone Lauren. There is help out there for you. Talking to someone and praying it through with them can make all the difference. It's time you let God change how you see yourself. I might even be able to recommend someone for you to talk to when we get home. He's been doing this kind of counselling for a long time."

"A man. I don't know Harry. I think I might prefer to talk to a woman. If I even decide to go ahead. Now that I realize I have some issues, I might just keep it between me and God," Lauren said as she began to panic. Harry was pushing her further than she wanted to go.

"That's up to you, but Steven's very good at what he does. I've received God's healing through him myself and so has Louise."

"Well thanks. I'll think about it" Lauren said desperate to change the subject. This probing hadn't been what she expected on what was supposed to be a social evening out.

"Harry, are you bothering Lauren?" Louise asked as she turned away from her conversation with Pat and focused her attention on her husband. Seeing Lauren's distress, she reached across and lightly tapped Harry on the chest.

"I hope he didn't upset you. He's always doing that to people. Asking them questions that lead to tears. Leave the poor girl alone Harry."

"It's all right," Lauren mumbled. "But if you'll excuse me for a minute, I just need to go to the ladies." Pushing back her seat, Lauren walked quickly to the bathroom, hoping that no one else was in there. She just needed a minute to compose herself, and the last thing she wanted was other people asking questions. She was a very private person and she didn't ever want anyone to see that she didn't have it all together. Harry was lovely but the conversation had taken her out of her comfort zone, and she was grateful to Louise for rescuing her. Digging into her purse she found a tissue and dabbed her eyes. She took several deep breaths, fussed with her hair a little and touched up her lipstick. When she felt ready, she took one last deep breath and opened the door of the bathroom. As she approached the table she saw that Harry was deep in conversation with Pat and that her dessert had been cleared away. Jamie saw her and called her over to the fireplace where he was standing with Daniel and Felicity. She joined their conversation, centred on which private schools were best in the area. Their children attended an exclusive College in the city, while Jamie and Lauren's were at a local Christian school. It didn't take long for Lauren to feel grateful that she had chosen a Christian education over the exclusive one the Lawson children were receiving. The pressure those kids were under sounded intense and even Felicity felt that she had to perform to live up to the high standards set by the school and the mafia mothers, as she called them.

Back in their room later getting ready for bed Jamie noticed that Lauren wasn't her usual self.

"You ok?" he asked.

"Yep. Just tired. It's been a long day of shopping."

"I saw you talking to Harry earlier. It looked intense. He didn't upset you, did he?"

"No, not really. He just asked some questions I hadn't expected. But it's all right. I probably started the conversation. Um, Jamie. He talked about someone named Steven. It couldn't be the same guy you mentioned a few months ago. The prophesy guy?"

"It probably was. Steven moved to Harry's church recently. Why? Have you changed your mind about counselling?"

"With him. No. But isn't it strange that they know each other?"

"No. I think they've been friends for a while. Steven was the one that recommended tonight's winery for dinner tonight. He lived here before he moved to Australia."

"But you haven't met Steven, have you? You just talked to him that one time on the phone."

"I've met him once," Jamie admitted. "He came to one of our board meetings. He prayed for us. It was no big deal."

"Why didn't you tell me?"

"Because last time I mentioned him you weren't very receptive Lauren. I didn't want to start a fight over nothing. And let's be honest. You aren't that interested in what happens at Gideon as long as the money keeps coming in."

Ouch, she thought. He really does think all I care about is money.

~ ~ ~

It had been chaos at the airport, getting everyone checked in. After a weekend of shopping, wives were transferring their overweight baggage into their husbands' suitcases hoping to avoid paying for extra fees. But once they were on the plane, all belted in and ready for take-off, Lauren began to relax. She had loved New Zealand and hoped to make it back there one day, but she was ready for home. She was looking forward to seeing the kids and most exciting of all, her new kitchen went in next week. As the plane pulled out of the terminal, she opened the novel she had meant to read this weekend. She hadn't finished the first page before Jamie decided he wanted to talk.

"So, tell me. What was your favourite part of the trip? We didn't get much of a chance to see each other over the last few days."

"Well the highlight for me was the spa."

"Of course it was. That was Harry's idea. He's very invested in all the wives getting to know each other better. Did you enjoy the private tour of the art gallery in Picton? It's normally closed on Sundays, but Harry pulled some strings and arranged a private tour."

"Um. Well actually I didn't go," Lauren admitted. "You know how I feel about modern art. If it's not a painting of something real, then it's just a lot of mess to me."

"Well, don't tell Harry. He put a lot of work into your schedule. What did you do instead? Sit and read?"

"No actually I didn't," Lauren responded, annoyed that she had to clear her schedule with Harry. Someone she barely knew and who was a good ten years younger than her.

"If you must know, I went to church. There was a Baptist church close to town, so I walked there. The girls understood. In fact, I'm surprised Harry hadn't ordered us all to church."

"We didn't have time. We had a lot on our agenda and barely got through it."

"I can't imagine what was so important that it took almost three days to talk about. Doesn't Gideon Solar pretty much run itself, with Harry and Jules on sales and you doing the numbers? I saw you through the conference room window and it looked like you were all just sitting there taking a nap."

"We were probably praying about our next step. Harry and Pat like us to spend time with God before we make decisions. We want to invite Him into every step of this project, and if we do another one, we will invite Him into that too. Anyway, how was the service. Small town church couldn't have been too thrilling."

"Actually," Lauren smiled, "it wasn't too bad. The music was kind of old. Like it was from the nineties. But the sermon was fantastic. Very old-school and biblically based. Not like some of those airy-fairy podcasts you keep insisting I listen to. And I met a lovely woman. She *was* from this century because she's a blogger. She said she writes about parenting, being a Christian woman in a changing world and the pitfalls that go with it. I really liked her, so I think I might look her blog up when I get home. I wrote her name down somewhere but then I shoved it in my handbag, so I'll probably never find it again. But it shouldn't be too hard. Blenheim's a small town and I remember her first name. It was Alice."

Chapter eight

As Jamie pulled into the carpark of Living Waters Church Lauren realized just how much she didn't want to be here. Lately, it seemed that every event they went to had something to do with Gideon. Today it was the baby dedication of Josh and Ashley's new son. Ashley had announced the pregnancy a few months after the first retreat, and it was hard to believe how quickly the year had flown by. Everyone had been excited by the first Gideon baby. Lauren was just glad they hadn't been required to wait around the hospital while Ashley gave birth. While it was nice to feel that they were a part of something, the commitment to Gideon was becoming suffocating. Sometimes she just wanted to say no to the monthly social dinners and stay in on a Saturday night in her pyjamas watching a movie. Instead she had to dress up and pretend to enjoy the food at the latest pretentious restaurant she was dragged to. The other Gideon girls were talking about starting a fortnightly bible study together and while she agreed a bible study group was a great idea, she already attended one with friends she had known for years. Jamie had suggested it would be better if she swapped groups and studied with the Gideon girls instead.

That was not going to happen. They were already beginning to lose touch with some of their long-time friends. Especially the ones who had asked too many questions about Gideon. Lauren knew they were concerned about the changes they had seen in Jamie, but he thought they were jealous of his new friends and their changed financial status.

From the car Lauren could see Patrick and Maria entering the church. Harry and Louise waved as they exited their car and waited for Lauren and Jamie to grab their coats and a baby present for two-month-old Bailey.

"So first time to Living Waters?" Harry asked Lauren after he had kissed her hello and had given Jamie a bear hug.

"Yeah it is," Lauren nodded.

"Well you are going to love it. There is such an atmosphere of God here. We prefer to keep it quiet and low key, letting the Spirit move as he wants."

"Um sounds great" Lauren replied thinking, *what a ridiculous remark. Let the Spirit move. Since when did humans let God do anything?*

"And we're hoping you'll love it. You guys and Lawrence and Janine are the only ones in Gideon who don't attend church here. Maybe God's calling you to a new church family."

"Well you never know," Lauren shrugged, "but we've been at our church for years, and I like it there. The kids have friends, we both serve, and Jamie's on the board. Being in business together doesn't mean we have to do everything together."

"Maybe," Harry said. "But it might be better for Gideon if every part of our lives were in alignment. Why don't you just sit back and see where God takes you today. He's brought you here for a reason. Perhaps he has something new to show you."

"We're very open to considering a change," Jamie announced, taking Lauren completely by surprise. They had never discussed this.

Not once. And she certainly wasn't considering a change. What was Jamie talking about?

When they reached the front door they were quickly separated from Harry and Louise. Several people gathered around them, but this didn't surprise Lauren. Harry was so charismatic, he had a gift of making people feel special. And Louise was very beautiful. It wasn't hard to see why people wanted to be around them. They left them to it and Jamie found a seat near the centre of the church. Pat saw them from the front row and walked down to say hello. More hugging, more kissing.

"Lauren, are you looking forward to our second retreat? I can't wait to get up to the Daintree."

"Didn't Jamie tell you. I'm not coming this time."

Pat turned to Jamie. "Ah no. He didn't say a word. This is a surprise."

"Emily has her exams a few weeks after the retreat. I couldn't possibly leave her then."

"She's a big girl. Year twelve, right?"

"Yes Pat. Year twelve. The most important exams of her life" Lauren confirmed. "I need to be home."

"Come on Lauren. It's a few days. We need you at the retreat. It would be a shame for you to miss out on what God has for you. How can we change your mind?"

"Good luck with that," Jamie mumbled under his breath.

"I wish I could be there Pat, but my kids come first. Even over Gideon."

"You know this isn't about Gideon. It's about God and what he has for you." *Fantastic*, Lauren thought. This argument had been going round and round the house for weeks. Lauren was furious that Jamie was going at all, let alone expecting her to abandon her daughter at such a crucial time. She thought he should be at home too, supporting Emily, but he had chosen his brothers over his own daughter's needs. And now Pat was challenging her on her decision as well.

"Sorry Pat," Lauren said, her fake smile not reaching her eyes. "You'll have to fill me in later on what I missed out on. My kid comes first."

By the time the service started Lauren estimated that there were about one hundred people in the church. They ranged in age from parents with babies and toddlers, to a few elderly people. The front two rows were taken by the Pastor and the other Gideon members and their wives. Harry, obviously an important member of the church, sat next to Pastor Isaac. Isaac was an old friend of her and Jamie's from a previous church years ago. When he had started Living Waters they had decided against joining him. They had been content where they were and because the new church was further away it hadn't made sense. But now it seemed Jamie was considering a move and without even asking her what she thought. As the musicians started playing an unfamiliar song and the worship leader welcomed everyone to the service Lauren leaned over to Jamie and whispered, "what did you mean when you told Harry we're open to a change? I don't want to move churches."

"I didn't say we're definitely doing it. It's just something I want to consider."

"But I don't want to consider it. I'm happy where we are. You haven't even mentioned this to me. Don't you think you should? I thought we were here for a baby dedication. And nothing else. Now I feel like you had an ulterior motive bringing me today."

"Let's talk about this later," Jamie quietly replied as he stood and started to sing along. She didn't know the words to the song, but he seemed to. Lauren tried to sing too but found herself distracted by the ever growing worry she had been experiencing lately. For months she had felt like she was slowly losing control of her life. It was hard to put her finger on exactly what was different but there had been a shift in their lives. Jamie was changing. He used to be able to make decisions quickly and decisively. Now it took him weeks. He had also become more introspective, analysing everything that happened in their family, always looking for a reason why someone said or did something. Nothing was taken at face value. He was praying more, which should have been a good thing but some of the subjects he expected her to pray about were just too ridiculous. Every little decision had to be taken to God. He had even wanted her to pray about what colour the floor tiles in the new kitchen should be. She was quite sure God had better things to do with his time than concern himself with the colour of her floor.

Beside her Jamie was processing his own thoughts. He had been so excited to have a reason to get Lauren to come to Living Waters. All he wanted was for her to give it a chance. But like always, she resisted anything new or different. She was so stuck in her ways, refusing to budge even a little. Couldn't she feel it? It was so peaceful here. People swayed slowly in time to the music, quiet and restful in God's presence. The atmosphere was perfect for allowing people to enter into worship. He wanted to be here, and it would bring about more unification at Gideon. Harry didn't think they would be able to move forward with new projects until everyone was in alignment. Jamie was ready. He just needed to convince his wife.

Lauren's mind wandered, as did her eyes. Most people were engrossed in the worship, but it was one of those songs that Lauren didn't like singing. It was all about what God had done for me. Calling it worship wasn't right because there was no worship of God. She had noticed more and more of these types of songs creeping into the church. Even their church had started singing some songs that barely mention the name of Jesus. They sounded good, but looking around, it was almost like people were in a trance. They sang the same lines repeatedly while the music slowly built to a crescendo. When the song finally ended they began another one and this time she knew the words. She had begun singing when she started to feel like someone was watching her. Trying not to be obvious she darted tiny glances around the room. Everyone seemed to be engrossed in the worship and at first it didn't appear that anyone was looking at her. But as she turned slightly to her right, she saw a man two rows down. He wasn't worshipping either but staring in her direction. Maybe five years older than her, his brown hair fell in waves around his serious face. His piercing blue eyes didn't smile as they caught hers. Lauren had made an effort to look nice for today, but men didn't tend to notice her. And while she was in a church, standing next to her husband, it was incredibly rude to be looking at her so intently. Not that she had any idea what he was thinking. Maybe he thought he knew her from somewhere, but she was quite certain she would remember him if they had ever met.

Lauren dragged her gaze away from his and continued singing while she tried to ignore the uncomfortable feeling as the stranger continued to stare at her. After one other song the baby dedication began. Josh and Ashley's family surrounded them while Isaac prayed and asked the congregation to support the Gordon family as they raised little Baily. Then to her surprise Harry stepped forward and preached. As he spoke on loving one another Lauren tried to focus. On the surface his message sounded fine. She couldn't find fault with anything he said but as he continued, she felt there was something lacking. There was no doubt he held the room captive with his words. He spoke to the congregation the way he had spoken to her in New Zealand. Soft, gentle questions, leading them along a journey. A few funny stories weaved together with the odd bible verse thrown in for good measure. But there was no depth. There was nothing she could take away and think on. Nothing had challenged her or convicted her. *If I'm honest with myself,* Lauren thought, *that had been uninspiring.*

At the end of the service Jamie and Lauren made their way over to Josh and Ashley. Lauren handed Ashley their gift, a powder blue hand knitted blanket she had found at a farmer's market and been unable to resist. It wasn't particularly practical, but it was much easier to be impractical when it wasn't your baby. Jamie quickly fell deep in conversation with Harry, probably congratulating him on his sermon. As the boys talked amongst themselves they were joined by Patrick, Daniel and Stuart. Almost the whole gang were here, they were just missing Lawrence and Janine who somehow managed to avoid most of the Gideon social events. Lucky them.

From the corner of her eye Lauren saw the man from earlier approaching the group. Ignoring the women, he made a beeline for Jamie. She watched as they shook hands and fell into what looked to be a serious conversation. Their body language said that they knew each other, and Lauren decided that perhaps he was a client. As least that explained why the man had been looking in her direction. It wasn't her he was staring at but her husband. Standing alone in the crowd of women, as they ooh'd and ahh'd over the baby, Lauren knew it would be rude to not join Jamie's conversation and introduce herself to the man. She took a few steps closer, placing her hand on Jamie's elbow to get his attention. When he turned to her, he smiled and said, "Just the person we were talking about."

"Me?" Lauren exclaimed. "Why would you be talking about me?"

"Lauren, this is Steven Wilson. I'm sure I've mentioned him to you before."

"Ah, sure. I remember. Jamie told me you used to go to Tim Rawlings church." So this was the counsellor Jamie and Harry had mentioned to her. She hoped Jamie wasn't going to bring up the idea of her seeing him for counselling again. She had made it very clear to him she had no interest. "So how do you two know each other?"

73

"He's a friend of Harry's," Jamie answered, not giving Steven a chance to speak. "We met at a Gideon meeting once when Harry asked him along. And guess what?" Jamie said, his voice loaded with excitement. "He has a word from God for you."

Lauren didn't know what to say. She didn't want to be impolite, but she didn't know Steven. The last thing she wanted was him speaking over her. Her stomach began to churn with warning, and she wished she could say thanks but no thanks. Meanwhile Jamie was smiling like this was the best thing that had ever happened to her.

"Err, um, thanks" Lauren stumbled, "but we really need to get going." She clutched her bag closer and pulled on Jamie's sleeve. "But it was nice to meet you."

"It will only take a minute. And it's important," Steven said, speaking to her for the first time. "We can find somewhere private. And it'll be ok. Jamie can come." Steven strode off in the direction of the staff offices with Jamie following quickly behind. Lauren felt rail-roaded as she slowly followed, knowing she had no choice. The men found an unlocked door and entered a small room that contained nothing more than a desk and a few office chairs. Steven put his phone down on the desk and asked Jamie to do the same.

"I prefer to record the words God gives me for people and I recommend you do the same. That way you can listen to it again. It can be overwhelming, and you might miss something," he said in a strong New Zealand accent.

"I don't know how to do that," Lauren replied. She was starting to feel physically sick.

"I'll do it" Jamie said as he fiddled with his phone, swiping through the apps until he found the one he was looking for. "Got it. You're all set." Steven took a few seconds before he began.

"Firstly, God wants you to know how special you are to him. He has plans for your life. Soon he will have a new gift for you but before he can reveal what it is and let you operate in it, he needs something from you. Instead of running from place to place, planning every little thing that happens in your life, he says it's time to stop. He wants you to spend your time with him, soaking in his presence so you will be ready to receive what he has for you. He wants you to completely give yourself over to him. If you don't, he can't trust you with what he has in store for you." Steven leaned back in his chair and turned off the recording function on his phone. Lauren took that to mean he had finished with the word from God.

"Um, thanks," Lauren said, not sure what else to say. This was the first time anyone had ever given her a prophesy before, and she wasn't sure what the protocol was.

"Thank you Steven," Jamie said as he too turned off his phone. "Isn't that exciting Lauren."

"Sure," Lauren replied unconvincingly. "I might just need some time to process all of that."

"Well don't leave it too long" Steven said as he stood. "It would be a great shame if you missed out on what God has in store for you." And before another word was said Steven stood and left the office.

As soon as they were in the car after saying their goodbyes to everyone, Jamie turned to Lauren. "Wasn't that fantastic," he proclaimed. "That was just so spot on."

Lauren shook her head at her husband. "Really? I'm not so sure."

"Of course it was. You are always running around doing something. When was the last time you just sat with God?"

"I don't think Steven was talking about taking half an hour. I got the feeling he expects me to spend my whole day soaking, whatever that means. I can't do that. It's not practical and I don't think it's biblical either."

"Steven doesn't expect anything from you. He was speaking for God. He's the one who wants you to stop and take time out for Him."

"I do take time for God. Just not the whole day. I have things to do, children to raise."

"Please don't dismiss this Lauren. It was an important word for you. It would be good for you to let go for a change and relinquish control of your life."

"If I tell you I'll think about it can we change the subject?" Lauren asked.

"So you'll think about it?"

Lauren looked over at Jamie and gave him a nod, but he wasn't convinced she meant it. Harry held Steven in great esteem and since he had been coming along to the board meetings he'd had some amazing words for the other guys. Jamie could see that the hand of God was on him. In the beginning when Harry had first bought Steven along to a meeting, Jamie had had a few reservations. Jamie thought the prophesy Steven had given him all those months ago hadn't been quite right but after spending time with him at Gideon he had begun to change his mind. But it was a conversation with his Pastor that had cemented the idea that Steven was a true prophet for him. Pastor Simon hadn't met Steven, but he said he had heard only good things about him. So over time Jamie had come to trust him. It was a shame his wife couldn't be as open to giving someone a chance as he had been. Maybe Lauren wasn't as perceptive as she thought she was.

"By the way. Why didn't you tell me you had met him?" she asked. "I hope you aren't keeping secrets from me?"

"No, I'm not keeping secrets from you. I met him just the once," he fibbed, not wanting her to get all bent out of shape. "I guess it slipped my mind. I just hope he didn't feel insulted by you. You weren't exactly polite."

"What do you mean I wasn't polite. I sat there and listened to him even though I know nothing about him. I told you before I didn't want any kind of counselling from him because he has no qualifications and now he's giving out prophesies as well. I felt cornered by the two of you. In future please back me up. If I say I need to leave, it's for a good reason."

"Lauren, he's a prophet. You should feel honoured that God spoke to you through him."

"A prophet? Is there even such a thing anymore? I know people can have a gift of prophesy but to actually claim to be a prophet," she said as she made air quotes. "Like in the Old Testament. That's a big call. Is that his job description? Prophet."

Jamie turned the key over and started the car. He could see that there would be no reasoning with her today. She was in one of her moods, and when she got like this she was irrational and said the most ridiculous things. He decided to drop the subject. He would bring it up again when she was back to her normal self. Although lately that wasn't very often.

~ ~ ~

Two days later Lauren sat in the backyard. She saw weeds that needed pulling and a hedge that could do with a trim. It was eating her up inside not being able to tend to her garden. But she had promised Jamie that she would give the prophesy a chance. She had listened to it again and hadn't changed her mind, but she wasn't willing to completely dismiss it. What if it was God? And so, for two days she hadn't picked up a book or spent time taking care of the garden. Two of the great pleasures in her life. Instead she had sat, waiting on God to come and spend time with her. Unfortunately, it felt forced. This wasn't bringing her closer to God, if anything, he felt more distant. She watched bee's dancing through the roses she had planted two years ago and heard birds singing over the distant hum of traffic. Lauren thought of how she felt when she worked in her garden. Like she was helping God care for his creation. How could that be wrong? Calling out loud, hoping that no one but He could hear her, she cried "God why do I feel like this? If this is what you really want from me, I need you to tell me yourself." And deep in her heart she heard that familiar voice say to her, you didn't have a good feeling about this man. Why are you listening to him? Instantly she felt the weight of depression that had settled on her over the past few days lift. She knew that word hadn't been for her, hadn't been what God was saying at all. She picked up the secateurs that were always close by and started to cut back some spent roses, talking to God and listening, as she always did when she was alone with him in her garden.

Chapter nine

Jamie felt himself begin to relax as he drove his hire car out of the Cairns airport carpark. He still had over two hours of driving before he reached his destination, a retreat in the Daintree rainforest, but he didn't mind. Driving soothed him. Here he was in control and being on his own meant he could listen to the music *he* liked and there was no one to argue with. Because that's all he seemed to do these days. At home Lauren raged about the time he spent working on Gideon, which to be fair to her, was most nights. And when he wasn't running the numbers on new projects that were being considered, he was out with the guys at one of their fortnightly dinners. He was physically and emotionally exhausted. Being pulled in two directions was taking its toll. He loved his wife. But why did she need to be so obstinate? If she could just let go and get on board with Gideon's vision, she too would become excited at the direction it was taking and they would be all in, together. Unfortunately, she refused to see past the money, to the calling that had been placed on his life and the life of the others. It had become so much more than a way to make money. Their goal was transformation for the people of God in Australia, a freedom they never knew was possible.

Maybe it would even spread to the world beyond. How could a person *not* be excited by that?

He had already missed out on the first day of the retreat. He had left buying his plane ticket to the last minute, hoping and praying that Lauren would change her mind about coming. But she had dug her heels in and refused to even consider leaving Emily alone for the four days they would be away. He thought back to the way she had cried when he refused to stay home too. When the tears hadn't worked, she became childish, throwing what amounted to tantrums. And when the tantrums hadn't swayed him, she reverted to that old punishment of hers. Silence. They had barely spoken for weeks and the tension in the house was so thick you could cut it. He knew it wasn't good for Emily or her exam study but hopefully with him out of the house the atmosphere would improve for a few days. By the time he'd given up any hope for a change of heart in his wife, Jamie could only get a flight arriving in Queensland a day later than everyone else. Because of her stubborn, selfish behaviour he was missing out on what God was bringing to the others. He had received countless texts from each of the Gideon boys, Harry in particular, telling him they wished he was there, and filling him on what he was missing out on. Harry had said that Steven had a prophesy for him that was going to change his life, which excited Jamie more than anything. Finally, God was bringing something for him. And unlike his wife, he was going to embrace it.

Steven coming to the retreat had been another argument. Well more than one actually, and he wondered if that was the real reason Lauren had refused to come. When she found out Steven and his wife were going to be there she had gone ballistic. Typical Lauren. She had formed an opinion of Steven and no matter what he said or did, she was sticking to her first impression. The woman was unmovable. He dreaded telling her that Steven had been on staff for a month, but he was going to have to do it soon. If she found out from someone else, he would be accused of lying to her. And that wasn't his intention. He just didn't want to give her another reason to argue with him. Something needed to change because they couldn't go on like this. Her refusal to give even an inch when it came to the subject of Steven was damaging their marriage and he wasn't sure how they were going to fix it. He had no intention of leaving Gideon. It was a huge part of his life. It wasn't about the money for him anymore, unlike Lauren. For him it was firstly about the growing relationship he had with God and secondly the friendships with the other guys. He was closer to God than he had ever been, but Lauren was letting her hostility towards The Prophet close her heart and mind to what God was doing. She needed to grow up and accept that she was wrong about Steven. And even if she wouldn't admit to being wrong, she needed to give him a chance to prove himself.

~ ~ ~

The view out of the living room was spectacular. The house, built on the side of a hill, was situated high amongst the trees and it reminded Jamie of the tree house his father had built him when he was ten. He could make out the sound of a nearby waterfall and the birds were as loud as they were plentiful. It was hard to believe that there was pollution and war on the Earth when all you could see and hear was the world at its most peaceful. Humans did not have dominion here, nature did, and Jamie was certain that if people ceased to exist, the rainforest would swallow up the beautiful building they were staying at in a matter of days and weeks. It was impossible to feel anything *but* peace here and he was sorry for Lauren that she was missing out. She loved to be outside with nature. Maybe not the snakes that he had been warned about, or the huge spiders, but the ancient trees and ferns would have sparked ideas in her head and given her the inspiration she needed for the fernery she was planning for the garden at home.

The wives had left for Cape Tribulation straight after breakfast. They were going to stop at the Aboriginal Culture Centre and check out some of the quirky craft shops. They weren't expected back until after lunch so the boys had all morning to discuss what direction Gideon would take in the next twelve months. Steven had also asked for some time to pray and wait on God so they could hear what He had to say. Jamie settled into the couch hoping that Steven would finally share his prophesy for him. By the time he'd arrived at Ribbonwood Lodge yesterday, named for a rare flower found in the Daintree rainforest, he'd only had time for a quick shower before they all headed out for dinner. Harry had put together some notes for him on the discussions that had taken place the day before, but he also shook his head when he told Jamie he should have been here. Jamie knew Harry was concerned that he had missed out yesterday and more importantly that he had been unable to convince Lauren to come. He felt like he had let Harry down and was going to need to try harder to convince Lauren that it was important she be part of all the Gideon events.

Music played quietly in the background as Harry began to pray and invite God into their discussions for the morning. He asked for God's wisdom and that each man would be open to hear from Him. Jamie felt all the anger and frustration of the past few months slip away as he focused on the soothing music and Harry's melodious voice. Half an hour must have passed as one by one the men bought words of encouragement for each other and declarations of God's blessing over Gideon. Bringing the quiet time to an end, Harry turned the meeting over to Steven and asked if he had any words for them individually or as a whole. Steven stood from his chair and took a few steps until he was standing in front of Jamie. He asked him to stand, and as he did, the others in the room quickly gathered around him in support.

"Jamie," Steven spoke, "I feel like God wants to talk to you about direction. Have you been hearing anything from God about this?"

"I haven't heard anything specific," Jamie answered as he shook his head, "but I don't think I'm doing what I should be. I'm working harder than is good for me and I'm not even sure I'm doing the right job anymore."

"So why don't you ask God where's the best place for you to be spending your time?"

Jamie closed his eyes and within a second opened them again. "That's easy, Gideon. But I don't know how I can make that happen when I've got so many other responsibilities."

"Why don't we all ask God on Jamie's behalf what he should be doing?" Steven suggested, "and then share with the group what you've heard."

The men took their seats and settled in, closing their eyes as they each silently sought God for Jamie. Harry had turned up the music, choosing a favoured song, the lyrics repeating over and over, lay it all down, lay it all down. God wants all of you.

After fifteen minutes of a wonderful time soaking in God's presence and letting the Spirit wash over the room Pat said, "I'm hearing 'let go'."

Josh quickly followed saying "I'm hearing 'it's time for a change and you need to break off entanglements'."

Daniel concurred telling Jamie, "I'm hearing, 'sell your practice'."

"I feel that God is saying that you should talk to your business partner about what it would look like to free up some of your time," Stuart said.

Harry asked Lawrence what word God had given him for Jamie. Lawrence said he heard nothing but that wasn't unusual. Lawrence had resisted Harry's attempts to draw him into a deeper relationship with God. A man who valued reason above feelings, Lawrence hadn't made much progress when it came to hearing God's voice. Harry looked over to Steven who raised his eyebrows ever so subtly, none of the others catching their silent communication. Then Harry asked Jamie what God was saying to him?

"It's really hard for me to distinguish my own voice from God's Harry but I'm feeling like I really want to get out of the accounting practice."

"Well I think you *are* hearing from God because I'm hearing the same thing. 'Time to change direction'. There's definitely a need for you to work at Gideon full-time. With the solar business, the Foundation and the new projects we're looking at there's plenty for you to do. Harry turned to the group and asked, "Is everyone in agreement with that?"

There was a resounding yes in the room. All of the men, except Lawrence who remained silent, were excited that Jamie was going to break free from the Accounting Practice that was holding him back. But as Harry began to rough out his role on the white board, Jamie's excitement quickly turned to fear as he realized he wasn't going to earn enough to cover all his financial responsibilities. Feeling a physical sinking in his stomach, he interrupted Harry saying, "the problem is that the full-time salary you're suggesting at Gideon isn't going to replace the income I earn from the practice, not even close."

"So you're going to let money get in the way of what God wants to do in your life?" Pat asked. "Don't you see how much God has blessed us so far. Surely you can't doubt that he's going to continue that blessing when you're laying down everything for him."

"Yeah but that blessing's not predictable, unlike the monthly bills that keep coming in."

"So ask God if you trust him with your finances," Harry prompted.

Jamie closed his eyes, exhaling gently, as he quieted his mind so he could hear God's voice. A minute or so ticked by as Jamie silently asked God if he trusted him. Ashamed of himself he told the group "I'm hearing 'no', I don't trust Him."

Steven suggested "Ask Him, why not?"

Jamie said, "I'm hearing 'fear'."

"What are you afraid of?"

"Failing" Jamie answered.

"Failing at what?"

"Failing to live up to expectations."

"Ask Him, whose expectations are you trying to live up to?"

"Well I thought it would be Lauren's, but I'm hearing it's my own expectations."

"Ask God why you have set yourself such high expectations," Steven prodded.

"Because I need to prove to people that the decisions that I made years ago were right. That I was right and that I will be successful."

Pat asked, "what does successful mean to you?"

"It means being able to provide for my family and continue living the lifestyle we've become accustomed to."

"Ask God how he defines success?" Harry questioned Jamie.

Jamie paused and closed his eyes as he sought God. This was intense. He was digging away at the very core of who he was and why he did what he did. The process was both painful and elating because he knew he was about to get freedom from something. Something big.

"I'm hearing God say I'm asking the wrong question. He doesn't call us to be successful, but to have integrity and become more like Jesus."

"That's right Jamie. You've based your life on chasing a lifestyle that isn't what God wants for you," Harry concluded. "All he wants is for you to become more like his Son. So maybe it's time to lay down your agenda and walk on the path God's got for you."

The atmosphere in the room was electric. Josh echoed the others when he started praising God for the freedom He was bringing to Jamie. Someone started clapping, and quickly that action was repeated around the room. The men were bringing honour to God for his faithfulness and to Jamie, who was willing to step out and make a change in his life. Tears started welling up in Jamie's eyes as he said "I know that's what I need to do but I don't know if I can. What will Lauren think?" Jamie knew that he'd put his family in a position where they needed to earn more than most. Between the house, the cars, and the private school fees, their monthly outgoings were well above average. He couldn't go home and tell Lauren that they would now be earning half the amount he had been and that she would have to find a way to make do. It would be impossible.

Despite the excitement in the room, Steven could see that Jamie was still hesitating, allowing his fears to hold him back. Catching Harry's attention, he placed his palms together and placed them under his chin, the way a child would when they were praying. Taking his cue, Harry asked for the others to again pray for clarity for Jamie and that he would move past his fears. They laid their hands on him, calling for Gods peace about his situation. When their prayers came to an end Steven said, "why don't you acknowledge to God that you have been on the wrong path and that you need him to direct you."

Agreeing, Jamie said "Lord I realise that I have been running my own agenda and I'm sorry. Would you please take away the need in me to be successful in man's eyes and would you please give me your heart." His prayers didn't stop his mind from swirling though as his thoughts jumped from God to Lauren. But right now he didn't want to think about her. He knew it was time to step out in faith and do the right thing.

He made the decision to trust God, because after all, as Steven always said, God's got it.

Jamie could feel the love for him coming off the group and a peace begin to settle on him. This whole session had confirmed for him what he had been feeling. He couldn't go on as he had, running his Practice and working all night. He was more than happy to move on, and step full-time into Gideon. It was a dream come true. Finally, his passion for putting together deals would be fulfilled and he could end the daily monotony of tax returns and reconciliations.

But Steven wasn't finished hearing from God. He asked everyone to take their seats as he wanted to share what God had told him He had in store for Gideon.

"While I was praying about coming to this retreat God prompted me to check if any of you think you might have a problem with money?" he asked, as his gaze moved from man to man, silently challenging them to look within themselves and question if they were the one he was talking about. "While some of you are openly embracing the freedom that is being offered to you by God, there may be others that are holding back. I wonder if the reason that none of the new deals you have been pursuing have succeeded is because there is a block. I know God wants to bless this endeavour, but I feel that until each of you have let go of the strangle hold that money has over you, he may delay any move forward. Ask yourselves how much are you willing to let go and trust God fully? Are you willing to lay it all down for Him?"

"What does that mean, lay it all down? Are you suggesting that we give all the profits to the Foundation?" Daniel asked.

"That's not for me to say. You all need to ask God what it would look like to completely surrender everything. God doesn't ask you for part of your lives. He wants it all."

Jamie looked around the room. All were nodding, except Lawrence, as Steven spoke. Like Lauren, he'd had a problem with Steven, and he had argued that there was no need to hire him. He maintained that no legitimate business needed to hire a prophet. But he had been out voted. Harry's insistence that Steven come on board had caused a rift between him and Lawrence which was bringing division in Gideon. It was hard enough with Lauren refusing to accept Steven, but the brothers needed to be in complete agreement. Everyone else believed that Steven was exactly what Gideon needed and he deserved to be paid a wage that was equal to what Harry and now Jamie would be earning. Lawrence had refused to vote with the others, and it was the first time they had made a decision that hadn't had one hundred percent approval.

Jamie hoped he wasn't the one with a greed problem. Hadn't he just proven that by being willing to take on a job with Gideon and potentially cut his income by more than a third. While the thought of giving all the profit to the foundation didn't thrill him, if that was what God was asking, then what choice did he have? *He* wasn't going to be responsible for holding Gideon back. Besides, they needed to trust God for their provision, not Gideon. But looking at Lawrence's face he could see that he wasn't going to agree to giving all the profits to the Foundation. Maybe Lawrence was the block Steven was talking about.

Lawrence shifted forward in his chair, his hands shaking with anger. He listened as Steven continued to prophesy over Gideon, promising them that if they were willing to give up everything, God would bless them in other areas of their lives. He managed to remain quiet until Steven finished talking, but only just.

"No," he blurted out, looking each board member in the eye. "I will never agree to this. And neither should any of you. Can't you see how wrong this is? We're being hijacked."

Standing, Steven moved towards the door. "I think it would be best if you discussed this privately," he said. "I can only reaffirm that this is a word from God, not from me. I have nothing to gain but let me say, if you reject what God has for you, you may step out of his blessing." He backed out of the room and shut the door quietly behind him.

"Who is this guy and why are we listening to him?" Lawrence continued after Steven had left. "We don't know his background and we have no proof he is a prophet. I mean, where did you even meet him?" he asked Harry.

"I know his background," Harry countered. "I met him through a mutual friend, a Pastor who spoke very highly of him. He was a member of his church and did a lot of good things there, but God told him it was time to move on and spread his message. He's a good man with an amazing gift. And I agree with him. We must be willing to give everything away for God. I for one am more than willing to give all the profits to the Foundation."

"Well if you're foolish enough to do that, then that's your choice. But I won't be doing it. Twenty-five percent was pushing it. I came into this to make money. I have a family to care for and I intend to do that. I don't believe for one minute that God expects me to hand over everything to a Foundation that hasn't done anything so far except employ a man I don't trust."

"I'm sorry to hear that Lawrence" Harry gently responded. "Because as a group we need to have harmony. Won't you consider going away for a bit and praying about it. God will reveal his plan to you if you're willing to lay down your own agenda and listen to him."

"I don't need any time Harry. I have a brain, and it's telling me this is wrong. What I want is to know what everyone else has to say about this. Jamie, what do you think?"

"I agree with you that it's a lot to ask," Jamie paused knowing that giving all the profits to the Foundation would put his family in even more financial strife. "But I do think we should ask God if this is what he wants instead of dismissing the idea. I don't want to go against God's will. If this is what he wants, then what else can we do?"

"But how can you be sure that this is what God wants? He hasn't asked this of me. And I don't think he's asking it of any of us."

"Lawrence, maybe you should ask God why this is upsetting you so much," Daniel suggested. "I'll be the first to admit that I enjoy the kind of lifestyle that money brings. Does this mean I have a greed problem? I hope not. But if I do, I want God to expose it and deal with it."

"I feel the same way," Josh spoke up. "I do trust Steven. I've spent a lot of time with him recently and he's helped me deal with some serious issues that have been holding me back. I'm finally starting to live my life in freedom and I'm not going to let money issues creep in just when I've begun to move forward."

"You can't be serious. Are you really going to make this massive decision based on one conversation? One prophesy that I for one don't trust. Shouldn't you discuss this with your wives?" Lawrence asked. "This affects them too."

"I doubt Cynthia will care," Stuart answered. "We've already had plenty of money from Gideon. We've all got our initial investment back and then some. I think we should do it. Give it all away."

"I concur," Pat said. "But we all need to agree. We can't have one person holding us back and bringing disunity. It would be like having sin in the camp and that's the last thing we want. I hate to say it because we've been friends for so long, but Lawrence you need to decide if you're with us or not."

"Not," Lawrence declared. "I cannot, and will not, agree with this proposal. It's absurd. What are you going to be asked for next? Your homes, your businesses?"

"Nobody is asking for your home Lawrence. But if God did ask for it would you say no? This kind of dissent leaves us with no choice," said

Harry. "We can't force you, nor would we want to. Your decision is between you and God. But I think it would be detrimental to Gideon if we aren't all in alignment. I'm not sure there's a way we can have you continue with us on our journey if you feel differently than the rest of us."

"I think that's the first time we've agreed with each other for a long time Harry," Lawrence nodded. "I'll email you my resignation from the Gideon board in the next few days. I expect my dividends to continue to be paid when they are due. I won't rescind my twenty-five percent contribution to the Foundation. I agreed to it, probably mistakenly, but I won't go back on my word."

"Hey, wait a minute. Is that it? We don't agree on something, so Lawrence is out?" Jamie exclaimed. "We're all reasonable adults here, running a business together. We can't just kick someone out."

"It's okay Jamie," Lawrence said. "I want to go. This is no longer the right place for me to be. I'd rather use my time and resources on something I feel passionate about. All I feel for Gideon now is deep concern."

"So, you're leaving? Just like that. You're not even going to stay for the rest of the trip?"

"Obviously, I'm going to wait for Janine to get back from shopping, but yes. I don't feel I have a choice but to leave today if I can get a flight. You don't need us here, making everyone feel uncomfortable. I want to say thank you all for including me in Gideon. It hasn't ended the way I want but I don't feel any anger towards any of you. I really do wish you all the best." Lawrence picked up his phone and the Bible that he'd left on the coffee table. He gave the room a sad smile goodbye, opened the door and was gone.

Chapter ten

"Harry, are you seriously going to let him go?" Jamie asked as Steven quietly re-entered the room and took his seat.

"You heard him," Harry answered. "It's what he wants. And it's exactly what we expected. If you wouldn't mind explaining Steven."

"Harry's already aware of what I'm about to say but it will come as a surprise to the rest of you. God had set you a test today and he told me that one of you would fail. This was his way of removing the block from the group. He isn't asking for all the profits to go to the Foundation. If you remember my words, I never said that. But the discussion that followed has exposed the person that was holding you back. I suggest you take some time now and ask God how much he really wants."

A hush fell over the room as the men settled into their chairs and silently asked God to reveal how much of the profits He wanted for the Foundation. Harry was the first to hear from God. He felt that half was all that was being asked of them. This was quickly confirmed by Josh who agreed that yes, God was allowing them to keep half of the profits. Jamie hadn't heard anything but with everyone else in agreement that fifty percent of their profits would now go to the Foundation, he had little choice but to confirm that yes, he was in. Once the decision was formalized Steven retook the floor.

"This is a great day for Gideon. Today you were tested, and you passed. You were willing to give up everything. God is very pleased with all of you. Now he knows he can trust you. The blessings coming your way because of this will be more than you could ever have imagined."

"I guess," Jamie mumbled, more to himself than anyone else. He was going to go home in a few days and tell his wife that he was planning to sell his practice and that they were also going to receive a lot less money from Gideon. He was also going to need to find a way to explain about Lawrence leaving. He couldn't mention that it had anything to do with Steven. If she heard that she would take it as confirmation that her concerns about The Prophet were right. And even though he had agreed to the reduced wages and the increased profits to the Foundation, Jamie found it hard to be completely excited. He knew this was the right decision and while he was grateful that God had only asked for half, he wasn't looking forward to the conversation he had at home ahead of him. Why couldn't Lauren just let it go and trust him? Why did she have to fight him and God at every turn? It was her fault he wasn't happier about the decision he had made. She was stealing his joy from him. And he couldn't let her do that. It was time she supported her husband like the other wives did. They were going to need to have a serious conversation when he got home about what it looked like to be a godly wife. Her behaviour couldn't go on anymore.

When he heard his name, he was drawn back to the discussion that had been taking place around him. He looked up to find Harry staring at him.

"Sorry, what was that?" Jamie asked.

"The Lakemba site. Do you have those figures? We want to decide today whether we go ahead, and the girls will be back soon," Harry said, concern on his face as he looked at Jamie. "You all right mate?" he asked.

"Yeah, sorry. Just a little distracted," Jamie responded. Pulling his notes up on his iPad he began to lay out how much it would cost to buy the land and build six new factories on it. The investment would be huge, and he wasn't sure it was worth the risk. The area had been flooded with factories and as a result those with land left were expecting exorbitant prices for small blocks. He explained his concerns to the room, and he felt like he was making a strong case that they should pass on the project.

"Thanks for that Jamie," Harry said at the conclusion of his presentation. What we really need to do is pray and see what God thinks. If you have any words, please share them." Harry turned the music back on and the room regained the peaceful atmosphere that had been present before Lawrence had objected to Steven's prophesy. Jamie focused on praying about the new deal, but it was hard to hear from God when he knew buying the land wasn't a good decision. Daniel was the first to speak after a suitable amount of time had passed.

"I believe God is saying 'no' to this project. He has something much better for us in the future."

"Are you sure that's right Daniel?" Harry asked, tipping his head to the side. "Why don't you check again? Ask God if there is a block that's stopping you from hearing clearly." So Daniel quietly asked God again, and quickly came back to the group.

"Wow. God just gave me a download. I was blocked from hearing from him because I was feeling guilty about making money. But he says I don't need to feel that way. He knows I will steward it well and he needs people like us to manage his money for the kingdom the right way."

"That makes more sense," replied Harry, "Because I'm getting a 'yes'. But I'm also hearing that we are to offer them a lot less money for the land."

"I agree," Steven said. "God definitely wants you to move ahead. This will be the next project for Gideon. Now that there is no more dissent the path is cleared."

"I have a yes as well," said Josh. "We're not to concern ourselves with what the figures say. He has it under control. We'll get the land at the right price."

"I'm also getting a yes now," Daniel confirmed. "You're right Harry. I wasn't hearing correctly.

As one by one the others agreed that yes, the Lakemba site would be their next project, Jamie stayed silent. He knew the owners had already turned down more money than Gideon had decided to offer. If God really meant this for them, he was going to have to do something big to change the landowner's mind about selling for less.

The rest of the weekend passed quickly. Nobody openly discussed Lawrence and Janine's sudden departure. Jamie assumed that the wives had been given an explanation by their husbands. He decided he wouldn't tell Lauren over the phone. There would be plenty of time when he got home. And he wouldn't rush to tell her about the fifty percent either. It would be better to fight one battle at a time. The first one would be telling Lauren he was going to approach his junior partner about buying out his share of the accounting practice. Steven had sat beside him at dinner on the final night and talked Jamie through the opposition he was going to face. But he confirmed that if the enemy was opposing him then he must be doing something right. In fact, the more opposition he received, the more it validated that he was doing what God wanted. He told him that his parents wouldn't understand why he was giving up the security of his job. And your wife, Steven had told him, will be the loudest voice fighting the change that was to come. He said this would have nothing to do with Jamie but would be out of her own fears. He felt that the time was close for Lauren to face her insecurities and then she would be receiving the same freedom that Jamie had. But for a while the devil would use her to try and stop Jamie from stepping into his future.

Jamie was now certain that God wanted him working at Gideon. Over the last two days Jamie had let go of the concerns he had about finances and for the first time in years he felt excited about work. It had always been a dream of his to be a property developer. And because of Gideon he was being given the opportunity. Pat was also going to be working part-time in the office. He had the contacts in the building industry and in local and state government. He would be able to streamline any future projects and Stuart would probably be involved in the actual building of the factories if they got the land at the price Steven had told them. It felt like his life was finally coming together. If he could only get Lauren to spend some time with Steven and see that he really was a prophet, then everything would be perfect.

~ ~ ~

At home alone (again) in her quiet house Lauren had finished her to-do list and couldn't find anything worthwhile on television to watch. She pulled out her iPad and logged on to her new favourite blog. A few weeks ago she had found the receipt in the bottom of her purse that she had written down the name of the blogger she'd met in New Zealand last year. Lauren had read a few of Alice's blogs and had quickly become addicted. The writer had an honesty about her that Lauren appreciated, and she was funny too. Lauren had gone back to the beginning and was making her way through several years of Alice's writing. Most of the time it was upbeat, but tonight's reading had taken a very serious direction. Lauren took a sip of tea and settled into the corner of the couch while she reread Alice's words.

Dear Reader,

Today I want to tell you a story. It happened fifteen years ago and for a long time I felt ashamed of myself. But I have come to realise that it's time to share my experience so I can warn others. I have become aware recently that there is an increase of men who are claiming to be prophets. Let me tell you of the time I met my own so called 'Prophet'. He came into my life at a time when I was feeling unhappy with myself. I had a great deal of guilt about how I had conducted myself when I was a teenager. I used drugs and had been promiscuous. As a grown woman I found it hard to believe that God had really forgiven me. Even though I had a wonderful husband and family, I let my past hold me back. So when a man joined my church who offered counselling I jumped at the chance. Our Pastor highly recommended him and at first, he was helpful. I was able to pray through my issues and began to feel like I was going to be able to move on from my past. But as we spent more time together he took me down a path that could have destroyed me. He told me that God had given him a vision of my father abusing me. At first, I didn't believe it, but he told me to delve deep into my memories and focus on a time I was traumatised as a child and couldn't remember properly. I had never had a memory of my father being anything but loving to me. I did know from family stories that my mother had taken ill and been hospitalised when I was five. The Prophet confirmed that this was when my father had hurt me because we were alone in the house and he had the opportunity. I decided it must have been true and this was the reason I had been a troubled teenager. Furious

97

with my father and ready to confront him with accusations of abuse I told my husband. I am so grateful I spoke to him first. He already had concerns about the time I had been spending in sessions with The Prophet and had seen a change, not for the better in me. He asked me to tell him of the specific details of the abuse I supposedly received but I couldn't give him any. My memories weren't real. I thought I had been abused when my mother was ill, but photos of that time proved I had stayed with my aunt and she confirmed my father had spent his time at the hospital caring for my mother and I hadn't seen him for weeks. My mother recovered and we both went home. Can you imagine reader, if I had accused my father of these crimes? I would have destroyed our relationship. How did I allow myself to be taken in? Because I was looking for someone to blame for my previous bad behaviour. I had always considered myself a good judge of character but this time the wool had been pulled over my eyes. And so, I warn you. Be careful who you let into your life, especially in the role of counsellor. Because a wolf in sheep's clothing looks like a sheep. The bible tells us over and over to test the spirits and judge men by their fruits. I should have twigged that something wasn't right when it was allowed for me to meet in private with a man. Every church I know of bans this practice. I should have known that something wasn't right when I was encouraged to pay The Prophet. I now know the bible forbids Prophets to receive payment for their prophesy. You can find this in 2Kings chapter 5.

When my Pastor, a man who had known my father for many years heard where The Prophet had led me, he banned him from counselling anyone else in his church, knowing none of it was true. And before we knew it, he was gone. We never heard from him again and I can only hope he has ceased counselling and prophesying. Steven if you ever read this you are not the only one to blame. I should have known better and discerned that this was not of God. And readers, use your own discernment when encountering people who claim to be prophets. I was taken in. Don't let it happen to you too.

I was lucky that my husband saw through the lies. If someone warns you, take heed. The bible tells us in Deuteronomy 13 v 3 that there will be false prophets and God allows it to test us. This is one test you don't want to fail.

It couldn't be, Lauren thought as she finished reading Alice's story. New Zealand wasn't that small. There must be more than one man running around the country claiming to be a prophet with the same name. But the story felt too familiar to her. And she knew it had been Steven who had got them some special favours when they had visited last year so he must at least know people who lived in the Marlborough area. Wouldn't that be too much of a coincidence? But it would be worth reaching out to Alice to get a description of her Steven. Maybe even a surname. And if it was the same man then maybe Alice's story would be enough to get through to Jamie. She had barely heard from him while he was away in Queensland and their conversations had been stilted. More and more she felt like he was keeping secrets from her but the more she asked, the more he clammed up. Now she wished she had never agreed to invest her money. They had been fine without Gideon. Now there were days they barely had a civil word for each other. She knew it would be easier to let her concerns go and just fold. Let Jamie make all the decisions and immerse herself in the Gideon lifestyle. She knew it would make Jamie happy. But she couldn't. If she did life as she knew it would be over and it just wasn't something she could do. Lauren scrolled to the comment section at the bottom of Alice's blog and sent her a message. Jamie would tell her she was wasting her time and it wasn't the same man. But what if it was?

Chapter eleven

A one-sided war raged between Jamie and Lauren. It was one sided because Jamie no longer fought back. He knew it was pointless to defend Steven. Lauren had made up her mind a long time ago and nothing Jamie said would make any difference. It was up to God now. Sometimes they would have weeks of peace before a simple comment or piece of information would set her off and then it was days of tears and ranting. Eventually Lauren would calm down and they would have a short ceasefire. But the peace never lasted long. Lauren felt betrayed and Jamie was on tenterhooks waiting for the next time she exploded. Lauren, for her part, tried to keep her feelings about Steven to herself. But sometimes she would learn something new that would make her so angry she couldn't control herself.

Alice, the blogger Lauren had contacted, confirmed that the Steven she knew was the one and the same. When Alice learned what was going on at Gideon and that Steven had essentially become the head of the organisation, Alice encouraged Lauren to stand her ground. Lauren had confronted Jamie with the evidence of Steven's Modus Operandi, but he had dismissed her concerns. When Jamie asked Steven about Alice, he was completely open, and he had a perfectly good explanation and Jamie believed him. Steven confirmed that he had never once told Alice her father had molested her, that revelation had come from her own memories. He had been nothing more than her guide as they waded through her pain together. He also disclosed to Jamie that Alice's father was a wealthy man and John, Alice's husband was expecting a large inheritance to come his wife's way when her then elderly father died. John knew if his wife made any kind of accusation of abuse there was a chance she would be cut out of the will. Motivated purely by money and not his wife's welfare he'd convinced Alice to back away from her allegations. Unfortunately for Steven and his ministry, John had wielded a great deal of power in their church and had convinced Pastor Bill that Steven was not a true prophet. John said that Steven had planted false memories in Alice through prompting and suggestion and Bill had sided with John. Jamie could see that Steven had truly cared about Alice and had been deeply worried about her mental health. But there had been nothing he could do when Pastor Bill removed any authority Steven had, telling him he no longer had his support for the releasing sessions or for him prophesying in church. Steven told Jamie he felt it was best for everyone if he moved on, and God had used the church's rejection to relocate him and his family to Australia. Here people were more open to his ministry. He'd told Jamie he felt sad for Alice, she was missing out on the freedom that God had for her but there would always be people who rejected him for reasons he had no control over. It just proved that he was doing the right thing. And Jamie knew from Steven and Harry that Satan only attacked people who were doing God's work. The more opposition Steven received, the more it validated what he was doing.

Jamie had tried to convince Lauren that she was wrong to believe Alice's story, even though Alice told Lauren everything Jamie had heard was a lie. In the end they had let the matter drop for the sake of their marriage. Jamie so desperately wanted his wife to accept Steven as her prophet. Then she too could receive the same freedom he had, the freedom she was so in need of. He couldn't understand why Lauren didn't see how damaged she was and that if she would just let go and receive healing, she would be a new person.

Lauren made all sorts of other allegations about Steven. Jamie knew it was all about perspective and Lauren's was wrong. Yes, Steven earned double what their Pastor did, but his whole life was now dedicated to furthering God's kingdom through Gideon. He didn't have the time anymore to go out and work elsewhere and he had a family to support. Lauren couldn't understand why a business even needed a prophet on staff. What was he doing all day to earn his keep? She had searched the scriptures to find an example of another prophet who modelled what Steven was doing but couldn't. Old Testament prophets worked for and were paid by either the King of the land, or the temple treasury. They prophesied over the Nation of Israel, often warning them of impending doom if they didn't return to God. They didn't go about promising individuals' wealth and emotional freedom in exchange for a fee. *That,* Lauren thought, *was nothing better than fortune telling and it reeked of manipulation.*

And when Steven wasn't in the office controlling Gideon, he was flying around the globe to church conferences much to Laurens disgust. She thought it was nothing more than a paid holiday for him. Jamie said this was so he could both learn and be recharged so that he could better guide the Gideon organisation. Harry was always by his side, having turned over the selling of the solar panels to Jules and Aaron, a member at Living Waters, who had recently come on board at Gideon. Lauren didn't know how Harry could stand being around Steven all day but where you found one, there was the other. Someone had even coined a name for them. Harven, just like Brangelina or Tomcat. Two names into one. Together Harry and Steven had made it their mission to direct Gideon through prayer and prophesy. Jamie said it was what the Apostles did in Acts, giving themselves over to prayer and ministry of the word. But Lauren didn't think the Apostle Paul had been praying for someone's business all day in exchange for money. And it wasn't just Steven's large wages that made her antenna go up. Someone had purchased new cars for both Steven and Lucy. To her that just looked like a payoff. Jamie disagreed, saying it was God's blessing on them.

Lauren had experienced Steven's interference play out in her own life. Six months earlier, after the retreat in Far North Queensland, with Steven's help, Jamie had sold his accounting practice to his junior partner. Steven had been involved throughout the whole process. He had worked with both partners as they came to a decision about how and when Jamie would leave. Steven helped them hear from God about the price and the timing of selling the practice. Along with weekly payments for the practice, Jamie had retained a few old clients which meant that they had enough money to live on. After insisting that Jamie only worked part-time at Gideon and maintained those few clients, Lauren had agreed to the sale because Jamie said it was what he wanted, but she wished Steven had been kept out of it. Jamie on the other hand was grateful for Steven's help. He was the happiest he had been in years. Yes, he was earning less money than he had before, but he was living the dream. Every day he was excited to go to work. Unlike home, there he was accepted, and surrounded by men with the same vision and desires that he had. There he could weigh up the pros and cons of a deal, something he loved doing. And then together they would take it to God.

~ ~ ~

Lauren watched Jamie across the breakfast table. Another one-sided argument had just taken place. She was exhausted by them, both physically and mentally. A single tear slid down her cheek and she wiped it away, hoping that Jamie hadn't seen it. Not that he cared anymore. He just sat there, staring at her silently, never fighting back. At least when they had yelled at each other she had felt like he was listening, was at least engaged in what she had to say.

Today's argument was of course about Gideon. Jamie had asked her to pray about making a clean break and working full-time at Gideon. She knew it was a terrible idea and would leave them in financial trouble and Jamie without any connection to what was going on in the real world. He would be completely trapped in the Gideon bubble. But when she told Jamie that, and reminded him that their agreement was that he would only be there part-time, he had just sat there, tilting his head to the side the same way she'd seen Harry do it when he was listening. He didn't defend his decision or say a word, he took everything she threw at him, which only made her feel like a naughty child being placated by a parent. It was almost impossible to fight him, but she wasn't quite done yet. Yes, she was tired and worn down. But this was still her life. Her gut told her that nothing about what was going on in Gideon was good and she still heard that quiet voice of God telling her to stand up and not give in to the pressure. She would never agree to Jamie working full-time at Gideon.

Chapter twelve

" Thanks for coming tonight," Jamie told Lauren as they drove into Pat's driveway.

"I didn't really feel like I had a choice Jamie. I hope this doesn't go on too long. I've got a cold and quite frankly I'd rather be snuggled up in my jammies in front of the TV."

"Well I still appreciate it. And it won't be too long. Steven said it will only be about two hours. Then you can do all the snuggling at home you like." Lauren hadn't been lying when she said she felt like she didn't have any choice coming out tonight. She couldn't put her head in the sand and hope that everything would be all right. That meant going to all the dinners. She had already agreed to go to this year's retreat but her reason was not so she could connect with the others and receive this freedom they were all obsessed with. It was so she could see exactly what was going on. It had even meant a change in churches for Jamie and Lauren. After eight years at their local Baptist church they had made the move to Living Waters last month. Lauren had never had a desire to attend Living Waters but one night as she was praying, she felt very strongly, that even against her objections, God was prompting them to move. Jamie was thrilled that God had told her it was time to move and taken it as a sign that she was close to accepting Steven as her Prophet. It had been horrible telling their Pastors. Friends for years, they weren't angry, but they were concerned. Lauren had confided in Elizabeth, her Pastor's wife many times about her concerns and Elizabeth also believed that the situation was becoming dangerous even though her husband had given Steven his blessing earlier. He had changed his mind about Steven recently, but it was too late. Jamie was beyond hearing anything but praise for his prophet.

Attending Living Waters had been eye opening for Lauren. It had shocked her how disrespectful Steven was during the service. He usually sat down the back of the church, not engaging in the worship. She would often see him with his arms folded, a sneer on his face, or looking at his iPad. One service when Harry was leading the church in communion, she noticed he had been interrupted by a message on his phone. After looking at it, Harry laughed the interruption off to the congregation as not being able to work his technology. But at the end of the service when all the Gideon boys were standing around chatting, Harry had shown everyone the message he'd received during communion. Steven had sent him a picture of a monkey making a rude gesture. They all laughed, commenting that wasn't it good that The Prophet didn't have a religious spirit. That was, all of them except Lauren. Communion was a time of great reverence, not the time to be distracting the speaker and someone who considered themselves so Godly shouldn't been sending something so distasteful to anyone.

Tonight's meeting was something new. Steven and Harry had decided it was necessary to hold a monthly meeting with all the Gideon members, their wives and the staff and their wives. There were also a few others that had been invited through their connection with the Foundation. It was essentially a home group. At first Lauren had said no, but after she decided it was important to keep tabs on what was happening at Gideon and attend everything she was invited to, she agreed to come. Seeing for herself what went on was the only way to be sure her intuition was correct. And if she had been wrong about Steven all this time then she would deal with it. But it was going to be a tough gig to convince her.

"Come in, come in," Pat said as he opened the front door. This was the first time Lauren had been to his home and it was beautiful. Built during the Victorian era, it retained all the original features but had been lovingly restored. An open fire roared as they stepped into a spacious lounge room. Most people had already arrived, Lauren and Jamie being a few minutes late. This told Lauren just how much she didn't want to be here. Normally she was never late anywhere because it made her crazy. But tonight, she had dragged her heels, dawdling over the dishes while Jamie hurried her along, complaining about Sydney traffic.

After accepting the offer of a tea from Pat's wife Maria, Lauren took a seat on a beautiful tufted couch. It was obviously old but had been refinished and recovered in a soft beige linen. It had a matching partner and several wing chairs of the same fabric. An ornate mirror hung over the curved mantle, which had been painted a glossy white to compliment the high skirting boards and picture rail that ran around the room. The artwork looked original, even to Lauren's uneducated eye. Picturesque scenes of Sydney's beaches and the Australian bush had been chosen to complement each other and the room. The atmosphere was warm and inviting and Lauren felt herself relax. Perhaps tonight wouldn't be so bad after all. When Maria brought Lauren her tea they fell into an easy conversation about local universities. Maria and Pat's son had also finished school last year and had decided to take a year off to travel. He would be starting University the following year and had been accepted into an economics course. Lauren's daughter Emily had decided against a gap year and was already into her second semester at Charles Sturt University. She had been accepted to study Naturopathy and was loving her course. Oliver was in year eleven and still couldn't decide what he wanted to do when he finished high school. Lauren told Maria she thought he would probably go into a trade which would suit him much better than studying at Uni.

When Josh and Ashley arrived, habitually late because of the now one-year-old Baily who didn't like being left with a baby-sitter, Harry called the room to order and opened the evening in prayer. After he prayed, he asked everyone to take the time to soak in the presence of God. He suggested they empty their minds of all their worries and doubts and connect with the Father. He turned up the music that had been playing quietly in the background. It wasn't a song Lauren recognized but she found it soothing. The lyrics spoke of God's father heart for his children. She settled back into the couch trying to get comfortable. Apart from the music and the ticking of a clock, the room was silent. Trying to follow Harry's instructions she began to silently pray. She thanked God for who he was and for his love and forgiveness. She asked for His covering over her family and asked that He continued blessing Gideon. After what seemed like ages she peeked to see if everyone was done. Steven had his iPad out and looked to be writing something down but for all she knew he was checking his emails. Everyone else was completely still, eyes closed, and completely focused on their prayers. She closed her eyes again after taking a quick look at the mantle clock. They had only been praying for ten minutes but it felt much longer. Not a fan of the long drawn out prayer sessions that Harry loved, she shuffled in her seat trying to get comfortable. *The couch might be pretty to look at* she thought *but it wasn't very cosy*. Which was probably a good thing, with the warm fire, the quiet ticking of the clock and her cold, there was a good chance she would fall asleep if she sat silently for too much longer. A new song began, very much like the last, a lilting melody with soft voices harmonizing. Lauren tried to concentrate on God but the longer this went on, the more her mind wandered to the things she need to do tomorrow. Hopefully prayer time would end soon.

Jamie was silently begging God for a breakthrough in Lauren. For months, he had been waiting for healing and freedom to come to her. Lauren hadn't been the only wife to have misgivings about Steven. Maria hadn't liked Steven when she first met him, and she and Pat had more than one argument about him being part of Gideon. Not like the fights he and Lauren had. He was the only one to have to endure that kind of opposition. But now Pat's wife had become more accepting of Steven. And Felicity who originally believed that yes Steven was a prophet but thought he wasn't as respectful of women as he should be, and had asked Daniel to keep him away from her, had now changed her mind. She too had let go of her misgivings about him and had been having releasing sessions so she could work through some of her issues. It was happening for the rest of them, just like Steven had said it would. Lauren was the only holdout. He felt responsible for her and was desperate for her to accept that Steven was a prophet and had authority over her. God had given Jamie authority over her when they married, and Jamie had willingly come under Steven's authority. He heard the music quiet, knowing this was a cue that the prayer time was over for now and either Harry or Steven were about to speak.

It was Harry who took the floor. Firstly, he thanked everyone for being here and then began to explain the reason for the evening.

"As you probably all know," he started "these meetings are intended as a home group only. We'll be gathering together once a month. This isn't a church and we have no intention of starting one. We already have one of those. This is a time to come together with our wives and explore what God is saying to us. When Gideon started, we men were all in different places, but God has drawn us closer to him and closer to each other. We want that for you too," he said as he looked around the room at each of the women there. "We believe that He has a role for you, and we don't want even one of you to miss out on what He has in store. It's so important for all of us to be in alignment. We need our women to be on board with us, it's not just up to the men anymore. For Gideon to move forward we must be in this together. That's the reason we've decided to do these meetings. We want to bring you in and have you be part of the decision-making process. We value your opinions. And as you can see, we have also asked Aaron who works in sales and his wife Pamela here tonight. If they are going to be hanging around Gideon, we want them to also have some input. Eric and Gabby are probably strangers to you but will be involved with the Foundation through their connection's in Thailand, so we invited them along too. We do have a bit of housekeeping to attend to tonight before we get started. I assume you are all aware of Jules who was on our sales team. Unfortunately today we had to let her go. I discovered that she had stolen about twenty solar panels for the new house that she was building." Jamie's head shot up in surprise. This was the first he was hearing about this.

"Are you sure Harry? She was a fantastic salesperson. And really nice. I can't imagine her stealing anything."

"I found the invoice myself this afternoon hidden in her desk. She had zeroed out the amount owing. I guess that way she could account for the panels without paying for them."

"Shouldn't we have discussed this before firing her," Jamie asked.

"If everyone had been in the office we would have, but Steven and I prayed about it and decided she needed to go immediately. Who knows what else she might have been planning?"

"Did you call the police?" Josh questioned, ever the Solicitor.

"We decided against that. We didn't want a scandal or the stress of a court case. She knows what she did was wrong and without a reference from us she's going to find it hard to find another job. That's punishment enough. Anyway, that's enough unpleasantness. He paused and looked over to Steven. "Do you have anything you want to add?"

"I wanted to say just how excited I am about tonight," he said, completely ignoring the shocking news that had just been shared.

"Harry's right. This is not a church, but we felt it was very important to have our wives be part of our vision and the great things that are happening at Gideon. Let me say that there will be many people that want to be part of this thing we are doing. But for now, we are only including the people who have been invited here tonight. Make no mistake. This is exclusive. Other people will look in and want what you are receiving here tonight. Please don't think that it's okay to invite friends or family to these get-togethers. This is by invitation only."

You've got to be kidding, Lauren thought. God isn't exclusive. And no one here was any more special than anyone else. What an ego Steven had, assuming others would want to be here because of him. She wanted to laugh out loud at the absurdity of what he was saying, but she could see that he was deadly serious. Trying to rearrange her features to neutral, Lauren focused on Steven who was still talking.

"While we were praying, God downloaded two things to me. The first is that there is a real need for physical healing here tonight. There is a person who is having trouble with their back and there's another person who is having trouble with their hearing. But I'm not the person who will be praying for you tonight." Steven pointed across the room to Lauren and said "God's told me you have a gift of healing. Tonight, it's time to use that gift and bless others with it."

If Steven had told Lauren her hair was on fire, she couldn't have been more surprised. She knew it wasn't true. While she believed anyone could pray for another and if God wanted to, he could bring complete physical healing, she had never done it, or even had a desire to. Lauren knew she had a gift of discernment, but healing, no. And she really didn't like being put on the spot like this. What was she supposed to do? Go with it and make an idiot of herself. Or refuse and embarrass her and Jamie. Either way she couldn't win.

Jamie on the other hand was thrilled. *This could be the thing that brings her in,* he thought. He had never considered that she had a gift of healing, but Steven heard from God. He would know. Watching his wife, he saw her confusion. He could always tell what she was thinking, and he could see she didn't know what to do. *Please don't embarrass me,* he silently thought.

Her mind still spinning from Steven's revelation and not seeing any way-out Lauren croaked out a quiet "Okay, I guess so." Before she had a chance to gather her thoughts, Josh shot across the room.

"I'd love you to pray for me. Steven's right. I've been having back problems," he said as he sat on the floor at her feet. Well God, she said in private prayer, it's up to you now. Please help. Gently laying her hands-on Josh's shoulders she began to pray out loud.

"Dear God," Lauren began, feeling like God was indeed directing her prayers, "thank you for your son Josh. Thank you for the love you have for him. I ask that you come and fill the places in his life where he feels like he didn't have the same kind of love from his Earthly father as he has from you. This has caused him to feel rejected and often not good enough. Please let him see himself the way you see him. Let him find a release so that he can let go of all the tension that manifests as physical pain." And for forty-five minutes, one by one, others sat at her feet and asked for prayer. She prayed for healing to come where there had once been rejection and hurts caused by others. She prayed for those who could only look at the world with an analytical mind and not hear what God was saying to them. She prayed for those who were holding back because they didn't feel in the deepest parts of them that they were ever going to be good enough. She even prayed for those that were striving to be the best and expected perfection from themselves, causing anxiety brought on by what they believed God and others thought of them. She asked God to bring rest and healing. Some cried and all thanked her for her prayers.

By the time people stopped asking for prayer, Lauren could hardly speak. Her throat was hoarse because of her cold and she was ready to go home to bed. She felt overwhelmed by what had just happened and needed to be alone so she could sort out her feelings about it. She didn't even remember most of what she had prayed. She could only hope it had been God who had directed her and her prayers. Unfortunately for her, Steven wasn't done for the evening, and regained control of the meeting.

"That was amazing Lauren," he said. "It was beautiful to watch you open yourself up and be used by God to bring healing and freedom to so many people. It brought tears to my eyes. But God isn't done yet tonight." He looked across the room to Stuart's wife.

"The second thing God's told me is that you have a gift of prophesy Cynthia. Tonight it's time to tap into it and prophesy for some of the people here tonight."

Cynthia looked even more surprised than Lauren had. Shaking her head, she looked down at her folded hands. But if she was hoping that Steven was going to drop it, she was mistaken.

"Cynthia you need to look past your fears and step out and do this." He stood up from his chair and walked towards her until he was standing directly in front of her.

"This isn't a time for you to be shy. God requires you to stand up and begin to operate in the gift He's given you," Steven pushed. The room had fallen silent as they watched the scene unfold. Cynthia continued to refuse Steven's command, while Steven urged her to step out in faith. Lauren kept waiting for someone to speak up and defend her. Cynthia had said no and that should be enough. Why wasn't Stuart telling Steven to stop. But he sat by, watching as his wife continued to refuse. People began glancing around the room, uncomfortable with the direction the evening had taken. Minutes passed while Steven refused to back off. Waiting for someone else to intervene clearly wasn't going to happen, and Lauren opened her mouth to tell him to leave her alone, when Cynthia squeaked out a quiet "fine."

"Good. God's told me you have a word for Aaron. So, if you could step up Aaron and Cynthia if you join him, you can bring God's word for him. Just close your eyes and tell us the picture you see," Steven suggested as Aaron moved into the middle of the room in front of Cynthia.

Cynthia closed her eyes as everyone in the room waited for her to speak. The men, including Stuart looked excited. Finally, their wives were finding their place in Gideon. God was using them to bring healing and prophesy. What else would he do? The other women in the room shot furtive glances at each other, hoping they wouldn't be the next one singled out.

"I don't see anything," Cynthia finally said after minutes had ticked by.

"Give it some more time. Be patient and it will come. You need to silence your fears and let God speak through you."

"I guess I see Aaron on a surfboard ... Out on the waves. Doing what he loves," Cynthia stammered. "Maybe God's saying he loves Aaron's feeling of freedom when he's out there. He's proud of him because he brings that freedom to his life and his family."

"Good. That's a start. Does anyone else have anything for Aaron?" Steven asked. As a few people stepped forward with more words for him, the tension in the room broke. Lauren looked at her watch. It was eleven thirty. They had been here for four hours. No wonder she was exhausted. Catching Jamie's attention, she tapped her watch and gestured her head towards the door. He shook his head no and continued to listen to the words people had for Aaron. It took another fifteen minutes before people were done. And then finally Harry closed the meeting with a short prayer. Wanting to make a quick getaway wasn't on the cards as people began to thank her for her prayers. It was almost twelve o'clock before Jamie and Lauren made it to their car.

"That was amazing darl," Jamie exclaimed as they pulled out of Pat's driveway. "I can't believe you prayed for all those people. You've never done anything like that before."

"I know right," Lauren answered. "I don't know where it came from." She felt like she had been outside her body and someone else had taken her mouth over and spoken on her behalf. Was it possible that Steven had been right, and she did have a gift of healing? He had prophesied that she would be given a new gift from God more than two years ago. Was this it? And if he was right about this, could it be possible that she had been wrong all along and he really was a prophet. She was going to need to think about what had occurred tonight. If she was wrong she was going to owe some people an apology. Needing a change of subject, she asked,

"What did you think of what happened to Cynthia?"

"It was ok. Bit awkward but it turned out all right."

"I didn't like it. Steven bullied her until she gave in."

"It wasn't that big of a deal. That's just Stevens way. When he hears from God he sometimes has to push a little so that he can bring break through to people. It would have been a missed opportunity for Aaron if she hadn't prophesied and for Cynthia too."

"Maybe. But the way he did it. I was ready to say something. I can't

116

believe Stuart let his wife be talked to like that. I'm glad that didn't happen to me."

"That's because you stepped out straight away. He didn't have to push. I'm proud of you."

It was nice to not be arguing with Jamie about Gideon and Steven, Lauren thought. But what would have happened if she had refused to pray for others. Would Steven have pushed and bullied her too? And would Jamie have sat by the same way Stuart had? Not defending or protecting his wife the way he was supposed to.

Chapter thirteen

Another Wednesday night, another boring meeting. Lauren tried to concentrate on praying. She really did. But telling her it was time to pray and for so long felt forced and orchestrated. There was nothing organic about it. It was the same as it had been the first two times with everyone sitting in silence. Soaking, as Harry called it, everyone was expected to enter into the presence of God. Lauren didn't feel it, but she wasn't convinced that it was because she wasn't holy enough, but that God didn't have anything to say to her right now. She cracked open one eye and looked around the room. Everyone was off in their own little world, one or two swaying to the music that quietly played in the background. It was more of the same repetitive melodies that Harry favoured. Songs about Father God and what He had done for the writer. A lot of it's all about me and very light on actual praise to God. Others had their hands outstretched as if they were trying to attract some sort of special power. It reminded Lauren of a documentary she had recently watched on meditation and resembled very little of the prayer meetings she had experienced throughout her earlier Christian life. Yes, she agreed that

God was relational and wanted to spend time with his children, but to expect that he would show up on demand to download as Steven would say, was arrogant. Sometimes God would take weeks, months, years to answer a prayer. The Gideon family expected Him to answer immediately. She peeked a quick look at her watch and saw that forty-five minutes had already passed. Only an hour and a quarter to go before she could escape. After the second meeting last month, which had gone on forever, she had told Jamie that if they didn't leave at nine-thirty she would refuse to attend ever again. At least she hadn't been called on again to pray for healing at this meeting or the last. People had raved about her for weeks but after the initial high she had felt; she knew in her heart that she didn't have a gift of healing. Lauren hadn't said anything to Jamie because he would be disappointed, but she was positive Steven had got it wrong. And nobody had actually claimed to be healed because of her prayers. Resisting the urge to sigh out loud she tried to pray some more but she had said everything she wanted to say forty minutes ago, and her mind drifted to Jamie. They had been getting along reasonably well the last few months. They argued a lot less. Trying to give him the benefit of the doubt, Lauren had backed off criticising Steven and the way Gideon was being run. She had asked God to make it clear to her if Steven really was a prophet and that she was the one in the wrong. Send me a dream, reveal a bible verse that I've previously missed about prophets, have someone outside of Gideon speak highly of him to me, she had asked God. Something, anything that would convince her that she was off the mark and he was all he claimed. So far God had been silent, and she had nothing but her own intuition to trust. If he was a false prophet, she had to believe that at some point he would trip up and be exposed as a fraud. She prayed often that if he was a fake Jamie and the others would see him for who he truly was. But as it stood now, the men were infatuated with him, hanging off every word he uttered and following whatever instruction he told them God had given him.

Finally, Harry brought the prayer time to an end. One hour to go and then she could escape.

"Thanks everyone for being here," Harry said. "Tonight we're going to do something a little different. After months of prayer and seeking God, we finally have our answer for the direction that Gideon will take." Harry dragged over a white board that had been tucked away in the corner and picked up a pen to write with. *What's he selling now,* Lauren thought? This reminded her of the time they had been invited to check out a new business opportunity in the nineties. After two hours of talking points their neighbour finally revealed that he was inviting them to join Amway. She had felt conned then and she was getting that same feeling now, that she was about to be sold something she didn't really want.

"The lads are aware of what I'm about to tell you and now it's time to share our future plans for Gideon with you all. We thought about discussing this at next week's retreat, but we decided to get it out of the way now. Then we can spend our four days away focusing on God." Pulling a marker out of his pocket, Harry looked ready to teach a class.

"There are three parts of our organisation. The first thing to come was Gideon. God gave us an amazing business opportunity that has provided us with a huge amount of money. I think that we would all agree that we have been amazingly blessed financially. We could walk away now, happy with what we have received. But early on we decided to continue to look for more opportunities. The right one hasn't presented itself yet, but we feel it's very close." Harry wrote Gideon on the board and then drew a circle around it.

"From Gideon came the foundation. The reason we started it was to further the kingdom of God. We have been able to help fund a school in Thailand for girls that have been rescued from the sex slave industry. We will continue to donate five thousand dollars a month to the good work being done there," Harry announced with a look of pride. *That's all,* Lauren thought? Five thousand dollars a month to what was yes, a great cause but the Foundation had millions of dollars. What was being done with the rest of the money? It was definitely time for the girls to get involved and make some suggestions of what could be achieved with all that money.

Writing Foundation on the board next to Gideon, he circled that word also, the second circle overlapping the first one.

"Tonight, we want to let you in on the last part of what we are doing. If you have been unsure why we employed Steven I want to put your minds at rest tonight. Steven has an amazing gift of prophesy. We've all seen it at work. But some of you may be unaware that he also uses that gift to provide counselling. All of us lads have benefited from spending time in the padded cell which is what we lovingly call our counselling room," he smiled at his bad joke. "A couple of the girls have also begun receiving healing through Steven and it's our desire that everyone here will use the counselling offered to get the freedom God wants for them. That's one of the reasons that we want to keep all of this exclusive for now. Anybody who is part of what we are doing here needs to be willing to move forward, putting their past behind them and move towards God's freedom. It can be painful at times and the commitment to changing and letting go isn't for everyone. Soon, when we are all in alignment, we will invite others who have the same desire for the things of God that we do. But for now, we will be focusing on this group receiving freedom." Beneath the words Gideon and Foundation Harry wrote the words Break Free. Again, he circled them, overlapping with the other two circles. Above that in large letters and underlining it twice he wrote the words The Collective.

"What I've drawn here tonight is our new logo for The Collective which is the banner that all three entities will come under. In the past our focus has been on making money. And there's nothing wrong with making money. But God has been very clear that we need to change our motivation for wanting to make that money. The foundation was originally a side thing. But now it will be our main activity. Gideon will exist to fund the foundation, which will in turn fund our counselling arm Break Free. Because ultimately that's what we're here for. To help people break free from their past. God singled out each man to be part of this and by extension, their wives. And when we were ready to receive Him, God brought us Steven. God is using him to change lives, one at a time. Our desire is to take this model of receiving freedom and influence Christians all over this country and eventually the world."

Jamie looked over at Lauren. As usual she looked less than impressed and he hoped she wasn't going to ask any awkward questions. He had hoped she would be excited with the direction The Collective was going. He had seen firsthand the work that was being done in Thailand. Last month he had spent a week with Harry and Steven in Bangkok setting up procedures and checks and balances to ensure that the money they were sending every month was being used wisely. The trip was unlike anything he had ever experienced in his sheltered life. The scale of the poverty that he saw put into perspective how very rich they were. Money that he had given to the foundation was helping to educate girls who, without them, would probably have no opportunities and would eventually return to a life of prostitution to feed themselves. Now they could have almost any future they wanted. How could Lauren begrudge those poor girls that? Every time the foundation came up she got angry. The word furious didn't even begin to cover how she had felt when he finally told her that fifty percent of all profits would be now be going to the foundation. She refused to see that they didn't need the money for themselves and were being asked by God to be part of something amazing. She had everything in life she needed and most of the things she wanted. He had come to realise that if anyone in Gideon had an issue with greed it was her. And the fuss she had made when he told her he would be travelling with Steven and Harry had been ridiculous. It was reminiscent of the early days when she would fight him on Gideon and use everything in her arsenal to control what he did. Steven told him she was operating out of fear and that he should ignore it. What she was afraid of, he couldn't figure out. And it had been a life changing experience that had opened his eyes to the poverty and evil in the world. It was so wonderful to know that he was doing some good out there and to be truly free of the issues that had been holding him back. Tied down by his need and desire to earn a huge income and to live up to a standard that wasn't realistic. Steven had been instrumental in helping him let go of his issues with money and status and Jamie would be forever grateful.

It had only taken one session with Steven and Harry for him to pinpoint the first time he had decided he wanted to be wealthy. When he was eight years old, he had been staying with his parents at his Aunt and Uncle's house in Perth. Uncle Robert had been a very successful businessman at the time with a string of pharmacies throughout Western Australia. With Steven's guidance, he was taken back to the time he first recognized true wealth. Jamie had been overawed by the Peppermint Grove home. His mother had repeatedly reminded him and his little sister Amelia not to touch anything, not to make a mess on the frighteningly white carpet and to be as quiet as they could. Thankfully Uncle Robert had been much more relaxed than his mother and had seen the little boy peeking into his home office as he worked. Inviting him in, he had placed him in the chesterfield chair behind the desk and let him spin it round and around. He would never forget the smell of the leather that beautiful chair was made from. When Jamie was too dizzy to think he stopped spinning and took in his surroundings. The walls of the office were lined with books, there must be almost a million of them Jamie had thought at the time and the desk was so fancy. He didn't think his mother would ever let him do his colouring on it. But the view out the window had been the thing that stayed with him. Overlooking the river, from the second storey window, he could see yachts sailing by. He wasn't close enough to make out the people on them, but he bet they were having fun. He'd never seen a yacht before, except on the television when there had been a story about the Sydney to Hobart race and the prices they had talked about in the story had seemed huge to the little boy. Jumping off the chair and running to the window to get a closer look, he had asked his Uncle if he had a boat too. "Of course," had been Uncle Robert's answer and from that moment on, Jamie knew that if he wanted special things like a boat of his own and a house where he could look at the water every day, he was going to need money. Lots of it.

As the years passed by he studied hard so that he could get good grades. He recognized that his Dad did very well, but he wanted to do even better. He wanted to be like his Uncle Robert. When the time came to decide what he wanted to study when he finished high school, he and his parents had only discussed careers that would make him wealthy. They had discussed him becoming a doctor but the thought of being around sick, germy people had freaked him out and he wasn't going to have the grades for it anyway. He didn't want to be a lawyer because that would mean talking in front of people in a court room which was definitely not his thing. After much debate about how long he wanted to study at Uni, what sort of grades he was likely to achieve and how much money he would be able to make when he qualified, he had decided on being an accountant. And that was what he become. Not a decision based on his passions or what God wanted for him. But a decision based on money. And now that he knew this and understood how that day, looking out over the water in his uncle's office had moulded every decision he made, he was ready to let it go. Being at Gideon was everything he wanted now. But he was still going to have to convince Lauren that letting go of his remaining clients was the right thing to do. She was still refusing to even consider the possibility that he should be at Gideon, now The Collective, full-time. He'd told her that they didn't need to worry about money. If he was doing what God had called him to do, then He would provide everything that they needed. Unfortunately, it fell on deaf ears.

Across the room Lauren was tapping on her watch. It was nine-thirty and she wanted out of here. Catching Jamie's eye, she tilted her head towards the door. Jamie had explained to Steven and Harry that they would be leaving early and although Harry wasn't thrilled, he had agreed it would be all right this time. He'd finished his presentation anyway and was asking if anyone needed prayer so now was a good time to leave. They had another hour, maybe two left in the evening and Jamie knew Lauren would keep her word. If they didn't go now, she wouldn't be back. After a wave to the room, they gathered their coats and quietly slipped out Pat's door. They had barely left the driveway when Lauren launched into yet another one of her tirades.

"Is that all you spend the foundation money on? Five thousand lousy dollars a month in Thailand. There must be several million dollars available for use. You could be doing so much more with it."

"We will. We just haven't come across the right project yet. The last thing we want to do is waste it," Jamie replied.

"Yeah right. Steven's wages come out of there don't they? He's probably making sure it all gets saved up so he can earn his astronomical wage for another decade. And seriously what's with that name? The

Collective. That has to be one of the stupidest things I've ever heard."

Well she has me there, Jamie thought. He had argued that the banner name over all the entities sounded wrong, but Steven had been adamant that that was the name God had given him and the others had accepted it immediately.

"The name's not important Lauren. What's important is the good work that's being done. Have you given any further consideration to having a session with Steven? I'm happy to sit in with you. I know you don't feel comfortable being alone with him. Or Harry could join you. You like Harry."

"Yes I like Harry. But no. I am never going to join them in the, what did they call it, the padded cell and have Steven poke around in my mind," she snorted. "I'm just glad we got out of there early. At least you kept your word this time."

~ ~ ~

"I think that went well tonight," Harry told Steven as they loitered in Pat's driveway, leaning against Harry's car. "I think the wives were very receptive to the plan of shifting focus from business and concentrating our efforts on Break Free."

"They were. Well, all but one. I still have concerns about Lauren. She isn't progressing the way she should be and that's holding Jamie back from completely letting go and committing fully to The Collective. She practically dragged him out of there tonight. And every time she does that he misses out. It was the same as the retreat last year. Because of her he missed the first day."

"Don't worry about it," Harry reassured him. "We'll have plenty of time next week at the retreat for her to see what God's doing. There won't be any talk about business. We'll just focus on God and let him do what he needs to do to bring about a change of heart in her."

126

"And we'll introduce what we discussed last week. About the dream I had?" Steven asked.

"We will. But gently, gently. We don't want to push too hard, too fast. We'll talk about your dream a little. Plant the seed. And then God will do the rest."

Chapter fourteen

❝ Are you ready to go down?" Jamie asked Lauren.

"Can't we stay here and have a nap? I'm so tired," Lauren moaned. "I promise nobody will miss us." The bed looked so tempting and it had been at least a week since Lauren had slept properly. Worrying about this weekend had kept her tossing and turning every night. And now that they were here, she was even more nervous. She had made promises to Jamie and while she intended to keep those promises, Lauren didn't want to.

When they had arrived she had been astounded at the beauty of the property where they would be spending the next few days. She might not agree with what was going on at Gideon, but they certainly never skimped on the accommodation. After stowing the luggage in the walk-in wardrobe Jamie joined Lauren at the window to look out over the property. The sun sparkled playfully off the water of a dam that was large enough to be a small lake. A rowboat tied to the pier looked inviting and Lauren wished she could spend the rest of the day floating across the water with nothing more on her mind than trying to figure out what kind of bird that was chirping happily in a nearby tree. Now that boat would be a lovely spot to have a nap. Unfortunately, they had orders to follow and were expected in the main lounge room in fifteen minutes for the first session of what she thought was going to be a long, long, long, long weekend. At least their surroundings were beautiful. When Jamie had told her they would be hiring a country house on a horse stud owned by the brother of one of his few remaining clients, Lauren had pictured tiny rooms with rickety beds and one bathroom to share. But the eight-bedroom homestead had been built with luxury in mind. Each bedroom had a king-sized bed with its own ensuite and was decorated in muted beiges and whites with the occasional soft pastel cushion or throw rug. Nothing took away from the emerald green grass and the manicured gardens full of precision clipped hedges outside their window. This was her first time visiting the Hunter Valley, but she hoped it wouldn't be her last. The small town of Scone was surrounded by farms and was famous for its horse breeding. Full of heritage listed buildings Lauren hoped she would get the chance to spend some time in town shopping in the unusual stores that were often found in country towns.

"I think they will miss us love. And Harry wants to get started on time, so we get through todays agenda before dinner."

"You do realise if he spent less time sitting around soaking and just got on with it we could probably get through twice as much and I'd be a whole lot less bored."

"Don't forget you promised to give this weekend a chance and especially Steven," Jamie reminded her.

"I know. I'll be nice."

"Not just nice. Try to listen for God when He speaks to you. And engage with the rest of us. No preconceived ideas."

"All right, all right. Let's just get this over with." Inwardly sighing, Lauren wished she could take her promise back. She had told Jamie she was going to give the next three days a go. Instead of complaining about

Steven, she was going to try and get to know him better. And even if she didn't like him, that didn't mean he wasn't a prophet. Unless proven otherwise, she was going to accept that he did have a gift and did hear directly from God, at least for the next three days. Because like it or not, he was in her life and Jamie thought it was unfair to base her opinion of him on her gut feeling and one not quite right prophesy several years ago.

Downstairs, the lounge room where the sessions were going to take place was just as beautiful as the rest of the house. Pat was adding a log onto the already roaring fire, as Harry fiddled with the sound system in the corner. Most of the couches were already occupied, everybody else having arrived earlier than Lauren and Jamie, so she chose a wing chair while Jamie squeezed in on an oversized two-seater couch with Stuart and Cynthia. Music playing quietly in the background, Harry sat down beside Felicity as the chatter around the room ceased. Without needing to say anything, all attention focused on Harry, who as usual, took control of the meeting.

"Welcome everyone to our third retreat. This one is going to be different than the last two. Usually you girls go off to shop and see the sights. But this time we're including you in the important discussions about The Collective. We talked about it with you a little at the last gathering but over the next few days we will speak in depth about the future and direction we will be taking. We started throwing some idea's around at lunch but unfortunately Lauren and Jamie weren't there. I'll try and find some time to fill you in later," he said, directing his gaze at Lauren. "It's such a shame you weren't here. You missed out on hearing what God is doing in the lives of some of us."

Why did he do that? Lauren was at least ten years older than Harry, but he made her feel like a naughty child. It's not like she had refused to come down early so they could join in the fun at lunch. She had work.

130

Unable to find one of the other part-timers to cover her shift at reception today, she had no choice but to work this morning. Jamie had picked her up at twelve and they had driven the three and a half hours to Scone without a stop. She really liked Harry, but it bothered her the way he felt he had the right to tell her off. She was a grown woman with children and responsibilities. If that interfered with his agenda, then that was just too jolly bad. In any other circumstance, she would have told the person to pull their head in. But here with thirteen sets of eyes all focused on her, she could see their disappointment. Speaking up and explaining wouldn't achieve anything and would probably spark a discussion where they would spend hours trying to convince her that she was putting work before God. She often wondered if these people had any kind of grip on reality and what life was like in the real world. Realizing she wasn't listening, she focused on Steven who had picked up where Harry had left. *I'd better pay attention,* she thought, *or I'll be in trouble again. I might end up in the naughty corner.* Although it might be preferable to having to listen to this all day. Smiling to herself, she noted, if they followed the rule that TV's *Nanny Jo* enforced for punishing unacceptable behaviour, she would have to sit one minute for every year old she was. Forty-three minutes of silence sounded wonderful about now.

"We weren't sure we were going to be able to make the timing work but as usual, God intervened, and we are pleased to tell you that we have been able to fly Alan and Florence Jones in from New Zealand. For those of you who don't know who they are," Steven continued "Alan was and is my mentor. He taught me everything I know about prophesy and trained me when he saw the gift God had given me. I owe everything to him and his wife Florence who guided and nurtured me and Lucy through the many tough times and rejections we have faced. In the face of opposition they always stood with me and encouraged me to never give in. Because of them, The Collective is here today. They will be flying in from Auckland tonight and tomorrow they will be with us for part of the day. They will be prophesying over each one of you and sharing their story with us."

"Something for you to prayerfully consider is how much each of you will contribute to their ministry," Harry said. "I'll make sure you all have their bank account details before the end of the retreat so you can easily make a deposit to them. They are being very generous with their time, so it would be great if your gift reflected that."

Catching Jamie's eye, Lauren gave a tiny shake of her head that he would recognize as a no. The last people she wanted to give money to were the ones that set Steven on the world. But instead of agreeing Jamie lifted one finger up. Pulling her phone out of her pocket, Lauren texted the words one hundred to Jamie. Looking at his screen, he frowned and then started typing. One thousand appeared seconds later on her phone. Fat chance, she shot back and then put her phone back in her pocket, not wanting to continue the ridiculous conversation any longer. If they all gave one thousand dollars, and these people were likely to give more, that was a hefty pay packet for one day's work with free travel and accommodation to Australia.

"Now because of Alan's visit tomorrow we are going to need to jam a bit more into today's session and Sunday morning. It might be best if you all plan to be here a little longer on Sunday as we have so much to get through." Most nodded in agreement but Jamie shot Lauren a glance and shrugged his shoulders. They couldn't stay longer because they had promised Jamie's parents they would come for dinner for his Mums birthday. She had already been disappointed that they wouldn't be there on Saturday with the rest of the family but if they cancelled Sunday dinner, she would be devastated. Great, they were already in trouble for missing lunch today. Now they would be in trouble for leaving on

Sunday as well. These guys needed to stop taking themselves so seriously and realise people had lives outside of The Collective.

"Steven and I have spent weeks seeking God in preparation for this," Harry said as he picked up his Bible from the floor. "The verse He gave us to focus on this weekend is found in Hebrews thirteen, verse seventeen. Before we come together and discuss what this verse means I'd like you to find a quiet place for the next twenty minutes and read this verse over a few times. And then I'd like it if you could pray about it. You might have a word from God for yourself, or even another person. Sit with that word and let God speak to you. We'll meet back here shortly, and we can share together what God has revealed to you." As the room quickly emptied Jamie and Lauren met in the centre.

"We can't stay longer on Sunday. You know how these things go," she told him. "We could be here till five o'clock."

"I know but I don't think we have a choice. I'll call Mum and apologize. She'll understand."

"No, she won't. And I'm not cancelling on her. It's her birthday. We've already given up today and tomorrow. That's enough. If they don't like it, it's too bad. We made a commitment to family and I intend on keeping it."

"Umm guys, is there a problem," they heard from the door leading outside to the gardens where a few of the others had chosen to go and pray.

"No. No problem Harry. But unfortunately, we won't be able to stay longer on Sunday. We need to leave at twelve as originally planned," Lauren explained.

"Are you sure you can't stay a little longer?" Harry asked. "What's more important than what we're trying to achieve here this weekend."

"Sorry Harry. We have plans," Lauren answered, not giving Jamie a chance to speak. "You'll just have to save the world without us. Now if you'll both excuse me, I need to go and read this verse." Harry stepped aside as Lauren pushed past him through the door. She walked towards the little pier she had spied earlier out of her window trying to calm her racing heartbeat. She didn't want to upset or embarrass Jamie, but Harry and Steven expected too much. They had already given so much money to the foundation. Jamie had sold his practice and worked for them and now they seemed to want every last minute of their time as well. She felt like she was being swallowed up by The Collective and soon there would be nothing of her left. Reaching the pier, Lauren carefully climbed into the boat. There was a chill in the air, but the sky was clear, and the bright sun cancelled out some of the cold. Pulling out her Bible she quickly found the verse. She read it twice, hoping she had read it wrong the first time. What blatant manipulation. *Obey those who rule over you, and be submissive, for they watch out for your souls, as those who must give account. Let them do so with joy and not with grief, for that would be unprofitable for you.* Are they serious? Lauren had no problem submitting to those God had put in authority over her. But that was the point wasn't it. Those *God* had put in authority. It was clear to her that this verse had been chosen today to bring those that were resisting Steven under his control. But Lauren didn't accept that he had any authority over her. He wasn't her husband, or her Pastor. Jamie might have given Steven authority over him but not for one minute did Lauren believe that authority passed down through Jamie to her. And where in the Bible did it say that a prophet had authority over *anyone*. Steven was just some guy that had come from nowhere and taken over the lives of everyone involved in Gideon.

"God," she cried out, overwhelmed. "I don't understand any of this. My husband is no longer the man I married. And the blessing that you brought to us is turning into a nightmare. I don't know how much longer I can go on." Finally giving in to the tears that had been threatening,

Lauren began to cry. Her throat, clenched from staying silent, tightened as her tears turned to sobbing. She could barely breath and gasped for oxygen as she tried to get herself under control. Minutes passed as her sobbing slowed and she was able to catch her breath. "Please God. Please open Jamie's eyes. You know he won't listen to me," she asked. Hearing nothing but the wind move through the trees as the water gently lapped against the boat, Lauren began to feel calm again. She might not be hearing God, but she knew his promise. He would never leave her. This season that she was in had been the worst of her life. But it couldn't last forever. Either she would see that Steven was genuine, or he would be exposed as a fraud. She would just have to wait it out. Wiping the tears from her face, she turned towards the house when she heard her name being called. Jamie was beckoning her and pointing at his watch. Checking the time, she realized the twenty minutes was up and she was expected to return with the others. As much as she wanted to stay here in the sunshine, that would be rude and would only cause another argument with Jamie. Climbing carefully out of the boat, she started walking towards her husband. When she reached him, he could see the smudged mascara under her eyes and knew she had been crying.

"You okay?" he asked.

"Yeah, I guess so. But if you don't mind, I'm going to take a minute to fix myself up in the room."

"But everyone will have to wait for you."

"Then they'll have to wait won't they. Or tell them to start without me. I don't care" she said as she walked towards the front door. If she went through the lounge everyone would see that she had been crying and the last thing she wanted was to be grilled about what was wrong. Sneaking up the stairs, she could see that everyone else had returned and were engaged in a lively conversation. In her room, she quickly wiped away the panda eyes and touched up her foundation. Feeling more like herself and looking less red and blotchy, she made her way back downstairs to the lounge. Everyone turned towards her as she entered and took the last seat in the room.

"We were just discussing the verse and what everyone received from God when they read it," Harry explained. "Did you have anything you wanted to share?" he asked Lauren.

"No. I'm good thanks," she replied

"It looks like you've been crying," Felicity said. "Are you sure there's not something you want to tell us?"

"No. It's private. Just between me and God."

"You're in a safe space Lauren," Ashley said kindly. "We are all here to grow together and maybe something God told you could help another. We'd love it if you could share."

"I'd really rather not," Lauren answered feeling everyone's eyes on her as she wished she could disappear into the floor.

"Can I share something with you then?" Lucy asked. "When I was praying I had a very clear word from God about you."

"Oh, umm. Maybe we should talk about it later," Lauren replied. She didn't want another prophesy and this time it would be public.

"It's nothing too private Lauren. And someone else may benefit from hearing it. God told me that He wants you all to Himself. He's jealous of your time, and desires to have a closer, deeper, relationship with you. But one of the things that's getting in the way is your job. Maybe it would be helpful if you could spend the next few days asking God what He thinks you should do about working. I believe He will have something to say to you about it."

"What if we all took a few minutes to ask God for Lauren what she should do in this situation," Harry suggested.

"Oh, that's really not necessary," Lauren stammered. "I like my job. It gives me some independence and gets me out of the house."

"Why do you feel you need independence?" Harry asked as he gently tilted his head and stared at her in that very Harry way. "Is it because of what you went through when you were a child with your fathers gambling. Does it make you feel more in control if you have your own money? Control is just an illusion Lauren. Perhaps that's why God wants you to let go of your job. So you will have no choice but to trust him. It would also mean you could spend more time with him, drilling down to why you do the things you do and feel the way you do. It could be very helpful for you to spend some time with Steven. I'm sure he would love to help you."

Doubtful, Lauren thought. She had agreed to give Steven a chance but there was no way she would go into the padded cell with him and let him get inside her head. And after he'd betrayed her by sharing their private conversation about her father to everyone here, she wouldn't be confiding in Harry again anytime soon. Her father's gambling was something she kept to herself and he had just blurted it out.

"Well maybe that's something to consider," she lied.

"Good," Harry smiled. "Now let's all take a minute to pray for Lauren and see if God has anything else to say. And then we can get back to the verse." Everyone closed their eyes and sat silently for a few minutes. Pat was the first to speak up.

"I'm hearing that God really loves you Lauren and he's wanting you to receive the freedom he has for you."

"I'm hearing the same thing," Daniel confirmed. "You're holding on so tightly to your job because you're afraid to let go and trust God. He's got it."

"Giving up my job was the best thing I ever did," Louise said. "It gave me the time to really focus on God and move into the future He has for me. He's saying this is your time." After a few more confirmations from others the room fell into silence.

137

"That's very encouraging everyone. And thanks for sharing. Does anyone have anything more for Lauren?" Harry asked. When a few people shook their heads and nobody else added anything to the conversation Lauren breathed a quiet sigh of relief. It was weird, she noted. All of the wives except her and Cynthia didn't work. Ashley had small children so that made sense, but Felicity had quit her advertising job late last year and Maria had left her job teaching kindergarten earlier in the year. Granted, they probably didn't need the money. Pat was loaded but for as long as Lauren had known her, she had always said she loved her job and didn't do it for the money. Lauren was aware that both of them were spending a lot of time with Steven receiving counselling. *I wonder if they were encouraged to leave their jobs too. Another good reason to keep working,* she thought. *That way I won't have the time to spend getting freedom.* And anyway, they actually needed her to work now that Jamie had taken a pay cut.

"Then let's move on," Harry continued. "Does anyone have anything they would like to share about the verse we read earlier in Hebrews?"

"It was a real challenge for me," Daniel started. "I've always been a man who controlled everything in my business and very rarely listened to advice from others. But I'm realising that by holding on so tightly I've removed God from any decisions I've made. It's time I fully gave myself, my family and my business over to those that God has put in authority over me. As our prophet Steven, that's you. And Harry, as our Apostle that includes you to. I'm no longer prepared to make my decisions alone. I want you to speak into everything I do."

"I'm sorry, what did you call him Daniel?" Lauren asked confused.

"I called him Apostle. Harry's an Apostle."

"Like in the bible?"

"Yes like in the bible. We were studying the five-fold ministries and

138

realized that Harry has the mantle of Apostle on him. Steven is the Prophet and Pat has the gift of Pastor," Daniel confirmed.

"I see," Lauren replied thinking she was going to need to find out what the five-fold ministry was.

"I think the thing is, that in society today, we are so spiritually disconnected," Josh said carrying on the conversation like everyone understood that Harry was indeed an Apostle.

"We have such a this-is-mine, I'm-not-sharing attitude, that we have lost touch with what God wants for us. And not just financially but in how we selfishly go about our day to day. He puts leaders in our lives to guide us and correct us when we step outside of God's will. And often it's hard to know what God's will is. That's why I feel so honoured to have Steven and Harry in my life. When I get it wrong, think I'm hearing something from God that I'm not, they are there to get me back on the straight and narrow. I thank God daily that He has bought you both into our lives. I think it's fair to say that Ashley wasn't completely on board at the start but now she can see that this is from God." Ashley nodding in agreement with her husband, affirming what he had said.

"I agree," Ashley continued. It's been a struggle letting go of how I thought I should live my life. There's been a few things I thought would go differently. We had planned to travel next year but Steven helped us hear that God had something better for us. And look at what we would be missing out on if we were to take off for three months. The growth and the friendships that have come from being part of The Collective. If any of you have any doubts, I encourage you to take them to God or talk them over with Steven. I know my mind is at ease."

"I agree," said Pat. "I think part of the problem is that people see authority as control. But in the same way that our children needed guidance when they were little, so do we. Life is a journey and sometimes we take a wrong turn. I embrace the correction I sometimes need. I too feel blessed to have Steven in authority over me. Many Christians are fumbling their way through life, making poor decisions, with no direction. I don't want to live that way."

"Thank you all for your contributions," Harry spoke. "It's getting on time wise and we have dinner reservations shortly. I think this session has been very productive and given us all something to think about. Tomorrow we want to get an early start. Alan and Florence will be here about eleven, so if we can all be ready for breakfast at nine, that will give us some time to pray together before they arrive. I'm so excited to hear what they have to bring for us. So be back here in an hour and we'll make our way to the restaurant together."

People left the room quickly after collecting their phones and bibles. Lauren and Jamie didn't speak until after they had shut their bedroom door behind them.

"That was fantastic wasn't it?"

"If you say so," Lauren answered.

"I think it's a great idea, you giving up work. It would give you the time you need to really work on yourself."

"I think I'm just fine thanks. I've told you before that there's no way I'm having any sessions with Steven."

"But you said you would think about it."

"I was lying Jamie. I'm not giving up my job. I'm not spending hours and hours with Steven and Harry. I like me just the way I am. And you used to like me this way too. I'm not about to become some pushover who lets those two run my life. And you seem to forget we need my wages. Since you took such a hefty pay cut."

"Are we going to have this argument again? We can draw money from the dividends we receive. You're exaggerating about being in trouble financially."

"The dividends are not for living on. They're to pay off the mortgage and get rid of debt. And what happens when the last solar panel sells? No more dividends. What happens then?"

"Something else will come up. I keep telling you, God's got it."

"You do keep telling me. But every time you find a good deal Steven and Harry say no. And when they say yes, the deal never goes ahead because they get the price wrong and won't negotiate. At this rate there will never be another deal. Anyway, what do they know about business? Do they ever listen to you?"

"Of course they listen. But in the end, it's up to God what deals we do or don't do. And they hear from God much clearer than the rest of us. I trust them."

"Well more fool you," Lauren whispered under her breathe as she headed towards the bathroom. She couldn't argue anymore. She was physically exhausted from the lack of sleep and the crying and she still had the whole night ahead of her – of being nice and giving Steven that chance she had promised.

Chapter fifteen

"Can I have everyone's attention please?" Harry said as he tapped his spoon on the side of his coffee cup. "The girls did the cooking this morning, so the boys are on clean up. If we could all be in the lounge in half an hour, we'll get started. Alan and Florence will be arriving at about eleven, so we can get a quick session in before that."

As Jamie picked up Lauren's empty breakfast plate, he leaned over to kiss her on the cheek. For the first time in a long time he was feeling optimistic about their future. Last night's dinner had gone fantastically. Lauren had sat next to Steven and Lucy, keeping her promise to try and get to know them better. He had only been able to catch snippets of their conversations over the noise of fourteen adults laughing and talking but she had been smiling and engaged. Later she had told him that she'd had fun and enjoyed the conversation with the two of them. Steven had told her about growing up in New Zealand and how he had come to know God. Thankfully nothing controversial had come up and Lauren was much more relaxed than she had been yesterday. She had even agreed to let Alan and Florence prophesy over her if they had a word for them.

"Ready for today?" Harry asked as Jamie handed him a stack of plates for the dishwasher.

"I'm excited. I really feel like Lauren's ready for a breakthrough."

"I agree. But I am a little concerned at her unwillingness to stay later tomorrow. I'm worried that you both will miss out on what God's doing if you rush off. It would be good if you could convince her to stay till we finish. Nothing's more important than being in the presence of God and hearing what He has to say."

"I know. But she's made up her mind that we're leaving at twelve. And to be fair, that was the original plan. I promised my mum we'd be home in time for her birthday dinner."

"But surely if you stayed just an extra hour or two you would still have plenty of time to get back to Sydney. We don't want to have anyone missing from the final session. If you can't get her to agree, we're all going to have to finish up at twelve. We can't move forward if we aren't all here together and in agreement. What about if we did finish on time but you came to lunch after with everyone. You could still be back by six."

"I'll ask. But I can't promise anything."

"I'm sure you can convince her. We need everyone together and that includes our wives. And you *are* the head of your home," Harry reminded him as he closed the door to the dishwasher and turned it on.

He's right, Jamie thought as he finished wiping the kitchen bench. *I am the head of my home, and my decision should be final. But I won't bring it up,* he thought. *I'll just drive to the restaurant tomorrow. That way there won't be a scene here and by the time we get to the restaurant it will be too late for her to do anything about it.*

Fifteen minutes later everyone else was present as Lauren settled into her usual seat in the lounge. She looked over towards Harry, expecting him to put on the music quietly and lead them into another prayer time. Instead Steven cleared his throat and began to speak.

"Recently God has been talking to me and Lucy about our living situation. Most of you would be aware that our house isn't suitable for holding meetings. It's not large enough and it's very run down. I'm excited to tell you all that God had told us that we are going to be receiving an upgrade. We don't exactly know what that looks like yet, but he's told us it will be within the next six months."

"I can confirm that," Lucy continued. "In a dream he told me that we are about to receive a massive blessing in the way of a new home. It will be soon, and it will be much closer to the city and the rest of you."

"That sounds so exciting guys," Harry said. "I think everyone here would be in agreement that we want our prophet to be blessed. I'm sure we all look forward to hearing more about this in the future. We don't have long before Alan arrives, so I've decided to open up the floor and let anyone bring what they are feeling to the room." He looked across at Steven and gave him an almost undetectable nod. The seed had been sown. Soon The Prophet would have the house he deserved.

"I have something to say," Felicity said. "I don't know how the other wives feel but I don't know where I fit in here. It's like the wives are along for the ride but we aren't really participating in any of the decision making that's happening."

Woohoo thought Lauren. Finally, someone was brave enough to speak up and say something.

"I agree with Felicity," Lauren nodded. "This all started out as a business and that was fine for you guys to run it. I didn't feel I had anything to add to that. But now things are changing. This is becoming much more than a business and we're expected to go along with everything you decide. You never ask us what we think about the foundation or the direction of Gideon."

"Would you say that you don't think the guys value our input Lauren?" Felicity asked, "Because I don't."

"That's exactly it," Lauren answered. "Like you boys have had an invitation to a party and … I don't know, we didn't get our own invitation. We don't know the destination of the party or what we're supposed to wear, or what the party's even celebrating. You have an official invite and instead of being asked ourselves we're just your plus one."

"Nail on the head," Felicity smiled across at Lauren.

"So, what exactly are you girls looking for?" Harry asked.

"I'd like some say in how the foundation money is spent," Lauren suggested. "There must be a lot of it by now and yes the money being spent in Thailand is fantastic but maybe we should be giving more. I've also noticed that you and Steven seem to be going away overseas to a lot of conferences. I'm wondering if that's being paid for by you personally, or if the foundation is paying for that. I mean, if you want to go away, that's fine. But is it fair to expect us to pay for it?"

"I'll take this," Steven said. "To answer your question about who pays for our travel overseas. Yes, it is paid for by the foundation. That was agreed on by the whole board early on. We aren't going for fun. Attending these conferences is part of our job description. We are away from our families working, learning and growing so we can bring back God's anointing to you. In regard to you girls having some input into decisions made about the foundation money, we agree. We were going to bring this up tomorrow, but we'll do it now. What we are proposing is that you have your own monthly catch up. I know you talked about it in the past, but nothing ever came of it. Now we believe it's important that you get together. Read the same books that we're reading and get together to discuss what you learnt. Maybe start with the five-fold ministry book. That way you will understand the five roles of Apostle, Prophet, Evangelist, Pastor and Teacher. It will help you identify your own gift and roles. And then, when we can see that yes, you are on the same page as us, we would love to hear your ideas for the foundation.

"We could have the catch up at our place," Ashley offered. "That way I don't have to drag the baby out."

"Thank you Ashley. I'll leave it for you girls to sort out the details. Jamie, if you could set up a yammer group for the girls so they can communicate with each other I'd appreciate it."

"Sure," Jamie nodded.

"Thanks for that girls. It's good to know how you're feeling. I think I'll wind up this session, grab yourselves a drink and have a stretch. I think I just heard a car door, so be back in fifteen minutes and we'll get started.

Lauren stood up, stretching for a minute. At least that session hadn't been boring for a change. She felt a hand on her shoulder and turned to find Felicity standing behind her.

"Hey, I just wanted to say thanks for backing me up. I wasn't sure if I should say something, but I think that went well."

"Maybe," Lauren replied. "I'm not sure I agree with the foundation paying for all these trips Harry and Steven keep taking. Nobody else gets to go. And seriously, how many conferences can you do in a year? They've been to three so far and two of them were overseas. That's a huge cost."

"Oh, I don't care about that. There's heaps of money and God will just keep bringing more. I just didn't like feeling excluded by the guys. And now we won't be," she smiled. "I'm going to get a coffee. Can I get you anything?"

"Thanks, but I'm fine. I have a water," she said raising the bottle of spring water in her hand. Walking out of the french doors that led to the garden, Lauren felt the warm sun beat down on her face. The view was just breath-taking, and she savoured the quiet. It didn't stop her mind from racing though. Yet again she felt like she had been *handled*. And what was all that about Steven getting an upgrade? He was on a great wage, but it took two very good incomes to even come close to affording a mortgage in the inner suburbs. Lucy didn't work and they must already have a mortgage on the small house they lived in now. They had only lived there for a year or so and if it was as run down as they had suggested, then they wouldn't have much equity. *Nope, not my problem,* she thought. I have enough worry about paying my own mortgage, let alone worrying about someone else's. That would be for Steven and Lucy to work out.

Fifteen minutes later everyone had reconvened in the lounge. Their guests had arrived and were talking with Steven and Lucy. Alan was a small man, thin and greying at the temples. Probably in his late sixties, he had a pleasant face that had weathered under the Australian sun. Florence looked like a typical Grandmother. Short layered hair, coloured a non-descript brown that had probably come in a bottle from the supermarket and the requisite floral skirt that looked like it had been in her wardrobe since the eighties, aged her. Catching her staring, Florence smiled at Lauren and she instantly felt comfortable. Florence reminded her of her mother in her later years. Perhaps this wouldn't be too awful. And maybe these two were the real deal. It might be all right to be prophesied over by them. Everyone took their usual seats. It didn't take long for humans to get into a routine and on the first day everyone had claimed a favourite place in the room. An extra couch had been bought in for their guests and they too took a seat. Steven made their introductions and then each person went around the room and told Alan and Florence their names. Half an hour later they had told their story of how they had come to move in the prophetic and how they had mentored Steven for years and helped him develop his gift. They explained the importance of having someone in each of their lives who could guide them in whatever gift God had given them. Everyone needed someone who would challenge them and expose the areas of their lives that needed healing. They also reiterated how important it was to come under authority of another and to be accountable to that person. Lauren listened carefully, wanting to give both Alan and Florence her full consideration. Surely such nice people wouldn't support someone who was working outside of God's will. But listening to Alan talk hadn't done anything to convince her that Steven was the one that should have that authority. She was happy to come under a *Godly* authority. She had always come under the authority of her Pastors over the years. And she knew she was supposed to come under Jamie's authority. That was becoming harder and harder to do as she felt that he no longer had her best interests at heart and was more interested in what The Collective needed and wanted. But she had gone along with everything he had done so far, albeit reluctantly. It was just Steven that she was saying no to. She didn't think she would ever believe he had any right to have authority over her. She was sure he was claiming something that wasn't his.

One by one Alan called each couple to the front of the room. He and Florence prayed and prophesied as the others watched on. When she realized that the prophesies would take place in front of everyone else Lauren had been a little taken aback. Shouldn't this be done in private? As they revealed problems within the marriages of the couples and tears flowed, she felt like she was watching a very weird soap opera. She didn't want to be privy to other people's problems and in return she didn't want them knowing about the difficulties that she and Jamie were having. When Alan called her and Jamie to the front of the room it took all her courage to stand up in front of them and take Jamie's hand as instructed. After hearing what they had to say to everyone else she had changed her mind about being part in this.

"Understand this, says the Lord," Alan began. "My hand is upon you and I love you. You feel like there is turmoil in your lives. There are struggles and at the moment you are not on the same page. There is misunderstanding and division. But I will bring you back together on the same page. This is going to be a new season and I will give you new tools to work with. Don't be in opposition with each other but cast your cares upon me and I will bring you back together." As Alan continued speaking, repeating the theme of division in her marriage, Lauren felt tears begin to slide down her face. Not tears of relief that they were being told that things were going to be okay and that soon they would come back together, which was no doubt what the others watching on were thinking. These were tears of humiliation. Yes, Alan was correct. There was division in their marriage. Nothing had been the same since Steven had entered their lives. But she had never spoken to anyone involved with Gideon about how she felt about what was going on and the disunity it had bought to her marriage. And here was a complete stranger announcing to The Collective that they were having problems. This was private, just between her and Jamie and it was for them to work out for themselves with God's help. Privately. Not to be shared with a group of people she didn't know that well and who she wasn't sure she could trust. What was stopping this from becoming gossip. She realized Alan had finished speaking when Jamie squeezed her hand. He led her back to her seat as Lucy handed her a wad of tissues to dry her eyes with. Not wanting to catch anyone's eye she sank as low into her chair as possible and bowed her head. Alan spoke over the last two couples, but Lauren was no longer listening. She didn't want to hear anymore. How could this man think it was okay to reveal peoples secrets publicly? He might have been right in his prophesy but that didn't take away the embarrassment Lauren was feeling. He should have spoken to each couple alone. Instead it had been turned into a show. And instead of feeling comforted, she felt like a loser with a bad marriage.

Harry bought the session to an end after the last prophesy was complete. Alan and Florence were going to stay for lunch and then return to Sydney for their flight. Harry reminded everyone that he had texted the bank account details for Alan and not to forget to make a generous donation for their ministry. About to stand up and find somewhere private to collect her thoughts before lunch, Lauren felt a presence and looked up to see Pat standing over her.

"I am just so thrilled for you," he said. "That prophesy was just amazing, and you are about to receive so much freedom. You must be so excited."

"Um. I'm not really sure what to think," Lauren stuttered. "This session wasn't quite what I was expecting."

"You shouldn't have expectations when it comes to God. But it was an amazing prophesy. For both you and Jamie. I can't wait to see the changes that are coming to your life."

"Yeah, well, we'll see I guess," she answered, wondering if he had heard the same thing she had. "I s'pose we should go and get some lunch," she said as she stood.

Lunch was a rowdy affair. Everyone else seemed to be high on the morning's events. Why did no one else appear to be upset by having their dirty laundry aired for everyone to see? People had been admonished for the troubles in their marriages and from the sounds of it she and Jamie weren't the only ones in trouble. Maybe she was being too sensitive. As Ashley had said yesterday, this was a safe place. But it didn't feel very safe to Lauren.

~ ~ ~

Dinner was another fancy affair. A private room had been booked and Harry had pre-ordered all four courses. It was typical of him. Now people weren't even allowed to decide what they would eat. Sandwiched between Lucy and Felicity, Lauren craved a quiet evening alone with Jamie so they could talk through what Alan had said to them today. He was sitting next to Steven across the table from her, but the chatter was so loud that they couldn't hear each other. After the first course had been bought to the table, oysters – yuck, Lucy noticed that Lauren wasn't eating.

"Not a fan Lauren?" she asked as she helped herself to more from the share platter that had been placed before them.

"No, they creep me out," she answered as she wrinkled her nose in disgust.

"Have you even tried one? I've noticed that about you. You're not very flexible. Once you decide on something, that seems to be it."

"Yes, I have tried them. And I didn't like them. It's no big deal. More for you. And what do you mean I'm not flexible?" she said giving Lucy a questioning look.

"It's been noticed that you aren't moving toward freedom like the rest of us. You won't have any sessions with Steven, you don't want to socialize with us. I've considered popping in to visit at your home, but I've never felt that I would be welcome."

"Nobody pops in to my house. It's just not the way I do things. Even my sister would never do that. If you rang, and it suited me at the time, then a visit would be lovely."

"That's not the way friends do things. And we are going to be friends. We can't go forward together in The Collective otherwise. And because you keep resisting moving forward in The Collective, you're holding everyone else back. Take for instance yesterday. Several people had a word from God for you about giving up your job. Instead of embracing God's word, you fight it, refusing to listen. That's just not going to cut it."

"That's a bit harsh Lucy. Just because someone has a word for me, doesn't mean it's necessarily right. I love my job. I don't want to quit it. And I don't see how my working interferes in any way with Gideon. I don't have anything to do with the business."

"I'm not talking about Gideon. I'm talking about The Collective. All these people here are moving toward a goal to change the world. But we all need to be together and of one mind. We can't have any dissention. So, I want to know what you're going to do about it," Lucy said with a warning note in her voice.

"What do you mean, what am I going to do about it? I'm not going to do anything. It's none of anyone's business whether I work or not. It's my decision. Not yours, not Stevens, yes Jamie's but that's all. I'm forty-three years old. I don't have to answer to you, or anyone else here."

"I think you'll find that's wrong," Lucy whispered quietly in Laurens ear. "It's time you accepted that you need to come under Steven's authority and do what you've been told." And then she turned to Ashley who was sitting on her other side and started up a conversation. Lauren felt a blush rise up her throat and onto her cheeks. Nobody had heard any of the exchange between the women and she doubted anyone would believe her if she told them. Was Lucy threatening her? Over something that was none of her business. What kind of people had they become involved with?

~ ~ ~

"You're very quiet tonight," Jamie noticed as they drove the short trip back to the farmhouse after dinner had finished. "Everything all right."

"Sure. It was just noisy in the restaurant. I guess I just need some peace and quiet."

"We are pretty loud when we all get together. Sorry about the oysters. Was the rest of dinner okay? It didn't look like you ate much."

"It was fine. I guess I wasn't that hungry. I'm just looking forward to going home tomorrow and back to normal life. These retreats are a little overwhelming. I'm not used to spending so much time with other people." Lauren had decided she wasn't going to discuss what had happened tonight with Jamie until they left tomorrow. Because if he didn't believe her then they would end up in another fight and she didn't want everyone else to hear it. More fuel on the fire proving her disobedience towards The Collective.

~ ~ ~

Lauren looked at her watch. It was eleven thirty. In half an hour, she was getting in her already packed car and getting out of here. If Jamie didn't want to come with her, then he could catch a ride with someone else. But there was no way she was staying a minute longer. The morning had been typical. Harry had played his hypnotic music that while soothing, focused on what God could do for the singer and never spoke of His power or His majesty. The discussion had come back to how the wives could become more involved going forward, but it had all been superficial. Read the books the boys were reading and spend more time together. Lauren had tried to steer the conversation towards the foundation earlier but had been shut down. If she was going to bring it up again it would have to be now, before they finished for the day. Gathering all her courage, she cleared her throat and spoke.

"Guys, I really want to get back to discussing what is being done with the foundation money. I'm concerned that it isn't being used the way it was originally intended. We have an opportunity to make a difference in people's lives but if it's whittled away on trips and conferences then we won't be able to help anyone."

"Is there somewhere in particular you want to see the money go?" Harry asked. "Because if you have a proposal, you are welcome to bring it to Steven and myself. We will prayerfully consider a request, if it fits the vision."

"I don't have anything in particular in mind right now but I'm sure if we girls put our heads together we could come up with some causes that

153

are close to our hearts. Don't forget that money came from all of us, not just the boys. I really think we should have a say in what's done with it."

"I don't think that's the way to look at it Lauren. They money doesn't belong to us. It belongs to God; we are just the stewards. But by all means, discuss it with the others and get back to us with a proposal."

"I will. But I think you need to be prepared that we won't always agree with you on how it should be spent." Lauren's last comment went unnoticed by the room. Harry had already moved the conversation on to where everyone was meeting for lunch after they left the farmhouse. The only person still looking at her was Steven. He leaned towards her and quietly whispered,

"Well I guess I'll allow you to be wrong, just once." Turning away from her, he addressed the room.

"There's been a lot of talk this weekend about where everyone fits in. We've talked about invitations. Well today I'm making that invitation official. Who here is willing to accept God's invitation to The Collective? Who is all in? Who is willing to lay down their lives and desires for the future God has for us inside The Collective? It's time we all made a formal commitment to The Collective." It took a minute, but one by one people began to raise their hands and say out loud that yes, they were in. Even Felicity and Maria, who in the past had had reservations about Gideon and The Collective. Lauren and Jamie were the only ones that didn't raise their hands. She felt every eye in the room on her.

"Lauren?" Harry asked. "Do you accept our invitation to be all in?"

"I … I need to think about this. I need to spend some time in my garden with God and pray about it." The room fell silent and Lauren could see Steven in particular was furious with her for not saying yes, but after what he had just said to her what did he expect.

"Well you can come and weed my garden if you need some extra prayer time," Cynthia joked, breaking the tension in the room. With Lauren receiving all the attention, nobody had noticed that Jamie hadn't put his hand up either. People began to gather their phones and Bibles and ten minutes later the house had been vacated. Lauren was able to hold the tears in until the car pulled out of the driveway. Jamie noticed that she was crying but didn't comment. What on Earth had upset her this time? They had had a great time, she had got her way and the retreat had finished on time. Flicking on the indicator to turn left out of the driveway towards the restaurant for lunch he began to follow the other cars.

"Where are we going? Sydney's in the opposite direction."

"Lunch. With everyone else. Harry thought it would be the perfect way to end the retreat."

"Pull over now."

"No"

"Pull over now," Lauren screamed.

Jamie slammed on the brakes and pulled over to the shoulder of the road, taking the unsuspecting Stuart who was behind him by surprise. He swerved out to the other side of the road, thankful no one was coming the other way and gave Jamie a confused look as he pulled ahead. Jamie turned to Lauren, furious.

"What is your problem? You've behaved ridiculously all weekend. Crying and arguing. You've embarrassed me and now you're making us late for lunch. I've had enough of your behaviour."

"I am not going to lunch. If you want to go, ring one of your buddies to come and get you, but there is no way I'm sitting at a table with those people, pretending everything's all right. You might consider those people to be your friends, and The Prophet your leader but I don't. Lucy attacked me last night at dinner. It was humiliating. I cannot sit there and pretend everything's all right. Because it's not. And all that

155

invitation business. They can take their invitation and stick it. I want no part of The Collective." Lauren was sobbing by now, her words coming in short bursts as she tried to breath.

"What do you mean she attacked you? Physically?"

"No of course not. She had a go at me about my job. Her comments felt like a warning. I don't think there is actually anything she can do about my job, but she's made it clear she's never going to accept that I have one. And then today when I told Steven that I wasn't always going to agree with him about the Foundation money he told me that he would let me be wrong just once. And I know you'll think he didn't mean anything by it, but it felt like a threat to me. Who does he think he is? His ego is out of control."

"He's a prophet. He hears from God, and God is never wrong."

"You can call him a prophet all you like but I don't agree. I gave him a chance this weekend, but I haven't changed my mind. I think he's a con artist and you idiots have given him control of your lives and your money. And that prophesy yesterday. It was horrible having everyone know that we're having problems. That was private."

"We weren't the only marriage they talked about. Everyone is having problems at the moment."

"And that makes no sense. If everyone's receiving all this so-called freedom, then why are all our marriages such a mess. Now please take me home. I cannot go to lunch. I don't care what excuse you use, just get me out of here." Sighing, Jamie took his phone out of his pocket and taped out a short text. *Sorry but we can't make it to lunch. Lauren's getting a migraine.* He hit send and then checking the traffic did a U-turn and started back towards Sydney. As he drove he heard the occasional sob from his wife. What was he going to do? They would never accept that Lauren was choosing not to be part of The Collective. Somehow, he was going to have to get her to change her mind. Because more than ever he was convinced that his future and that of his family was tied very strongly to his brothers. And if Lauren wasn't in alignment, then they both would have to leave Gideon and The Collective. Somehow the enemy had got on something that had been said to Lauren with love and she had misunderstood it. Lucy was a nice woman. She would be horrified if she knew Lauren was upset by her probably very innocent comment. And as for Steven's words. He had most likely been bringing correction for Laurens rebellious nature. She had questioned The Prophet about the foundation, and it was only right that he put her back in her place. Please God he begged silently. Please show her the way. Please let her receive the freedom she so desperately needs.

~ ~ ~

"Where's Jamie and Lauren? They left before me," Steven asked Harry as they walked into the restaurant. Steven had been looking forward to eating here all weekend. He had developed some very expensive tastes since he had become part of Gideon. The restaurant had received two hats and the last review in the Good Food Guide had been outstanding. And the wine. He had only dreamed of being able to afford such a luxury in the past. But now. And he didn't even have to pay for it. God had blessed him with generous benefactors and if he happened to mention how much he enjoyed his glass with lunch, surely someone would feel honoured enough to buy him some to take home. And if not, Gideon was picking up the tab for lunch. Why not add a couple of bottles to the bill?

"They're not coming. Apparently, Lauren has a migraine."

"I doubt it. She seemed fine earlier. She's probably sulking because I gave her a dressing down earlier."

"Did you? Good. She's becoming a real problem. Her attitude is holding everything back. I wish she would come to the realization that we only want the best for her. She, more than any of them, needs to receive the freedom God has available. I'm beginning to think that she's operating under a Jezebel spirit and until we can remove that influence from her life, there won't be any more projects for the foundation. She's becoming a real stumbling block for us."

"We'll talk to Jamie at the men's retreat. It's only two weeks away. And we will pray for her. Ultimately, it's God's job to change her heart and show her the future He has for her.

Chapter sixteen

ince they had returned from Scone, life had been hectic for Jamie and Lauren. Oliver's presentation ball was on Monday night and their week had been filled with preparations for the big night. Oliver had a final suit fitting and still needed to find a suitable gift for his dance partner Haley. There was still one more dance practice on Sunday morning to attend and then after Monday it would all be over. Lauren had finally found herself a dress and had organised a girl to do her hair and makeup. It was Friday night and all she wanted to do was curl up on the couch with a glass of wine and watch something funny on the telly. An old favourite of hers was on at eight-thirty but before Notting Hill started Jamie had settled on a travel program. He loved watching these kinds of shows. Lauren wasn't a fan of holidays and this was as close as he was going to get to seeing the world. She always had some excuse to stay home. They couldn't really afford it, or the kids were too young to leave, or she couldn't get out of work. Personally, he thought she resisted because she was afraid. She didn't like flying and she liked her routine. A holiday would take her out of her comfort zone where she wasn't in control. When the perky host of the show announced that they were doing a special on Fiji he inwardly groaned. Fiji was on her list of 'absolutely not' places in the world. Years ago, her sister had stayed in a resort on a Fiji island and told her that it had been infested with cockroaches. Just hearing the word cockroach set Lauren off. Growing up in poverty, one house that they had rented had a healthy population of the revolting bugs and she had always been terrified they would find their way into her food. A friend had once told her that cockroaches liked to settle in people's ears and that had triggered nightmares for months. She had told him over and over she was never going to Fiji. Well he might not ever get to visit it, but he could at least see what he was missing out on. Lauren sat in her favourite chair, reading a book and only looked up occasionally to pass comment on the resorts that were featured on the special.

Fiji was just as beautiful as he'd imagined, and he was sorry he wasn't ever going to visit. Maybe he could convince Lauren to take a trip to Queensland once Oliver had finished year twelve next year. They could celebrate not having to pay anymore school fees. As the show progressed, he could see that it was one big advertisement. It featured resorts for people on a budget, people with families and even a week-long cruise. There were packages with free flights, or kids stay free. None of them interested him. When the show was almost over, he decided that maybe Lauren was right. The scenery was beautiful but who wanted to pay for the privilege of eating bad buffet food with OPC's (that was what Lauren called Other People's Children), while they ran amok with their clueless parents smiling on, not realising their unruly children were ruining everyone else's holiday.

Picking up the remote to change channels so Lauren didn't miss the start of her movie, Jamie paused, captivated by what he saw on the screen. At the same moment Lauren put down her book and shifted her attention to the telly. The host of the show began to describe a place so amazing, so beautiful that it must be Heaven on Earth. A resort that only had forty-five private bungalows and no one under the age of seventeen was allowed. The bungalows were luxurious, some with their own private plunge pools overlooking the beach, and some that were built over the sea. Now *that* was the way to holiday.

"Oh my gosh. I want to go there."

If Lauren had announced that she was getting a tattoo and joining a motorcycle gang Jamie would have been less surprised than by her declaration that she wanted to get on a plane and go there.

"Did I hear you right? You want to go to Fiji?"

"I want to go to that resort. I don't care what country it's in."

"Then let's do it."

"Are you serious? Just drop everything and run off to Fiji. Can we afford it?" Lauren asked.

"We have the money and we're due another dividend before Christmas." Jamie rewound the television to the details of the package the resort was offering. It was not going to be a cheap holiday, but you get what you pay for and perfection was costly. Lauren quickly found the resort's web site on her phone, taking a closer look at the rooms and the restaurant.

"When can we go? Cause it needs to be as soon as possible. Just you and me, no kids, no Collective."

"So, you're serious. We can go? Don't toy with me woman," he joked

"Not only do I want to go but I think we need to. We haven't been away alone for years."

"Then I'm going to email Julia, The Collective's travel agent, right now and ask her to book it before you change your mind. Let's make it extra special and book business class tickets."

"Only way to travel," Lauren smiled.

161

Jamie pulled his phone out of his pocket to email Julie when he was hit with a feeling of panic. He realized they hadn't prayed about this holiday. They couldn't possibly do something like this without seeking God first. He was very aware that several Gideon members had cancelled holiday plans when Steven and Harry had prayed and God had told them it wasn't a good time for them to be away, or He had something better for them in the future.

"Lauren, I don't feel comfortable going ahead with this without praying first. Do you mind if we take a sec and ask God about this trip? And the timing of it?"

"Sure. Of course we should pray." Lauren muted the TV, all thoughts of watching Notting Hill forgotten.

"Dear God. We have an opportunity to get away together, but we don't want to do it if it's not your plan for us. Please give us a yes or a no on whether we should go to Fiji. And if it's a yes then when should we go?"

"Heavenly Father," Lauren asked, "is it all right with you if we take some time and money for a holiday? I think it would be a good thing for us but if it's not your will or timing then we won't do it." As they waited quietly on God, Lauren felt a peace about the holiday. A date dropped into her mind. Opening her eyes, she saw that Jamie was still quietly praying. She reached for her phone and checked that she was indeed free on the dates she had heard. November was usually filled with end of year school events and she did have work. Breathing a sigh of relief, she saw that from the eleventh of November for the next seven days her diary was clear. They would need to be back for the nineteenth because Oliver had his graduation ceremony for a course he had been taking throughout the year. But the package was for six days so that would be perfect. And Ellen the other receptionist had asked Lauren to fill in for her a few weeks ago and promised she would be happy to cover for her anytime in the next few months.

"How did you go Lauren? Cause I heard a yes. I'm just not sure when we should go."

"Eleventh of November is the date. Check your diary. I bet that week's clear." Grabbing his phone from the coffee table, Jamie pulled up his diary. "I have a board meeting on the ninth at Cornwell Finance and I'm due at J and R on the twenty first, but I have nothing at all booked in between. That would be the perfect week to go away. I'll easily be able to take a few days off from Gideon. I'll even get holiday pay."

"So, we're going?"

"Yep, let's book it. I'll email Julia now."

"I can't believe it. We're actually going to do this. A week with nothing to do but lounge by the pool and read. Nobody asking me for anything, nobody nagging me. No picking up dirty clothes off Oliver's floor and no cooking for a week. It sounds like Heaven."

~ ~ ~

When Jamie woke the next morning his first thought was of Fiji. His second thought was of Harry. He might have asked God, but he hadn't run his plans past the guys and given them the opportunity to pray about and speak into whether or not this trip was the right thing to do. Lauren was still asleep, so he slipped out of the bed quietly and left the bedroom. It was late, already eight-thirty but if Harry didn't want to pick up on the weekend then he wouldn't. Finding his number in contacts he hit call and waited as the phone rang.

"Jamie, mate. What's up?" Harry greeted him.

"I just wanted to run something by you. I hope it's not too early?"

"I've been up for hours already. Watched the sun rise while I prayed."

"Good, glad I'm not disturbing you. Thing is, Lauren and I are planning a holiday and I thought I better run it past you before I pay for it."

"Oh. You haven't said anything about wanting to take a holiday."

"It's sort of a spur of the moment thing. We saw something on telly last night and we thought why not."

"And did you pray about it? Ask God what he thought of you taking off right now. It's a busy time for The Collective. There are a lot of changes and we really need you around at the moment."

"We did pray about it and we both got a firm yes. God even gave Lauren the dates and they work perfectly."

"And yet you're asking me, so you obviously have a check about it. Are you sure you really heard a yes? Because I feel there's something on this. Why would God want you away at such a pivotal time? I think this might be the enemy trying to interfere with our plans."

"So you think we shouldn't go?"

"I think you should bring it to the group on Monday. We can pray with you and that way you will know what God is *really* saying."

"I won't be there Monday remember. It's Oliver's presentation ball that night. I'm coming up the next day. I should be there by nine."

"Can't you come earlier? I'm concerned you're going to miss out if you're not there with the rest of us."

"Harry we're hosting the after party. I'll have kids at my house till two in the morning. And there would be no point driving down after the ball. I need some sleep if I'm going to be driving almost three hours."

"Perhaps you shouldn't be throwing the party. This week's retreat should be your only priority."

"We hadn't booked the retreat when Lauren suggested we have the party at our place. It's been months in the planning, and we didn't want to disappoint Oliver and cancel it. And I'm only missing breakfast. Stuart won't be there till nine either, so just hold off on discussing anything important until we arrive." Hearing the bedroom door open he whispered a quick goodbye to Harry and hung up. He didn't want Lauren knowing he was seeking Harry's guidance on their decision.

"Sleep well?" he asked.

"Fantastically."

"Do you still want to go to Fiji? You haven't changed your mind or thought of a thousand things we should be spending the money on."

"Nope. I can't think of anything I'd rather do, or anywhere I'd rather be. I don't know about you, but I desperately need this break. Have you checked your email yet? Has Julia got back to you?"

"No. Not yet. I don't expect to hear from her till Monday."

"Hopefully we can get flights and a booking for those dates. But as you're always saying if God's in it, it'll all work out."

"Hmm," he smiled as he nodded. But he couldn't shake of the sinking feeling that they wouldn't be going. Because recently when anyone bought their holiday plans to the group Harry and Steven heard from God that it wasn't the right time. The only couple to leave the country, apart from Steven and Harry and their wives, was Stuart and Cynthia. They had travelled around the US for six weeks and Harry had been openly hostile to Stuart about the trip, asking him to cancel it or at least cut it short. Stuart had refused, not caring if Harry approved or not. Jamie knew he would never go against what God told the group and if the past was anything to go by, they would hear a no. He looked into the kitchen where Lauren was mixing eggs and cream to make scrambled eggs while she hummed happily to herself. How was he going to break the news to her? And how was she going to react?

~ ~ ~

Jamie yawned as he drove down the M1 towards Port Stevens. He had got off to a late start and the traffic was horrendous. Harry wasn't going to be happy with him if he wasn't there by nine am. Unless the traffic cleared, chances were he was going to be at least half an hour late. It had been worth it though. Oliver had been thrilled to have the after party at their place. Lauren had made sure there were no gate crashers and none of the kids had even tried to bring alcohol in which had to be a first. All the parents had been on time to pick up their kids but by the time they had cleaned up a little and wound down after the big night, it had been almost three before he had fallen asleep. When the alarm had gone off at six, he had hit the snooze button and rolled over. He hit snooze two more times before he managed to get up. Three and a half hours was not enough sleep and he wished he could call Harry and tell him he wouldn't be there until tomorrow. But when he imagined the disappointed look Harry would give him, he'd dragged himself into the shower in an effort to wake himself up. He'd been driving for an hour when his hands-free rang and he saw Stuart's name flash up on the screen in the car. Pushing the talk button, the radio which he had turned up loud in an effort to keep himself awake silenced, and Stuart's booming voice filled his car.

"Hey mate. I'm just letting you know I'm going to be late. Traffic's horrible."

"I'm going to be late too. The google map is red for kilometres and I got a bit of a late start."

"That's not like you. You're usually early."

"I only got three and a half hours sleep. I found it a little hard getting out of bed."

"Oh yeah. The dance thing. How did that go? I'm surprised Harry didn't suggest you ask the school to change the date to suit him better."

Jamie chuckled. Harry had suggested that maybe it wasn't necessary for Oliver to attend the ball, but he assumed it had been a joke. But now, he considered that maybe Harry had been serious. He hated to admit it but maybe Lauren had a point. There was a little too much interference in their home lives from Steven and Harry. Speaking of which.

"Can I run something by you Stuart?"

"Sure. It's not like I have anything else to do. What's up?"

"Lauren and I are thinking about taking a little vacation to Fiji. I'm just concerned the others won't think it's a good idea."

"Who cares what they think? Fiji's beautiful and you should get away with your wife. It won't do any harm if you take some time and in fact it'll do you both some good. You work hard and you haven't had a break since Gideon started."

"But shouldn't I take into consideration what God has to say? Lauren and I prayed but it's not the same as when God speaks to the group. What if we got it wrong and were not supposed to go?"

"You're taking a holiday. It's not exactly a life changing decision. It's what, a week or two out of your lives. I think Gideon will be fine without you."

"I know but Harry and Steven don't seem to like people going away."

"Jamie. When Harry tried to stop me from going away I shut him down. It's none of their business what you do with your free time and they're hardly ones to talk. Haven't they just got back from Europe with their wives? Steven and Harry always seem to be overseas. It would be pretty hypocritical of them to try and stop you from having a break. We all need to get away once and a while. Take that wife of yours and have some fun."

"Thanks. I appreciate your input. I'm probably making a mountain out of a mole hill. A holiday would be a good idea."

"It's a brilliant idea. Don't even give it a second thought. I'll see you when we get there. Bye." Stuart hung up and the radio resumed, the music from the easy listening station soothing him. An old favourite came on and Jamie sang along to True and thought about going to Fiji. It would be good for them and that would be good for The Collective. He might be able to convince Lauren that she was wrong about Steven while they were away without all the distractions of home. There was another gathering coming up next week and she had said there was no way she was going. He hadn't said anything to the others about the fit she'd thrown after the retreat, just stuck to the migraine story. But her absence from next week's meeting would be noticed and he would have to explain. He might be able to invent an illness this time but that wouldn't work for the gathering next month. He needed her to accept that The Collective was a major part of their lives now. The miles flew by as the traffic cleared and at twenty past nine Jamie pulled into the driveway of the conference centre. It wasn't quite as flash as the house they had rented last month for the retreat with the wives, but it looked nice from the outside. As Jamie pulled into a parking spot he saw Harry walk out from the front door towards him. Had he been in there watching for him? Jamie took off his seat belt and opened his door as Harry strode towards his car.

"Where have you been? You're late."

"It's twenty minutes Harry. We're here for four days. It's not that big of a deal."

"It's not the time. I'm concerned about your attitude. I don't think you're taking this seriously."

"You're kidding, right? I've hardly had any sleep and I won't see my family for the rest of the week. I think that's taking it seriously."

"No, I'm not kidding. You need to be all in but instead you're letting family commitments take precedent. God has to come first in your life or you'll be in danger of missing out on what He has for you. Just leave your bags and check in later. Here's Stuart. Can you tell him we're in room B off the foyer."

"Sure," Jamie said, surprised by Harry's outburst. Bit of an overreaction. Stuart parked his Range Rover next to Jamie's car, hoping out and going to the boot to get his bag.

"Leave it," Jamie told him. "Harry's asked us to check in later.

They're all waiting for us. And just so you know. He's not very happy with us being twenty minutes late." Stuart rolled his eyes as he closed the boot of his car.

"We've got days here. The guy needs to calm down a little." The men walked through the foyer and saw conference room B ahead of them. When they entered the room the others were already seated. The windows overlooked the golf course, but Jamie doubted he'd be allowed to get a round in.

"Welcome everyone," Harry began. "We've got a packed agenda for the next few days but this morning we wanted to spend some time in prayer. More than anything it's important to encourage each other and bring up any concerns we have. You need to come today with an open heart for what God is doing and what he has to say to you. Steven and I agree that The Collective is about to make a breakthrough but for that to happen we need to let go of everything that is holding us back and put God first. Firstly, does anyone have any prayer requests?" Harry looked around at each individual, challenging them to bring up any issues that would get in the way of hearing from God.

"I have something I'd like the group to pray about with me," Jamie said. "Lauren and I have planned to take a week's long holiday to Fiji but before I book it, I want to confirm that this is God's timing."

"Jamie has already spoken to me about his holiday, but the decision was made in the spur of the moment and without prayerful consideration. We all know how important it is to bring everything we do before God."

"That's not quite right. I did pray about it with Lauren."

"Sure. But you know how powerful it is when we all hear from God together. We're your brothers and we want nothing but the best for you" Harry said. "Let's all bow our heads and spend some time praying for Jamie."

The room fell into silence as each man earnestly asked God what Jamie should do. Josh was the first to speak.

"Jamie, God's saying that this isn't the right time for you to be away. There are so many important decisions coming up and you're needed here for the time being. He has an even better holiday planned for you in the future."

"God knows you're afraid to tell Lauren no," Daniel continued. "But making a stand for what God wants is the breakthrough that she needs to get the freedom you desire for her. When she sees that God has something better, her eyes will be opened to the truth of who God is and what he wants for her. Don't be afraid. God is holding you and her in his hands and he won't let you down."

"God definitely wants you here for now. He's saying that taking this holiday now would be a poor substitute for what he wants to give you later, when the time is right. Trust him with Lauren. She's so close to seeing it but first she may need to feel some pain before she truly understands Gods love for her. At the moment, she's operating under a selfish spirit. She can only see what she thinks is best for her. But when she understands her part in The Collective, she will fully give herself over to Gods will," Harry concluded. Opening his eyes, he asked if anyone else had any prayer requests before they moved on.

"I believe God wants us to pray about all of our wives. I feel there's a real spirit of opposition to The Collective. I believe that Jezebel is operating through some of them and we need to put a stop to that. If that spirit gets on us, God won't be able to use us to fulfil his will," Steven said. "Until *all* our wives are safe God won't move."

"Um, what do you mean by Jezebel Steve? Like the wicked queen from the Old Testament?" Stuart asked.

"I'll take this one if you don't mind" Harry said. "The Jezebel spirit *is* named after Queen Jezebel. It comes into churches, organisations and marriages and causes havoc. Its goal is to separate us from God by destroying the church. Once a woman is affected by this spirit she will refuse to come under Godly authority. She will dismiss prayer and prophesy and she will become demanding and manipulative. But people fall under her spell because she seduces them, especially men, if the person she is inhabiting is beautiful. And she's a master at controlling others and often gives her own false prophesy's while dismissing God's true prophets. Does any of that behaviour sound familiar?" Harry asked. "Because I know I've seen it happening in The Collective with some of the women. Who here hasn't had their wife argue with them about authority. Who here hasn't had his wife dismiss a prophesy from Steven." Harry looked around the room and saw that a few were nodding, including Jamie, whose own wife had been the worst offender. But now he would know what he was up against.

One by one each man prayed for his wife and for the wives of their brothers. They asked God to cut of ties to Jezebel and free the minds of The Collective's women, bringing them under the authority that God had given Steven and Harry. As they prayed, a sense of excitement fell on the room. They could feel barriers being broken in the spirit world and they had an absolute assurance that break through with the wives that were resisting was imminent. Nobody named names, but Jamie was sure it was his wife they were praying for. All the rest of them seemed to be on board with The Collective now. He could see why the others would think Lauren had a Jezebel spirit controlling her, but the last thing she was, was seductive or manipulative. And what Harry had left out of his description was that men could also have a Jezebel spirit.

They continued to pray throughout the morning, asking God to bring deals for Gideon that would further fund the foundation and the work Steven was doing in Break Free. Lunch was bought in at one o'clock and by then Jamie was exhausted. The lack of sleep and the emotions surrounding having to tell Lauren the holiday was off were taking their toll. Before he had a chance to talk himself out of it, he sent Julia an email from his phone instructing her not to go ahead with the booking. After all the words he had received from God today it would be disobedient for him to even consider going away right now. And he had faith that Lauren would ultimately receive freedom from his decision.

Chapter seventeen

 Can you get that?" Lauren yelled to the family room. She could hear her phone ringing but wouldn't make it from the kitchen in time. The ringing stopped and she could hear Oliver talking.

It was probably Jamie. He had only been gone since this morning, but he usually checked in around this time when he was away. Lauren continued to serve up dinner, she had cheated tonight and was feeding her family chicken, chips and coleslaw from the Charcoal Chicken down the road. Even though she hadn't worked, she had dragged herself through the day exhausted. It had been well after two before they had finally got to bed last night and as quiet as Jamie had tried to be when he got up several hours later, he had still woken her. Why he couldn't go to the boys retreat a day later was beyond her. Poor thing must be so exhausted, especially after a day of sessions with Harry and Steven. Although they spent the better part of their day sitting around soaking with their eyes closed. Maybe he got a nap in. She knew put in the same situation she would have been asleep in minutes. Oliver came into the kitchen and handed her the phone.

"Dad," he said as a statement and then picking up a plate from the bench, went and sat at the small dining table.

"Hi love, can you hold on a sec? Oliver could you please tell your sister dinner's ready."

"Emily," Oliver roared, "Dinner."

"Thanks Oli. I could have done that myself." Turning away for some privacy, Lauren picked up a chip of her plate. Being tired always made her extra hungry.

"Sorry I'm back. How's it going?"

"It's going. I'm exhausted."

"So, go to bed. I'm sure they can spend an evening without you. Just explain you only got a few hours' sleep. You should have driven up tomorrow, or at least later in the day like I suggested. It was dangerous driving that tired."

"I'll be all right. We're having dinner here at the conference centre, so I'll sneak off early."

"Did you hear back from Julia? I was expecting you to forward her emails with the flight times and confirmation that we could book the holiday for the dates we wanted."

"I did hear back from her. And the dates were fine."

"Woohoo," Lauren shouted as she began to do a happy dance around the kitchen. "I can't wait to go. Nothing to do but relax, no kids, no cooking or cleaning."

"The thing is," Jamie paused, desperate to not have to tell her what he had decided. "I asked the guys to pray about the holiday to see what God was saying about us going away right now."

"Why would you ask them? We prayed about it and God said yes. Seriously Jamie, it's none of their business."

"I think that maybe we heard wrong. Because they heard a no from God. They said He's got something better in store for us later. So,

I've told Julia not to go ahead with the booking … We're not going to Fiji."

It took a second for Jamie's words to sink in. And as they did, Lauren felt like her heart was falling out of her chest. Her worst fears about The Collective had finally been realized. She had hoped and prayed for the last two years that Jamie would come to his senses and see that he'd got caught up in something dangerous and pull away. In time she'd hoped they would be able to laugh about The Collective and she would tease him about how close he had sailed to the edge of craziness. They had been married for twenty-three years. They had children together and had survived all sorts of ups and downs in those years. But they had always been together in it all. He had been her first priority and she had been his. But not anymore. He had made a vow to forsake all others for her and he had just broken it. He may not have cheated on her with another woman, but he had put his *brothers* first. And in doing so he had betrayed her by choosing them. She felt huge tears slip down her face and then she was no longer crying but weeping. She hung up her phone and then flicked it to silent. She would not be talking to him again tonight. She didn't care if she never spoke to him again. It was over, this was the last straw. She was done with him.

"Mum, what's wrong," Emily asked, standing at the kitchen door. "What's happened? Is Dad all right?"

"He … I don't know. We can't go away like we planned."

"So if you can't get a booking, make it for a different time."

"It's not that," she whispered, her throat closing over and her breath ragged as she tried to gain control. This was not how she wanted her daughter to see her.

"Then what?"

"We're not allowed to go."

"What do you mean you're not allowed to go. Who said?"

175

"The Collective said."

"Don't be silly. Just ring Dad and tell him you're going. I'll do it if you like. He's just being stupid. Maybe he doesn't realise how much this holiday means to you."

"He knows. It's just not important enough to him. The Collective comes first."

"I wish you wouldn't call it that. It's a stupid name and all the people in it have clearly lost the plot. What's it got to do with them anyway, where you go and what you do?"

"I don't know Em but to your dad, what they think matters the most." Picking up her plate she opened the bin and began scrapping her food in. The thought of eating made her sick and she didn't think she would be able to swallow, even if she was still hungry.

"Hey, I would have eaten that," Oliver protested as he dumped his empty plate on the bench.

"Not a good time Oli," Emily warned. "Put your plate in the dishwasher and then go and watch telly."

"You're so bossy. Stop telling me what to do all the time." Finally noticing Lauren's blotchy face and the tears dripping onto her shirt, he asked "What's wrong with Mum?"

"Dad."

"Oh, what did he do this time?"

"Just go and watch TV. I'll be in soon." Watching her brother's retreating back Emily turned to her Mother.

"Do you want a hug?"

"I appreciate that but not right now. I just want to be alone. I need to sort out what I'm going to do."

"What you're going to do? What you should do is take the trip on your own. Or we could go together. I'll be finished Uni by then. That would serve him right. We'll take off and have the best time ever without him."

"No, I mean what I'm going to do about my future. Because I can't go on like this."

Shocked, Emily realized that her mother was taking about leaving her dad. Things had been tense for the last three years since they had become involved with Gideon, but she hadn't realized it was that bad.

"You don't mean you're getting divorced? You can't split up over a holiday. I'm sure you can fix this."

"It's not looking good Em. It goes much deeper than that. But it's not your problem and it's not appropriate for me to discuss it with you. Sorry, I shouldn't have said anything."

"Well you let me know if you change your mind. I'm here to listen, even if you think I am only a kid. I better go and check on Oli." Emily took a plate of dinner with her not knowing how she could help. Her parents had always been together. It was other people that got divorced. Not them.

"Thanks love," Lauren said as a shudder ran through her body and she realized she was going to lose control again. Grabbing the box of tissues from the bench, Lauren cast her gaze around the room. She had spent weeks designing her perfect kitchen, waited months for it to be installed and had dreamed of cooking future Christmas dinners in it for her children and maybe even one day her grandchildren. As she saw the beautiful range with four separate ovens, the two dishwashers she had always wanted and appreciated the classic decisions she had made on style and colour, Lauren realized that soon this might be someone else's kitchen. If they split up they would never be able to afford to keep this house. She'd probably end up living in a run-down rental miles from the city. Flicking off the light, she left the dishes for tomorrow. She quickly made her way to the front room that the kids never used. Here she could be alone to cry and plan what she was going to do because there was a very good chance she would soon be a divorced woman.

~ ~ ~

"You alright mate?" Josh asked Jamie. He was sitting alone in the conference room, even though everyone else had gone back to their rooms to get ready for dinner. Josh had been heading to the dining room when he noticed Jamie through the open door.

"I don't think I am. I just told Lauren that I cancelled the holiday. She did not take it very well."

"It'll be fine. We prayed about it. God's got this. She might be mad for a while, but she'll get over it. And she's so close to the breakthrough God has for her. Maybe He's just allowing her to be broken before he can rebuild her the way He always intended her to be."

"Maybe."

"So she ranted at you for a bit. God will work on her heart and she'll see he has something even better for her."

"But she didn't rant or rave. She didn't say a word. She just hung up. I've tried calling back over and over but she's not picking up." As he spoke his phone started ringing.

"I'll bet that's her now," Josh said. Jamie looked at the display and saw that it was Emily. He hit accept as Josh gestured towards the door and waved goodbye, giving him the privacy he needed.

"Hi Em. What's up?"

"What's up?" she screamed down the phone. "What's up? What did you do? Mum's a mess."

"I'm very, very sorry mum's unhappy. She's upset about some news I had to give her. I'm sure she'll be fine tomorrow."

"She's not going to be fine tomorrow. She's talking about splitting up."

"We're not splitting up. It's just a misunderstanding."

"Then you need to come home now and sort it out."

"I can't do that Em. It's very important that I spend the week here. I'll be home on Friday afternoon. It'll all be fine."

"I don't think so. She's barely stopped crying and she's got out the budget folder and her calculator. I saw her checking out the price of units online. Why would she be looking for somewhere to live if it's all going to be fine?"

"She's overreacting and so are you. I promise you we are *not* getting a divorce."

"Well you might want to check that with her and soon. I don't know what you were thinking but you're an idiot. You need to come home now and sort it out. I don't blame her for being furious at you. You're being a complete jerk."

"Don't talk to me like that Emily. I'm still your father," he said being careful not to raise his voice.

"You might be my father but you're being a terrible husband." And with that final statement Emily hung up on Jamie.

He decided to try ringing one more time but not Lauren's mobile. If he rang the home phone maybe she would pick up. But the phone rang and rang until the answering machine picked up and he heard his wife's happy voice asking him to leave a message after the beep. He declined, knowing there was nothing he could say. He would try again tomorrow when she had calmed down. Gathering his Bible and jacket he stood up from the chair he had spent most of the day on when his phone pinged. Hopefully it wasn't Oliver texting to tell him off as well. But when he saw that is was from Lauren his heart lifted. Maybe she'd had a change of heart. But as he read he realized he was wrong.

Stop ringing me. Stop ringing the house. I don't want to talk to you and don't bother coming home at the end of the week. You are not welcome here anymore. You have taken something that is essentially a job and turned it and your partners into your new family. I hope you'll all be happy together. I have had enough.

~ ~ ~

Jamie tossed and turned all night. Even though he was exhausted, his sleep had been broken by horrible dreams. He couldn't remember them fully, but he had a sense of being chased through the night and each time he woke he remembered the text that Lauren had sent. And he knew her. When she said she had had enough, she meant it. They were not the empty words of someone who was trying to get her way. He had tried to keep it together during dinner last night and the guys had been encouraging, telling him they would continue to pray for Lauren. They really believed that her eyes would be opened to the truth that The Collective was God's plan for her life and that once she got freedom she would be a changed woman. But Jamie was a realist. He'd been hearing this freedom promise for two years now and all that had come from it was pain and heartache. He didn't think the freedom was coming anytime soon and for the first time he was beginning to question whether this was the right thing for him and his family. He had cried out to God, begging Him that if The Collective was the path that He wanted them on, then He would intervene and change Lauren's heart. But God was as silent as Lauren and it began to dawn on him that something was very wrong here. And in giving The Collective his all he had broken his wife's heart.

~ ~ ~

Several hundred kilometres away Lauren had slept but when she woke she felt sick and foggy. A bottle of wine would do that and as a headache settled in she groaned. She was supposed to be working today. Picking up her phone she sent a quick text asking if Susan could cover her afternoon shift at the law firm. The last thing she wanted to do was see anyone today. At least she knew some good lawyers. As a rule, they didn't handle family law, but they knew others who did. Because a night's sleep had not changed her mind. Her marriage was over. They would need to find a way to make it amicable for the children's sake. Especially Oliver, who would be starting his final year of high school soon and didn't need the disruption. But continuing on with the tension in the house wouldn't help him either.

Emily had driven Oliver to school and Susan had agreed to work for Lauren today. She tried to keep herself busy to take her mind of its swirling thoughts by catching up on the washing. She stood in front of the telly, making her way through the ironing pile but she found it impossible to focus on what she was watching. Over and over she ran the figures through her head. They would have to sell the house. The mortgage wasn't as big as it had been as they had paid almost half of it off. And the renovations they had done must have added value. The market was hot, and they should be able to sell quickly but she would never be able to afford anything in Paddington on her wage. Even if she worked full-time, she was going to have to move further from the city. That meant changing schools for Oliver and that wasn't fair when he only had a little over a year to go. He would have to bus in which would be added pressure and time. At least there wouldn't be a custody battle. Emily was nineteen and at seventeen Oliver would have a say in where he lived. She hoped he would choose her because one of her biggest fears was that he would fall under the influence of The Collective. So far, she had done her best to insulate the children from it. But if the kids decided to live with their dad, she wouldn't be there to protect them. Panic rose as she considered Harry and Steven getting their hands on the kids. Suddenly Lauren felt a weight in her head, like her brain was expanding and there wasn't enough space inside her skull for it and she was overtaken by dizziness that threated to topple her. Falling into a nearby chair, she tried to breathe but her heart was racing, and the dizziness increased. *Am I having a stroke?* she thought as she called out for Emily. Hearing the panic in her mother's voice, Emily ran from her room where she had been studying.

"I don't feel right Em. Something's wrong."

"What Mum?"

"I don't know. Something's wrong with my brain. I think I need to go to the Doctor."

"Let me call them." Emily picked up her mother's phone and quickly found the number to their local GP. Her mum must be sick if she wanted to go to the doctor. Lauren preferred to deal with illness and aliments the natural way and usually refused a doctor if she was sick. A few years ago, she had suffered from pneumonia and the doctors hadn't been able to help. The antibiotics they prescribed didn't work and she had lived with violent coughing for months. A trip to the naturopath had her feeling much better in a few days and healed in a few weeks. She hadn't visited a doctor since and swore she wouldn't unless she needed a bone set or something stitched up. So being asked to be taken now must mean that something was very wrong.

Lauren could hear Emily in the background talking but she couldn't make out the words. She wasn't in pain, but the dizziness continued and increased. She feared if she stood up she would not be able to hold herself up. Finishing her call to the Doctor's surgery, Emily removed her mother's slippers and slipping some shoes on her and helped her out of the chair. Holding her up, she walked her to her car, telling her the Doctor was expecting them. *I'm frightened*, Lauren thought. *I've never felt anything like this before.*

During the short drive to the doctor's surgery Emily tried to reassure Lauren that this was nothing serious and everything was fine.

They bypassed the waiting room and were quickly ushered to a treatment room where their Doctor was waiting for them.

"It's been a while since we've seen you Lauren. I hear you're not feeling so good this morning."

"I don't know what's wrong with me. I'm dizzy and I feel like my heart's beating out of my chest. And my brain feels like it's going to explode."

"Are you experiencing any pain?" he asked as he wrapped a blood pressure cuff around her arm.

"No and I haven't. But I just feel wrong." Lauren felt the cuff tighten as her Doctor pumped and then it released.

"Well your blood pressure is very high." Placing his fingers on her wrist he could feel that her heart was indeed racing.

"Lauren, have you had any significant challenges recently. Maybe financial problems or problems in any of your relationships?"

"My husband and I have been having some serious issues. I've been considering a divorce, so I guess yes, you could say I have a problem in my relationship."

"And is this a recent decision?"

"Yes. I decided last night."

Nodding his head, he pulled over a chair and sat down.

"The good news is you're not having a stroke. Or a heart attack. But you are having a panic attack."

"I don't think so," she said indignantly, "I don't have panic attacks. I'm perfectly sane."

"You may not have had them in the past but today you are. And it has nothing to do with being insane. You're facing something very traumatic. How long have you been married?"

"Twenty-three years."

"That's a long time. I need to ask, has there been any violence in

183

the home? Is that what's leading to the marriage breakdown?"

"No, never," she responded, shocked. Jamie had never laid a hand on her. "My husband has decided to take his life in a different direction. One I can't accept. It's hard to explain, but I can't stay with him anymore."

"Ok. We can always talk about this further and I am happy to refer you to counselling. A third party might be able to help you work out your differences. For now, I want to prescribe an anti-depressant. It's not a strong dose but it will help you feel calmer. We don't want your blood pressure going off like this again. And I can also give you something for the dizziness. I don't want you driving for a few days. It could be dangerous if this happens again." Looking across to Emily who had stood quietly in the corner during the examination he asked, "Did you drive Mum here?"

"Yes, and I can help picking up Oli from school. And I can drive her to work. A few days off Uni won't hurt."

"No work this week. No stress of any kind if it can be helped. You understand Lauren. I want you to be kind to yourself. And get the prescription filled. It'll help."

"Thanks, but I don't want to take anti-depressants."

"Just take the prescription. You might change your mind if things get worse. And feel free to call me if you want that referral."

"Thank you Doctor Marshall. I feel so silly wasting your time for nothing."

"It's not nothing Lauren. Panic attacks are real, and they can feel like something serious is happening in your body. You did the right thing coming in. Please take it easy. I'll leave the prescription and a medical certificate for your employer at reception for you."

Rising from the chair, Lauren noted that while she still felt dizzy, it wasn't as bad. The initial fear that she was seriously ill had passed and knowing that she began to feel calmer. Never before had she felt so out of control and was relieved that she was beginning to feel more like herself.

Before taking her mum home, Emily had stopped at a chemist and had the prescription filled. But Lauren had already decided she wasn't going to take the anti-depressants. Her life might be falling apart but she didn't want to become addicted to any kind of medication and she needed to be clear headed and in control for what was coming next. She was quite sure there was nothing Jamie could say or do to change her mind. Princess Diana had said there were three people in her marriage. Lauren finally understood what she meant, although it wasn't just one person in the middle of her marriage. It was a whole bunch of them, and Lauren knew there was no longer any place for her unless she was willing to give in, give up and accept the invitation from The Collective. And that was never going to happen.

~ ~ ~

She had lost count of how many times Jamie had called. He had stopped leaving messages by Wednesday night but had persevered with trying to get a hold of her. Ignoring him had worked at first but she didn't want him coming home tomorrow and needed to make that very clear to him. When the phone began to ring again her finger hovered over the answer symbol for a second before she pressed it.

"Finally. I've been trying to get you on the phone for days."

"What do you want Jamie?"

"I want to talk to you, sort this out."

"There's nothing to sort out. You made your decision when you chose The Collective over me."

"I haven't chosen The Collective. I've put God first in my life. Isn't that what the Bible asks us to do?

"Steven is not God."

"Of course he isn't. But he hears from God and he's guiding us in what God wants for our lives."

"That's your opinion. You know what I think, and I have from the start. He's nothing but a con man who has you all completely snowed. I used to respect you. I don't anymore. I used to think you would stand up for me and our family, but you've become a puppet and Steven's pulling the strings. I don't know why he cares whether we go away on holiday or not. He probably doesn't want you to go because then he's no longer able to control you. Time away might give you some perspective once you're removed from his influence. You might actually see the truth. That this has become like a cult. You do whatever he says, whether it's good for you or not. You've given him half of our money. Doesn't that ring any alarm bells for you?"

"I haven't given him our money. It goes to the foundation."

"And who controls that? Do you have a say what's done with that money? Do I? No, Steven decides."

"And Harry. They agree together and the board signs off on what God has told them."

"And have you ever disagreed, said no to one of their proposals?"

"No. We trust them."

"Well more fool you. I can't take this anymore. I didn't sign onto Gideon to be anything more than an investment. It's been hijacked by your false prophet who saw a group of men whose good intentions made them ripe for the picking. I'm not going to be part of it. I don't accept their invitation and I want nothing more to do with them. I'm taking my life back. I no longer have any hope that you will see the truth and that's why I've been looking for a lawyer. We can't stay married when you won't put me above The Collective. I have begged and pleaded with you to open your eyes. I have screamed from the roof top that something is very wrong but all I got from you was deaf ears. And I can't do it anymore. I'm physically and mentally exhausted. Don't come home tomorrow. I'm done with you." Lauren hung up the phone and turned her attention back to the show on the telly she had been trying to watch. She couldn't follow the story line as she replayed the conversation over and over in her head. She felt a sense of relief at having said what she did. It wasn't her intention to hurt Jamie, he used to be her best friend. But she wasn't going to risk losing her soul and her relationship with God for a man who loved other people more than he loved her. Because he must, to be willing to risk everything they had built over the last few decades.

~ ~ ~

It had been a long week, but it was over. Four days away from home with the guys had been far too long and the consequences of it could change his life forever. But not if he could help it. Jamie was only fifteen minutes from home when he left a message on Lauren's voice mail that he would be there shortly. He was going to make her listen. Because she wasn't going to believe what he had to tell her. He was still reeling from what had happened today. For the first time he finally understood what Lauren had been fighting against and the scales had fallen from his eyes. It was time to go home and save his marriage.

Chapter eighteen

L auren knew Jamie was home before she heard the key in the door. Clarkson and Hammond circled excitedly at the front door barking. Jamie fell to his knees patting the dogs, knowing that they wouldn't calm down until they'd had at least a few minutes of his time. When he had finished being greeted by the dogs, he made his way through the house to the family room where he found Lauren slumped in her chair, glass of wine in her hand. She was completely focused on watching the news and didn't bother to acknowledge him.

"Hi love," he said as he leaned over to kiss her. Swaying away from him, Lauren put her hand up in protest.

"What are you doing here?" she asked. "I think I made it very clear that you are not welcome. I suggest you go and stay at Harry's. Maybe he'll feel sorry for you and take you in."

"I'm not going to Harry's. He's the last person I want to see right now. It's you I need to talk to."

"Well too bad, because I don't want to talk to you. And as I wasn't expecting you, I didn't save you dinner."

"I don't care about dinner. I have something very important to talk to you about."

"Jamie, this is not my first glass of wine tonight. It's not going to be my last. This is not the time. I have had the worst week of my life thanks to you, which makes you the last person I want to talk to. Just go away." Lauren took a sip of her wine, ignoring him. Jamie stood there for a minute, wondering how and when he was going to get her to listen to him. It was obvious that it wasn't going to be tonight, but it would need to be soon. With every minute that slipped by he was becoming more distressed at what he had seen and heard and desperately needed someone to talk to. Someone who would understand. Lauren turned her attention back to the television, dismissing him. Disheartened, he went in search of his children. Emily's room was empty, but he found Oliver watching YouTube clips on his computer. Any other day Lauren would be in here telling Oli to turn them off and get on with his homework. *I guess it shows just how upset she was if she was letting Oli slide on this,* Jamie thought.

"Hey Oliver," he said trying to get his son's attention. "I'm home."

Dragging his eyes from the screen he glanced at his father who was standing in his doorway.

"What are you doing here? Mum said you wouldn't be back."

"Well I am back. Your Mum and I have some things to work out, that's all."

"Good luck with that. All she's done this week is cry. And Em had to take her to the doctors. She had some kind of melt down. You really stuffed up this time."

"I know that. But I think I can fix it."

"If you say so," Oliver shrugged his shoulders, turning back to the computer, conversation over.

"Is your sister home?"

"Nup. She's out at a movie."

Leaving Oliver to his YouTube, Jamie went to the kitchen. He had told Lauren that he wasn't hungry, but his growling stomach told a different story. He opened the fridge, hoping to find something he could heat up. After his long drive the last thing he wanted to do was go out again in search of food. He was surprised to see the fridge full of leftover pizza and Chinese takeaway. Lauren almost always cooked dinner, but it looked like this week had been different. What was it that Oliver said about her going to the doctor? A melt down? That wasn't like her. After putting a few slices of pizza on a plate and into the oven, Jamie returned to the family room to give talking to his wife another go. This might not be the right time to discuss what had happened during the week, but he needed to know that she was all right. Standing in front of the television to get her attention he asked,

"Oli said you had to go to the doctor this week. Are you sick?"

"I don't think that's any of your business. Now if you don't mind, you're in the way," she said, craning her neck to try and see around him."

"You are my business. You're my wife and I love you. I want to know what happened while I was gone."

Lauren scoffed, "you want to know what happened while you were gone. Fine. I'll tell you what happened while you were gone. I had a panic attack. Sensible, always-in-control Lauren had a complete meltdown and it was the most terrifying thing I've ever experienced. I thought I was having a stroke. I couldn't breathe and it felt like my head was going to explode. I hope you're proud of yourself. The doctor put me on anti-depressants so thank you very much for that. Now if you don't get lost I think I might be ready for my second attack."

"I'm sorry that happened to you. It was never my intention to hurt you. If you'd just let me explain I'm positive we can work this out."

"I really don't care what you have to say anymore. I can't listen to the same regurgitated rubbish from your prophet."

"Fair enough. I deserve that. But umm, do you think you should be drinking when you're on that kind of medication?"

"I think you've lost the right to come in here and tell me what to do. And I'm not stupid. I would never mix alcohol with medication. I never said I *took* the pills. I don't need them because *I'm not depressed.* I'm angry and looking at you right now makes me want to punch you, but I'm not the one with the problem. You're the one who needs help. You can't even recognize what's right in front of your face. One day you're going to look back and realise what a complete fool you are."

"I know, and that's what I want to talk to you about. And if it makes you feel better, then do it. Punch me, hard."

"I'm not going to hit you Jamie."

"You should."

Putting her empty wine glass on the coffee table, Lauren stood up.

"I'm going to bed. Obviously, you have no respect for me, or you would just go away like I asked. So I'll leave instead." But as she walked past him she curled her hand into a fist. Right then she did want to hit him, so hard right in his face. She knew it wasn't the answer, violence never was, but the rage she felt was so close to the surface. And so was the hurt. Surprising herself she felt her arm rise and connect with his arm. Jamie didn't retaliate. It hadn't hurt him, but he hoped releasing some of that anger made her feel better. She looked at him one last time and he saw fresh tears gathering in the corner of her eyes. He had known that he had hurt his wife, but in that moment, he truly understood how deep it went. Even with what he had to tell her, if he could get her to listen, he wasn't sure she would ever forgive him for what he had put her through.

~ ~ ~

Lauren could feel Jamie's presence in the bed when she woke the next morning. He must have slipped in at some point after she had gone to sleep. Quietly she left the bed and the room. She needed a cup of tea and to do a little research. Before she had gone to sleep, she had decided that just because Jamie wasn't allowed to go away, didn't mean she had to miss out. She might not be going to Fiji, but a few days at a spa on her own would do her the world of good. A facial and a massage were exactly what she needed. And some time away from this mess. Selling the house would mean weekly open-for-inspections. And there was the inevitable call from the real estate agent asking if people could come through at a moment's notice. It would fall to her to keep the house perfect at all times. And it wasn't really ready for sale yet. They still had to pull down the old fibro shed in the back corner of the yard. Hopefully it wouldn't be too difficult. Lauren was certain the vine growing over it was the only thing holding it up. Most of the concrete floor had turned to dust so they wouldn't need to jackhammer that up either. Thankfully it wasn't made of asbestos so they could do it themselves, but it was too heavy a job for her to do alone. Unfortunately, she would either need Jamie's help, or they would have to pay someone to do it. As she poured water from the boiled jug into the teapot, she could see that Sydney was going to be putting on a beautiful day for them. They could get the shed down today, plant a few trees in its place, and she could have a real estate agent in to value the house in a week or two. Jamie was just going to have to find somewhere else to stay. His parents would probably take him in for a while. Sitting down in front of her computer she googled nearby spa's. There were several that had stay packages and she sent off an email to two asking for prices and availability.

"Morning," she heard as Jamie shuffled into the kitchen.

"Good, you're up," Lauren said as she turned away from her computer. "You're pulling down the shed today, so make yourself some breakfast while I have a shower."

"Lauren," he sighed. "We really need to talk. The shed can wait."

"No, it can't. We won't be able to sell with that eyesore in the backyard. I know we talked about putting up a new garden shed on the same spot, but I don't want to spend any more money on this house before it goes on the market."

"We don't need to sell. A few more dividends and it'll be paid off."

"Yes, but where are you going to live? Cause you're not staying here."

"If, after today you still want me to go, I will. But you can keep the house. You love it. And all the work we've done. I don't want it to go to waste on someone else."

"You don't seem to get it. I don't want to live here in our forever house alone. It will have too many memories, most of them bad. I'll find myself something smaller that I can maintain on my own, and anyway, we can't afford this house and somewhere else for you to live."

"If you would just listen to me you might realise none of this is necessary. You can't make such an important decision when you don't have all the facts."

"If you want to talk, you can do it while you work. I doubt I'll be able to stop you. But don't think it will make any difference. The Collective and I are through. And you're part of it. So we're through too."

She could be so stubborn, he thought watching her retreating back as she walked to the bedroom. But if it took pulling down the old shed to get her attention then he would do it.

~ ~ ~

Gloves on and pruning shears in hand, Jamie began to snip away at the ivy covering the shed. It was going to take more than one trip to the dump to get rid of all of the foliage and rubble. It was a shame they couldn't just burn it, but with houses so close to theirs, they couldn't take the risk of an ember catching and burning down the neighbour's home. Lauren was working beside him silently, determined to get this done. Taking a deep breath in Jamie knew this might be his only opportunity to get her to listen to him.

"You were right," he admitted, not just to Lauren, but himself. "Everything you said about Steven and The Collective. It was spot on. I've … I've been such an idiot."

Lauren stopped pulling at the foliage and stood up to give her back a well-earned stretch.

"If this is because I want a divorce Jamie, then don't bother. The Collective and your brothers" she said as she made air quotes with her fingers, "mean everything to you. They have become your world and I don't want to have you lie to me and pretend they aren't just to save our marriage. I don't want you that way because you'll end up resenting me. I can't live like that."

"It's not that. Not at all. Some things happened while we were away that have made me question everything. And not just Steven, but the whole thing. When I tell you, you're going to get really angry. Even angrier than you already are."

"I doubt that's possible, unless you tell me you've given the foundation all our shares in Gideon. Because there's no way I will ever agree to that. And even though you boys think you can run this thing anyway you like, I actually own half of the shares, and when the court finds out that my inheritance paid for them, you won't have a leg to stand on. And don't think I won't sue you. Because I will."

"Can you please let me explain what happened?"

"Fine. But do it while you work. I want this done by the end of the day."

"You know about the holiday. They didn't come out and say we couldn't go. But they told me God had something better. And I trusted what they were hearing better than us because we might be biased, hearing what we wanted to hear. They felt that this was going to be the catalyst for you getting freedom. That you would realise that you had been wrong about The Collective."

"Hmmm. Then they don't know me very well do they. And some prophet you've got there. He wouldn't know the future if it jumped up and smacked him in the face. Because if he did, he would have known I was never going to stand by and accept this rubbish."

"I agree. None of his prophesies about Gideon have come to pass. We haven't done the deals he said we would get, and deals I knew stacked up were vetoed by him. But they always had an explanation. They usually blamed the wives for having a Jezebel spirit, or the men for having a greed problem. Steven claimed God couldn't do what he'd promised until we fixed ourselves. And that's what this week was all about. Our greed problem."

"So he did ask you to give *all* the profits to the foundation. That way he gets control of all the money and you all accept that it's your fault because of greed."

"That's not what was proposed. Because if the money went to the foundation, then they wouldn't have been able to do what they wanted with it. The first suggestion was that we give a portion of our shares to Steven."

"What? For free? Sure, let's just give them to him," Lauren shook her head. "Does he want our house too? You can't give him your business cause you already sold that."

"Not our house no. But yes, it was suggested that we each give him a percentage of our shares so that he could be an equal owner. You know the verse in Matthew chapter twenty about paying the workers the same wage whether they started first thing in the morning or an hour before the end of the day. They used that as their justification. Harry said it wasn't Steven's fault that he had joined us later and he should have the same opportunity to earn dividends as the rest of us."

"But we *paid* for those shares. We took a huge risk. We could have lost all our money. And he gets to show up and claim part of it for free. Does Steven have any concept of how the real-world works? Please tell me you didn't agree to that. Because like I said, the court will see it my way. I don't have to give that charlatan anything."

"No, I didn't agree to it. Daniel did, almost immediately. He felt that if that was what it took to remedy his greed problem, then that's what he would do. Stuart felt the same way I did and said no."

"Well, good. At least someone has some sense left" Lauren said as she exhaled loudly. "But I'm guessing they didn't stop there."

"No. And to be honest I think it was a ploy. They probably understood they couldn't just transfer shares from one person to another without proper paperwork that would have to be signed by all of us *and* our wives. It wouldn't be legal otherwise. And I think they realized most of you girls would say no. They definitely had to know *you* would. So that's when they changed tack, and I think that was the plan all along. That's when they put the question to us about what it would look like to honour The Prophet."

"Honour the Prophet. That's a new one. And what did they decide it looked like?"

"Well I suggested that we could acknowledge him officially on our web site. Unfortunately they didn't go for it. That wasn't the kind of honour he was looking for."

"Let me guess. He was looking for the financial kind of honour?"

"Yes he was. Apparently, The Prophet deserves a lifestyle that includes a new home."

"Right … The upgrade. That sneaky freeloader. I knew he would never be able to afford a new house on his wages. Not the kind he expected that God was going to provide." Lauren stopped pulling at the vine and looked at Jamie properly for the first time since he'd been home. "And did you fall for it?"

"No. After our phone call on Tuesday night when you hung up,"

"Don't you dare tell me off for that," Lauren interrupted. "You got exactly what you deserved."

"I agree. I would have hung up on me to. But as I was saying, after you hung up, everything came crashing down around me. The guys kept telling me that this was when you were going to get freedom. But I couldn't see how. You were heartbroken, and I couldn't believe that God would use a husband to do that to his wife. That night I put out a fleece. I told God that if I got home and you had changed your mind and agreed about the holiday then I would believe that The Collective was His plan. But if you felt the same and wanted to leave me, I told God it was too much and I was out. I am not and will never be prepared to lose you for a calling, even if it did come from God."

"You know Steven would have a complete meltdown if he heard you speaking like that. It's not very holy."

"At this point I don't care what he thinks. I never told you, but when Steven first came along, I had my own doubts about him."

"You did? Why didn't you say something? We could have worked through it together. You were adamant that he was on the up and up."

"Not at first. I wasn't sure he was a prophet. The prophesy he gave you wasn't right and the one he had given me over the phone the first time I was introduced to him was so generic it had no value for me at all. So I thought if he could get it wrong for both of us then he was probably getting it wrong for others as well. And I was afraid of being deceived. Pastor Matthew had been speaking about deception in the church, so I was wary of everything I heard. But Steven started hanging around Gideon and Harry spoke so highly of him that I felt I had to at least give him a chance. I even approached Harry and point blank asked him if Steven really was a prophet. His answer was that he wasn't perfect, but he definitely had a gift and God had brought him into our lives. So when Steven came on staff and came with us to the second retreat, the one you missed, I decided that instead of worrying about being deceived I would trust God and give him the benefit of the doubt. And of course, the second I let my guard down was when I was deceived."

"Did you say anything to the others. Ask their opinion?"

"No because while I was questioning him privately, some of them were already having counselling from him. I didn't want to cause any conflict. I think that was one of the reasons I accepted him. I trusted their judgement, especially Pat's. And you know me. This had been my dream. I wanted out of my practice. And if I did what he said I would finally be doing what I always wanted. Working with a great group of guys, putting together deals. I was going to be a property developer. I've been talking about that for years. But we never had the money. With Gideon I was finally getting the chance to do it."

"But you could have done all that without Steven. Gideon was doing fine without him. You could have just voted no."

"I knew that if I had any objection to Steven that I would be out. Look what happened to Lawrence. He voted no to hiring Steven and within a month he was gone."

"But what about my opinion of Steven. I didn't keep it a secret what I thought? You trusted Pat and Harry's judgement over mine."

"I'm so sorry Lauren, I was completely wrong. But once I decided to believe in Steven, I put my blinkers on. No looking to the left or the right. Just straight ahead, hoping that everything I had decided to be true … Was. I had to be all in."

"Jamie, I'm trying to understand why this was so important to you? Clearly something was missing in your life, but what. Sometimes things were tight financially, but I thought we were happy."

"Yes I was happy with you, with our family. But I never felt fulfilled. I wanted more. A better lifestyle, the money to take off for a holiday at the drop of a hat like my clients did. I always felt like I was on the outside looking in. I helped make their businesses work but they were the ones who reaped the rewards. I thought with Gideon it was finally my time."

"And Gideon gave you what you were missing?"

"At first. But even in the group dynamic I still never felt good enough. Steven was The Prophet and Harry was The Apostle. They even decided that Daniel had an Apostle mantle over him, and that Pat was the Pastor figure in the group dynamic. All I ever was, was the Accountant."

"I'm so sorry you felt this way Jamie. I thought you loved it there."

"I did love it. But I don't think I'm going to be able to stay."

"Because of Steven. Can't you just ignore him? Get on with your work and bring your relationship with the others back to what they should be. Running a business together. Just stay out of the prayer meetings, do the books and collect your dividends. Nothing says we have to invest in the next project they find. Eventually it will come to a natural end and you'll find new work somewhere else."

"I wish it were that simple Lauren. But I can't be there. The environment is toxic. And you know just as well as I do. You're either all in or you're out. There's no room for compromise."

"But if you tell the guys how you feel they might see it too and decide to get rid of Steven. Just fire him. He doesn't have any shares thankfully, he's an employee. You could make his position redundant. Because seriously, what business needs a prophet?"

"It won't work. Unfortunately, Steven's not the biggest problem."

"He's not? Then what is?"

"Not what Lauren. Who? Really, it's all about Harry."

Chapter nineteen

"Harry? Over enthusiastic, nothing more than a big puppy dog, Harry?"

"Yes Lauren. Harry. He might come off like that at first but when you see through the facade Harry isn't what you think he is."

"But I like Harry. I mean, sometimes he drives me nuts with all the praying, but I always thought he was a great guy."

"I don't think you're going to feel that way once I explain to you what's been going on. I got a bit off track, but I was explaining what they thought it looked like to honour The Prophet."

"Right. He needs an upgrade. Carry on."

Jamie opened up an old camp chair they had dragged out of the shed before they started the demo. "It might be best if you sit down for this."

"I'm not going to like it am I?" Lauren asked.

"No. And there's no easy way to say it, so I'll just start at the beginning. Harry asked us all what it looked like to honour The Prophet. After my idea of acknowledging him on the web site was shut down and Stuart and I said no to giving him some of our shares, Steven did what he always does and stepped out of the meeting. That's when Harry told us that God had told him that the way to honour The Prophet was to purchase him a new home."

"I don't know a lot about foundations, but I do know they can't be used to purchase private property for an individual," Lauren pointed out.

"That's correct. And that gets us back to why they didn't ask us for more money for the foundation. Harry suggested that instead, we individually give Steven a cash gift from our next dividend."

"Nooo. You're kidding. They must know I'd never agree to that. We haven't even paid off our own home yet. I'm not going to pay for someone else's."

"And that's why it was suggested that we shouldn't tell our wives because they're not all safe yet."

"Safe?"

"Completely on board with The Collective," Jamie explained. Once you were fully in, we could tell you."

"But that's stealing. And lying. A marriage can't work that way."

"I know Lauren. And when Harry suggested it that's when I knew. Properly knew, that The Collective was not operating inside God's will. He would never want a husband to lie to his wife."

"And all you guys agreed to this?"

"I didn't. I stayed quiet and decided to see how it would play out. I already knew I would never say yes, but Josh was on board straight away. I know Pat and he would give Steven the shirt off his back if he thought he wanted it. And Daniel's so freaked out about having a problem with greed he'd try to prove he didn't by giving them whatever they asked for. I don't know about Stuart. He plays his cards pretty close to his chest. But he didn't disagree."

"So, let me get this straight. Harry want's you all to help Steven get into a fancy new house. What, like put in for the deposit? That's tens of thousands of dollars each."

"Oh no. Not a deposit," Jamie said. "The Prophet doesn't do debt anymore. When we first met him he had a massive amount of credit card debt and no equity in his house. But that was taken care of."

"I'm afraid to ask how?"

"I don't know exactly who paid what when it came to the credit cards, but I have an idea. What I do know is how his mortgage was paid out."

"Someone paid his whole mortgage?" Lauren asked, her eyes wide with disbelief. "Who could afford to pay out an entire mortgage. I know Lucy says their house is a bit of a dump, but still. That's a lot of money."

"It was. Around six hundred thousand dollars. And it wasn't paid by one person. It was paid for by money that should have gone into the foundation."

"You can't be serious? You all agreed that our profits went to paying out Steven's mortgage instead of going into the foundation. And other people paid out his credit cards."

"Yep. And bought him and Lucy new cars."

"Did we ever pay for anything? You didn't take our money and give it to him without me knowing?'

"No. I never did. But I think I was probably the only one."

"So everyone else had been lying to their wives."

"I don't know if they told them or not. But I do know they are being encouraged to lie now."

"By Harry."

"Yes. By Harry," Jamie confirmed.

"Let me get this straight. He wants everyone to put in enough to buy Steven a new house. How much?"

"Well right before we left, and that's the way he does it, so there's no time for more discussion, Harry showed me a picture of a house he had already picked out for Steven. It was over one point seven million. Steven might get seven hundred for the house he owns now. So they want us to put in about two hundred grand each to cover the upgrade, stamp duty and of course they can't take their old furniture with them. That needs to be new too."

"And what about the tax?" Lauren asked. "Someone would have to pay that. I'm assuming Steven wouldn't want half the money going on that."

"No. As we had earned the money and were giving it as a gift, we would be expected to pay the tax."

"But that makes a two hundred-thousand-dollar gift really almost four hundred thousand in actual cash."

"That's correct," Jamie confirmed.

"And Steven gets a free house. Actually, his second free house."

Jamie nodded.

"And if you disagree, you lose your job and your position inside Gideon?"

"That's the point. You can't disagree. We spent two whole days talking about and dissecting what it looked like to honour The Prophet. Anytime we suggested something different than money we were told to go back and ask God again. That's what Harry does. If you heard something different from God, then he suggests you heard wrong. He never comes out and directly challenges you, just asks you to try again. And after hours of this you do hear what he hears. Every decision we make has been like that. We think we're wrong because Harry's so holy and hears perfectly from God. But right now I don't know who or what I've been listening to. But once I decided The Collective was not from God, I stopped hearing anything. I think it was mostly our own voices wanting to be in agreement with The Prophet and The Apostle. At least that's what I hope it was and not something more sinister."

"Well I can tell you I never liked the way you all sat around emptying your minds. That's meditation, not prayer."

"I know. I realized that this week. I never recognized before but what's been going on was very similar to guided meditation."

"You said Steven always leaves the room. Why do you think that is?"

"It's so he can never be accused of manipulating our decisions. But he doesn't need to be there. That's what he has Harry for. It doesn't matter how long it takes. We sit there till we agree with his position. Because we always have to be in alignment. Supposedly with God, but in reality, we have to be in alignment with Harry. And I can't do that anymore. The only person I want to be in alignment with is you," Jamie said looking at Lauren with pleading in his eyes.

"I don't know Jamie. While I appreciate you finally being honest with me there's been so much damage. You've lied by omission and you've put your prophet and your brothers before me and our children."

"I know. And I'm so, so sorry. I think I'll be telling you how sorry I am for the rest of our lives."

"And what? I'm just expected to forgive you and forget all this ever happened. It's too much Jamie."

"It is too much. Don't forgive me. Not yet anyway. Just let me stay and prove to you that everything I'm saying is true. I have to get out of The Collective. I never want anything to do with it again."

"But how do you do that? We have shares. Someone needs to make sure we're being paid our dividends properly. Clearly we can't trust them."

"Oh, I don't think that will be a problem. I expect they will buy me out. They won't want me anywhere near them or voting on decisions as a board member. Because until they do buy me out, unlike Lawrence, I'm not going to resign. You're right, they can't be trusted, well Harry and Steven anyway."

"And what about your friendships? You've known some of them for years."

"That's up to them," Jamie sighed. "I expect they won't want anything to do with me once I challenge their prophet. And that's what I'll be doing when I go into work on Tuesday. I'll be telling them I vote no on the purchase of the land near the Blue Mountains."

"I thought there were no new deals on the table," Lauren queried.

"The land isn't for a Gideon project. It's being bought through the foundation. About ten acres. It's not Sydney prices, but it's still a lot of money."

"And why does the foundation need land?"

"Because The Prophet said so. He said it would be for all of us to use. We can go there to pray and spend time with God. But mostly I think it's for him. He likes to hunt and if he moves closer to the city, he won't be able to do that anymore."

"Or," said Lauren, "he wants it for the Freedom Centre he and Harry have been talking about. You know the twenty-million-dollar facility where people can come to get freedom. Or worse" she laughed cynically, "maybe they want to build houses on it, and you can all live together in a compound and Steven can be the leader and have many wives," she half joked, hoping for her friends' sakes that that would never be the case. Just the thought of it made her shiver in disgust.

"Harry would be the real leader. Steven would just be the figure head. Josh has commented more than once that Harry would make a great cult leader. They used to joke about drinking the cool aid. It doesn't seem so funny anymore."

"So you really meant it when you said Harry was the problem. But what does he even get out of it? Steven's the one reaping all the financial benefits."

"Harry has plenty of money, and quite honestly I don't think that's what motivates him. I think he genuinely believes he is doing God's will. But I've come to see him in a different light this week. He's ambitious. He want's that freedom centre to be built. If that happens, I think he believes he will have a world-wide ministry. Then he'll be famous. And he needs control. Something you said to me on the phone the other night really rang true. They hate it when anyone goes away with their wives and families. I think you were right. When we aren't with them day after day it's harder to control us. We make our own decisions and other people can influence us, especially our families."

"And maybe that's why they don't want the wives working," Lauren suggested. "Because then we're out in the real world away from their influence. And when you're working and socialising with people outside The Collective you can see how cultish it all is. And with no other income then we would be relying solely on Gideon. That would leave us with no choice but to do exactly what they tell us, or we'd be in financial trouble. That's how they hold all the cards. I don't think I was far wrong calling it a cult. And if it isn't one yet that's the direction it's heading in."

"And that explains why they were so invested in me giving up my other clients," Jamie realized. "They wanted me to be completely reliant on them. I'm still trying to figure out how I'll replace the income I'm going to lose. But at this point I'd rather sell up everything and buy a small house out in the country and teach accounting at the local high school than have anything more to do with The Collective. It's evil what's been happening. The manipulation and control. I think if anyone is operating under a Jezebel spirit it's not the wives, it's Steven and Harry."

"This is all coming as a bit of a shock. I've hoped for so long that you would finally see the truth, but I had given up. And for the record, I'd be happy living in the country. The kids might have something to say about it, but we could hang on here for another year till Oli's finished high school."

"Whatever happens with work we'll be out of The Collective as soon as I can get it done. And Lauren. I really appreciate you listening to me. You've been more understanding than I deserved. I just hope one day you will be able to forgive me."

"That's going to take time Jamie. Two years I've put up with this hell. You dismissed me, berated me and made me feel like I was going crazy. And you lied to me about what was really going on. I feel betrayed. We haven't had a real marriage since you let Steven into our lives."

"I know," Jamie admitted. "And I take full responsibility for it. But please give me a chance to make it up to you. From now on every decision we make will be done together and if we don't agree, then we don't do it."

"You can't ever do that to me again. Put others first in your life. And I don't mean God," Lauren clarified, "but other people. We should always come first with each other. Because it's felt like I've been cheated on. Not with another woman, but the hurt is the same."

Jamie's head dropped. The gravity of everything that had gone on weighed heavily on him. It would serve him right if she never spoke to him again and made him leave.

"I'm so sorry. Do you believe me?"

"I do. But I'm going to need some time to sort out how I feel. And in particular about Harry. I was so focused on Steven that I didn't realize what *he* was up to. I thought I had discernment, but this time I really missed the mark. I thought he was just overzealous. I never once thought he was running the whole show."

"They run it together really. Without Harry, Steven was a nobody. He went from church to church, and eventually they saw through him and asked him to leave. And without Steven, Harry was a great salesman, but he didn't have a spiritual hook with people. There was nothing to capture their attention. But together,"

"together they are the perfect storm," Lauren finished.

"So you understand. And maybe one day we might be all right?"

"For now, our first priority needs to get this mess sorted out. Then I can decide how I feel about you. But today I think the best thing would be some demolition therapy. Pick up that sledgehammer and let's get these walls down."

Chapter twenty

Every time Jamie thought about how close he had come to losing Lauren he sent up a prayer to God thanking Him for opening his eyes. He and Lauren had spent the entire weekend talking through what their options were, but until he told the others he was out they couldn't make firm plans. Knowing he couldn't put it off any longer he decided it was time to get the ball rolling. He dialled Pat's number, hoping their long-time friendship would mean he would at least hear Jamie out.

"Hey Jamie. I was just thinking about you," Pat answered his phone with. "How's it all going? Sorted out with Lauren?"

"That's why I'm ringing. Is this a good time? I don't want to take you away from anything, but I need to discuss something with you, and I didn't think this could wait until next time I'm in the office."

"All good. The girls went out shopping after church, so I'm just reading the new book Harry recommended. Have you started it yet?"

"Ah no. Haven't had a chance. I just wanted to have a chat about what went on at the retreat and how I'm feeling about it."

"Wasn't it fantastic? Being able to drill down like that to our issues and get them out in the open. I feel so free now that I've dealt with my greed problem. This time I think I'm done with it for good. And I'm excited to be honouring The Prophet with a new home. If anyone deserves it, it's Steven."

"But aren't you concerned about telling Maria? They're asking for a lot of money. Wouldn't that be better spent on your own mortgage?" Jamie knew that Pat's mortgage was huge after he had fully renovated his home last year and he had told the bank he would be paying off a lump sum when the next dividend was paid. Pat had sold out of his other investments when he started working for Gideon believing that he needed to focus solely on The Collective, so like Jamie, he was now earning less and needed the dividends to make ends meet. If he gave the next one away to pay for The Prophets house where would that leave him?

"God's got it Jamie. You know that. Money's easy to come by. But being part of The Collective, not many people get an opportunity like this. And I'm not worried about Maria. I'll tell her when she's ready to hear it. She's so close. Like Lauren. We just need to keep praying for our girls. Speaking of which. Lauren's all good? With you cancelling the holiday?"

"No, she isn't. She hasn't changed her mind, which puts me in a bit of a dilemma. If God is asking me to sacrifice my wife for The Collective, then I'm afraid it's too much to ask."

"God isn't asking you to sacrifice your wife. He want's freedom for her. You know how it is. The more opposition you get, the more in line with God you are. The enemy is using her to get to you. You can't let that happen."

"I'm not sure I believe that anymore Pat. There shouldn't be division in a marriage. I can't see how God would want that. Even to bring freedom. But if you are right and that's what God wants, me breaking my wife's heart until she's free, then that's not something I want to be part of. It's asking too much of me and it's asking too much of her."

For a few seconds Jamie heard nothing but the sound of Pat breathing in and out slowly. When he did reply it was exactly what Jamie had expected and he knew he was going to hear it more than once while he was extracting himself from The Collective.

"I'm really worried for where you're sitting Jamie. You've gone home and Lauren has done whatever she can to manipulate you into to going on the holiday anyway, against what God told us. She's not the right person to talk to Jamie. We're all aware that she has some serious trust issues that Harry believes stem from her father. And she's always refused to come under Steven and Harry's authority. And now it sounds like she won't even come under yours. You shouldn't process this with her. You know better than that. She isn't safe yet."

"Careful Pat. That's my wife you're talking about."

"I know. And look at what she's doing. She isn't being obedient. You don't talk to her," Pat spoke, quietly and controlled the way Harry would. "You know better than that. You talk issues through with your brothers."

"I don't think The Collective is the right place for me to be Pat."

"You're just scared Jamie because you think you might lose your wife. That's never going to happen. She's just trying to get her way. You need to stand up to her. It might be painful now but in the long run it *will* bring her freedom. We have your best interests at heart. *She* only cares about what *she* wants. Take some time. Pray about the situation and I'll be praying for you too. But please don't ring Harry. He's left with Louise for Bali this morning and he deserves a break. We'll discuss this further tomorrow in the office." *How ironic*, Jamie thought. Everyone else has had their holidays questioned and most have been cancelled recently, but there's Harry, on yet another one. What's that, the third so far, this year.

"I won't be in tomorrow," he said, "I'm out at a client. I'll see you Tuesday."

"That's part of the problem. It's time you gave up these other jobs. You don't need the distraction of these outside influences. The Collective should be your priority. I'll see you Tuesday and don't worry. Together we can sort this out. God really does have it."

The phone call had gone as expected. Pat was so invested in The Collective that Jamie wondered if he would ever see the truth. Lauren wanted him to go into work on Tuesday with guns blazing and lay that truth out on the table. Tell them that he had changed his position on Steven and no longer believed that he was a prophet. She thought that he was influential enough to get through to the boys and that would be enough to get Steven out of Gideon. Jamie knew better. It was going to take something big to open their eyes. For him it had been nearly losing his wife. But until something major happened, nothing he said would change their minds. And Jamie would become the outsider. Especially with Harry manipulating them.

~ ~ ~

Driving through the traffic on Tuesday morning Jamie felt a heaviness and dread unlike anything he had ever felt before. *I'm going into battle,* he thought. *For my family and our spiritual and financial future.*

"God, if I'm wrong about The Collective, if I'm way off about Steven and Harry this is the time to tell me." Jamie prayed as he listened for God's voice but all he heard was the sound of traffic and the occasional horn as people became frustrated with their normal commute through Sydney's clogged roads. But in the silence, he decided something. Lauren's philosophy was that if you had a situation and God

wasn't talking, move forward in the direction you believe is right until
He does speak. Otherwise nothing would ever get done. As long as it
didn't contradict the Bible it was unlikely you would go wrong. She
argued God had given each of them a brain and a conscience. He
expected them to use it. So that's what he would do. He knew in his heart
that this thing was no longer Godly, and it was time to get out. Whatever
that looked like.

Pulling into the car park of the Gideon offices, he tried to calm
himself. His heart and his brain might know this was the right thing to
do, but they hadn't been able to communicate that to his churning
stomach. He wished he could turn around and go back home. Maybe
resign by email. But this wasn't a situation that could be dealt with by
email. And when he told them what he decided, it would inevitably be
followed by hours of prayer and discussion. The only saving grace was
that Harry was away for the week. While it infuriated him that Harry
was off on holidays *again*, at least he wouldn't have to confront him.
Harry had a way of turning your words against you until you were so
tied up in knots, that you didn't know what you believed anymore. And
while Jamie finally saw him for the skilled manipulator that he was, he
wasn't ready to face him yet. It was still too new, and he wasn't strong
enough. Grabbing his briefcase from the passenger seat, he locked his
car and headed for the front door of the office. He could see that Pat's
car was here, as was Daniel's, which was unusual because he normally
only came in for the Friday board meetings. I guess they're rallying the
troops. Taking a deep breath, he opened the door and headed for his
desk. He put his briefcase down beside his chair, taking only his phone
and his Bible, and made his way to the meeting room where he could see
Pat, Josh and Daniel were waiting. He hadn't expected Josh either. He
also only came into the office on Fridays for the weekly board meeting,
and that was if he wasn't in court for the day. They must be taking this

very seriously if Josh had been called in. Steven wasn't there, which surprised Jamie. Maybe he thought the guys could handle it themselves and it was no big deal.

"Please take a seat Jamie," Pat suggested. "I've told the others about our conversation on Sunday and they're as concerned for you as I am. I'm hoping you've had a change of heart since we last spoke."

All eyes were on him, and he was glad they couldn't hear is heartbeat thumping as he took his usual chair. He had spent hours in this room, praying and strategizing with these guys. They had formed a deep bond, real mates and he had never experienced anything like it before. So how did he explain what he had decided to them? They had spent the last two years building something together, and now he had to tell them he was out and was walking away from them. That he wanted no part of what had brought them all together and yes, made them brothers. How do you leave a family without causing hurt? But then he reminded himself that they were willing to let him sacrifice his real family. This, the mission, was something he no longer believed in.

"No Pat, there's been no change of heart. After last week, I went home knowing that what is being asked of me by The Collective is too much. And if it's God asking, then I'm sorry but He's asking too much as well. I'm not willing to lose my wife because of The Collective."

"I think before we say too much that the best thing to do is pray," Daniel said. "Bring this to God and let him speak to you. Okay?"

"Sure," Jamie replied. "Of course, I have no problem with that." Daniel took his phone out of his pocket, and a minute later he had blue-toothed music into the speakers. At first the men asked for God's guidance, asked him to help Jamie make the right decision. But slowly they quietened down as the music became more repetitive, more hypnotic. Cracking open one eye Jamie noticed Josh and Daniel. They had slumped in their seats, off in their own world, arms outstretched, and Jamie saw what Lauren had been talking about. They looked like they were meditating. And not on the word of God like the bible told them to. There had been an inside joke when they were trying to make a decision about 'kumbyaing this thing until it was done,' but now that saying took on a much darker meaning. Were they even praying to God, or had some other spirit taken them over? Half an hour passed as the others soaked in the presence of God while the music played quietly in the background. Slowly, as Jamie watched, they seemed to come back to the room, eyes glazed as they began to focus on the here and now.

"That was amazing, being in the presence of God," Pat said, his comment aimed at Jamie. "Surely you can't deny that He was here with us. I can't even begin to understand why you would want to give this up, not bring your family along so that they too, can experience Him this way."

Jamie knew it was pointless to try and explain what he had felt while they had been soaking. He hadn't realized until now just how much they had changed over the last year. Josh had recently gone to see a hypnotist, and nobody had questioned him. Maria was doing yoga and claimed it helped her connect with God. Lauren had challenged her, but Maria had defended herself claiming the way she did it had nothing to do with the Hindu religion. How had he not noticed the new age practices that had crept into The Collective. Now that his eyes were opened Jamie could no longer stomach the soaking. He quietly asked God to forgive him for ever being part of this. They weren't connecting to God, but he couldn't deny they were connecting to something. No wonder it had been so easy for Harry and Steven to manipulate them. Whatever they were connecting to probably kept them from seeing the truth. And now they were sitting here waiting for an explanation from him about his change of heart. If he told them what he was really thinking they would think he had lost his mind.

"As I explained to Pat on Sunday, I believe that The Collective is no longer the place for me or my family. One of my deep concerns is this thing about honouring The Prophet. I have been very recently reminded of a story I read in the bible a few months ago and I actually meant to ask Steven what he thought of it, but I never got around to it. It's a story in 2 Kings chapter five. It's about a Syrian commander named Naaman who had leprosy. It was recommended to him that he travel to Israel and find the Prophet Elisha who can heal him of his disease. So he goes to Israel and Elisha tells him to bathe in the Jordon river seven times and he'll be healed. At first, he refuses, thinking it was a waste of time because he could bathe in the much cleaner rivers at home, but his servants talk him into giving it a go. And of course, he's healed. But it's this verse that concerned me, and I've re-read this story several times over the weekend to make sure I'm reading it right." Jamie flipped open his Bible to where he had marked the page, but before he had a chance to read, Steven came bounding up the stairs and sat next to Jamie.

"What's going on guys? It's almost a full house here today. Can't stay away from the place?"

"Actually, Jamie was telling us a story from 2 Kings," Pat said. "He was about to read us a scripture. Go ahead Jamie."

Could Steven's timing have been any worse? He had hoped to bring this to them privately. Steven was not going to be happy with what he had to say. But then again, he needed to hear it, and it was better he heard it firsthand, instead of from one of the others who might spin it.

"I was about to read verse fifteen and sixteen from chapter five. *'And he returned to the man of God, he and all his aides, and came and stood before him; and he said. "Indeed, now I know that there is no God in all the Earth, except in Israel; now therefore, please take a gift from your servant." But he said. "As the Lord lives, before whom I stand, I will receive nothing." And he urged him to take it but he refused.'* The story goes on to tell how Elisha's servant Gehazi ran after Naaman, after his gift had been refused, and told him that Elisha had sent him to receive payment on behalf of someone else. Naaman happily gave him talents of silver and fine clothing which Gehazi then hid for himself. Then he went back to Elisha and lied when he was asked where he had been. But Elisha the prophet knew where he had been and what he had done. He told him that Naaman's leprosy would cling to him and his descendants forever. You might ask what this story has to do with anything. The story is about the prophet refusing to take payment when Naaman received healing from God through him." Pausing, knowing what he was about to say would not be received well, and especially by The Prophet, Jamie looked down at his Bible, wishing that Steven wasn't sitting right next to him. "I believe it's unbiblical for a prophet to receive payment for healing or prophesy, which is what's happening here at Gideon."

Looking up and catching his eye Jamie thought Steven looked like a deer in the headlights. I guess The Prophet didn't see this coming.

"Have you spoken to Pat in the last few days?" Jamie asked him.

"No, Lucy and I took a few days away, you know, to make up for being away last week. We got back last night."

"Ok. The guys here know that I've had a change of heart about The Collective. I just don't feel that it is the right place for me or my family to be anymore. And as you might have ascertained from the story that I just read, I'm no longer of the opinion that we should have a prophet on the payroll, let alone fund the upgrade of his house."

"I think this is all coming from Lauren," Pat jumped in before Steven had a chance to reply to Jamie. "She's upset because he cancelled their holiday and she had an overreaction to it. And he's too scared to tell her about upgrading your house Steven. It's the same old problem of greed. And once you got it out of your life Jamie, it moved to your wife. She's operating under a Jezebel spirit, trying to control you. I told you on Sunday, you don't talk to her, you only talk to your brothers" Pat spat his words at Jamie, his voice dripping with rage.

"Let's take a minute guys," said Daniel calmly. "Obviously Jamie has some concerns. I don't share them, and I don't think anyone else does. But we shouldn't dismiss them. I think the best thing is for you to go and spend some time alone with God. I don't think it would be helpful for you to go home. That's clearly a toxic environment and you won't hear from God there. Find somewhere you feel at peace and can take the time to process this properly. It's obvious that things at home aren't great and that will be influencing your feelings. That isn't the best environment to make a decision. We love you both and want what's best for you. If you still have concerns after spending the day with God we can talk about them in a few days and sort them out. Take the rest of the day off, and we'll reconvene this meeting on Friday when everyone is here. How does that sound?"

"I did have a couple of urgent things I need to do, things that need paying. But sure, after that I'll take your advice. I'll spend some time with God alone."

"That reminds me," Pat said, his voice controlled, but his face tight with anger. "I had an email from the real estate agent. The deposit for the land is due tomorrow. So can you please load that up before you go."

"Actually, on that. Sitting where I am at the moment, I don't feel like I can agree to the purchase of the land for the foundation. I think it needs to go back to the board and be reassessed before we go ahead with it."

"The decision has been made Jamie. We are buying it," Steven said, speaking for the first time since Jamie had told him how he felt about what was going on.

"But *my* decision has changed, and I at least want the chance to discuss it with the others. We can deal with it on Friday at the board

219

meeting." Jamie knew realistically that the others would never change their mind. Steven and Harry had told them that God had set the land aside for them. No one else would go against their wishes. But he wanted to be on record as objecting.

"But we'll receive late penalties if the deposit is not paid on time," Pat argued.

"They won't charge penalties, but if they do then we'll deal with them. It's only a few dollars. Better than making a mistake with hundreds of thousands of dollars on land we don't have any use for."

"I see," Pat said. "I can see there's not much point trying to talk to you at the moment. I hope you can get your head straight in the next day or two."

"And guys," Jamie said as he picked up his Bible and his phone before he headed to his desk to do the required work, "I recommend you tell your wives about the money for Steven's house. I've told Lauren about buying Steven a house and I can't guarantee she won't tell them before you get a chance. She feels very strongly that it's wrong to keep this a secret."

From the window near his desk as he finalized the wages for the week before he left as Daniel had suggested, Jamie saw Steven exit the office. He had his phone to his ear and was talking animatedly into it. He paced around the car park as he talked, looking very concerned. He's probably talking to Harry Jamie thought. I'd love to know how that conversation went but he had a pretty good idea because Steven did not look happy.

~ ~ ~

"Miss me already?" Harry asked when he answered his phone. It was a rare day that Steven and Harry didn't see each other, let alone talk, but Louise had said that she wanted some time on their own and the two had agreed to keep the communication while Harry was away to a minimum.

"We've got a problem with Jamie."

"What now?" Harry sighed. "He seemed fine last week. It's Lauren isn't it? Is she still sulking about the holiday, so he's given in and decided to go anyway?"

"I don't know if he's going or not. He never said. It's much worse than that. He's decided he doesn't want to be part of The Collective anymore. And he doesn't think I should be paid my wages anymore. He found some obscure story in the Old Testament, that I've never read, about a prophet who refused payment when he healed someone, and he's read it to the others this morning, trying to convince them that prophets shouldn't accept payment. What does he expect me to do? Live on air."

"No one expects that. You earn your wages and without you Gideon would never have done so well. And what can he do about it?" Harry reassured him. "It's a board majority vote, and you know the board always goes with what God tells us. It'll all be fine."

"It's not just that. He's told Lauren about the house. He said you all better tell your wives about the money because he can't guarantee she won't tell them herself. That woman has been nothing but a thorn in my side. She won't come under any authority and argues with everything. And now she's finally getting Jamie on her side."

"Look, realistically we would have had to tell them at some point. And you know what women are like. If one knows, they all know. So tell the guys to let their wives know it's happening. The other are completely behind getting you that upgrade God promised, so don't worry about it. The problem is going to be if Jamie actually leaves The Collective. You know this is an all-in, exclusive thing. We can't let him stay on the board of Gideon, especially if he's trying to influence the others.

"He's already refusing to pay the deposit on the land. He wants to take it back to the board on Friday. Just two weeks ago he was completely behind the purchase. What if he convinces the others to change their minds too?

"Don't worry about it Steven. God held that land for us. He's not going to let it slip through our fingers because of one person's flawed opinion. Jamie's stumbling a bit at the moment but with our help he'll come to see that he's wrong. He obviously has a few concerns and we have Lauren to thank for that, but we'll all get through this and will be stronger for it.

"I don't know. I think it's bad. He's made up his mind to put his wife before God. And he has so much influence with others. What if he does talk them out of buying the land? We have plans for it."

"Stop panicking Steven. He doesn't have as much influence as you think, and he can't beat God. Even if he gets the others to agree to vote again the outcome will be the same. They won't change their minds."

"You're right. They weren't supportive of him when he bought it up this morning. But what about outside of The Collective? He's Daniels accountant. If he does leave, he'll still have influence over him at Racers. That could bring us out of alignment."

"If, and I'm sure Jamie will be brought back into the fold once he realizes, he's wrong, but if he does leave then I'm sure Daniel won't want him in his life anymore. All we need to do is remind him someone who's willing to walk away from God shouldn't be trusted with something so important as advising him on how to run his business."

"Let's pray Daniel see's it that way."

"He will. We also need to keep Living Waters in our prayers. The church is on the cusp of real breakthrough. I would hate to think Jamie would try and interfere there and spread rumours about us."

"How could he have any influence there. He's only been attending for a few months and I don't think he knows that many people there."

"You're forgetting he's known Pastor Isaac for years. And Isaac has the same trouble as Jamie – his wife. They're both operating under Jezebel and if those two got together it could cause problems for us."

"I'm not worried about that," Steven said. "Isaac placed me in authority over him. His wife is off licking her wounds after we called her behaviour out. She's become a toothless tiger. I'm much more concerned about the damage Jamie could do here. We can't have any dissent on the board."

"We'll buy him out if we have to. From what you've said he wants to go anyway. We've known all along that Lauren was the one holding us back. This might be a blessing in disguise. God's way of getting her out. It's a shame she's taking Jamie with her, but if that's the way it has to be let's not fight it. We don't need someone who's not one hundred percent committed to us hanging around and causing trouble. I'll be back next week, and we'll deal with him then. And in the meantime, I'll have a word with the others about the land, make sure they vote the way God wants them to."

"Okay," Steven sighed with relief. "At least we have a plan. And Daniel suggested to him to take the day, spend some time alone with God. Hopefully he hears from Him and realizes the mistake he's making, and this all goes away. Although I have no idea what to do about Lauren. The woman's my worst nightmare."

"People split up all the time. If he stays in The Collective they might die a natural death. And we should each spend some extra time praying for Jamie, really bring this situation to God. Because you know He's got it."

Chapter twenty-one

"I can't believe I was so stupid."

"I know."

"I'm so, so sorry for putting you through this."

"I know."

"What are we going to do?"

"Now that I don't know," Lauren answered from across the dinner table. The kids had disappeared to watch telly half an hour ago, but Lauren and Jamie had been unable to move, Jamie sighed and dropped his head into his hands every few minutes. The shock was wearing off and now he was coming to grips with the consequences.

"I'm so glad you made me keep the clients I did. Can you imagine if I'd given them up? But I'm still going to have to go out there and get some more work."

"We have money Jamie. And a lot less debt than we did at the start of the year. Before you start panicking why don't you wait and see what the board decides to do."

"You're right. And they can't fire me yet. None of them are capable of doing my job so they'll need to find a replacement."

"See. Nothing to worry about. What I'm really interested in was how you went today after you left work?"

Breathing out yet another sigh, Jamie pushed his empty plate forward and rested his elbows on the table.

"I don't know. I mean, it was fine. I found a lovely spot in a park not far from the office to pray and it was nice and quiet. But the praying? It was hard. I think I'm hearing God, but I can't be sure. There's so many jumbled thoughts up here," he said as he pointed to his head. "I'm so confused. I mean, I haven't changed my mind about The Collective. It's toxic, I have no doubts about that. But these guys were, are, my friends. And they really, really believe it. They think I'm the one who's got it wrong. I don't think I'll ever be able to get through to them. They're so blinded. And then that email Josh sent around. I could believe he would actually put that in writing."

"What email?"

"That's right I didn't show you." He picked up his phone from the table and tapped the screen until he found the email Josh had sent about an hour after Jamie had left work for the afternoon to think through his decision and get back on board with The Collective.

"You're going to love this," he said as he handed her his phone.

"Hi Guys," Lauren read aloud. "I've been thinking about today's discussion regarding the purchase of Steven's house. We probably can't go ahead with paying for it without telling our wives. That means we'll need to tell them what's going on. It wouldn't look good if they found out from another source. But telling them doesn't mean we can trust them. I don't even fully trust my own wife. They aren't all safe yet, so we'll have to proceed with caution, but be firm. Steven is getting his upgrade. Josh." Lauren read the email again, silently this time as she let the words sink in. She guessed it was a dig at her. But putting it in writing and then sending it to all the Gideon guys, including Jamie wasn't bright.

She would have expected more discretion from a Solicitor. She could easily send this to Ashley and how would she feel, knowing that her husband was discussing her like this.

Handing Jamie back his phone she said, "I've already decided I'm not going to say anything to the other wives."

"You're not? That's a surprise. I thought I'd come home and find out you'd already done it."

"It's not the right thing to do. Our marriage nearly came to an end and I think there's already conflict going on with Daniel and Felicity. Yes, she accepted Steven's invitation to be all in, but I'm not sure she understood what she was doing at the time. I don't know where the other girls stand, but to find out your husband is not only prepared to take a huge chunk of your money and give it away is bad enough. To find out he's prepared to lie to you about it is even worse. I don't want to be the one who tells them. It's between husband and wife. No-one should come between a marriage and if The Collective can't understand that, I do. Don't get me wrong. I want to tell them. I should forward this awful email to them right now. But what good would it do? I won't be responsible for causing trouble in someone else's marriage. If I'm asked, I'll be honest. But until that time, I'll keep silent on this matter."

"I doubt you'll be asked. I'd be surprised if you hear from any of them. You said no one called you last week when you were in a mess. The guys all knew what was going on and would have said something to their wives. And yet not one of them reached out to you. I think it's safe to say the friendships are over. When they don't get the answer they want from me at Friday's board meeting they won't want anything more to do with us."

"Well I'd rather be out than stuck inside that horror show. Who needs friends anyway?" she smiled thinly, knowing she didn't really mean it.

"You've got me."

"I do. Now help me do the dishes," Lauren said as she pushed back her chair and picked up her plate. "I've been thinking about something. If this isn't from God, The Collective, then where is it coming from? Is it some other spirit masquerading as God? Because the guys, and especially Steven really believe they are hearing from someone. Unless he's actually has a condition, like schizophrenia or something, which I don't think he has, *something* is speaking to him."

"I know. Watching them today while they prayed, they looked so out of it. I felt sick when I realized I used to do the same thing. I spent quite a bit of time today when I was at the park asking for forgiveness for allowing myself to be so deceived."

"And you're still certain? You really, really believe The Collective is wrong? Because I don't want you here under false pretences. I've said it before, but this can't work if you change your mind later and blame me for you leaving The Collective.

"I really, really believe it."

"Ok. Just checking," Lauren said as she stacked the last plate into the dishwasher.

"Jamie, maybe we should ask God."

"Ask God what?"

"What spirit this is operating under. Know your enemy and all that."

"We could but I don't trust my hearing anymore. I think I hear from God, but I could be completely wrong. I'm not sure I'll ever trust the hearing thing again."

"I understand that. I'd be sceptical too if I'd been deceived the way you have. And it makes me so angry that they messed this up for you. I hope that eventually you will be able to recognize God's voice again. But *I* trust *my* hearing from God. I haven't been brainwashed like the rest of you. I stayed away from all that soaking stuff that I think has really screwed you all up."

Lauren put down the sponge she had been wiping the bench with and quietly began to pray.

"God, you are the Almighty. Everything in Heaven and on Earth is under your authority. Thank you for opening Jamie's eyes to Steven and Harry and revealing that The Collective is not from you. I ask that you share with us what spirit is controlling them so that we know what we are dealing with. Thank you God." Instantly the word witchcraft dropped into Lauren's mind. *That can't be right,* she thought. I don't see them standing around in robes chanting and sacrificing goats. They might be dangerous, but I can't imagine them actually cursing us.

"Did you hear anything?" Jamie asked.

"I did, but it doesn't make sense. I heard witchcraft. You haven't seen anything like that, have you?"

"Well no. But on the last day of the retreat I remember thinking that it wouldn't surprise me if Steven pulled out that hunting knife he always carries with him and made us take a blood oath of brotherhood. I wasn't going to have any part of that."

"Yuck that thing was filthy."

"Yeah it was," he smiled. "So, witchcraft you say. That's a big call."

"I know. I think I'm just going to tuck that away for a bit. I certainly have no intention of running around accusing people of being witches."

"Good idea. They already think I've lost the plot and you're under the influence of a Jezebel spirit."

"And when you don't change your mind, they won't be happy. They'll say I'm controlling you. How will you handle it?"

"I'll go to work like nothing's changed. I won't try to convince them that they are wrong about you. What's the point. But I still have a job to do and I intend to do it well. And then on Friday at the board meeting we'll discuss what's going to happen with my shares. I can only hope they'll want to be rid of me and offer to buy me out. They certainly won't want me hanging around, voting against them. Everyone has to be in agreement, and by agreement, I mean going along with whatever agenda Harry and Steven have. I'm dreading Friday but at least Harry will still be away. I was furious that he took this holiday, right after suggesting that *we* shouldn't go away, but now I think it's a Godsend. I really, really don't want to have to deal with him and his scheming. He'll turn everything I say around on me till I don't know up from down. I'm not ready to face him yet."

"Go sit down love and watch something silly on TV. Take your mind off it for a bit. I'll finish up the dishes and join you soon."

"You sure?"

"Yep. You've had a rough day. It won't take me long."

A minute later Lauren could hear Jamie laughing. He'd joined the kids and it sounded like whatever they were watching was just what he needed. *Good*, Lauren thought. Now that the kitchen was clean there was something she wanted to look up. Sitting at her new study nook just off the kitchen, she opened google on her computer and entered the words spirit of witchcraft in the church. She was surprised to see how much had been written on the subject. Clicking on page after page she found two kinds of threads. One was about churches that had been infiltrated by witches to cause trouble and bring Pastors undone. But it was the second kind of articles that really piqued her interest. There were lots of books and articles written about the spirit of witchcraft inside the church and para-church organisations like The Collective. The main character-istics of witchcraft operating in a Christian environment were control, manipulation, domination and intimidation. So much of what she was reading was exactly what she and Jamie had been through. Authors wrote of people feeling they could not make simple decisions without running it by their leader, not being able to make day to day choices like a normal adult did. They explained how witchcraft hid itself behind legitimate ministries and surrounded itself with Godly people while it drew them in until it had complete control. But the article that stood out the most to her was one that stated that a prophetic gift that was not properly stewarded could easily give way to witchcraft. This answered the question that had come between her and Jamie for the past two years. Was Steven a prophet or a fraud? Even now Jamie believed that Steven truly thought he was a prophet and that he was doing God's work. What if he had started out with a prophetic gift but had become corrupt along the way, Lauren asked herself. If, and Lauren still wasn't sure, if he did have a gift, his desire for financial gain could have left a door open for witchcraft to creep in. Because the behaviours that she saw in him and Harry were the same as those she was reading about. What they wanted from the members of The Collective went beyond submission to a Godly leader. They wanted complete control. Clearing the search, she typed in the words how do you know if you are in a cult. There were pages of articles and she read them one after the other. And what she read only convinced her that she had been right. The Collective was on the verge of becoming a cult. The only thing missing was telling the women what to wear and sexual sin by the leaders. The control, the exclusivity, how they had convinced everyone to give fifty percent of the profits to the foundation that was being controlled by Steven and Harry was textbook. And how Steven and Harry believed they had a special gift when it came to hearing from God. It reminded her of the quote from the George Orwell novel *Animal Farm* that she had read in high school – *all animals are equal, but some are more equal than others.* They had created a group where everyone had a vote and a say but Harry's and Steven's votes and opinions were the only ones that mattered. Like a cult, they had tried to come between her and Jamie when she refused to step into line. The brothers first above everyone else. Jamie was walking away but what about the other guys? What about *their* wives and families? Were they ever going to wake up and see The Collective for what it really was, or would they willingly remain trapped under the pretence of the Godly mission? Lauren jumped as she felt a tap on her shoulder.

"Earth to Lauren. I've been trying to get your attention."

"Sorry. I didn't hear you. I've been doing some reading."

"Uh oh. That sounds dangerous."

"You know how I said earlier that God told me The Collective was operating under a spirit of witchcraft, but I thought that didn't sound right. Well I was wrong. The reading I've done, and it's come from heaps of different sources, all say that witchcraft presents as control. Complete control of others, manipulation to get their way, and total authority over others. Does that sound familiar?"

"It sounds exactly like Steven and Harry. They're always talking about submitting to authority."

"Combine that with how a cult works. Again control, with the leader believing they have a special gift from God. And the exclusivity that Steven talks about, people wanting to join The Collective but not being allowed to. And giving of finances. Millions have gone into the foundation and Steven and Harry control that. The others don't stand a chance because they don't see what's happening to their lives. They feel special being part of The Collective and believe that God has a blessing for them through Steven. They have no idea how they are being used. And I think that even includes Steven and Harry to an extent, because they are just as deceived as the rest of them. They don't see anything wrong with what they are doing and think they're bringing freedom when they are actually bringing bondage. No wonder they don't understand why you want out," Lauren stated. "What I don't understand is why would God let this happen to people?"

"I don't know darl. Maybe it's a test to see if you fall for it or can discern a false teacher. The Bible is full of warnings about this," he surmised. "I've been thinking that before I go into the meeting on Friday I could use some advice from people who are outside of the situation. I can't talk to Pastor Isaac. Most of the church board is from The Collective, and I get the feeling the church does whatever *they* want. Do you remember Martin Foster? I trust him and he's been around churches for a long time. His advice could be invaluable."

"Do you think he'll talk to you? It's been a few years since you've seen him. Since you did the accounting on the deal when he bought those old warehouses to convert."

"We stay in touch a bit. I've run a few ideas by him when deals have come up for Gideon. Which of course have all been shot down by The Prophet. It's late now so I'll give him a call tomorrow. Speaking of which. I'm off to bed. I'm going to need some sleep if I have to face them tomorrow."

~ ~ ~

The rest of the week had gone slowly for Jamie. Steven had stayed out of the office, which took some of the pressure off him, but Pat had been in and out all week. He'd been polite and hadn't mentioned Jamie's mutiny against The Collective, but the easy-going friendship had disappeared. They had always enjoyed each other's company and being able to work with Pat in the office, trying to put new deals together, had been a dream for Jamie. He hadn't missed the monotony of tax returns and monthly reporting for his clients. He had finally been doing what he'd always wanted but now he was going to have to walk away. Not just from the business side of Gideon, but the guys. Their friendships had become so close and their lives and their families had become so intertwined that it was hard to tell where work stopped, and friendship began. But that was gone. They would never be able to agree to disagree about The Collective and stay in each other's lives. If you reject The Prophet, you reject them all. Daniel had pulled him aside before he left on Tuesday and told him nothing between them would change and that he still wanted Jamie working for him at Racers, where they manufactured high end bicycles, but Jamie couldn't see Harry and Steven letting that continue. He had, for all intents and purposes, become their enemy.

Jamie was relieved it was Friday. He was dreading the weekly board meeting but at least they would know where he stood. From there everyone could move on. And this time he was going into the meeting with some crucial advice from his old friend Martin. He and Lauren had met with Martin and his wife Eva on Wednesday night. Eva, it turned out, was incredibly discerning and when they told them the whole story of what had been going on in their lives, the first thing she said was that The Collective was operating under a spirit of witchcraft. For Lauren that was confirmation that she had heard correctly from God. The second thing they told them was to run! Trying to find a compromise, staying in Gideon for work and having nothing further to do with The Collective wouldn't work. Witchcraft was a strong spirit and in their weakened emotional state they weren't in a position to take it on. Jamie wanted to fight. He wanted to find a way to get through to the others and save them from Steven and from Harry's influence. But for now, fighting wasn't an option. Jamie was going to take Martin's advice and get out as quickly as possible.

And for the first time Lauren and Jamie heard the phrase spiritual abuse from Martin. He explained to them that Steven and Harry had claimed an ungodly authority over the group and then used it to manipulate and control others to forward their agenda, not God's. God didn't need Harry to build a Freedom Centre for people to attend so they could receive healing. God would bring healing into a situation when it was the right time and not when The Prophet said so. He told them that other typical traits of spiritual abuse were members being rebuked if they didn't do exactly what was asked of them, criticised for missing meetings, and encouraged to check with the leaders on personal decisions. And a classic tool of spiritual manipulation was telling people they were no longer going to receive God's blessing if they left the group and would be missing out on what God had for them. Eva revealed that this in fact was speaking a curse over the person. Jamie recognized that all these tactics had been alive and well inside The Collective. They also pointed out how manipulative it was when a person came to you with the God told me this statement. There was no real argument against that. If you disagreed, you were either calling them a liar or saying that God was wrong. You were left with no comeback and had to believe whatever they claimed.

But it was the story of Steven asking everyone at the Scone retreat if they were all in minutes before the meeting ended that troubled Eva the most. She reminded them of the story in Joshua chapter nine when Joshua and the men of Israel made a peace agreement with the Gibeonites. The Gibeonites set out to fool Joshua into thinking they were friends from a far-off land, not their neighbouring enemies. They convinced Joshua to quickly make an agreement with them for peace and told him they came in the name of The Lord thy God. Joshua and the men of Israel did not seek Gods will on the matter and by the time they found out the Gibeonites were in fact their enemy they had to keep their word and did not go into battle against them as they had been originally told to do by God. So Israel was trapped in a treaty with an evil nation that fooled them, and most certainly did not come in the name of God. Eva said that the same way that Joshua, a Godly man had been fooled, so had the Godly members of The Collective. Steven didn't give people a chance to go away and pray about the agreement they were entering into with him and Harry. And because they had agreed immediately and without prayerful consideration the wool had been pulled over the eyes of all those that said yes. She believed that if Lauren had given in to peer pressure and said yes, even if she hadn't meant it, she too would have been blinded. And that's why she believed that Jamie had finally been able to see the truth. He too hadn't accepted their offer to be all in. After the dinner, when they got home, Jamie and Lauren had prayed to cut off all soul ties with members of The Collective and had asked God to break any curses spoken over them.

After putting his briefcase on his desk, he walked slowly up the stairs to the board room. Everyone except Harry was present and he wondered how long they had been there strategizing before he had arrived. They will have wanted to fill in Stuart who had been missing on Tuesday.

"Take a seat," Pat suggested. "I think you'll agree we have a lot to discuss today. But before we get started, I think we should take some time in prayer. Josh if you don't mind starting us off."

"Heavenly Father, we come before you today in conflict. A place we never thought we'd be. Please come now and speak into this situation and remove the barriers that have divided us. We ask for your peace and your wisdom and please bring us back into alignment."

"God," Daniel prayed next, "Please be with us today as we work through Jamie's fears and insecurities. Please show him how he's being used by the enemy to bring division to The Collective. Open his eyes Father, let him see the truth. And please open Lauren's eyes as well. Let her see that she is wrong and bring her the freedom she desperately needs, and quickly God."

One by one each man prayed, asking God for wisdom, alignment and his blessing for The Collective. As always, the same repetitive, hypnotic music played in the background. Jamie used to love this music, had felt it bought him into the presence of God, but now, it made him sick. He silently asked God to forgive him for falling under the spell of these songs. He knew they were sung in churches all over the world and people believed they were worshiping God. And yes, the music was beautiful to listen to and it was easy to be swept away by the emotion of the words, but people were being fooled. A favourite of Harry's was playing now, and it took all of Jamie's restraint to not jump up and turn it off. An entire song that was about God's love for *us* and not ours for him. A song written about the created, not the Creator. It wasn't true worship. As he peeked around the room he saw each man had assumed their usual position. Sinking into their chairs, eyes closed and hands outstretched, ready to receive. All of course except Steven. Jamie had never taken much notice before of how Steven didn't participate in worshiping God. But thinking back, he realized Steven was always tapping on his iPad, or making notes while the others gave themselves over to the music. Even in church he sat down the back, arms folded, with a grumpy look on his face. He very rarely joined the others in prayer either. For someone who believed he was a prophet and heard from God, he didn't seem to have much interaction with Him.

A few minutes later as another song came to an end Pat stood up and turned off the music. Slowly the men seemed to come back from wherever they had been, but they looked a little dazed, Josh in particular. Pulling himself up in his chair he took a deep breath in and after releasing it he said,

"That was an amazing time of worship. I could feel the presence of God so strongly it was like he was sitting right next to me. I just felt so enveloped in his love and in particular his love for you Jamie. He's told me that this is all going to be ok. He said you are exactly where He wants you and doing what He wants. You've got a little side-tracked this week but it's time to let your fears go. Give yourself completely over to Him."

"I appreciate your encouragement Josh, but the problem is that what's being asked of me is not to completely give myself over to God. I have no problem with that. What you're asking of me is to give myself over completely to The Collective. You want me to give up everything, including my family, if it came to that, for your cause. And guys, I'm just not prepared to do that."

"No one's asking you to give up your family, even though the Bible does say that if you do you will be rewarded later," Josh continued. "What is being asked of you is to bring your family along. Bring them under the Godly authority He's given to Steven. We've all had some trouble with getting our wives on board. They've been resistant. Even Ashley has had her moments. But she can see how much I've changed, how much closer I am to God now. The Collective has been good for our family."

"And I'm happy for you," Jamie lied. He knew that Ashley and Josh fought like cats and dogs, had seen them going at it in public. And if they behaved like that in front of other people, what was happening at home?

"You know my wife Jamie," Pat picked up where Josh had left off. "She can be stubborn and independent. A lot of the time in the past she made the decisions in our house. And she's been almost as resistant to The Collective as Lauren is. When I told her about the troubles you are having at home, I'll be honest, we had a horrible fight. But through that she had an amazing breakthrough. She said she wasn't going to fight it anymore. She told me that if being in The Collective and coming under Steven's authority was what it took to stay in our marriage, then that's what she would do. She said that she felt like an eagle whose wings had been clipped. And that's what you need to do with Lauren. Bring her under authority. It's what's best for her."

"But I don't want Lauren to feel clipped. How is that love? I feel so sad for you right now Pat. Why would you do that to your wife? Force her into something she doesn't want."

"You obviously haven't read Psalms!" Steven exploded. Jumping up from his chair where he had been quietly watching the exchange between Jamie and Pat, Steven looked wild. He leaned over the table and began to poke his finger in Jamie's face. "God says we are to come to him with a broken and contrite heart. If Pat had to break his wife for her to get freedom, then that's what he had to do. And you, you should be doing the same. By allowing your wife," he spat the word like he was disgusted at the thought of her, "to control you with her threats to leave is not being head of your home. She does what *you* tell her, and *you* do what *I* TELL YOU," he screamed. "Because *I* hear from God and this is what He wants."

Jamie had never seen Steven so completely out of control. He'd seen him come close to anger when the group wasn't hearing from God the way he wanted. But Harry had always been there to gently direct them towards Steven's wishes while managing his frustration. Unfortunately for Steven, Harry wasn't here. And the true Steven had shown his face. Looking around the table he saw that no one else was alarmed at the outburst. They all sat quietly while Steven ranted about obedience and for a moment Jamie saw behind the physical into the spirit world what was really happening to his friends. For all their talk of freedom, he saw them wrapped in chains, their arms bound at their sides and their eyes were coved by the grotesque hands of demons. *Thank God my eyes were opened,* he thought. *Thank God Lauren never gave up her fight. Because the others don't know what they have gotten themselves into.*

Jamie just sat there and looked at Steven. "You haven't got anything to say have you? Because you know I'm Right!"

"No," replied Jamie. "I'm just waiting for you to calm down. I have no intention of engaging with you while you're in this state. Don't you know the Bible say's a gentle answer turns away wrath? I have no desire to fight with you. Obviously, I see The Collective in a different light to you and we are never going to agree. What you are asking of me and my family is too much and I can't be a part of it anymore."

"So what? You're walking away from God. You'll regret it one day," Daniel predicted. "He asks for our all, you can't just do the parts of being a Christian that suit you."

"I don't believe that what is happening here is what God wants. And if it is then it's too much. So yes, I'm walking away. Not from God, but from The Collective. I'll keep working at Gideon until you can find someone else and we'll have to work out what to do about my shares. But after that I will be leaving."

"Well I can tell you; you won't be staying on the board with the attitude you have right now," Steven told him. He had taken his seat and regained control of himself, but his voice was still angry, and his words were spat like bullets at Jamie.

"That's not how it works in the real-world Steven. Until everything is financially resolved, I will be staying on the board. But for now, this meeting is over. I have work to do, as I'm sure the rest of you do." His heart pounding, Jamie turned away from The Collective, sad that it was ending this way. But they couldn't see it. They had no idea the bondage they were in, and until they did, he knew he couldn't convince them that The Collective was dangerous and had nothing to do with God.

Chapter twenty-two

L auren looked out over the tranquil water as she lounged on the lanai. The book beside her forgotten as she sunk into the quiet. Occasionally there would be a helicopter landing, or a boat docking and the staff would greet the new guests with a welcoming song, the strains of the ukulele floating across the clear blue water. Everyone was welcomed this way and from the moment you stepped onto the island your every need and want was catered to. Fresh flowers were placed in their room every day and it was by far the cosiest and cleanest hotel they had ever stayed in. Cool dark timbers were offset by white linen on the bed and the vaulted ceilings helped keep the room cool, even in the November heat. From the magnificent meals in the restaurant, to the cookie dude who brought fresh chocolate chip biscuits to their room every afternoon, the resort was perfection.

"How long was I asleep," Jamie asked as he roused himself from the nap he had been enjoying beside her on the lanai. Built for two, they could see the ocean, and say hello to the occasional person who wandered by, or they could close the blinds for privacy, but as there were less than one hundred guests on the island, they barely saw a soul. Even in their private pool, they could see the sea, but because it was below the beach line, no one could see them as they swam.

"About an hour I think," Lauren answered. "Relaxed?"

"Completely" Jamie answered with a gentle sigh. "I've made a decision."

"You have. And what might that be? I thought all future decisions were going to be made together."

"I think you'll like this one. I've decided that we're never going home. We can just live here forever and never go back to Australia. I'll work from here if they won't let us stay for free."

"As wonderful as that sounds, do you think you might miss the kids?"

"Eventually. But we can face-time with them. Or they can come here to visit us in Fiji."

"Probably not a solution, I'm thinking. As wonderful as this is, we have to go home and finish this thing once and for all."

"I know. And the sooner the better. I'm not sure how much more I can take."

Jamie was still at Gideon doing the accounts while they looked for someone to take over his job. They had interviewed a few people, but because someone had to be Steven approved it might be months before they found the right fit. Everyone was polite, but the tension in the office was unbearable. It didn't help that they were still trying to agree on a buy-out figure for Jamie's shares. It was easy enough to value the cost of the remaining solar panels. The hold up in negotiations was the future overheads for Gideon. They had to consider how much money would be spent on running the business. Unfortunately for Jamie and Lauren this also included all the retreats and expensive dinners for the next year or two. And without Jamie there reigning in the spending he was sure Gideon's future costs would blow out way more than he had originally projected. If they did then that would be on the remaining members. He wasn't going to pay for two-hundred dollars bottles of wine. And neither was Lawrence. When he heard that Jamie was leaving the Gideon board he had insisted on being bought out too. He had been comfortable while Jamie was handling the money but didn't trust the others to make sure he was paid fairly, especially with the stranglehold Steven and Harry had over them.

Re-booking the holiday to Fiji had been the easiest decision they had ever made. The dates they wanted were still available and although it was a lot of money to spend before they knew the outcome of the buy-out, Lauren and Jamie agreed the holiday was priority number one after what they had been through. Dealing with their church situation hadn't been as simple. They knew they couldn't stay at Living Waters. With Steven appointed prophet over the church, a stacked board and Isaac giving authority over himself and by proxy over all church members to Steven, if they continued there, they would still come under Steven's spiritual umbrella. They had meet with Isaac within days of Jamie's decision to leave The Collective because they knew Harry would sugar-coat the facts and Isaac would never know the truth.

Lauren could still see the look of surprise on Isaac's face when they told him that they were leaving Gideon and Living Waters. Trying to explain it had taken over an hour.

"I don't understand guys," Isaac had said. "It was only two months ago that we sat at your kitchen table and talked about you joining the church. Lauren you said God had told you to make the move. Are you saying now that that was a wrong decision?"

"No Isaac I'm not. By being at Living Waters I saw things that confirmed for me that Steven wasn't on the up and up. I mean, I was already sure, but seeing him at church and being part of The Collective's community inside the congregation proved to me how dangerous it had all become."

"What do you mean dangerous? Our church is thriving with Harry and Steven's leadership."

"Maybe. But our family wasn't thriving under their leadership," Jamie said. "I nearly lost my marriage because of The Collective." Isaac looked from Jamie to Lauren waiting for an explanation.

"Isaac, I was planning on divorcing Jamie. I couldn't stay anymore knowing that he had chosen The Collective over me. My mental health was taking a battering, and as for my spiritual health, I wasn't going to risk my soul. It wouldn't be Steven standing before God on judgement day, and it wouldn't even be Jamie. It would be me, there alone, giving an account for my actions. I couldn't stay in something I knew was not from God."

"Oh Lauren," Isaac said shaking his head at me. "You know how God feels about divorce. He hates it."

"I know. But I didn't feel I had a choice. Jamie broke the covenant relationship we have. He went outside our marriage. I know, I know. He wasn't cheating on me with another woman. But that's what it felt like. That I was being cheated on. And I wasn't going to be allowed to stay married to Jamie without being all in with The Collective. And there was no way I was giving in. I've come out the other side bruised and battered. But I can also say I stood up for God. I held my ground and I held onto my convictions. I didn't let myself be fooled by a false prophet and false teaching."

"False prophet? Come on Lauren."

"Yes. False prophet. Maybe he once had a gift of prophesy. I honestly don't know. But now, no way. He's a con artist. Out for the money. That's why he latched onto the Gideon boys. He saw dollars and took them for everything he could get."

"Do you seriously think I would let someone have authority over me that I didn't trust completely? Give me a little credit. I've been Pastor at this church for almost a decade. I would never do anything to jeopardise the spiritual health of the members."

"I thought that too Isaac. That my family was everything to me and I would protect them no matter what," Jamie replied. "But I didn't see what was right in front of me. Steven and Harry have fooled us all. Lauren fought tooth and nail to make me see, but I didn't want to. I trusted them and I was very, very wrong."

"But what's made you change your mind? From what Lauren's said she was always wary of Steven. Something else must have happened because last week you thought he was your prophet."

"I can't go into details. I don't feel it's my place to divulge private information, but Harry and Steven brought us a proposition that I knew instantly was wrong, and they asked us to lie about it to our wives." Jamie and Lauren had decided not to say anything about Steven's upgrade. They knew it would come out eventually and people would wonder how Steven had been able to afford such an expensive house. Let him answer their questions. And besides, if it got out, something might be said to the other girls before their husbands were ready to tell them about the two hundred grand they were about to give away.

"My advice to you Isaac," Lauren counselled. "Always follow the money."

"Well guys. I can't say this hasn't come as a shock. If you ever change your mind you will always be welcomed back with open arms. I can see that you think your decision is right and I won't argue with you." Isaac looked at his watch. "I have to get going. Adelaide needs me to pick her up at an appointment. Her car is on the fritz again."

"Oh no. What's wrong with it?" Lauren asked.

"Automatic transmission. It's going to cost around two thousand dollars to fix, and unfortunately that's not in the budget this month. So for a bit we're a one car family."

"Well please pass on our love to her," Lauren said. "It's a shame she couldn't be here this morning."

"I will. And don't be strangers. No matter what, we're still friends and I hope you both find what you're looking for."

Lauren and Jamie hadn't been back in their car for more than a minute before Jamie said what Lauren was thinking.

"I can't believe it. His board members are delighted to shell out a million dollars to buy Steven a house when he already has one, but they can't chuck in a few hundred bucks each to get their Pastors wife's car fixed."

"Maybe they don't know about it."

"Felicity and Adelaide are best friends. Of course she'd know."

"Then we should pay for it. They're our friends. Getting their car fixed is the right thing to do."

"Are you sure? It's going to be two thousand dollars."

"I'm positive. I know I seem to have a bit of a reputation for having a greed problem, but this is exactly the kind of thing I'm thrilled to be paying for."

"All right. I'll text them and offer."

Isaac had been surprised by Jamie's offer to pay for the car repairs, but he had accepted. Two days later when he met Adelaide and Isaac at the mechanics to pay for the repairs it had been Adelaide who asked if he had time for a coffee and a chat. Lauren had been at work and missed out on the enlightening conversation, but he conveyed it back to her that night. Lauren and Jamie hadn't known but before they joined Living Waters, Adelaide had been forced to step down from her leadership role in the church. Steven had felt, and Harry agreed, that she was under the influence of a Jezebel spirit and was holding the church back. If she wasn't prepared to be delivered of that spirit she could have no influence over her husband or anyone else in the congregation. Adelaide had been devastated by the accusation. She knew she wasn't under the influence of any spirit, but at Isaac's request she had quietly stepped down from her role in church and Harry became the person Isaac relied on for guidance and support. She had felt no different than Lauren about what was going on with The Collective, she had just been quiet about it. Jamie couldn't believe that Isaac had let his wife be accused like that based on Steven's word, but then it hadn't been any different for him. He was just as guilty of letting his wife suffer the same emotional and spiritual abuse as Isaac did. And he could see that Steven wasn't very inventive with his accusations. Any woman that challenged him had the same problem.

Adelaide had been very interested to hear from Jamie what was going on inside The Collective. It confirmed everything she believed about Harry and Steven. Before, she had been alone in her concerns for Living Waters. Finally, there was someone else who might have a chance at getting Isaac to rethink the authority that he had given Steven over the church.

As predicted a few days after they had met with Isaac, Daniel asked Jamie to join him for a coffee. After a few minutes of awkward small talk Daniel had told him that he no longer felt it was appropriate for Jamie to be on the board of Racers or do his accounting work. Daniel felt that he couldn't trust him anymore, and although it was Daniel speaking, Jamie could hear Harry's voice. Daniel was just regurgitating the excuses he would have been told to give. What he hadn't predicted was that Daniel asked him to attend Racers annual Christmas party the following month where Daniel would announce Jamie's retirement from the company. Daniel was telling the staff that Jamie had decided to go in a different direction. Lauren had been disgusted that Daniel would have the gall to ask that, knowing it was to cover himself with the other Racers board members who had great respect for Jamie and wouldn't under-stand Daniel's reason's for letting him go. As always Jamie had been gracious and accepted the party invitation. Lauren wasn't sure she should go. There was no guarantee she would be able to behave herself. But she was considering it, knowing it might be her last chance to see Felicity.

The only incident that had made Jamie laugh in the office was the day Steven brought in a plastic chain with hooks. Sitting under the stairs where he had been moved to as a punishment, Jamie had had a first-class view of Steven hooking on the chain to the stair rail and across to the other side like a barrier. Curiosity had got the better of him and he asked Steven why he had done that. Steven had informed him that upstairs would now only be used for him and Harry to do the releasing sessions. No one would be admitted without prior permission. They needed their privacy. Instead of making him look authoritarian it made Steven look ridiculous. The top floor had a glass railing, anyone in the office could see up there, and hear all the conversations that took place. It was just another not so subtle way to point out that Steven and Harry were above everyone and the rest of The Collective bowed to their demands. Watching Steven attach the plastic chain across the stairs, he saw what a fool he really was, so full of self-importance. When Pat had explained to Jamie the purpose of the chain, just in case he hadn't heard and would dare to go upstairs without permission, Jamie hadn't held back. He'd told Pat how stupid the whole idea was. Anyone could unhook the five-dollar chain and walk up the stairs. And besides he'd said. Every word could be heard from downstairs. If they were so desperate to keep secrets from the rest of the team they had better keep hanging out in the padded cell. Pat had sulked for the rest of the day and hadn't spoken more than two words to Jamie for the rest of the week.

~ ~ ~

As she roused from her nap in the cool of the room, she'd had more naps here in a week than in the last five years, Lauren could feel eyes on her.

247

Jamie was sitting on the armchair he had claimed as his own the first day on the island, a smile on his face, one she hadn't seen in a long time.

"What?"

"It's done. Settled."

"Is it what you expected?"

"Yes. Enough to pay out the mortgage and any tax, and a little set aside to finish off the house."

"When?"

"By the end of the month. We'll be out on the thirtieth of November. Which means there's a reason they want me gone, but at this point I just don't care. I want me gone too."

"So, we'll be free?"

"Completely free."

"But the others?"

"I tried. They didn't want to hear it. Maybe in time they will realise. And we can pray for them. But they've made their decision. They believe Steven is a prophet, their prophet."

"Well more fool them."

"Yes. More fool them," Jamie said, but his heart was broken for his friends.

Chapter twenty-three

“ So, do you want to hear the latest?”

"Spill," Lauren replied as she peeled potatoes for dinner. Every once in a while, Jamie came home with a new piece of information about The Collective. Some of it made her angry. Like the time that they found out Harry had relocated an old friend from America to Australia. They paid for the flights and all the other costs involved in moving from one country to another. The friend was now employed by The Collective as worship leader for the gatherings which were now taking place weekly. And all paid for by the foundation. How anyone could think that this was a legitimate use of foundation funds was beyond her. They were supposed to be helping the poor and extending the kingdom of God. If they had spent the money feeding the homeless in the inner city, or providing shelter to battered women and children, then Lauren would have been glad the foundation had been created. But this was just another con on The Collective members. Paying for a worship leader for less than a dozen people. Most churches couldn't afford to pay their worship leader, it was a voluntary role. At the rate they were spending the money she had hoped that it would run out soon and Steven would leave in search of greener pastures and their friends would be saved. But Jamie assured her there would still be millions in the kitty, just waiting for Steven to further his own kingdom here on Earth.

But once in a while they heard something that gave them hope. Both Jamie and Lauren had thought the Living Waters Church was a lost cause. With Harry at the helm, they had seen the church heading in the direction of New Apostolic Reformation theology. Lauren had never even heard of the NAR movement before she began researching the role of prophets and apostles in the local church. What she came across had shocked her. All across the western world there were men who were popping up in churches declaring themselves prophets and apostles. They wheedled their way in and ingratiated themselves to the church leadership. She had seen it happen firsthand with Harry and Steven, but she quickly realized they were just two in a long line of men deceiving Christians all over the world. She started listening to the teachings of these prophets and apostles so she could see for herself exactly what they believed. Some of the teachings she came across in her research were straight from eastern religions and the new age. There was one very popular church that took part in a practice called grave soaking where people would lie on the graves of deceased Christian leaders. They believed that some of the anointing was left with the body and could be soaked up by the person lying on top of the grave.

She'd also watched videos of church services that looked no different than the meetings Hindu yogis presided over with people rolling around the floor acting like they were drunk, shaking and screaming. These people believed that the Holy Spirit had come upon their congregation, but Lauren had learnt that this was a counterfeit holy spirit called Kundalini. The Holy Spirit never calls for people to lose control of their bodies or their senses. The Bible calls for the saints to have self-control and be sober but these churches, in contradiction to the Bible, encourage people to be drunk in the spirit. The Bible says that God is not the author of confusion, but of peace. He bought order out of chaos when he created the world. What was being seen in these churches was anything but order and peace. Many of these prophets and apostles claimed God had a new revelation for his people, one that did not appear in the Bible, displaying an arrogance that was astounding. The Bible was no longer the authority for these churches. The prophets word came first.

These prophets didn't seem to be accountable to anyone. One prominent leader in America who claimed to have the gift of the prophetic had left his wife and children for another woman, but few called out his sin and the prophet continued on with his work. Not the kind of Godly example that leaders were called to. And it didn't matter if their prophesies were wrong. People still trusted them, but in the meantime real people were being harmed when a prophet was mistaken and gave people words that couldn't actually be from God because God never gets it wrong. There were accounts of people losing their homes and businesses because they did what a prophet had told them. But people were so desperate for signs and wonders that they believed whatever they were told. With claims of gold dust and feathers falling in their churches and the prophets taking authority, God had been removed from his rightful place as Lord over all, and was treated more like Santa Clause, good for bringing people blessings but not worthy of worship or obedience. Many of God's people had lost their discernment and couldn't see that many of these prophets were wolves in sheep's clothing.

But thankfully, Living Waters church had escaped. After Lauren and Jamie had left The Collective and the church, Pastor Isaac had had a change of heart. After learning of Jamie and Lauren's defection from The Collective, Adelaide had spoken out and fought back against the claims that Steven had made that she had a Jezebel spirit. Jamie and Lauren continued to pray for the church, even though they no longer attended, and God answered those prayers. Isaac saw that Living Waters was being taken in an unbiblical direction. He recognized that Steven and Harry were the ones who were really running the church and took responsibility for being the one who had given them the authority to do it. Backed by the board members who weren't part of The Collective and who had also become concerned about the direction the church had taken, Isaac told Steven he was no longer allowed to attend the board meetings or prophesy in the church. He wasn't being asked to leave the church, but he would no longer have any authority. Harry and the other Collective board members had fought it, but they were out voted. Steven left the meeting that night quietly and only attended services a few more times before he disappeared forever from Living Waters. Lucy had been the one to cause a scene. Present at the meeting removing Steven from authority, Lucy had stormed out of the building, throwing accusations at Isaac that he had broken his promise to protect Steven from any opposition. Isaac had never made such a promise but there was no reasoning with the hysterical Lucy. She never stepped foot in the church again.

It took longer for the rest of The Collective to leave, but eventually every single one of them did. One by one they resigned from their role as elder and were replaced by prayerfully considered candidates who had been wary of Steven and even spoken out against him and his unbiblical theology. Rumours sprung up about what was going on and why so many prominent families had left the fellowship but when Isaac asked the church for forgiveness for allowing the situation to arise the rumour mill died down. Isaac steered the church back to God and biblical teaching. Oddly, Harry was the last elder to go. Perhaps he thought he could change Isaac's mind and return Steven to his role as prophet. But more likely he was recruiting the people he wanted to join The Collective. Young, impressionable people, desperate to do the work God had for them, but naïve. Without a strong grounding in the Bible, and the lure of charismatic leaders courting them, those invited felt special and left the church, joining the now weekly gatherings.

More than one desperate parent had approached Lauren and Jamie looking for answers. They had decided right from the start that they wouldn't gossip about what had happened, but if asked directly they would be honest about The Collective. They were never able to quell the fears of the parents. They could only tell them the truth, but it came as no real news to these people. They could see their children moving away from them. One daughter had given up her career teaching when Steven told her it was God's will, and now she and her husband were struggling on one income before they had even had a chance to buy a house or start a family. Another's son had closed the successful business that he had been building for several years and had gone to work for The Collective. Unfortunately for him, he wasn't earning nearly as much as the Prophet or the Apostle, and with a baby on the way, and working upwards of sixty hours a week for The Collective, he too was in financial strife. Families were divided and nothing their worried parents said could change their children's minds. All they could do was pray for their eyes to be opened. And as predicted, The Collective became just like any other run of the mill cult. Control, money and more control. But at least Living Waters had been saved.

And now Jamie had more news to share. As always, Lauren hoped it was good. She waited patiently for the day he came home to tell her that their friends had seen the light and left. It had been months now and The Collective was still there, doing their damage.

"They got their upgrade," he announced putting down his brief-case on the bench.

"Who got their upgrade? What upgrade?" she asked, a little confused.

"Steven and Lucy. They said God would get them an upgrade and they got it. And let me tell you it's more than your average home."

"Harry actually pulled it off. Do you know if the others paid for it, or did they have to get a mortgage?"

"Nope. No mortgage."

"How did you find that out? I can't imagine you rang old Stevie and you two had a lovely chit-chat about his finances."

"No of course not," he replied with a smile. "But do you remember Ellie? Nice girl from Living Waters who left with her husband to join The Collective. I ran into her dad today while I was getting lunch and he told me Steven had moved into a new house. When I got back to the office I did a little digging. I used a few tricks I know and was able to find out his new address. And then for the grand sum of nineteen dollars I did a title search which told me that there was no mortgage on the property. And then because I had the address, I did a web search to find out how much the new property went for. And you might want to sit down for this."

"How much?"

"His new house cost one point nine million dollars, give or take and stamp duty on top."

"Shut up."

"I wish I could."

"Well when Harry goes after something he gets it."

"Yep. Each family would have needed to give him about two hundred and thirty thousand each to cover it. Some might have done more; some might have done less. I doubt we'll ever know the break down. But he got his upgrade for nothing. And it's in his name, so no one can ever take it away when they realise how deceived they were. They have no claim to ownership."

"I can't believe it. He's conned them all. I ... I ... I don't know what to say. I'm speechless."

"Well if you think you're speechless now, wait until you see it. Obviously it's not in the centre of the city. They bought in Leichhardt, but it's big and it's been fully renovated. It's actually really beautiful. A dream home." Jamie pulled out his laptop from his briefcase and in a minute had a picture up on the screen.

"You've got to be kidding me," Lauren sighed under her breath. It was spectacular. A Californian bungalow with formal English gardens in the front. Hedges pruned to perfection with standard roses lining the driveway. Lavender encircled a beautiful magnolia and there was even a swing on the front porch so the owner could sit and watch the world go by. The inside pictures were just as lovely. High ceilings with original features were complimented by a sleek new kitchen. It had beautiful timber floors throughout and with four bedrooms and three bathrooms it was more than they needed. Anyone would be proud to call this place home. And now Steven would. Proof in his eyes that God had blessed him. And proof for others too. But she had to wonder how many fights had taken place privately in the homes of the other Collective members. It was a massive amount of money to give to someone, and each family would have to have been in agreement with the others. That would have been an uphill battle, and something that Lauren would never, ever have agreed to. And on top of the gift, they each still would have to pay the tax due.

"Harry's good isn't he," she told Jamie. "Getting everyone to agree to buy this for Steven. I hope it doesn't put them in too much financial trouble."

"Yep he's good. I can hear him in my head, quietly persuading me that this is how God wants us to honour The Prophet."

"I'm so relieved you got out."

"Me to. I still can't believe how close I came to losing you, our life together. Sometimes I think I must have gone mad for a little bit there."

"But it didn't happen. And we're good."

"Yes, we are good," he said as he closed his laptop, wishing he could completely close this chapter in his life. But every time he thought it was over, something else popped up and he was reminded all over again how close he'd come to losing everything.

Chapter twenty-four

S teven settled into his favourite new chair. He had always wanted a Chesterfield wing chair and now he had two. Harry had insisted on paying for the new furniture, telling him that they would both be using the room to strategize The Collective's next moves so they might as well do it in comfort. He picked up his glass of Chivas regal and swirled it, loving the sound as the ice clinked against the crystal. Maybe it was time to upgrade to a more prestigious brand. This had been his drink for years, but traditions could change. Besides he could afford it now. And didn't he deserve the best?

Looking around the room, Steven breathed in the luxury. What more could a man want? The magnificent old desk that had been refinished to perfection, the built-in shelves that were filled with books he would probably never get around to reading, but that were necessary to complete the look of the room, and the smell. Leather and expensive cologne mingled together gave the room a rich ambiance. His study was a reflection of how far he had come. No longer the sometimes prophet who had to work disgusting farm jobs to make ends meet. He was respected and revered by successful men and they were honoured to support him with their finances. And with his and Harry's plans coming together, one day he would be recognized all over Australia. Maybe even the world. It would take time, but Harry had told him that was okay. With his help, Steven was learning patience and how to influence people. It came naturally to Harry, he was skilful at handling people. Gently, gently he spoke, but there was no room for dissent. In the past Steven had overreacted when a Collective member had stepped out of line, but Harry had shown him that people responded better when dealt with kindly. Yes, he reminded them that they were in danger of missing out on everything God had for them if they challenged him or The Prophet, but he did it with love. That was Harry's gift. To draw people in and make them see the error of their ways. That a course correction was needed. And it happened very rarely now. The Collective members understood their obedience was key to the future plans they had. And with The Collective about to take the next step they needed everyone to be on the same page.

"Can I refresh your drink?" Harry asked Steven. He had something to discuss with him, and he needed him mellow. Steven had a habit of over-reacting when he felt challenged. More than once Harry had needed to step in and calm Steven down when he flew off the handle. How he had responded to Jamie when he decided to leave The Collective had been a perfect example. The timing of his holiday in Bali had been disastrous and Harry was sure that if he had been in the meetings with Jamie, he would have been able to manage the situation. Jamie would never have left if he had been there. Harry often prayed that God would help Steven grow in this area of his life. Not that he would ever tell Steven that. His job was to keep him calm and connected to God so he could hear from Him. If Harry pointed out that he still had one or two faults he needed to work on Steven would sulk for days and then he would be no good to anyone. And with this new situation arising, Harry needed him to stay right out of it. Besides, he knew exactly how he was going to handle it.

"Sure" he replied as Harry brought the decanter to him. "One more can't hurt."

Harry poured generously, adding more ice cubes from the sterling silver ice bucket that had been a housewarming gift from Stuart and Cynthia. Everyone in The Collective had been so generous when Steven and Lucy had moved in. Getting this house had been a hard-fought battle with the offer they made before the auction rejected immediately by the vendors. Steven had been shocked. God had told him the price he was going to pay, promised him that he had been keeping the property for him all these years and that all the renovations had been done for him, in advance. When they failed to secure the house for the price Steven had heard from God he had wanted to walk away, and actually questioned whether he had heard wrong. But Harry refused to be beaten and after wrangling more pledges of finance from the others, they went to the auction. When the price went over what he had secured he kept bidding, believing that this was the house God wanted Steven honoured with. And in the end, they were the successful bidder. He'd had to put in more of his own money when a resounding no came from the others when he requested additional funds. They had their own mortgages to pay and families to support and couldn't afford another cent. He'd backed down, realizing he had pushed too far. But it was worth the extra hundred grand it had cost him personally. He had it to spare, and now Steven had a tangible symbol of God's blessing on his life. He told the others a private donation had come in to cover the short fall, and that wasn't a lie. They just didn't know it had come from him.

"I've been hearing some chatter recently," he started as he took a seat on the matching chesterfield couch. "It seems that Jamie and Lauren are talking to people about The Collective."

"I doubt anyone's listening. No one cares what that has-been has to say. Who would even take him seriously anymore? Couldn't stick it out with God and rejected his blessing because he was scared of his Jezebel wife."

"While that might be the case, they do know a lot about us. And they are bitter and angry. And bitter and angry can do damage. And some people *are* actually taking what they have to say seriously."

"Who? If anyone in the inner circle is talking to them they need to consider how much they want to be part of The Collective. This is special, ordained by God, and they don't want to get left behind."

"So far there's been no damage to The Collective," Harry responded. "But I know they have been approached by Ellie's parents. They wanted information and advice."

"And did they give it?" Steven asked, his earlier peace disappearing quickly.

"They talked. I don't know what they did or didn't say, but Ellie's father continually makes comments to her about being controlled and giving up her life. But you know as well as I do that Ellie's thriving in The Collective. She's coming forward in leaps and bounds with God. We're the best thing that ever happened to her. She told me she was very upset that her parents spoke to Jamie, and asked them to stop interfering in her life. I think that if they keep up the nagging, she'll eventually break away from them.

"And has Jamie been talking to anyone else?" Harry knew he had to tell Steven the information he'd learnt. If he found out later that Harry had been keeping secrets, there would be trouble. It was always best to limit Steven's knowledge and let him get on with hearing from God, but this time he had to tell him everything.

"I heard they were around at Aaron and Pamela's a month or so ago." Aaron had worked for Gideon selling the solar panels with Jules and had lasted for another six months after she had been fired. He had left not long after Jamie's defection, unhappy with being expected to take part in the gatherings outside of work time and hadn't had the respect he should have had for Steven. The men had never really got along, and the office had felt better once he left. Unfortunately, he had been a brilliant salesman and sales had slumped to an all-time low without him.

"I told you we shouldn't have let these hangers-on be part of the gatherings. Exclusive I keep telling you."

"We need more people Steven. We can't move forward without them. Don't worry about Ellie. She knows she's following the will of God. Aaron and Pamela are gone and don't have any influence anyway. We're better off without them. And I've been talking to Peter and Cassandra from Living Waters. They're nearly ready to make a decision and I am certain they are going to join The Collective. And yes, they both know that being in means all in and nothing less. They told me they love coming to the gathering and want the same things we do. To follow God's will. And they will bring others. They have influence in their circle and he's very successful. They're both excited to contribute to the Freedom Centre when we start building."

"Good, good. No damage done then. Lauren and Jamie can gossip all they like. It doesn't sound like anyone of importance is listening anyway," he said standing and walking towards the decanter, empty glass in hand.

"Well, that might not be the case. It seems," Harry paused, wishing he didn't have to reveal his next piece of information, "that Lauren has been in contact with Felicity."

"Whaaat?" Steven screamed, thumping his glass on the desk, making a ding on the perfect surface. "How did that happen?"

"Girls talk I guess. And they knew each other outside of The Collective. It's only been texts as far as I know, but Louise saw one when they were out shopping together last week. She only saw it for a second, but it looks like they are planning a get together. All four of them."

"We can't let that happen. I don't want Daniel being influenced by Jamie. I thought that relationship came to an end when Daniel fired him."

"So did I. It's very important that they don't spend time together. Daniel is going so well at Racers thanks to you and your advice. His business is booming and he's contributing more to The Collective at the moment than anyone else. Pat's investments have taken a dive in the market and every time I mention money he cries poor. And now that we have cut his Gideon hours back to only one day a week he's getting even more sensitive about the subject. As for Stuart, he's off on holidays every few months with Cynthia, wasting money that should be coming to The Collective. And you know as well as I do. When they go away, we seem to lose influence. I don't know why they don't stay connected to God when they leave the country, but it does seem to be the case. But we can't say anything to him. He's already sensitive about the subject of holidays and when I brought it up last time, he told me he was going to go wherever he wanted. I don't want to push it. That was what tipped Jamie over the edge."

"That was what tipped Lauren over the edge you mean. That woman started all of this. Before she got her nose all out of joint everything was going fine. Jamie understood his place. He was happy to wait until God had something better for him. And now he's gone and he's talking to people about us. There's no loyalty. I know he's the one who got in Pastor Isaac's ear."

"We don't know that. It was probably Adelaide who got him all stirred up. I don't know why we have such trouble with the women in the group?" Harry sighed. *Well I do*, he thought. Jezebel. That evil spirit influencing the women, causing dissent. But he wouldn't bring that up tonight. That would send Steven into an hour-long rant about the place of women and how they all rejected their husband's authority, and then his. It was time to wrap the evening up, tell Steven how he had decided to handle the Jamie situation once and for all.

"Calm down Steven. It's going to be fine."

"I hope so. I know we have the foundation, and we can move forward with some of our plans. But we can't do everything we want with it. Auditors and the Government putting their two cents worth in. We need donations. Ones without strings attached."

"And we'll get them. Joshua has been incredibly generous with you. Look at all the furniture he bought you. And Lucy's new car. Didn't even give it a second thought. And Daniel will be fine. We made sure of that. Jamie no longer has any influence inside his business, and I bet nothing comes of this dinner business. Louise will talk to Felicity and remind her that Lauren's nothing more than a gossip. It won't even go ahead. And I've decided how I'm going to deal with Jamie."

"How? Do you know someone that can have a word with him, get him to back down? Praying that he just goes away quietly doesn't seem to have worked."

"We don't need anyone else," Harry declared. "Because I'm going to take care of it. It's time Jamie was put back in his place. And I know just the person to do that. Me. Jamie and I are going to have a little chat."

Chapter twenty-five

"I think I'm going to be sick."

"No, you're not. This is going to be fine," Jamie said as he pulled into Daniel and Felicity's driveway. "We're friends. We have their best interests at heart. And don't forget. This was their idea. They want us here."

"I just hope we can get through to them."

"So do I. But don't count on it. Daniel's completely committed to Steven and The Collective. He's convinced that he is a prophet."

"Arh. So stupid. I can't believe a smart man like him can be so taken in," Lauren groaned. "I guess we'd better get this over with," she said as she opened the car door. "We can't sit here forever."

Lauren and Felicity had been texting each other for a few weeks. Lauren had seen something funny on Facebook that reminded her of Felicity and tagged her in it, hoping it would open up the lines of communication. It had worked and the two had shared a few conversations about the problems Lauren had with The Collective. Lauren recommended some books to Felicity that explained how to recognize a false prophet. She didn't know if Felicity ever read the books, but at least she had given her the information. It had been Felicity that had suggested that the two couples meet for dinner and clear the air. Jamie and Daniel had been friends for years and she didn't think it was okay for the friendship to end because of The Collective. But Lauren had hesitated at first, not wanting to see Daniel. After the debacle of the Racers Christmas party last year, Lauren was still so angry she didn't know if she could be in the same room with Daniel and remain civil. It had been almost a year since the party, but the betrayal she had felt on Jamie's behalf hadn't left her. Watching Jamie standing up with Daniel, being given a parting gift for his service for over ten years while Daniel lied to his board and employees had sickened Lauren. She had left the party, locking herself in the toilets so she could cry in private. She hadn't wanted to make a scene, but Lauren had been unable to hold back her tears. Jamie had handled it much better, saying goodbye to the people he had got to know over the years and graciously accepted the watch Daniel had given him. Lauren hadn't returned to the party once she got her emotions under control but had waited for Jamie in the car. She hadn't trusted herself to not start crying again. And now she was going to have to force herself to be polite to Daniel when all she wanted to do was tell him what she really thought of his behaviour.

The first ten minutes of the evening went as expected. They exchanged info about how their kids were and what they had been up to and Felicity showed them pictures of a recent trip they had taken to England. She didn't say it out loud, but Lauren hoped they had got permission before they booked the holiday. But when they sat down to eat at the massive dining table the conversation petered off.

"This all looks delicious Felicity," Lauren said trying to fill the silence.

"Thanks, but it was a team effort. Daniel did the steaks on the barbeque. Anyway, let's get started before it goes cold."

Jamie looked out at the view from Daniel's hilltop home. He remembered when they built this house years ago. They had been friends then, and Jamie was also working for him. But now conversation was difficult, and he recognized that their easy-going friendship was never going to be the same, even if they could come to some sort of understanding about The Collective. Hoping for some sort of inspiration he was rescued by Felicity.

"We might as well get it out in the open. That's why you're here right. So we can talk about The Collective. How are you guys doing now that you've left? Any regrets?"

"We're doing great," Lauren jumped right in. "Absolutely no regrets. It's wonderful to be able to live our lives without needing to get permission for every little thing we do. We can go where we want, when we want. We can be friends with whoever we want and spend our money any way we like. And what about you Felicity? How's The Collective treating you?"

"Oh, you know. It's fine. A lot has changed since you left. I think Steven and Harry realized that they might have pushed people a little far. It's much more relaxed now."

"So they learnt they shouldn't be trying to control people's lives so openly you mean?"

"They were never trying to control anyone's lives Lauren," Daniel argued. "This has always been about hearing from God and doing His will. Steven helps us hears from God and corrects us when we hear wrong. He want's what's best for us."

"Well he thinks he hears from God. But how often is he wrong? I know the one time he gave me a prophesy it was a load of rubbish. Thank goodness I dismissed it and went on with my life."

Daniel paused for a moment, taking a bite of his dinner before he answered her.

"Maybe Steven misunderstood the vision he had. He's not perfect. Or maybe you misunderstood what he said."

"I didn't misunderstand. He made me record it and I listened to it several times. I followed his advice for a few days but all I felt was anxious and disconnected from God. The minute I decided it was wrong I felt a great sense of peace. Isn't prophesy supposed to edify and encourage? It didn't do that."

"So he got it wrong once. That doesn't mean he's not a prophet." He's helped us all so much. My life is better for having him in it."

"Is Felicity's life better?"

"Sorry?"

"Is Felicity's life better? Because we heard about the verbal abuse that she received from Steven, in front of the rest of The Collective."

"Who told you about that?" Felicity asked, her voice unsteady as tears suddenly threatened.

"We heard it from more than one person, it doesn't matter who. I was so devastated for you."

"What happens at the gatherings is supposed to be private," Daniel exclaimed. "You should never have heard about that." Ignoring Daniel, Lauren turned her attention to Felicity.

"So it's true then, what we heard?"

As one single tear slipped down her check Felicity put down her fork to wipe it away.

"Yes it's true."

"And no one stopped him, not even your own husband? That must have been horrible."

"It wasn't … Great. To be honest," Felicity paused, "it was one of the most humiliating things to ever happen to me. I've never been accused of something like that before and especially not in front of other people."

"From what we've been told, and please correct us if we're wrong, he accused you of being under the influence of a Jezebel spirit. He called you disobedient and rebellious to Daniel."

"That about sums it up. But it wasn't just the accusation. It was the way he did it. Like I was a naughty child who needed punishing."

I've been there before, thought Lauren, but it had been Harry dishing out the rebuke in her case.

"Why would he think you've been disobedient to Daniel. And if you were, shouldn't that be a private matter between the two of you?" Lauren said, this time as her gaze swung towards Daniel.

"The brothers discuss everything," Daniel said going into defence mode. "We have no secrets. How else can they know what to pray for, what issues people have? Felicity and I had been having a few problems and the guys have been an amazing support system, the way they were for Jamie."

"Yeah, thanks for that by the way. Your interference in our marriage was fantastic," she replied sarcastically. "Would you have let anyone else talk to your wife like that?" Lauren challenged.

"Well no, but Steven isn't just anyone."

"Daniel, come on. It shouldn't matter who it was. You stand up for your wife. It's your job to defend her. Especially against baseless accusation like the one he made."

"But Steven was right. Felicity wasn't coming under my authority and it was causing problems for us."

"Mate, Steven is obsessed with authority. And have you noticed that any woman who doesn't agree with him seems to have a Jezebel spirit? He's incapable of accepting that women have opinions, and a right to speak out if they see something wrong in their own homes and families," Jamie said. "Lauren and I have come to the conclusion that he actually hates women. That's why he reacts so badly to them, and why instinctually they don't like him. If anyone has a Jezebel spirit, it's Steven. That would explain why he responds so badly when he's challenged or feels like he's losing control, especially when a woman is involved. Be honest Felicity. Do you like Steven?"

"I'm not going to answer that Jamie. He's a prophet and he deserves respect."

"Even after he humiliated you like that?" Lauren asked.

"I know that you think he's a con, but Lauren I really do believe he speaks for God. He has a gift and I need to learn to come under him and The Collective."

Lauren sighed. She had hoped she would be able to get through to Felicity, but like Eva had said, when Felicity put her hand up and accepted the prophet's invitation at the retreat, she had made an agreement. And now she couldn't see the truth.

"Look," Daniel said. "I probably should have intervened. Steven may have gone too far. But we're doing much better now as a family. We don't fight as much, and Felicity accepts that we are part of The Collective."

"And you were fine buying him a house Felicity?"

"Of course Lauren. God's blessed us so much. Why shouldn't we be a blessing to others."

"Buying someone a fancy house is a lot to expect though. I never would have agreed to it, even if we had stayed in. He earns a huge wage. If he wanted a fancy new house why didn't he go and get a mortgage like everyone else in Australia has to."

"You seem to think that Steven pushed this. Apart from the word he got from God that he was going to get an upgrade, he never mentioned it again. He was deeply moved that we all put in and paid for his house. Harry was the one who championed it, and he gained nothing and put in just as much as the rest of us. I don't know why you think Steven's conning anyone?"

"Because Daniel, that's what they do. Steven suggests something to Harry, and Harry his henchman manipulates and pushes until Steven gets what he wants. Yes, I know it doesn't seem like that's what's happening. But if you hear something different than Harry, he makes you go back to God until you hear the same thing he heard. And while it doesn't appear like Harry gained anything, he did. Even more control over you. Steven wants material goods and Harry want's power and recognition. Together they both win," Jamie articulated. "We were coerced into giving the foundation fifty percent of the profits. That never should have happened. And it's done very little good. It mostly goes to paying wages for Steven and Harry. Oh and of course your new worship leader. What's that about?"

"The gatherings are getting bigger. We needed someone to lead worship and none of us had any talent. I don't see anything wrong with paying David a wage. He gave up a lot to come here. And don't forget that at the time you had no problem with giving half of the profits to the foundation."

"And I was wrong."

"Can I ask what Steven does all day Daniel?" Lauren asked. "Because the rest of you aren't there most of the time, so he can't be counselling you all day or praying with you."

"He's praying and listening by himself. Or with Harry. And they go away a lot to get perspective and spend time alone with God. They give up time with their families to do it for us. They should be compensated."

"Two hundred thousand dollars a year each. Do you think that's reasonable? I know of Pastors living on a quarter of that. And nobody in their church is paying off their houses and buying them an upgrade so they can live in luxury. None of this is normal or biblical. He's basically a fortune teller and you're paying him for it," Jamie said. He had finally been able say to Daniel what he had wanted to say for a year.

"You can't exactly complain Jamie. You did pretty well out of Gideon."

"Yes we did," Jamie agreed. "God's blessing has been amazing. But we took a risk and invested cold hard cash. The seven of us started Gideon and it was doing very well. We didn't need a prophet to come in and tell us what to do."

"You know that's not true Jamie. Steven had words from God about how to proceed in Gideon. Without him we wouldn't have done so well."

"And how's sales at Gideon going now?" Lauren asked.

"They're a little slow at the moment. But Steven said it's about to pick up. And I'm not worried. Racers is doing brilliantly. God is still blessing us. We have a beautiful home and everything we could need. Why should The Prophet have any less?" Daniel asked.

It was a beautiful home. Lauren thought. Paid for by Daniel's company that made racing and recreational cycles. Daniel had taken a fledgling company left to him by his father and turned it into something that was internationally respected. He took a risk during the 2006 Melbourne Commonwealth games that was still paying off today. A little-known rider from Wales whose cycle had been damaged during training for the mountain bike race had reached out all over Australia for someone to loan her a replacement. No one in Australia had heard of her, and there wasn't time to have another bike sent from Britain before she was due to compete. But Daniel had decided to take a chance on her, his only request being that if she did well, she would tell everyone where she got her bike from. She didn't medal but had done so much better than anyone had expected, including herself. She sang the praise of Racer's to everyone who would listen, and now they made bikes for top athletes all over the world. But the real money had started coming in when Daniel created a mid-line range of cycles. Weekend warriors who wanted a piece of equipment with a prestigious name on it but couldn't afford the many tens of thousands for the top of the line, one-of-a kind, carbon bike. And Jamie had been there, by his side, through it all. Guiding him through the complicated tax laws, helping him employ the right staff to run the office and sitting on the board of the company for over a decade. Steven had had nothing to do with the success of Daniel's company.

"I am glad Racers is going so well. But you do understand that you were successful long before Steven came along."

"We know," Felicity said. "But after Jamie resigned, Daniel needed some guidance and advice. And Steven has been that for him at Racers."

"Felicity, is that what you think? Jamie didn't resign. He was fired."

"No he left. He told Daniel that it wouldn't be the right thing to do, working there anymore now that he wasn't part of The Collective. He didn't want to make things difficult for us. You were at the party. We said how sad we were to see him go. But it was his choice."

"I'm sorry Felicity, but Daniel asked Jamie to leave. He told him that he could no longer trust him and that he didn't have his best interests at heart anymore. Going to that Christmas party was torture for me. Watching Daniel lie to everyone."

"I didn't lie Lauren. We decided it was best to sever our business relationship."

"So you didn't tell my husband that you could no longer trust him? Someone that had been there with you all those years and never steered you wrong. He made sure you set up all the tax structures properly so you could maximise your profits. He's saved you thousands and thousands of dollars over the years, and then one day, that's it, he's gone. Do you know how that made him feel? Do you know how that made me feel? His integrity is everything and you questioned it. He didn't fight you on leaving. He resigned and went away quietly because you asked him to. But he didn't quit, and after you promised him that nothing would change. You did this."

"I'm sorry Lauren. I should have handled it better. I can only apologise and ask for your forgiveness."

"What about me?" Felicity asked. "You know how upset I was about Jamie leaving. I relied on him to tell me how things were going in a way that I understood. He never talked down to me like other Accountants had. I'm sorry Jamie," she said turning towards him. "I would have done something if I'd know the truth."

"It's all right Felicity. Daniel was half right. It probably wouldn't have worked out. Steven would have been in his ear about me the whole time. It would have been uncomfortable for all of us. And for what it's worth I don't think that Daniel truly believed that he couldn't trust me. Those words didn't come from him. They would have been straight from Harry."

"Oh no. Harry wouldn't have done that. He would never steer us wrong."

"Oh come on Felicity," Lauren said. "Harry's been manipulating us all from the beginning. Bringing in his false prophet to back up whatever he said and did. He's always wanted to build a ministry. And with Steven telling you all what to do and what to give, that's probably going to happen. The next move will be to start their own church. Exclusive of course. And with everyone under the thumb. Cause you can never challenge The Prophet."

"I've told you, he's not a false prophet. He's the real deal and you know as well as I do that they said they will never start a church."

"I don't get it Felicity. He humiliated you and yet you keep standing up for him."

"Things have changed. And he's never done that again to anyone. I might not like the way he goes about things, but I have never doubted for a moment that he's Gods prophet."

"But Felicity. He's wrong all the time. The bible says that a prophet must be right every time they speak on God's behalf. The people were told to take a false prophet out and stone them. I know we can't do that today, but to just believe him even when he is found to be in error is crazy."

"That was the Old Testament Lauren. No one expects him to get it right one hundred percent of the time now. He's human. And humans make mistakes."

"But God doesn't. And if he was truly speaking through Steven there would be no error. God wouldn't be changing his mind every ten minutes. Steven tells you God said to do this, and when it doesn't work out suddenly God has had a change of heart and now it's going to go this way. That's just not how it works. Steven is covering his behind every time that he gets it wrong."

"You expect too much Lauren. I truly believe he is a prophet."

"Well I truly believe he's a con artist who has you all fooled. With Harry by his side manipulating you all."

"I'm sorry Lauren but I just don't believe that. Harry's a great guy. I think we're just going to have to agree to disagree."

"I guess we will Felicity," Lauren said realising that she was never going to convince her friend of anything different.

They went on to a safer topic and talked about their kids for a while, but shortly afterwards Lauren and Jamie said their goodbyes and left. Nothing more was going to come from the evening. They had tried to warn them about The Collective one more time and failed.

~ ~ ~

"That was just ... I don't have any words."

"I thought I would be able to get through to Felicity."

"I did too. Especially after what Steven did to her."

"But she believes. They're so blind. It's like he's put some kind of spell on them. I don't think we will ever be able to convince them. What is it going to take?"

"I don't know."

"Well I can't put any more emotional energy into Felicity. I can pray for her, but that's all. It's like banging my head against a brick wall. They're just so …"

"I know Lauren. And Daniel," he sighed. "It's just so …"

"Frustrating?"

"Yes frustrating. But so … It's such a waste of their lives."

"Maybe one day they'll get it."

"Maybe" said Jamie, but he couldn't see how.

Chapter twenty-six

J amie could see Harry through the window of the coffee shop. It had been over a year since he had been here, and it was one of the things he had missed when he left Gideon. Many hours had been spent here with the guys, discussing new deals they were considering, or just grabbing lunch and hanging out. He would probably never have those kinds of close male friendships again and he admitted he felt a void. The dinner with Daniel had showed him that they were unlikely to go back to the rapport they'd had in the past. They might catch up again, but the relationship would always be strained. The Collective was too big a chasm to cross.

Opening the door he could see that nothing had changed. The scent of coffee was strong, and Emilio was still behind the machine doing the barista thing. He made the best coffee around and Jamie had been looking forward to drinking one all week. When he had seen the text from Harry asking for a meeting Jamie's first instinct was to pretend he hadn't seen it. He had been ignored by everyone with the exception of Daniel so why bother giving them any of his time, and frankly, what good could come from seeing Harry? But after talking it over with

Lauren he decided he was now strong enough to face him. And since his conversation the other day with Gideon's former employee Jules he was more convinced than ever that Harry had no power over him anymore.

Jules had phoned him out of the blue a few weeks ago. She had asked to meet him in person, cryptic about why on the phone.

"I didn't steal those panels," she said the minute she sat down at the table in the coffee shop where they had agreed to meet.

"Okay," Jamie said, thinking so much for a hello or some small talk. "I only know what Harry told us. Why don't you tell me what really happened."

"I loved working at Gideon. I was making great money, and you guys were so nice. You were all a bit religious for my liking, but you never pushed your beliefs on me. At first it was the best job I'd ever had."

"So what changed?" Jamie asked.

"Things just started getting weird when Steven started working there. I'd be in the kitchen making a coffee and he'd just kind of sidle up beside me. He never touched me, but he was always staring and standing too close, and he'd tell me that God had the perfect man for me. My prince charming. I tried to laugh it off and told him I wasn't looking, but he kept bringing it up, asking personal questions about my private life. When he finally told me that the perfect man was right in front of me, I finally got the message. He was talking about himself."

"Did he actually say he was your perfect man?"

"No, but the way he suggested it," she answered shuddering at the thought of those piercing eyes staring at her, not blinking, not looking away. It had been she who had broken eye contact with him, feeling sick at the thought of him coming anywhere near her. She had rushed past him, running into Pat in the hallway. An old family friend, he could see that something was wrong, and trusting him, she told him what had happened. Pat's concern had quickly turned to anger, but not at Steven. He told Jules that she had misunderstood Steven and was overreacting.

"How long after this happened were you fired?" Jamie asked.

"The next day."

"And you didn't take any panels? Harry showed us the invoice with a zero-balance owing. Did he fabricate it?"

"No. I took the panels. But only because Harry told me to."

"He told you you could have five thousand dollars worth of panels?"

"Yes. I was looking in his desk drawer for a stapler one day and I saw an invoice with no name on it for a house lot. There was no charge, just a delivery address. And of course, perfect timing, he came back into the room and saw what I was looking at. He said that all Gideon members had been given some panels for their houses and this was the invoice for his lot. The invoice was just so that the panels would be accounted for during stock take."

"That was true. We were all given a house lot before we started making any dividends. It probably was his invoice. I don't understand why his name wasn't on it though. I did those invoices myself."

"It couldn't have been his invoice. The delivery address wasn't his. I dropped him home once when his car was at the mechanics. It was in a completely different suburb."

"Right," Jamie said, as it dawned on him that he might have his answer to why his budget had been out by thousands. The remaining physical stock had matched exactly what the ledger said they had on hand, but the money coming into the bank didn't match the recorded sales. He had asked Harry at the time, wracking his brain to figure out where the fifty thousand dollars had gone, but Harry told him it must have been an invoicing mix up and said not to worry about it. Jamie had spent hours going over the figures trying to find the mistake he must have made but was never able to solve the problem. But if Harry had been raising invoices for panels that nobody was paying for, then he finally had his answer.

"And then Harry told me I should have also been given the same number of panels as you guys and he sat down at his computer and raised an invoice for me. But instead of charging five thousand dollars for them, he charged me zero. At the time I thought he was incredibly generous. He said not to mention it to anyone because he preferred to keep his giving a secret. I thought it was odd that I couldn't thank you all, but Harry was such a great boss that I agreed."

"And then you complained to Pat about Steven?"

"Yep. The next morning Harry called me into his office and pulled out a copy of my invoice. He told me that you had been going through all the invoices while looking for some missing money and found that I had delivered a house lot of panels to myself and not paid for them. He said that they couldn't have a thief working at Gideon, but if I went quietly, he wouldn't call the police. Needless to say I was shocked. I had thought he was so nice. I tried to argue with him, but he told me if I wasn't gone in the next ten minutes, he would make it his mission to see that no one ever employed me again. But if I left quietly, he would supply me with a glowing reference and talk me up to future employers. I knew what he was doing, but I didn't have a choice. I had those panels, and I didn't pay for them. It was his word against mine."

"Did he give you that reference?"

"Yes. By the time I got home it was waiting in my inbox. I got another job within the week and tried not to think about what had happened. But when I heard from my mum who is friends with Maria, that you had left, I decided that I needed to tell someone. To be thought of as a thief, to have my integrity questioned was too much. I wanted someone to know the truth."

When Jamie had told Lauren Jules's story, she had asked what he had been wondering. What had Harry done with all the missing panels? And now that he was here, Jamie was going to ask him.

"Hey Jamie. Long-time no see," Emilio called out. "Are you still drinking latte's?"

"Always Emilio."

"Then I'll have one of the girls bring it over."

"Thanks. Is it still five dollars?"

Emilio waved his hand as he shook his head. "Don't worry about it. Gideon still has a tab going. You guys are my best customers."

Jamie thought about insisting on paying, but Harry had been the one to call the meeting. He, or actually Gideon could shout this time. He made his way to the booth in the back that they had always sat in, relieved that as promised, Harry was alone. That had been one of Jamie's conditions for the meeting. No Patrick or Josh, and definitely no Steven. Harry was going to be enough to contend with today. Half rising as he approached, Harry stuck his hand out to shake Jamie's.

"G'day Jamie. Thanks for coming."

"Not a problem Harry," Jamie replied as he slid into his seat.

"I'm sure you are wondering why I've asked you to meet with me today."

"Well it did come out of the blue."

"Sure, and I think it might be best if we skip the pleasantries and I get straight to the point." Harry paused as Susan, Emilio's wife slid two coffees onto the table. Jamie thanked her and took a sip. It was still as good as ever.

"I've been hearing that you and Lauren are talking about The Collective. A lot. And as a brother in Christ I thought it would be best to approach you privately about your gossiping. It's a terrible sin, gossip, and it can do a lot of damage. And I can't have you out there doing damage."

"Ah, gossiping. That's a pretty strong accusation. Who exactly are we gossiping to?"

"I know that you've been speaking to Ellie's parents among others."

"Ellie's parents came to us, very distressed, worried about her being in a cult. I wasn't going to lie to them. She's left Living Waters Church and become a member of The Collective. What was I supposed to say? Don't worry. It's all fine. I'm not a hypocrite. I told them the truth. If you want to call that gossip go ahead. I call it informing someone of the dangers that lie ahead for their child."

"She's hardly a child Jamie. She's a grown, married woman. Her parents need to let her go and make her own decisions. And I would caution you against using the word cult. The Collective is no such thing."

Jamie took another sip of his coffee, thinking through his answer before he spoke. Nothing had changed. Harry still spoke in that quiet voice, head tilted to one side, lulling a person into believing he was nothing more than a kind soul who wanted the very best for you. But Jamie knew better now. Although spoken gently, Harry's words had a threatening undertone. Not that it mattered to Jamie. He was no longer under Harry's control.

"Are you still exclusive?" Jamie asked. "Or can anyone come along to the gatherings? Can Ellie invite her parent's so they can see what's going on?"

"Just because we are careful about who we allow to attend, and who we choose to associate with doesn't make us a cult. Do you even know what a cult is? You can't just throw a word like that around. All you'll do is scare people and for no reason. Ellie has never felt better, but you've filled her parent's heads with all sorts of rubbish which isn't doing anybody any good. And you need to stop it. Now," Harry said, his voice rising above his normal volume.

"Does The Prophet still demand complete obedience? Is he still claiming authority over everyone in The Collective?"

"You mean the God given authority Steven has. I've heard you think he's being controlling, but that's not the case. Everyone comes under someone's authority. Children under their parents, wives under their husbands, and husbands need to come under the authority of someone who has an anointing on their lives. Otherwise they have no accountability."

"And who is Steven accountable to Harry? And what about you? Whose authority do you come under?"

"What if you're wrong Jamie?" Harry replied, side stepping the question like a seasoned Politician. "You tell people that Steven is a false prophet. And I've even heard that you are telling people that we are under a spirit of witchcraft. How do you think God feels about you saying such things about a man of God? His chosen man. Remember when we studied what happened to Miriam and Aaron when they spoke out against Moses. Miriam angered God so much that he gave her leprosy. I'd be very careful if I was you."

Jamie held out his arm for Harry to see and turned his palms over to emphasise his point.

"Nope, no leprosy here."

Harry gave Jamie the small smile that he had come to loath towards the end of his time at The Collective. It never quite reached his eyes and the recipient knew that they had made Harry angry. He wouldn't yell or fly off the handle, but you knew you were in trouble.

"But there might be other consequences Jamie. Your health might take a turn for the worse. Or your finances. We warned you when you left The Collective that you were walking away from God and the blessing that He had for you. You didn't listen and you will have to live with the consequences. We have gone on from strength to strength. But what about you? How's life for you these days out there in the world all on your own?"

"For starters Harry, you can keep your threats. I don't accept your predictions of illness or failure over my life. And not that it's any of your business, but my life is great. My marriage is stronger than it's ever been. I have plenty of work coming in, and we've found a church that actually preaches the gospel. No one is shoving pop-psychology down our throat's dressed up in Christian lingo and with God's guidance *I* decide how *I* and my family live." Jamie smiled back at Harry, his voice calm. Two could play at this game.

"Well time will tell who is right. But you should be very careful about what you say and who you say it to. And speaking of which. Lauren needs to back off from Felicity. I know they have been corresponding. She's not being helpful. And Felicity is probably too polite to tell her she isn't interested in her anymore. The friendship ended when your wife made you leave The Collective."

"I'm not going to tell Lauren who she can or can't be friends with. And if anyone else asks me about The Collective I'm going to be honest. And don't think I'm not aware that you have been doing some gossiping of your own. Telling people they should stay away from us. Telling old friends and colleagues that we're dangerous. But do you know what? You're the one who's dangerous. You and Steven both. And exposing false doctrine isn't gossip. In fact I have a responsibility to warn people."

"Then I guess there's nothing more to say here. I appreciate you meeting with me today. The outcome hasn't been as I exactly what I wanted, but I hope that we can walk away today with an understanding. No need for animosity between us. We are still brothers in Christ after all. Are we all good?"

"Hmm. All good? Well, if I see you on the street will I say hello? Sure. But will I ever be all good with what you are doing to people's lives, or with your false prophet, a wolf in sheep's clothing, then no, we aren't all good. And we never will be. Especially after I heard what you did to Jules. What did you do with all those panels Harry? Sell them? Probably not. You didn't need the money. Did you use them as a bribe? To get people on side, see The Collective vision."

"I have no idea what you're talking about. Jules was bad news. I wouldn't believe a word that comes out of her mouth," Harry said, but Jamie could see from the look on his face that he had rattled him.

"But I do believe her. Come on. Just between you and me. I know you took them. Gifts for friends perhaps?"

Harry stood up from the bench seat, hovering while Jamie remained seated. He had never realized just how threatening he could be before.

"Goodbye Jamie. I hope you see the truth one day. I'll pray that you do," he said and then he was gone, striding out the door and down the street towards the Gideon office. Well that was short but not so sweet. Jamie could only imagine the conversations that would take place about this meeting. He realized he didn't care anymore what they said about him. He had faced Harry and held his own. If he happened to run into any of the others, he would be fine with them too. He didn't need to hide in the shadows, afraid of their disappointment in him any longer. Having allotted an hour for this meeting he realized he had time to sit and enjoy for a while longer. He motioned to Susan and pointed to his empty cup. She came over and confirmed that yes, he would like another coffee.

"I'll add that to the tab," she said.

"You know what, Jamie said as he pulled his wallet out of his pocket and pulled out a ten dollar note. "I'd rather pay for both of mine if you don't mind."

Chapter twenty-seven

"Are you sure this is the place love?" Lauren asked. "There aren't any signs up."

"Why would you have a sign up if you don't want the general public knowing that you're here? This is definitely the building their new church is in. See that's Pat's car. And look. I told you Josh bought Lucy another new car. I wonder if she'll get a new upgrade every year."

"I was positive they were going to start their own church, but a tiny part of me thought they wouldn't be able to do it. I mean, don't you need to have gone to Bible College to be a Pastor. Harry never did that, and Steven would consider himself above getting an education when he has a direct line to God."

Jamie shrugged his shoulders. "Apparently not. They joined an association that only has a few churches under it, so it's all legal. Got to get that tax-free status. I've never heard of that particular association, but I'm guessing their criteria for signing up a new church can't be very strict. I can't imagine the Baptists or the Church of Christ taking them on. Too much oversight and The Collective definitely don't want that."

Jamie and Lauren were sitting in their car across the street from a row of factories. Their church service had ended early and they hadn't been able to resist checking out The Collective's new church. Only open for two months, Jamie had learnt from one of the parents that they kept in touch with, that Steven had prophesied that this church was only the first of many. They had plans to train up Collective members and plant them all over Australia and eventually the world. But with only twenty cars or so parked outside, Harry was going to need to let a few more people into the inner circle if that was going to happen. Even with the window up they could hear music playing, the tune a familiar one. It was Harry's favourite song and now Jamie would have it playing in his head all day.

"It sounds like they have a big band for such a small church," Jamie noted. "I know they have the worship leader Harry brought over from America, but I didn't think anyone from The Collective were musicians."

"Ellie plays piano remember. And Samuel from Living Waters is going there now. He was in the band and played the guitar."

"And his brother Luke was a drummer. If they got Samuel, they might have got to Luke as well."

"You don't think they targeted those people specifically because they were musicians?" Lauren asked.

"Well they didn't bring them in for their money. They don't have any," Jamie answered.

"But they are young and impressionable. Easy to control. And if they can use them as well, no wonder they pursued them."

"Can you imagine if we went in? Just walked through the door and took a seat," Jamie laughed. "It would be worth it to see the look on their faces."

"While that would be hilarious, I don't fancy having Harry man handle us out of the building. It would almost be worth it though. Steven would have a fit."

"A by invitation only church. How can such a thing even exist?" Jamie said shaking his head. "It completely defeats the purpose of a church. And did I tell you Harry has started attending the monthly Pastors meetings for the area? Isaac said it's really uncomfortable for him, but he doesn't want to go around bad-mouthing Harry. I can only hope he has no influence on anyone there. The last thing we need is more exclusive churches."

"Jamie, duck."

"What?"

"The door is opening. Duck."

Lauren and Jamie ducked down laughing hysterically at the thought of being caught spying, as Josh exited the building and walked towards his car. After a minute Lauren peeked a look and saw that he was already heading back into the church.

"All clear," she said. "Let's get out of here before the service ends and people start coming out."

Jamie turned the car on and did a U-turn towards the main road.

"I doubt anyone will be leaving anytime soon. Ellie's dad told me it's mandatory to stay afterwards for The Collective family lunch. His family has a tradition of lunch together after their church service, but Ellie doesn't go anymore. She's not allowed."

"Not allowed. And Felicity said things had eased off in the control department. More like they pretended for a while and regrouped."

"Yep," Jamie said. "They were just biding their time until the dust settled from us leaving. I also heard now they are running a group for all the older kids. Each month everyone is given a book to read, but they are coming out of NAR churches so you can imagine what those books are full of. How to be drunk in the spirit or high on Jesus and why it's your fault if you don't receive complete physical healing from God. Got to get those teenagers the same freedom as their parents. I'm so glad our kids never got mixed up in any of this."

"But by the grace of God."

"Amen."

Chapter twenty-eight
One year later

C hloe pulled the factory door open. Thankfully the air conditioning was on, because today had been horrible. It was one of those humid Sydney days that everyone dreaded. There was no sunshine, just an overcast sky that would later turn to rain, but without being accompanied by a cooling breeze. Tomorrow after the rain, the heat would be even worse. Weather like this made some people cranky and Chloe was one of them. She wished she had been able to cancel tonight's releasing session and was tucked up at home watching the new episode of *The Big Bang Theory* with a bag of barbeque chips and a diet coke.

Because Chloe couldn't stand taking part in these sessions with Steven and Harry. As far as she was concerned, they were a complete waste of time. She didn't have any major issues that she needed freedom from. What she was dealing with was just normal teenage stuff. So what if she and her mum butted heads from time to time. That's what happened between mothers and daughters. She was seventeen and still trying to figure out what she was going to do with her life. If anyone had a problem, it was her mum. She had been pushing her to do a law degree at Uni. Chloe couldn't think of anything worse, and she knew she wasn't going to get the grades for it anyway. And she already knew she didn't want to go to Uni. Most of the kids who went there had trouble getting jobs when they were done, so as far as she was concerned, it was a waste of time. Chloe was much more interested in doing something in the beauty industry. What she really wanted was to learn how to do professional makeup. With that qualification she could work in TV or movies, or even have her own business doing makeup for weddings and special occasions. If her mum had let her leave school last year when she'd asked, she could have already been halfway through her course. But that kind of job wasn't prestigious enough for her parents and they had insisted she at least finish high school at her exclusive girls College.

Now that she was seventeen and had her licence all she wanted was her freedom. Probably not the kind that Steven was always carrying on about, but to be able to choose what she thought was best for her life, without hours of discussion and even more hours of prayer, especially when she already knew what she was capable of and what made her happy. Chloe was the girl in school who others came to for advice and help before a big date or an important event. She knew how to help someone look pretty, understood what colours suited them best and how a change of hairstyle could give an ordinary girl confidence. Her parents thought it was shallow, but when Chloe helped one of her friends she knew it was about more than looks. Beauty might only be skin deep, but when someone felt happy about how they looked it made them feel better about themselves on the inside too.

And that's why she was here tonight. Because of the arguments between her and her mum about her future. When her dad, Pat, had suggested that she talk to Steven and try and find out the root cause of her issues with her mum, she had laughed and said there was no way she was doing that. It had taken for her dad to promise to pay for a trip at the end of year twelve to get her to agree to see Steven and Harry. They both spent a lot of time praying for her and asking lots of stupid questions she didn't have the answers to, but if it got her an all-expenses paid holiday then she would keep going. They had agreed to six sessions and this was number five. And when she turned eighteen, she had already decided there was no way she was staying at this church. She didn't like the way it had changed her dad. They couldn't do anything as a family anymore without checking if The Prophet thought it was okay. Every moment of his life was controlled by Harry and Steven and her family hardly ever did the fun things together like they used to. Her dad was always at the Gideon office having long meetings, or at church. Sundays were the worst. The service went on and on and then they had to stay afterwards for lunch. The only way to get out of it was to pretend she had heaps of homework, but her dad was getting suspicious of that excuse, especially when he got home and found her watching TV or texting one of her many friends.

Chloe thought that if anyone had to spend time with Steven and Harry in a releasing session it should be her parents. They were the ones who were constantly arguing, mostly about money. They tried to keep it private, but Chloe had overheard her dad say he wanted to give more to The Collective. Mum said they had given more than enough and why couldn't Harry just be happy with their tithes? As far as Chloe was concerned the sooner she was away from The Collective, the better.

Chloe walked through the foyer towards the stairs. Because they were expecting her, the stupid plastic chain was down, and she began her ascent. Music was playing like always, but tonight the lights were dimmed. Chloe always dreaded coming here, but tonight she wanted to run. One hour. That's all she was staying for.

"Hello Chloe," Steven said from the large couch they used for sessions. She had been told she could lie down if she wanted to, but that always felt a little to cliché for her. Normally Steven and Harry sat opposite to her but tonight Steven hadn't pulled any chairs over. *I hope they weren't both going to try and sit with her,* she thought.

"Um, where's Harry? I didn't see his car outside."

"Harry's not going to be able to make it tonight."

"Oh, you should have called me. Now I've wasted time I could be using to study. I guess we'll just have to reschedule for another time," Chloe said feigning disappointment, turning to leave. Steven patted the seat next to him.

"There's no need to do that. I'm perfectly capable of doing a session on my own, and besides, I've been praying for you all week. God has been downloading so much about you to me and I don't want to risk missing the moment. I think we are going to have a real breakthrough tonight."

"Oh, I don't know. Shouldn't there be someone else here? What about Lucy? Do you think she could come?"

"Lucy's busy tonight. And it's not necessary. You've known me for years. I'm like another Father to you. Come, sit."

Steven was definitely not like a father to her, Chloe thought. More like some creepy old weirdo. And something about the way he looked at her, especially lately had made her feel uncomfortable. But she took a seat on the couch, sitting as far away from him as possible, while she checked her watch. The hour couldn't be over fast enough.

"Normally we would start with prayer to bring you closer to God and open up your heart and your mind, but today I think we can skip that. I spent a lot of time this week focusing my prayers on you and God has revealed to me why you have such trouble with your mother. Do you have any idea? Has he been talking to you too?"

"Steven. I've told you. I don't have a problem with my mum. I love her. I just want some space and the chance to make my own decisions about what I'm going to do with my life. That's all. And I'm not feeling comfortable being here alone with you. I think it's best if I went home and we did this another time when Harry was here."

"Wait please Chloe. God is using me to give you the freedom that you need, and it wouldn't be very respectful to ignore what His Prophet is saying, would it?"

"No," Chloe mumbled. Steven was being stranger than usual tonight and her antenna was up. Something wasn't feeling right about this.

"God has told me that the reason you have so much anger towards your mother is because you are jealous of her."

"I am so not jealous of mum. She's old. And I've told you I'm not angry at her either."

"Then why do you fight with her so much?"

"We had a couple of fights. It's no big deal. We just don't see eye to eye on my future."

"You love your father a lot, don't you Chloe?" She felt a chill down her back. Even the way he was saying her name sounded wrong. Something was different about him tonight and she thought about just standing up and leaving. But her dad would have a fit. Honour the Prophet had been drummed into her for years now.

"Of course I love my dad. Everyone loves their dad."

"But not everyone loves their dad the way you do. And that's why you're so jealous of your Mother. If you were to be honest with yourself, wouldn't you like to have a relationship with your dad like she does."

"Eww. Yuck. Are you suggesting I have sexual feelings for my dad? That's sick. I can't even think about something like that without wanting to throw up. That is the grossest thing I have ever heard. I'm leaving."

Chloe grabbed her bag and was almost to her feet when Steven who had been creeping towards her slowly on the couch grabbed her hand and pulled her back down.

"Do not dishonour your prophet. Sit down," Steven said, his voice steely. "It's nothing to be ashamed of. All little girls love their daddies. But you're not a little girl anymore. And I know how you can get over this. If you were able to transfer those feelings for your dad onto someone else, you could move on and have the freedom you so desperately need. And I really want to help you move on Chloe." Steven leaned in towards her slowly as he said, "It's time you showed me the honour I deserve."

~ ~ ~

Jamie picked up his ringing phone, a look of surprise crossing his face. He held it up to Lauren so she could see who was ringing before he answered.

"Daniel. Hi."

"Hi Jamie. Long-time no talk."

"That's okay. What's up?"

"Um, is this a good time to talk?"

"Sure. We've just finished dinner."

"Is Lauren with you?"

"Yes she is. Why?"

"Do you think you could put me on speaker. I only want to have to say this once, and I think you both deserve to hear it first-hand."

"Sure," Jamie said as he hit the speaker button. "You're on. How can we help."

"Hi Lauren," Daniel greeted her.

"Hi Daniel. How's things?"

"Um. Actually things aren't so great at the moment. I have

something to tell you both, but it's going to be hard to do that. I'm not really sure where to start."

Lauren and Jamie looked at each other across the dining table and Lauren silently clapped her hands together and grinned. Hopefully Daniel was ringing to tell them that they were leaving The Collective.

"The Collective has been disbanded. We've also closed the church."

"I see," Jamie said, trying to keep the delight out of his voice. "That's ah, a bit of a surprise. You were all so invested in it. I'm guessing something must have happened for you to change your minds."

"There was a bit of an incident with Steven," Daniel sighed. Jamie recognized that sigh. He had done it a hundred times at least when he had left two years earlier.

"Right," Jamie said as Lauren pushed her chair back and started happy dancing around the kitchen.

"We weren't sure if we should tell you, but you seem to find things out anyway, and we thought it best if you heard it straight from us."

"What happened Daniel?"

"It seems that Steven made a move on someone during a session."

"Are you serious? Not on Felicity I hope," Lauren said as she took her seat, dancing time done. This was serious.

"No. Although that might have been better."

"Why? Who did he try it on. Not one of you guys?"

"No. Chloe."

"Pat and Maria's Chloe?"

"Yes."

"But she's what, eighteen."

"Seventeen."

"Seventeen," Jamie yelled. "I hope you called the police. Please tell me he's in custody."

"No. Chloe refused to press charges."

"Is she all right? He didn't, you know, hurt her?" Lauren asked.

"No. He didn't get the chance. What Steven didn't know was that Maria had enrolled herself and Chloe in a self-defence class last year. When Steven tried to kiss her she head butted him. And good. She must have broken his nose because when we got to the office the next morning there was blood everywhere. That's how we knew something was up. Chloe didn't tell her parents what had happened until they questioned her about it. She said she was too embarrassed."

"Pat must have wanted to kill him when he found out."

"Oh he did. As soon as Chloe told him what had happened, he was straight around to Stevens house, but it was too late. He was gone. No one knows where. He packed a bag and left. And because Chloe insists that we don't tell the police about this no one official is looking for him. We could probably get a private detective but what's the point. He's gone and no one here want's to ever see him again. Lucy's in a complete state. He didn't even leave a note, just up and left her."

"Daniel, have you checked with all the other girls that he didn't try this with them?" Lauren asked.

"We did. And no. Normally he wouldn't have even had the opportunity. But he and Harry were doing sessions with Chloe, and he told Harry that she had cancelled. So Harry didn't show up which gave Steven time alone with her. It never should have been able to happen."

"I told you those sessions were bad news. I knew it," Lauren said. She couldn't be happier that The Collective had come to an end, but this was not the way she'd wanted it. She and Jamie had always wondered if things would go this way. Something about cults always seemed to turn sexual. She thought it was because the men in authority felt they were above the normal rules of society and became warped by the power they had.

"Lauren, this probably isn't the time," Jamie said.

"No she's right," Daniel sighed again.

"How did Harry take it? He and Steven were best friends. Those two were joined at the hip. But I must say I'm surprised he let the church close. What will he do now?" Jamie questioned.

"Harry's gone too."

"What? With Steven?" Lauren asked.

"No. After we found out what Steven had done, we called an emergency meeting and Harry did fight to keep the church going. But we all told him we were leaving. I mean, how could we stay? Steven's behaviour was completely unacceptable in our eyes and in God's. If Chloe hadn't defended herself who knows how far Steven would have taken it? Harry lobbied to run the church on his own, promised that nothing like this would ever happen again, but it's like our eyes were opened. Suddenly, for me anyway, everything you said started to make sense. I don't even know where to start with the apologies."

"Daniel, you've had a shock. Apologies aren't important right now. As long as Chloe is all right. That's the main thing."

"She claims she's okay. From what Pat said something about defending herself made her feel empowered. We've all told her how sorry we were. Well, all except Harry. After our meeting about closing the church we didn't hear from him. Stuart and I went around to his place to make sure he was okay. There was a for sale sign up and we ended up having a very interesting chat with his neighbour. She said he and Louise packed everything up and left. He told her they were going to spend some time at a church in Northern California. That's where David, the worship leader he brought to Australia was originally from. Redding, I think. But she also told us something we are going to want to look into."

"About Harry?"

"Yeah. She was telling me how sorry she was that he had left and what a great neighbour he had been. Turns out he had been very generous with her. Apparently, her flowering gum nut tree over hung his property. It was dropping leaves and gum nuts into his pool. So he asked her to cut it back. When she refused, he offered her a house lot of solar panels for free. She cut back the tree and he gave her the panels. I'm hoping he paid for them, but I've been wondering if maybe he didn't. Do you know anything about stock discrepancies?"

"I do. But I think you'll find more than one house lot missing."

Daniel swore under his breath. "Well that might explain the panels on the house across the street from him. Mrs Andolini, the neighbour, couldn't wait to tell us that Harry had been in an argument about a car that was always parked opposite from Harry's front windows. It was an old piece of junk the son owned. He refused to park it in the garage, even though there was space. One day the kid started putting his car away, and a week later Mrs Andolini saw panels being installed."

"I asked Harry about the missing panels when I was still at Gideon, but he denied knowing anything about it and told me I must have made an accounting era. I was alerted to the situation recently by Jules. You remember her? Harry sacked her for theft. Long story, but she never stole anything. Harry was covering for himself, and for Steven. She was uncomfortable with the attention Steven was giving her. She went to Pat and next day she was gone."

"Ok. That makes sense. After the Chloe incident Pat kept saying, I should have listened to Jules. We had no idea what he meant. Now I guess we do."

"And both Steven and Harry have disappeared. Maybe Steven went back to New Zealand," Jamie guessed.

"Well his passport was gone. Along with about forty thousand dollars he had stashed in the house. He's left Lucy with nothing but credit card debt."

"But his credit cards were all paid out by Collective members," Jamie said.

"What can I tell you? He liked to live large. We had no idea he was spending so much money. And Lucy can't even sell the house because it's in Steven's name. Without any income and all that debt she's going to be in financial trouble very quickly."

"It sounds like it," Lauren said feeling sorry for her. She hadn't really liked Lucy, but no one deserved this.

"So what happens now?" Jamie asked.

"That's where you come in. If you're willing? We need someone to close down Gideon. We have sold almost all of the solar panels so that's not a problem. And you know we never got any other projects off the ground. No matter how hard, we tried nothing ever came to fruition. With what happened with Chloe I'm beginning to suspect God had a hand in that. Not letting any more money fall into Steven and Harry's hands. We need to get out of our leases for the office and the church and we need to deal with the foundation. There is still money there. What we need is someone to manage it and give it to some worthy causes. I don't have the time, and Pat's a mess. He's barely working. He feels responsible for what happened to Chloe. It's killing him that he didn't keep her safe, and that he trusted Steven completely. I don't know if he'll ever get over this. We all feel that way. If Steven really was God's man, he never would have done anything like this. I know I feel completely gutted. I can't believe I didn't see it. And Josh feels so betrayed. He looked up to Steven, treated him like father. With time I think he'll be all right, but he's very fragile at the moment. I can't ask for his help when it comes to wrapping this all up. Stuart's the only one who doesn't seem phased by the whole thing. I get the feeling he was looking for a way out for a while but didn't know how to go about it."

"I'm so sorry Daniel. I know how badly you feel, but I can tell you it does get easier with time."

"Maybe. Right now I have a lot of apologising to do. To you two.

To Felicity and my kids. And we'll need to get to the bottom of what happened to Jules and try to make amends. I barely know where to start. I trusted those two more than anyone. And all they cared about was themselves."

"Why don't we get together this week and talk it through, face to face," Jamie suggested.

"Yeah? Would you be willing to do that?"

"Sure. How about Wednesday. We can talk over what to do about the foundation."

"We can pay you. No one expects you to do this for free."

"We'll talk about when I see you," Jamie said.

"And please say hi to Felicity for me," Lauren chimed in. "I hope she's all right."

"Well she's angry about Chloe, we all are. And relieved that it wasn't either of our daughters. But she's kind of happy. I haven't seen her like this in years. It's like she feels … free."

Epilogue

Lucy and Steven took a seat near the back of the church. This was the third one they had visited in as many weeks. The first two had been a bust. Number one had been full of old people, most of whom looked like they weren't long for this world. The Pastor was just as old and Steven thought that while he would be easily handled, it wouldn't work long term. No one in the congregation would have had the money to fund his ministry. The second church just hadn't felt right. From the moment he walked in, he had known it wouldn't be the one. The Pastor had spoken about watching out for false teachers and prophets. And while Steven knew he was the real deal, the Pastor had used his pulpit to fear monger about prophets and the congregation clearly would not be ready to receive him.

As the singing came to an end Lucy and Steven sat down. He reached for Lucy's hand, wanting to remind her that he was happy she was here. She had been resistant to joining him in New Zealand at first. She didn't want to leave the kids, but at least she had eventually believed him that Chloe had overreacted and misunderstood his intentions. It had been harder to convince her this time though. The first time a girl had made an accusation against him he had been able to laugh it off. She had been unstable, and this wasn't the first accusation she had made about an older man trying something with her. That's why her parents had asked him to do releasing sessions with her. She had seriously needed help. And anyway. She had misunderstood him. He wasn't going to do anything to her, he just wanted to give her a reassuring hug.

Steven had told Lucy the only reason he left town so quickly after Chloe had broken his nose was because Pat was unreasonable when it came to his daughter. He would believe any ridiculous story the girl came up with. He thought it was best to give everyone an opportunity to calm down. He promised he would reach out to The Collective members when the time was right and tell them his side of the story. He reassured Lucy that he had never intended to leave her but had panicked and wasn't thinking right at the time.

Except that he had lied to Lucy. Steven was panicked, but he knew exactly what he was doing. After Chloe had head butted him and run out of the office, Steven had found a twenty-four-hour clinic in a part of town where a broken nose was nothing remarkable and had it set. He raced home knowing Lucy would still be out and collected the money he had put aside for emergencies, his passport and a suitcase of clothes. He'd spent the night in an airport hotel and taken the first flight out to New Zealand the next day. After a week of healing and figuring out his strategy, he had contacted his wife. He sure could have used Harry's advice about how to handle Lucy, because at first, she'd been unreasonable and refused to listen to him. He promised her that Chloe was lying but she wouldn't hear it. But once he sent Lucy half of the money he had taken from their hidey hole in the floor, she had calmed down and agreed to hear him out. His plan for them been for her to sell the house and join him in Whangarei. Being close to her parents had been one of his draw cards and he thought Harry would have been proud of that move. With the sale of the house in Leichhardt he told her there would be more than enough money to buy something nice here, fund their lives, and support the kids while they finished their Uni courses.

They still had the sticky situation of Chloe to work through because Pat had been in Lucy's ear, telling her that Steven's leaving was as good as an admission of guilt. Thankfully Lucy had kept her word to Steven and not told any of The Collective they were in touch, so they backed off and left her alone. That gave him the chance he needed to get through to her. It had taken time and many hours on the phone but eventually Lucy was convinced that he had done nothing wrong. When Lucy told him Chloe hadn't gone to the police that had been the thing that convinced her he really was innocent of the accusation made. He made her see that if he had done something wrong then Chloe would have pressed charges.

Relieved he'd convinced her, he quickly signed the papers so Lucy could sell their house and join him. Because the last thing Steven wanted was a divorce. It didn't look good for a man of God, and Lucy would have been able to claim half of their assets if she had left him. He needed every cent to continue living the life he had become accustomed to and deserved. Their house had sold in days, and with a quick settlement, Lucy had quietly sent their furniture back home, sold the cars, and set up the kids in a small flat near their Uni. Chelsea only had a year left and Jonathon had three. They could choose to join their parents in New Zealand or stay in Australia when they were done studying.

Dragging his attention back to the service, Steven could see that the room was mainly populated by ordinary people. But here and there he saw expensive jewellery, or a wife whose clothes were a cut above the rest. And with several hundred people attending, there were bound to be a few who would feel led to support a man of God. When the preacher, a man of about forty started speaking about hearing from God, Steven gave him his full attention. This was definitely someone who was on the same page as him. His excitement built as the Pastor turned the microphone over to the congregation, asking if anyone had a word from God that they could share. Steven closed his eyes and listened for God to speak to him. And there it was.

"Good morning," Steven greeted the room as he took the microphone from the previous speaker. "I hope nobody minds a stranger coming forward, but we're all brothers and sisters in Christ after all." He looked around the room, listening as God pointed out three men in the room that were going to help him.

"God has been talking to me this morning about your community. You have been stuck for so long, doing the same things year after year. But God has a new revelation for you. His Holy Spirit fire is coming to this city. You will feel His presence like you never have before. Hearts will be changed, lives will be changed. The dryness you are feeling will be replaced with a freedom you didn't even know was possible. Pastor, the revival that you have been earnestly praying for, is on its way. And this church is where it will start. So open your hearts, listen to them and listen to God. Because your lives will never be the same." Steven handed the microphone back to the Pastor and made his way down the aisle to his seat. He caught the eyes of as many people as he could, and before he knew it a few people started to clap. A few Amens rang out across the service and the sound of clapping grew until a few people stood and the worship team began playing a familiar tune. It was Harry's favourite song. He couldn't have asked for a clearer sign from God that he had found his new home.

When the service finished the Pastor made a bee line for Steven and Lucy, introducing himself and thanking Steven for the prophesy he'd given.

"That word you had for our church was so inspiring. We have needed to hear something like that for so long. And I have been praying and hoping for a revival. It truly was a word from God." He gestured over to another man about Steven's age, his hair peppered with grey wearing a watch that cost the price of a medium range car. Perfect, Steven thought. This was one of the men God had pointed out to him and Steven felt his pulse quicken. Just Anthony, the Pastor had asked Steven to call him, made the introduction.

"Steven, this is our head elder Harrison Parks. And Harrison this is Steven and his wife Lucy. They just recently moved into town." Harrison held out his hand and as the men shook Steven said "Great to meet you Harrison. I look forward to getting to know you better. But Harrison is so formal, and I feel like we are going to be great friends. Do you mind if I call you Harry?"

Author's Note

Dear Reader,

Firstly, let me say thank you for reading *The Collective*. While many of the details have been changed to protect people's privacy, and I have taken some liberties in altering the story, something like this did happen to me and my family.

When we came out the other side, we were confused and very lost. How had this happened to us? And, especially for my husband, how had he not discerned that he was being deceived? I needed to clarify for myself that we had indeed been fooled and that we had not made a mountain out of a mole hill. Over the weeks and months after coming out of the 'cult' we did a lot of research and the things we learned were very disturbing. I decided to write our story as a warning to other Christians. We discovered that this was happening in churches all over the western world and that we were not the only people being deceived. If only there had been some sort of check list we could have used to identify the danger we were facing.

Once I started digging, I discovered that there were warnings from other Christians out there. Several researchers helped us understand that what we had experienced was not biblical, and actually very dangerous. It is an insidious evil that is slowly infiltrating many churches. But what should you look out for and how can you protect yourself? First and foremost, you must know your Bible. Jesus and Paul warn us continually that there will be false teachers and those that call themselves prophets but are not, and we need to be able to recognize them. If you are concerned that you or your church is being led astray these are some of the red flags we have identified:

- A person who calls himself a Prophet. I'm not talking about a person with a gift of prophesy. Paul tells us in 1 Corinthians 12 v 10 that some will have a gift of prophesy. We were not faced with that.

- 'The Prophet' believed he heard directly from God and that he heard clearer than anyone else in the group. We had to defer to him and his authority.

- When it came to 'The Apostle', I found it very confusing. Did apostles still operate today, and should they hold 'office of apostle' in the church? Holly Pivec, who speaks often about prophets and apostles answered the question for me. An apostle was a man who walked with Jesus. There were 12 of them. When Judas betrayed Jesus and then died he was replaced by Matthias and he had also been a follower of Jesus and witnessed his death. Paul was the final apostle and he met Jesus on the road to Damascus. After the apostles died men were not appointed by the church to replace them. Men calling themselves apostle and appointing themselves is not found in the Bible. They will tell you that God is doing a new thing and bringing fresh revelation, even though this was not modelled in the Bible, which must be our source of truth.

- 'The Prophet' and 'The Apostle' continually told us to follow our hearts. However, the Bible tells us in Jeremiah 17 v 9 that 'The heart is deceitful about all things, and desperately wicked'. We were expected to check our brains at the front door and the word of God along with it. Everything was about experience. How do you feel, what is your heart saying? This was supposed to be God speaking to us. Unless it was different than what 'The Prophet' heard, and then we had to check again.

- The music in the meetings and in our church was all about the created, not the creator. This is not worship. The songs were all about me and what God is doing for me. And while it can be enjoyable (but potentially dangerous) singing along with the melodious, hypnotic music, how often do you check the words of a song and decide if you want to declare them or not.

- We learned the hard way to follow the money and the power. This should be something you hold to in all parts of your life, but it's very disturbing that we also need to identify it in the church. If someone is telling you that God has told them that you need to give to them, or their ministry I would caution you to be very suspicious.

- And if someone tries to control your life, and I'm not talking about a friend or a Pastor pointing out sin, but someone who tells you what to do with your job, marriage, education and money and expects you to comply without question there might be a problem. Spiritual abuse is a real thing, but it can be hard to identify as it can creep in slowly.

- If you think something isn't right talk to people you trust. We had amazing counsel from a Godly couple. Our good friends Elle and Rob recognized what was happening as soon as we explained the situation. They told us to get out and run. We followed that advice and it was one of the best things we ever did.

This is not a comprehensive list. It is a starting point for you to do your own research. Every situation will be different. But if you find yourself in a church that is changing, and people are popping up and wanting to take control it might be time to talk to your pastor. Ask God to open your eyes, and know the word. It can be painful, but in some cases you might need to find a new church. In the end you need to be responsible for what teachings you accept as truth, and for what your children also learn. Below are some bible verses that we found helpful.

- 2 Kings 5
- Deuteronomy 13 v 3
- Matthew 24 v 4
- Matthew 13 v 24 – 30
- 2 Corinthians 11 v 13 - 15

You can also go to my website for further information. www.rebeccapater.com.au

About the Author

Rebecca Pater has dedicated her life to raising her two sons with her husband. She wrote her first novel *You don't bring me flowers anymore* when she was forty. "For several years the characters had been taking up space in my mind and I decided the only way to get rid of them was to write their story." she said. Despite having never written a novel before, she wrote the first draft of Flowers in just three months. Rebecca surprised herself that she was able to complete a novel and that people loved reading it.

Rebecca was born in New Zealand in 1973 and immigrated to Melbourne Australia with her family when she was fifteen. She married her husband at nineteen years old and had both sons by the age of twenty-six. They live on a small property outside of Melbourne.

Website: www.rebeccapater.com.au

Facebook: www.facebook.com/becpater

Twitter: @PaterRebecca

Also by Rebecca Pater

You don't bring me flowers anymore - Westbow Press 2015

Beth is overweight, worn down and afraid she is losing her marriage. Can she rediscover the girl she used to be, the girl her husband fell in love with, or is it already too late?

Joan must face the shame of her birth and learn to believe that she deserves to love and be loved.

Jillian has been devastated by her husband's infidelity and must decide whether she can move on with him or start again on her own.

Caroline's life is forever changed by a tragedy that tears her family apart.

Four ordinary women whose lives will never be the same again. Where do they go from here?

Available from your favourite on-line retailer.